A SAGA OF THE WEST PLAINS TO ROLLA ROAD

TYRONE
DUST

To Jim Bargett — Thanks for your service to God's people at FCC.

Hubert Ray Sigler

Dec. 5, 2017

H. RAY SIGLER

CROSSBOOKS
PUBLISHING

CrossBooks™
A Division of LifeWay
1663 Liberty Drive
Bloomington, IN 47403
www.crossbooks.com
Phone: 1-866-879-0502

This book is a work of fiction. People, places, events, and situations are the product of the author's imagination. Any resemblance to actual persons, living or dead, or historical events, is purely coincidental.

First published by CrossBooks 10/11/2011

ISBN: 978-1-6150-7971-1 (sc)
ISBN: 978-1-4627-0571-9 (hc)
ISBN: 978-1-4627-1079-9 (e)

Library of Congress Control Number: 2011915854

Printed in the United States of America

This book is printed on acid-free paper.

Any people depicted in stock imagery provided by Thinkstock are models, and such images are being used for illustrative purposes only.

Certain stock imagery © Thinkstock.

Tyrone Dust would not have been possible without the editing and input from C. Keith Sigler, my older brother. He spent countless hours editing and questioning some things. His help was invaluable.

My daughter was also involved in a second editing of Tyrone Dust. Christina (Sigler) Lyrela's contribution was as monumental as my brother's.

My granddaughter Andrea Piorkowski was extremely helpful as well.

Joanne Vollmer was exceptionally helpful in the initial relay of vital information to the publisher.

Thanks must go out to the Tyrone one-room school graduates who meet once a year in Houston, Missouri. I will not name you all for fear that I will exclude someone. However, Marie (Sevege) Bradford was a fund of information about Tyrone and many of the people who preceded me in that fair villiage.

My cousin Tom Skaggs gave me names and insight into the book in our jaunts around the Tyrone enviorins. My Aunt (who is more like a sister) Freda (Weiler) Anderson was an immense help in understanding the "inside" information about the Weiler family.

My "Aunt" Marthie Ann (Sigler) Harrison (who was really a distant cousin), now, long since deceased, regailed me with stories of the old days and piqued my interest in the historical Sigler clan.

Thanks to Fred Evans, Terri Solorio, and Dr. Steve Drake for their helpful Theological Review and allowing some editing to make it possible for this publication of Tyrone Dust.

CHAPTER 1 -

Independence Day, 1931

Earl awoke from the chilling dream with a start. He sat up abruptly, swinging his feet from the bed to the floor. Fine beads of sweat found creases in his forehead, creating little rivulets of moisture. He could still see the arm of his good friend, Lonnie Bailey, nearly severed from his left shoulder but held in place by some remaining sinew and muscle, just missing death by scant inches.

The dream was too real to ignore.

"Lonnie, Lonnie," Earl muttered to himself, "how could you get yourself in such a fix?"

Behind him he heard the whimpered protest of his younger, half-brother Glen. "It's so early, Bud! Can't we just go back to sleep?"

Earl had forgotten his ten year old brother's "escape" to his bed from the night demons of his nightmares. He glanced out the window. It was very early. The morning sky was a light rose color from a sun hidden behind the curvature of the earth. He picked up the old alarm clock from the dresser by the bed. Just after five.

"Sleep some more, youngun," Earl said softly. He must hurry, he had big plans for the day. He had promised Eva he would pick her up by ten o'clock and maybe sooner.

Eva, the girl of his dreams. The first girl not to allow him a kiss on the first date. He wrinkled his forehead trying to recall how many times he had taken her on an outing before she allowed a discreet kiss, then fleeing for the safety of her house, a window in the house suffused by the yellow glow of a kerosene lamp, a matronly shadow passing between the lamp and window, Earl waiting until she was safely inside.

What a puzzle she was, Earl thought. She still would allow no intimacies as all his other girl friends had, much to his dismay. But was that love he wondered.

Shaking his head to clear it from such beguiling thoughts, Earl quietly slipped on his jeans and shirt, moving as silently as possible, on bare feet, down the stairs, through the pantry and to the back porch. He pushed open the screen door on the back porch very carefully because it sometimes squeaked to high heaven. He sat on the stacked stone steps to slip on his battered work boots. Rising, he broke into a fast trot toward the back yard gate, through it and on to the barn.

The sun was ready to peek over the horizon, now. The horses were far back in the pasture, just above the spring. Earl stopped at the barn door, whistling shrilly but got no response. He walked through the barn to the floored room that was used for tack and feed. He pulled a bridle off its peg and a bucket from another, filling the bucket about a quarter full. He sauntered through the breezeway for unloading hay to the back gate of the corral.

Leaning over the gate, Earl banged the bucket against the vertical brace in the middle. "Pidge, come and get it!" he yelled. He whistled again, at the same time giving the bucket another bang. Pidge's head rose from grazing, she wheeled in a half circle and came toward the barn at gallop.

Putting the heel of his left hand on top of the gate and holding the bucket high, he vaulted neatly, gracefully over it. He landed solidly on his high-heeled boots in the soft dirt on the other side, just as he would beside the head of a steer prior to wrestling it to the ground in a rodeo.

Pidge came to a sliding halt inches from the bucket proffered to her. She was his favorite mount, a big rangy mare with a blaze face and reddest coat he had ever seen on a horse. Affectionate and gentle, Earl thought sometimes that she would lie on her back and purr until her belly was scratched as if she was a cat.

Earl allowed the horse to eat the oats before he grabbed a handful of mane and slipped the bit in her mouth and the bridle over her ears and forelock. He buckled the throat strap in place. He briefly considered putting a saddle on but discarded the idea as taking too much time; too much urgency to his mission. He must warn Lonnie to hide for a day, a week, maybe much longer.

Pidge was anxious to go, as Earl led her through the corral, opening and closing the gates behind him, to the well beaten drive to the loading chute. He paused to glance around: the orchard on his left and the mill building on the right. There was a large depression by the big apple tree left from the collapse of a cistern where Grandpa Sigler's house had stood. He was standing just back of where the old mill building once stood. It had burned before he remembered, early in the century. The house had been so close by that the burning embers from the mill had ignited it as well.

Nearly an economic disaster for Tyrone, the mill was a large employer, Marcus had told his grandson before he died that the fire made him a believer in insurance because he borrowed money to rebuild. It was fortunate that the fire had occurred in the springtime when the need for ground animal feed had diminished somewhat. He rebuilt quickly and was ready as soon as the first winter wheat had been threshed. He'd even had to buy a new boiler and steam engine because the old one was ruined by the heat of the fire.

Earl vaulted to Pidge's back with the lithe ease of youth and vigor. Seated erect, having dark eyes and hair, a long v-shaped face, he very much had the look of the American Indian with his sun-tanned visage from all the outdoor work and play. But with the long aquiline nose, high bridge, he might have been a Semite from the near east. Given his mixed heritage, anything was possible. In looks he favored the Odor/Morgan clan but in build was more like his father, big boned, muscular, a little taller than the Sigler tendency.

The gentle Pidge tried to take her head, but Earl only allowed her to begin the trip to Lonnie's house in a warm-up trot. He headed for the road that bisected Tyrone from east to west. Reining Pidge in a westerly direction, he stopped just past the high point in town at the Sigler residence.

Tyrone was situated on a ridge separating a north flowing watershed from a south flowing watershed. This view never failed to elevate his spirits. He could just barely see Kings Mountain near Willow Springs twenty miles away, through the early morning misty-blue haze. The green of the forest contrasted with the white of the fog that settled into the creek valleys.

Earl gave Pidge a nudge with his heels and she broke into a full gallop but he reined her in to an easy distance-eating canter. He rode past the Winslow place, the Old German blacksmith, to a Tee where one must turn north or south. He went North a few yards to the gate to the Bailey farm they rented. He opened the gate while the horse stood tethered by the dropped reins as any well-trained ranch horse should. The entry was to a large open field. Seeing no cattle or horses in the field he left the gate open. He mounted quickly and let her run freely across the field to the farm road to the house, slowing to a walk, as it cleaved a grove of trees, because it became rough and rutted. Emerging to another open field, the Bailey house and barn was only a couple of hundred yards away. He pulled the horse to a stop in front of the house, looping the reins over a hitching post.

The house was a large, white-painted, frame clapboard, story and a half, dormers in front, with a wraparound porch. The early morning sun was just giving the green leaves of the oaks behind the house a sort of golden-green glow.

Earl hurried up the steps of the house and to the front door. There had been no sign of anyone awake, no telltale smoke coming from the brick chimney indicating that the kitchen stove had been lit. He hesitated to wake the whole house by knocking. He knew the door would not be locked, would the screen be latched? In the Ozark Hill Country, locking one's house was not done. It was a sign of distrust of your neighbors, inhospitable.

Cautiously, Earl reached out for the handle of the screen door, pulling it gently. It swung open with a slight creak. He walked on the balls of his feet so the heels of his boots would not thump along the wood floor. He glanced into the big living room with the stone fireplace, remembering the long winter evenings spent sitting in front of it playing checkers or Pitch or just talking, with the dancing yellow flames serving as the only light as kerosene lamps ran low on fuel along with money.

He ascended the open stairs to the second floor, which was more like an unfinished attic, where Lonnie, his brother and sister slept. For a modicum of privacy the sister slept on the right side and the boys on the other side. He remembered the times he had slept in that very bed with his friend and brother when the discord in the Sigler household became too great. He had left the home he had lived in his first years back in Missouri with his mother and step-father, filled with constant bickering but not the bitter arguments, vociferously waged in the Elmer and Sylva Sigler household.

He moved to the bed where both young men were sleeping. In the Ozarks it was not unusual for siblings to share a bed with two or more because people did not have the resources to build larger houses to accommodate additional beds. He noticed Lonnie was nearest him. Walking to the bed he shook him. Startled, he awoke.

"Get up! Get dressed!" Earl whispered as loudly as he dared. "Hurry!"

Now sitting erect in bed, brown hair tousled from sleeping, Lonnie whispered back, "What's up?"

"My dad knows! Come outside, quick."

By this tine Robert had roused and was sitting up in bed. "How did Elmer find out?" he asked rather loudly.

Earl raised a forefinger to his lips. "Not your business." Earl stood erect abruptly, hastening quietly to the top of the stairs and on out of the house. He walked far away from the house and stopped by a corral near the barn. Lonnie and Robert followed soon and were leaning against the top of the wood fence, one on each side.

Looking at Robert, Earl spoke rather crossly, "I thought I told you it was not any of your business."

"I know all about the birds and the bees. I won't say a thing, just listen, promise." Robert crossed his heart.

Earl glared at him and his face relaxed as he realized that this eighteen year old brother was really as socially mature as either he or Lonnie. Especially since he knew that Earl, himself, went out with very willful girls. He also knew that Earl had one child out of wedlock and another shotgun wedding of "convenience" that lasted until the child was born.

Elmer, a profligate himself, arranged for the first girl to go to Kansas City, paid all the costs, arranging to give up the child for adoption. Earl was not given the same treatment the next pregnancy, he and the girl were both two years older (seventeen and eighteen). His father had felt he was of an age when he might be better prepared for marriage and fatherhood, although Elmer's first marriage had not succeeded under similar circumstances.

Smiling at Robert, Earl said, "Okay. Stay but no interruptions."

Turning to Lonnie he said, "It took me a long time to convince my Dad not to come directly over here and shoot you down. I took the shotgun right out of his hands."

"Earl heard Robert gasp as he comprehended the seriousness of the situation. Lonnie's face had become ashen, as his Adams apple went up and down nervously, "How'd he find out?"

Lonnie looked down and away, "You dinnittellhimdidyou," his words began to run together.

"You know I'd never do that, Lonnie. You're my very best friend. Sylvia is not my mother." Earl paused and continued, "I didn't think of Sylvia as a woman of loose morals and you're going right along with her. And my father is no better."

He wanted to add caustically, "Had I known what kind of situation I would be coming to, I think I would never have left my mother and step-father's house. Maybe I wouldn't have made all the bad misakes when I wasn't grown up enough to handle them."

"That still doesn't tell me how he found out," Lonnie complained.

"Just relax," Earl said, "and I'll tell you. But promise me that you'll get lost somewhere for a while."

Lonnie nodded his assent.

Earl began quickly to relate the events of Friday to answer Lonnie's query.

CHAPTER 2 -

The Revelation

Elmer and Earl had returned from the West Plains sale barn with a large load of hogs, ready for market. They would unload and feed them well until noon on Sunday. The market had gone up two cents on Thursday and radio reports said the market was still strong. They would load up late Sunday night, take the hogs to East Saint Louis National Stock Yards, feed them lots of dry mash, then let them drink their fill before going onto the floor for sale, insuring maximum weight. Mondays had the highest volume of sales and, usually, higher prices.

Elmer loosened the bandanna from around his neck, mopped some of the sweat and grime from his face while unloading and moving the hogs into the confinement pen, and said, "Earl, go up to the house. Let Sylvia know we're back so she can get some supper on. I'll get some feed out of the mill."

"Sure, Dad." Earl turned to leave. He quickly walked to the house atop the hill.

Earl entered the house by the back door and shouted, "Sylvia." No answer. "Anybody home?" receiving no answer, he hurried back to the barn and corral area.

Elmer was sitting on the running board of the truck, when Earl came back.

"No one there, Dad."

"I know," Elmer said. "Right after I heard the screen door slam at the house, here comes Lucille to let me know they were at Mother's. Sylvia has gone off to Houston for some reason or another."

"I'm not much at cooking but there's lots of baloney left in the icebox from yesterday," Earl said, forlornly. He had a hunger for a hot meal.

"Good news! Mother wants us to come over for supper," Elmer said. "Pearl has been cooking something special. Help me carry water for the hogs and we'll head over there.

In a few minutes they were walking to Sarah Sigler's a half block east and a block north.

Ira Miller, Elmer's brother-in-law, was sitting on the front porch with Earl's two half-sisters and half-brother. At the sight of their father they jumped from the porch, led by the prancing Vivian. She gave her dad a big hug and a loud kiss on the cheek. Lucille, a willowy thirteen, but showing early signs of womanhood, eagerly stood waiting for her hug and kiss, with Glenn hanging back, not wanting to enter into this "girl stuff." Elmer walked over to him and put his arm affectionately around his shoulders. Glenn beamed proudly over this manly affection. All three children were fair-skinned and blue-eyed. Vivian was a strawberry blonde, having a generous scattering of freckles across her nose and cheeks. All three were somewhat shorter than the Sigler genes demanded, more resembling the Smiths. Glenn, facially, more resembled his Grandfather "Monkey Jim" Smith, although he had more of the Sigler temperament.

Ira rose to greet them as they stepped on the porch.

"Hello, Ira," Elmer said.

"Hello, Ira," Earl repeated, not using the title uncle, showing his contempt for a man all the Sigler men despised. They thought him a lazy ne'er-do-well who didn't merit the affection of their sister-aunt and had no real standing as a family member. There was a certain amount of unfairness because Pearl had fallen in love with Ira, and he did make some attempt to produce an income to maintain their childless household.

"Hello, boys," the greeting, while deflecting some disrespect back toward Elmer who was senior in age and more socially advanced or better educated, was cordial enough. "Come on in, I believe supper's ready."

In the Ozarks the evening meal was supper and the noon meal was dinner, usually.

"I need to wash up some," Elmer announced, "after handling hogs all day I feel nigh on as dirty as them."

"Me, too." Earl assented.

Elmer and Earl walked around the house to the back porch. A small table, holding a water bucket and Granite Ware wash basin, served as a stand just outside the kitchen door. They both scrubbed and rinsed until the water was exhausted.

"I'll go out and refill after supper, Dad," Earl said, "if that's okay?"

Elmer nodded and led the way into the kitchen.

All were seated around the table: Aunt Pearl on the left by the stove, still radiating heat from cooking; Vivian and Lucille on the side away from the door; Ira on the right by an empty chair; Glenn nearest the door with another empty chair.

"Come sit by me, Earl," Glenn said eagerly.

Earl knew that wasn't going to work. Elmer would be incensed if he had to sit next to Ira.

"No, your dad has been talking all day how he missed you three. He can sit by you and see his girls at the same time," Earl insisted. "I'll sit by the stove, it's not too hot for me. Aunt Pearl, you can cuddle up to your husband."

"I can't do that," Pearl said. "What if someone needs something off the stove. "I'd have to walk all the way 'round the table."

When Earl had eaten at his Aunt and Uncle's in the past, Ira had complained, "I cain't sit by the stove. It's too hot!"

"That's okay, Auntie," Lucille piped up, using a particular endearment common to their family. "If Vivian will trade chairs with me, I can do the fetching. I'm big enough to do that now." She squared her shoulders and sat up straighter.

After everyone was resituated, Pearl bowed her head. Waiting for quiet, she said a devout, humble prayer for the food, the blessings of the day and God's watch and care over the family. Even though she was the only overt Christian at the table, all heads were bowed in respect. She was the one who made sure the three young Sigler children went to Sunday School and church on a regular basis. Someone had described her as the happiest person they ever knew under very difficult circumstances.

After the prayer and filling their plates, the chatter about the mundane happenings of the day took the center of their attention.

Suddenly, in the middle of this hubbub, Earl noticed his Grandmother's absence. "Where's Grandma?"

"She'll be along dreckly," Pearl explained, " she got word that Missus Kidd was feeling poorly. She's her best friend," (as if everybody didn't already know). "She said she'd join us not long after we started eating."

"Earl," Elmer spoke up rather loudly, "I've made up my mind about something. I met a man at the West Plains sale barn today. He is selling out his herd. I'm going to take the hogs to Saint Louis Sunday night, Monday I want you to deal for them." He reached into his breast pocket of his shirt and pulled out a sheet of paper, reaching across the corner of the table to give it to Earl.

"There's a name and directions to his place," Elmer continued. There will be about thirty steers, a bull, and some older cows that he feels won't bring as much at the auction he intends to hold for his better cows, heifers and suckling calves. He's south of West Plains, near the Arkansas line. I'll give you a blank check. You figure how much to pay, buy them and trail them up here."

Elmer was an astute livestock trader who bought within fractions of a penny of market value. many traders were buying at a much lower percent because the market continued to fall as the depression deepened. Although Elmer took some losses, he watched the market carefully so that he continued to keep ahead but built his reputation for being the most fair trader.

"Okay, Dad." Earl looked pleased.

"You can ask Dillard Lay and George Bailey, just keep him sober, " Elmer smiled wryly. "Take three reliable trail horses and the two work mules for pack. Enough grain for four days and food for your men. Saddle the horses and tie them to the front slats. Tie the mules in the back with a separation gate between them and the horses. You'll have to ride all the way in the saddle because you'll have to put the feed and food in the cab, canteens, too."

Turning to Ira, Elmer said, "I'd like your help on this, too. Could you go down with them early Monday morning to take the mounts for the trail ride and drive the truck back. I've arranged to borrow a truck for that, since I have to take these hogs up."

As trucks became larger and more efficient, cattle were trailed less regularly, unless it was a fairly large herd of cattle. Since open range prevailed in most southern Missouri counties, larger herds would be moved to railroad shipping points for several more years this way until better roads were built.

It was galling for Elmer to have to ask Ira for help, but he knew the other men he could ask were not available over a holiday weekend.

"Would you do this for me, Ira," Elmer asked.

Ira looked at him in surprise and Pearl looked pleased.

"Sure," Ira said, chewing with his mouth open, food gathering at the corners of his mouth, "I'll have to close the shop." He was a rather handsome man with dark curly hair, almost kinky, average height, lean. He was glad to get away from the hum-drum of the barber shop with fewer and fewer customers all the time. Besides, he knew Elmer paid well.

Elmer gave his attention back to Earl, "There's three other consignments you can add to the herd along the way. John Huston will meet with you with fifty or sixty steers and some canners at Pomona. One or two of his boys will help trail to the home place or, even, to Rolla if you need them. You can overnight at Doug MacRae's by Willow and Grady's by West Plains, remember him?"

Earl nodded.

"On Thursday evening, Van Deventer, George and Charlie Bradford, McAllister and Patterson will meet you with another hundred or more head. You'll probably want to overnight there and you'll have a chance to visit your mother." Elmer raised his eyebrows, "any questions."

"Can we get there by Thursday?" Earl asked.

"You can but it won't be easy," Elmer answered.

Earl was pleased with the prospect of being able to see his mother. But he knew that it would be a strained time since he hadn't fully healed the rift between him and his step-father.

"Will I have to dye or paint brand them?" Earl asked (as the open range shrank and more cattle were raised in confinement, fewer and fewer were branded).

"No, Earl, that should all be done," Elmer answered. (Normally a good dye mark would last several weeks.) "I hope to have at about five hundred head to move on to Rolla a week from tomorrow. Pasture them at the home place. By the way, the rest will be consignment along the way. I'll give you list at the house this evening. We'll buy some more at the Licking sale barn. It would be good to arrive at Rolla with nearly a thousand head."

Earl was dumfounded, "Dad, that will be the largest herd we've ever brought there."

Elmer was going to say something more but the screen door squeaked as Sarah Sigler entered the room. All expressed their delight to see her, a short, rather matronly figure entering her sixties with dignity. She had a round face, blue eyes and graying brown hair.

Earl went to the next room to get another chair, still prickling with goose bump pride from the wonder of it. Being trusted with such a responsibility by his father was recognition of his maturation, adulthood. He returned and sat in the chair by the still warm stove. Lucille had already put down a plate and silverware for her grandmother.

The others lapsed into silence, as Sarah filled her plate and started eating, allowing her to catch up on the evening meal.

The silence was broken by Elmer, his handsome visage furrowed by a frown. He had blue eyes, full mouth, cleft chin, ears that had a distinctive crinkle on top, darkening blond hair. "Where's Sylva gone off to this time? She's been pushing the kids off on you too much lately, Pearl."

There was an inordinately long silence, the children shifted uncomfortably in their seats.

With the naiveté of all children, they could believe nothing bad about their mother or father. Lucille knew something was afoot but wanted it to just go away.

Sarah spoke first, "Sylvia went to Houston......with Goldie." The break in continuity was heavy in the atmosphere.

"Mother! You don't lie very well. 'Fess up. Who did she go to town with? " Elmer demanded.

A long silence was followed by another query by Elmer. "Kids, did Goldie come over today?"

All three mutely shook their heads, nearly in unison, Vivian mimicking her older siblings.

Elmer turned, glaring at his mother.

"Best you come outside, Dad," Earl said, rising from his chair, striding toward the door.

"Lucille," Pearl hastened to say, "there's two peach pies in the warming oven, get them out for your Uncle Ira, Grandma and the three of you," as she quickly followed Earl with Sarah not far behind. Elmer left the room slowly, reluctantly, with an inkling that he wouldn't like to hear what Earl would tell him.

Earl walked up toward the main road and to the three-sided well house where he couldn't be heard by his siblings. He stopped close enough to the structure so he could place his right hand against the side of the little structure, seeming to need its support.

Earl looked up as the three came to face him. He gazed forcefully, directly in his father's eyes. "Dad, thank you for your trust in me today." A catch in his throat slowed him, "What I tell you will hurt you. Me, too. Sylvia went to town with Lonnie Bailey."

As Earl's revelation made its impact, Elmer's face blanched, giving him almost a skeletal, skull-like appearance. As this disclosure seeped deeply into his mind, anger began to suffuse his face with brighter crimson. His jaws worked up and down, swallowing furiously, trying to contain his ire.

"That little son-of....." Elmer hesitated not wanting to use a crude phrase in front of his women folk. "I'll have to kill him!" he continued, rooted as a tree by fury, immobilized.

"Dad. You can't do that," Earl said, "Just think........."

"Why didn't you tell me, Earl!' Elmer's plaintive voice interrupted him.

"I didn't know myself until last night," Earl replied.

"You were with me all day and didn't say a word. Why?"

Pearl interjected before Elmer could say more, "I told Earl last night. I asked him not to say anything to you, just warn Lonnie off. He's about the only person Lonnie would listen to anyway."

"And I haven't had a chance to talk to Lonnie, Dad," Earl added, "You know how early we got up this morning to pick up a load of steers from the Bakers, get back here, unload and still go to West Plains."

"Mayhap, you just got what was comin' to you, Son," Sarah said softly, standing nearly behind Elmer, now.

Elmer spun on his heel, shouting, "You knew, too, Mother, and didn't tell me!" Globules of spittle formed at the corners of his mouth.

Sarah was a normally, quiet, self-effacing woman, but began one of the longest, accusatory statements she had ever made. "Is it any wonder with the way you and your father treated their women. I came out here, not knowing that Earl was going to blurt out the whole sordid mess. I just wanted to confront you with the fact that it has been three years since Marcus died. Pearl and I have yet to see any of our inheritance from the estate."

"But you knew. You knew!" Elmer repeated, rather pathetically, angrily, not heeding what Sarah had said.

"Yes," Sarah said, hesitating, "yes, I knew and I spoke to her about it, warned her to break it off. I knew if she wouldn't you would eventually find her out."

"Well, now I've found her out!" Elmer said vehemently, wiping the spittle from the corners of his mouth with his bare hand, in turn wiping it on his trousers. He turned to leave, walking stiffly up the road and up the hill toward the looming white house on the top of the hill.

16

They watched his progress up the hill. As Elmer turned into the driveway, Sarah spoke, "Earl, you must talk to him. Talk some sense to him." Knowing the Sigler temper, she added after a protracted silence, "He could really kill him, you know!"

"Yes," Pearl agreed, "You're the one he's most likely to listen to."

Earl nodded and walked slowly back toward the driveway by the mill and to the truck. He mulled over what he might say, the ominous burden slowing his steps. He opened the truck door and slid under the steering wheel. He reached for the dangling keys but then sat back in the seat, wondering again, how to begin, what to say. After a short interval, he turned the key on, put the gearshift in neutral, pressed the starter button the floor and the truck started, thankful that they had an electric starter now. He had his fill of cranking the old truck by hand. He drove to the house and parked by the Model A, nose in to the front yard gate, the whitewash peeling from the posts. He moved more quickly, now, feeling the urgency, up the flag stoned path, up the steps and onto the front porch. Opening the front door, he said loudly, "Dad, where are you?"

Earl could hear noises coming from the kitchen. He walked around the dining table and into the kitchen. Elmer was standing on tiptoe in front of the large pantry storage closet, a shotgun in his left hand, his right feeling around the top shelf where the guns and ammunition were stored. He pulled a .38 caliber revolver from the shelf and threw it back. Elmer had contended that he couldn't hit the broad side of a barn with it, that it was useless.

Earl stopped a pace from his father. "Dad, please listen to me!"

Elmer turned from his search, his eyes bloodshot, his mouth gaping open, his jaw slackly held. A vacant, haunted look dulled his eyes.

"Dad! You can't do this. They'll just hunt you down like an animal, throw you in jail, find you guilty, and fry your brain in the new electric chair in Jeff City. What of your children?" Earl waited for a response and continued, "Send Sylvia away, divorce, whatever. Not this! I'll make sure Lonnie leaves and never comes back." Earl paused again. "You can tell everyone you ran him off. Not this! Not this!"

Elmer still did not respond to this entreaty, staring blankly at Earl.

Earl held out his hand and moved closer, "Let me have the gun, Dad," he said firmly.

Surprising Earl with his meek response, Elmer held out the gun. Earl took it, his smile almost a grimace. He reached to the top shelf feeling for the gun case, found it and slid the 12 gauge into it. He placed it back on the shelf.

"Let's talk more about this," Earl said softly, turning to walk back to the dining room. He sat across from his father's accustomed place.

After a brief period Elmer slowly entered the room, trudging along as if carrying a great burden. He pulled out the chair and sat down heavily.

Earl and Elmer sat in uncomfortable silence for several seconds before Earl spoke. "I'm sorry this has happened and even sorrier that it happened with Lonnie. I thought he was my best friend but with this, I don't know." He paused. "But heaping one wrong on another is not the answer, Dad."

Elmer was silent for a long time. When he did speak it was with a hoarse, choked sound, nearly a Sob, "I shoulda done it seven years ago."

Earl looked directly in his father's eyes, a puzzled expression on his face.

Elmer continued, "No, not kill Sylva. I never told you this or anyone. I filed for divorce from Sylvia about seven years ago. When I told her she begged me not to because she was pregnant at the time. I just never carried through with it." Elmer didn't tell Earl that he had filed again for a divorce four years later but did not appear for the court date.

"I'm glad you didn't, for your children's sake," Earl said.

Elmer thought for a while before speaking again, "I do believe I made a big mistake not sticking with your mother, Mary. She was such a nice girl. But I was just too young to realize the mistake I was making."

It was Earl's turn to be thoughtful before replying, "What's done can't be undone. Besides, I wouldn't have two terrific sisters and brother." Earl grinned to show his sincerity and continued, "Just promise me, Dad, that you won't do anything drastic. Let me get rid of Lonnie my own way."

The clock on the shelf between the dining and living room chimed once. Earl looked at it. Eva had written him a letter early in the week to let him know she would arrive on the Frisco train at Willow Springs about eight o'clock. Here it was six-thirty and nearly an hour's car ride away to pick her up.

"Dad, please promise me you won't do anything," Earl said when his father's silence dragged on.

Elmer nodded almost imperceptibly and said quietly, "I just can't believe Sylvia would do this to me."

"Dad, I have to go pick up Eva at the train station in Willow. Will you promise me, really promise me, you won't go off and do something you'll regret and hurt your family."

Elmer nodded again, more emphatically, "Okay. I won't, Earl."

With great relief evident is his voice, Earl said, "Thanks, Dad. I'll be off then. I've got to take a quick bath."

Elmer sat morosely at the table as Earl went to the back porch and took a large wash tub hanging on a nail hammered into the wall by the washing machine. He brought it into the kitchen and began dipping tepid, warm water from the tank attached to the kitchen stove into the tub. He bathed quickly, disposing of the water by dumping it over the back porch steps. He hurried upstairs to change.

When Earl returned Elmer was sitting in the same place with elbows on the table, with his chin cupped in both hands.

Earl sat at the table, glancing at the clock. Ten minutes to seven. Still plenty of time to get to Willow before the train arrived. "You know how good Aunt Pearl's peach pie can be," he said, "Why not go down and get a piece?"

"No. I can't now," Elmer answered. "How can I face anybody?"

After a long silence, Elmer added, "I'm so shamed by it!"

Earl said, "Go over to Raymondville, Dad. See Ray Miles. He's a good friend. You respect his opinion." He hesitated, then continued, "I think he'll give you good advice."

"All right, Earl, I'll go over to Raymondville," Elmer said finally.

"Dad, I'd like to take a vehicle to pick up Eva. Do you want me to take the truck?" Earl asked.

A faint smile twitched at the corners of Elmer's mouth, "That wouldn't be very romantic would it, all that hog manure smell?"

"I guess not," Earl replied, pleased at his father's thoughtfulness and relieved that some of the angry tension seemed to have departed.

"I can drive the truck to Raymondville and pick up some feeder pigs at Jack McKinney's on the way," Elmer said. "You can take the Model A.

"Thanks, Dad." Earl sometimes drove the Plymouth on dates (Sylva had demanded it new two months ago. It was now in Houston).

* * * * * * * * * * *

"Well that's it, Lonnie. I stopped to reassure Aunt Pearl and Grandma that dad wouldn't do anything drastic. I heard the truck go off toward Raymondville well before I left Tyrone," Earl said, rather grimly.

Chapter 3 -

Earl

After starting the Model A Ford, Earl adjusted the choke just a bit when the car backfired noisily. The two miles from Tyrone to the West Plains-Rolla Road was occupied by the thought of the dire situation his family was in.

The West Plains-Rolla Road was still a well-maintained, important road between Willow Springs and Raymondville, despite the opening of the relatively new U. S. Highway that bypassed little communities like Pine Creek, Clear Springs, Grogan, Nagle, Tyrone, Big Creek and Yukon. It was much farther to make the big Western swing where larger towns like Cabool and Houston were more important connective points.

Since the road south past Nagle to North Jack's Fork valley was relatively flat with gentle curves, Earl pressed the accelerator near the floorboard. It, also, required less attention and his thoughts turned to Eva. Soon he was singing to the hum of the Model A. engine. He had a good singing voice, used to enamor young women with romantic lyrics of the period.

Earl slowed for the ford at North Jack's River, shifting to low gear.

Sometimes he splashed across in higher gear but he didn't want to drown the engine and be delayed. Even though the rock and gravel was fairly compacted with so much use, the narrower tires on the Model A made it possible to get stuck in the middle of the shallow stream so he kept the car moving steadily through to the dry roadway on the south side.

He began the ascent up the hill to the ridge. A rutted track entered brush and partial clearing, on his left, leading to the Cubbins Place where his mother and step-father lived. It had come up for sale while Charlie Bradford and Mary came back from Denver for Mary's father, Frank Odor's, funeral in late summer, 1924. He passed Granny Hostetter's, waving back when he noticed her sitting on the front porch.

At the Clear Springs ball field Earl saw Rol Patterson out smoothing the infield for a double header on Sunday. It would be back to back double header's for Earl since he would be playing with the Clear Springs team in Cabool tomorrow. It would be fun. He waved at Rol.

A mile down the road he sped by his old stomping grounds at Clear Springs school and store. He'd lived with Charlie and his mother over two years, working the farm, going to school and church at the school house and playing baseball at the diamond. His departure was a painful episode in his life. The images of the pretty little Brewer girl, the pregnancy, the horrific argument with Charlie over it and his move to live with Elmer. Then, Elmer's solution to the fifteen and seventeen year-olds' pregnancy problem was more than he could bear to think about. So he closed it out of his mind.

Atop the ridge that separated the two forks of the Jacks Fork River, he began his descent, passing the Van Deventer's place and down the steeper slopes to the South Jacks Fork river where Clear Springs flowed into it. He crossed a more treacherous ford. The footings, just above the ford, had just been poured for the new bridge for a new highway that would connect Willow Springs to U. S. 63 at Raymondville. It would make driving between the two towns much less arduous. It would lapse for lack of money.

The remainder of the trip was less familiar to him, the ford at Pine Creek easier, and fewer people he knew along the way. He took a couple of minutes to stop at the Weiler's to offer to take them to meet Eva, too. They declined because they had late chores, but expressed thanks for picking up Eva. Esther, Eva's younger sister wanted to come along but was denied by her parents. They felt Eva deserved to meet her new beau alone.

Earl would discover the Weilers were much different from their neighbors, beginning their day later, and, usually, finishing by lantern light in the evening.

Earl was at the train station ten minutes early. Since there was time to spare, he went across the street for a cup of coffee at the clapboard Horton Hotel. He sat at a stool at the counter drinking his coffee. When he saw raisin pie on display, a favorite of his, he decided that since he had missed out on his aunt's peach pie to order a piece.

Just as Earl was finishing the pie, he heard the train's whistle as it entered the west edge of Willow Springs at the highway crossing. He quickly placed money on the counter top to cover the pie and coffee with a little extra.

By the time Earl hurried across the street and onto the platform in front of the station, the Frisco engine was screeching to a halt, the brakes squealing, spouting steam, billows of coal smoke and flying embers from the prevailing westerlies showering the people gathered to meet the passengers rapidly disembarking.

Eagerly Earl looked up and down the platform for Eva, but she was not there. He heard the conductor announce a short layover for coal and water. The whistle would blow three times to announce the end of the interruption of their travel. Many were starting for the hotel.

"Earl, why don't you come aboard and help me with my luggage?" he heard Eva's voice behind him. He turned so quickly he nearly fell, his feet atangle. Her head and shoulders were out the passenger car window, smiling, alluring, with an impish twinkle in her eyes.

When Earl entered the car, he saw the soft-sided valise and an open top briefcase filled with notebooks and books. He was puzzled why she needed help with so little baggage. She moved close to him, putting her arms around his neck, her face bare inches from his.

"Hi, honey," Eva said.

"Hi," Earl said, nearly choking from the sudden emotion. It had been several weeks since he had seen her and letters weren't really sufficient.

Eva pressed her lips firmly to his and held them there, until he lowered his hand farther and farther down her back. Pushing his hand away, she said, "None of that! But now you know why I lured you in here. I don't like public hellos."

Earl nodded but continued to press as closely to Eva as he could without offending her sense of propriety.

Moving away, Eva grabbed her bags and thrust them into Earl's hands. Turning, she strode, back martinet straight, out of the passenger car. Earl fell into step behind her.

As they neared the Weiler house, sunset was imminent, the clouds already suffused with orange many times brighter than the fruit. The darker blue of the evening sky gave Earl's heart a flutter of awe at the magnificence of God's creation. "It's sure beautiful, isn't it?" Earl said.

"Why not stop here in front of the school," Eva said, "we can watch it from here" It was the little one room school Eva had attended as a child. She scooted across the seat, avoiding the gearshift knob, next to him. He took the hint and kissed her a couple of times. He parted his lips slightly the second time but Eva kept her lips firmly together. Preemptively, she pushed him away.

"Earl, you should know me by now. Please, don't try it again," she said emphatically.

"Yeh, I know," he mumbled.

"If I'm to be a teacher, I'll have you speaking proper English. It's yes, not yeh," she said firmly.

Earl had allowed the Model A to idle in neutral so it would be unnecessary to hand crank the engine.

"Okay. Let's Go," Earl said, putting the car in gear, avoiding Eva's knees since she was now firmly ensconced by his side, and disengaging the clutch.

When he stopped beside the Weiler house, Eva insisted, "Go on home and get a good night's sleep. I want you at your best on the field tomorrow.

"Won't your parents think badly of me if I don't come it?"

"If my parents see you once a day," she chuckled, "it's probably enough."

Earl's smile was enough to melt Eva's heart as he said, "What you're trying to say is: They already think I'm some sort of savage."

"It's not that, you silly man," she said, putting both hands to his shoulder and chest giving him a playful shove, as he was half-turning to face her. "They just think that I'm too young and inexperienced for you."

Earl's lighthearted manner evaporated, as he said, "I guess my reputation does precede me." He sat musing for several seconds before continuing, "All the things your parents 'think' may be true, but I am hopelessly smitten with you. There's no getting around it."

The evident sincerity was sobering to Eva as well. "I've discovered I'm in love with you, too. If I've not already conveyed that in my letters to you." It was her turn to be thoughtful before she continued, "You must get home and get your rest for the big double-header."

Feeling the exhaustion of the hard day's work, the emotional stress of his familial turmoil and the hurried trip to pick up Eva, he said, "Boy, I am all tuckered out."

"Before you go, Earl, I want to thank you for your last letter and the check for the train fare. I would have wanted to come home so much, I might have used up the money I need to finish out the summer semester at SMS. Thanks."

"That's okay," Earl said, "just consider it a present. And I don't even know when your birthday is."

Smiling, Eva said, "It's a long way away. December tenth."

"Then consider it a fourth of July present," Earl laughed, putting on his lighthearted demeanor like a well-worn hat.

"There you go again, getting silly, Earl," Eva smiled, offering her inviting lips for another farewell kiss, "People don't give Fourth of July presents."

Earl obliged.

"You be off now," Eva commanded, scurrying backward out of the car with her valise and school case. She turned at the sound of the screen door slamming shut. Brother Clyde was standing on the top step by the door. He waved and Eva waved back. Turning back to the car she shut the door and leaned over slightly, to look into the interior.

Earl noticed, for the first time, that the dress Eva wore was a rather dingy print that had seen too many washings, and that the collar was even a little frayed. She puckered her lips in an 'air' kiss. He did the same.

"Bye," he said simply.

"Bye," she said, her eyes glittering with excitement.

It was getting dark quickly now. He switched on the headlamps. Putting the car in gear, he sped away, gravel flying from the rear wheels.

Earl stopped at Aunt Pearl's to get the children. They were in the kitchen playing with some Tinker Toys. His aunt and uncle were ready for bed, waiting for someone to take the children away.

They looked up when Earl entered the country kitchen, which served as an all-purpose room. "I'm back," he announced. They all looked at him questioningly, wondering what had transpired between their father and half-brother. "Kids, put your things away and we'll be off for home," he added. They all were anxious to get home so they raced to the car.

He parked the Model A by the shiny new Plymouth, and noticing the truck wasn't in sight. When he entered the house, Sylva was at the table where he had left his father.

When Earl opened the screen door, a single kerosene lamp burned in the center of the table. Sylva looked up. Her lipstick was smeared above and below her lips.

The look of loathing she endowed Earl with was not masked. She had come to hate him because she feared he was supplanting some of the affection Elmer had for her children.

Lucille, Vivian and Glen hurried to their mother's side; Sylva rose to embrace them with genuine affection.

After a brief time, Sylva turned from her children to face Earl, "Where is he, Earl?" she demanded.

When he hesitated, Sylva vehemently repeated, "I said, where is Elmer?"

"He went over to Raymondville. He was picking up some pigs and stopping off to see Ray Miles," Earl replied and continued, "Why don't you kids be off to bed? It's a big day tomorrow."

"Earl, don't tell my kids to go to bed," Sylva said. "You're not their father. I'm their mother and I can handle it."

Earl stared at her without rancor. Her blond hair was rather tousled and her blouse was buttoned crookedly.

"Sorry, Sylvia," he said contritely, as he walked over to a small table by the sofa. He took a match from a small metal holder and reached under the table. Finding a metal brace he scraped the head of the match over it, sparking it to a flaring flame. He removed the glass chimney of the small oil lamp, pressing the match head to the wick. It caught the flame. He blew out the match, adjusted the height of the wick, replacing the chimney. Earl picked up the lamp.

As Earl turned with the lamp in his hand, Sylva said, "He went over to see that….."

Earl interrupted before she could say more. "I'll take Glen up to bed if you'll give the girls a light back to their room," his voice was a steely command. Sylva glared at him again but said nothing more as he proceeded into the kitchen with Glen following closely. He entered the pantry which gave access to a door at the head of the stairs to the upper story. There was a latch that clicked when it opened. He swung the door back, which squeaked softly.

When they were walking up stairs the step next to the top one creaked loudly.

The heat of the day had built up in the second story. Earl went from room to room opening all the windows and doors to cross ventilate. By the time he came back to Glen's room his brother was in bed.

"Hey, Bud," Glen addressed him with his favorite nickname, "would you leave the lamp on a while."

"Okay, Glen. I'll just turn it down a bit. You can leave it on all night, if you want." He turned to lower the wick to a low flickering flame. Earl moved the couple of strides to the bed and sat down beside his brother placing his hand in an affectionate gesture on Glenn's shoulder. "I'm sorry your mother and I don't get on better," Earl continued.

"It's all right, Bud. I understand. She's just afraid of you." Glenn was so sincere and insightful for an eleven-year old. "I love you like my own sisters," he added.

Earl felt a sudden surge of love for his little brother and he felt somewhat better despite the terrible circumstances generated by his father and Sylva. In the time living with them he had established a healthy sibling bond.

"Good night, Bud," Earl said.

"Night," by the way Glen's slightly slurred speech, Earl knew sleep was not far away.

Earl left the room and back down, directly, to the front porch. He sat on one of a pair of one-armed single chairs. It was wood lawn furniture that he and Lucille had moved to the porch during a big thunder storm two days before. The two of them, then, sat and watched the boiling clouds sweep over the hills and trees in the west. He heard the higher pitched voices of his sisters and the lower modulated one of Sylva. The voices subsided. Sylva's footsteps approached the door to the porch. She emerged from the house and saw Earl sitting in the faint glow from the lamps through the window.

Chapter 4 -

Sylva

As Sylva stood in the darker shadows of the porch looking at Earl, slouching so nonchalantly in the lawn chair, her anger flared, overcoming the fatigue of a long, difficult day. She was pretty cranky to begin with. It was a tough day, she thought, having to fight off Lonnie's advances. She explained to Lonnie that it was not a good time for it.

* * * * * * * * * *

When Sylva had returned, the house was dark and deserted. She, then, drove the three blocks to Sarah's house. She found that house dark, too, in the deepening twilight. She knocked on the door loudly, shouting, "Granny Sarah, where are my children?" Sylva called Sarah "Granny" because that was how she had addressed the grandmother she had known as a child. Sarah, on the other hand, preferred to be called Grandma Sigler. Her grandchildren had acquiesced but not Sylva.

The door opened so soon after her knock and query that Sylva was startled by it.

Sarah, standing in the darkness of the interior, was like a ghostly apparition in her white night dress and white nightcap. It was a favorite accoutrement, a lacy thing. Sometimes the nightcap would stay on until midday or after. The dress and cap seemed to float by themselves in the last light of the gloaming.

"They're not here, Sylvia. They went to Pearl and Ira's house."

Author's note: Sylva was called Sylvia in everyday address.

Sylva placed her fists on her hips, a favorite pose when she wanted to exude some authority, "Pearl told me she was coming over to help you this afternoon and that she'd be cooking supper for everyone here."

Sarah assumed a defensive posture, crossing her arms over her ample bosom, her tanned hands creating dark holes in the white raiment. "She was. She did," she said rather curtly. "Might's well let them stay the night. Pearl and Ira will bring them home in the morning"

Sylva turned to leave.

"Wait!"

The sharp command by Sarah arrested Sylva's departure.

"What now?"

The curtness of Sylva's questioning reply brought a whistling, in-drawn breath through Sarah's clenched teeth.

"Elmer knows. He was threatening to kill Lonnie," Sarah said angrily, quelling the ire boiling within her.

"Oh, no! Oh, God, no!" Involuntary sobs erupted from Sylva's throat.

"Earl talked him out of it," Sarah said quickly. "He stopped by to tell us he had."

Sylva turned quickly to leave, the relief of the news stilling the sobs and tears. She stopped again as Sarah said, "I told you Elmer would find out. There'll be hell to pay yet!"

Sylva started toward her car again, almost breaking into a trot before she got to the auto. The Plymouth started quickly and she sped up the lane past the old harness and saddlery shop on the corner by the main road. Sarah watched the car all the way to the big white house on the hill, illuminated by the waxing moon.

* * * * * * * * * *

Now, turning away, her indecision apparent, Sylva wanted to confront Earl about her children. He had picked them up from Pearl and Ira's without permission. He had ordered them to bed like an old mother hen. He had now insinuated himself in their private affairs. What could she say? She wanted to shout curses at him, invective she had heard between her parents before they had separated. Her mother had remarried and moved to western Missouri and her father had remained at the home in Arroll.

Her dilemma was solved by Earl as he spoke, in a quiet, sad voice, one she had never heard him use before, "He knows! Dad knows about you and Lonnie."

The lack of an accusatory note, robbed Sylva of some of the anger in her retort, "I don't give a hoot if he knows. I'm glad he knows."

After a long silence, Sylva continued, "Maybe, now he'll know how it feels. This has nothing to do with you acting like you are my children's parent. I'll have none of it. You'll stay out of my business, you'll stay out of my children's business. Any more of it and out you go." Winded by her tirade she hesitated.

"Yes, maybe he will know how it feels." Still speaking softly, Earl had risen from his lawn chair.

Sylva could sense a rising anger from Earl, nearly shouting at him now, she said, "You sent him over to Raymondville to that woman over there. That.....that Jana! You don't care how I feel. Elmer don't care how I feel. Sarah don't. Pearl don't. All of you hate me. Sometimes I think even my children hate me. They fawn over you and mind you better. Now you want to take away the one man I love." Sylva sank onto the wooden love seat, putting her arms on the arm of the love seat her head on her arms she began to sob and cry pathetically.

Earl sat back down, his anger subsiding. When Sylva's sobbing had stopped, he spoke softly, "Your children do love you. You're wrong about that. They want you to love them, to mother them, to mind you. They love Dad. They want him to be a father to them, to mind him. The two of you have been so caught up in your affairs that you've been ignoring them and they've turned to me for comfort, for a little parenting."

Earl paused and continued, "You love your children and I love them, too. Let's not hurt them."

Sylva sat up abruptly, extracting a handkerchief from a dress pocket she dabbed at her eyes and wiped her nose. "Well, Earl, you've given me something to think about," she said softly herself now. "Lonnie and I had intended to, to……." She stopped in mid-sentence, dabbing at her eyes.

"This is something you and Dad have to work out between you," Earl said. "He wouldn't listen to my advice anyway. That's the reason I encouraged him to go over and see Ray Miles. All I can hope for is that he'll talk some sense to Dad."

Sylva was silent for so long that Earl asked, "How did you and Lonnie get into such a mess?"

Again crossly, Sylva said, "Don't you get into my business, Earl."

The question jarred Sylva. Earl rose and went in the screen door to the living room. She remembered the early May day.

* * * * * * * * * * * *

It had been an unusually early Spring. Glen had been out exploring the dry creek to the west, it led south to the main part of North Jacks Fork. It was essentially dry because it only had a stream after a rain or from snow melt. It widened to some open glades. There were abandoned fields near an old unused farmstead. He enjoyed poking around the old barn and the remains of the house. He found wild strawberries.

Glen remembered Sylva's fondness for wild strawberry shortcake. He came back to the house in time for lunch with his mother and his sisters. They all thought it would be a grand time to pick gallons of berries for shortcake and preserves.

When Sylva and her children arrived at the valley glade patch, they found they were not going to be alone in picking berries. Lonnie Bailey was already there and had a bucket half full. He greeted them cordially and welcomed the company. He had discarded his shirt over an old fallen tree branch.

It was a warm day and Sylva soon lost interest in picking berries. She began to recall the time she had gone to the doctor in Houston about a feminine irritation, a burning and itching, only to find that Elmer had brought home an unwanted gift. She confronted Elmer with it. He'd laughed and said he'd been to the doctor with the same complaint. She was still furious over it and not even telling her.

The sweat sheened back, shoulders and arms Lonnie displayed, the muscles supple and pliant beneath the suntanned skin, brought to Sylva's consciousness that she was attracted to him. She was picking very few berries as she glanced at him surreptitiously. A couple of times Lonnie glanced her way and smiled at her. The second time, he blushed beet red. Sylva wondered if her glances were that obvious. The more she thought about it, she realized that this was her opportunity to get back at Elmer for bringing her that awful disease.

Sylva was sure that she was cured of the disease Elmer brought her but she continued the treatment. She knew the doctor, near her own age, rather enjoyed having a chance to examine her. She had known for many years that she was attractive to men but had always remained faithful to her marriage vows. Now she resolved to break those vows.

Sylva stood up and announced, "This patch is about picked out. There's another patch just down the valley. I'll take Lonnie down and show it to him. Glen can take you girls up to the patch by the old farm he was telling me about."

Glen jumped to his feet eagerly. "Okay, Mom. Let's go, Sis," he said, walking over to grasp Vivian's hand, pulling her to her feet.

Vivian jerked her hand away. "I want to go with you, Mom, " she said.

"I'll come up and find you in a few minutes. It's not fair for us to pick all the berries from this patch since Lonnie was here first," Sylva explained. "He should have his own patch again."

The crestfallen look Vivian bestowed on Sylva very nearly changed her mind. "Go on, honey," Sylva said, flapping her hands away from her body in a "go away" motion.

Vivian turned reluctantly. Glen, anxious to leave, bounded toward the hill with bucket in hand. Lucille followed without a word and Vivian moved along more slowly. She kept looking back as they proceeded up the hill, Glen stopping periodically to allow the girls to catch up. When they were nearly out of sight, Sylva turned to walk down the valley, following a livestock and game trail.

When Lonnie failed to follow immediately, Sylva turned around and said, "Come along, Lonnie."

As the trail was too narrow to walk side by side, Lonnie plodded along in Sylva's wake. They went through a copse of trees to a lushly green, grassy glade sprinkled with wildflowers. Sylva walked off the track into the most thickly carpeted grass under the shade of some trees. She stopped in the shade and turned. Lonnie stopped a few feet away.

Sylva had known the Baileys for about ten years, when they moved onto the farm just west of Winslows. The old man who had farmed it died and his widow had moved in with a daughter. The Baileys had rented it ever since, raising a few hogs, some beef cattle and George bred horses to donkeys to make mules. He was kind of lazy but was renowned as a horse trader. His wife was the major bread winner, selling imported lace, crystal and glassware around the countryside.

Sylva had seen Lonnie grow up. Now facing him, she could hardly shake the feeling that he was still a child. But he wasn't a child. He really needed a shave. He was a handsome boy, she thought, no, a handsome man. He smiled and opened his mouth to speak. She noticed that some of his front teeth needed filling by a dentist. Probably too poor, she thought.

"Where are the berries?" he asked.

Sylva had been so distracted by her study of him that the question took her unawares. "What? What did you say?" He had incredibly blue eyes and nice light brown hair, a genuine Anglo-Saxon, full attractive lips.

"I said. Where are the berries?"

"I'm the berries," Sylva said, moving closer to him.

About a half hour later, Sylva and Lonnie parted at the strawberry patch where they had met. Lonnie went off to another strawberry patch nearer his house but not before they had planned to meet the next Monday.

Sylva tramped up the hill in transported delight with a twinge of guilt in the recesses of her conscience. After a couple of shouts she located her children in the middle of a large patch of berries. Their containers were nearly full so they decided to pick until Sylva's much larger bucket was full.

It was Saturday, sale day in Willow Springs. Sylva was in a hurry now, picking berries feverishly. She was very hungry already with all of her vigorous activity. She knew Elmer and Earl would be back with a load of livestock from the sale barn. Elmer would be cross if supper was not ready. Then the two of them would likely go off Sunday night for East Saint Louis to resell their Saturday purchases or take some hogs they had been feeding in the big lot by the barn and old mill.

As Sylva considered Earl's question and how to answer it, her good feelings toward Earl began to evaporate, replaced by s slower burning, calculated anger.

"It's none of your business, Earl," she said, standing up abruptly, her fists on her hips in her authoritarian pose. "It's just one more example of how you've messed in my family's affairs and I'll not have no more of it."

Earl looked at her silently, searchingly, a puzzled expression on his face, before he said, "Whatever! Whatever you wish, Sylvia."

Now that she had apparently achieved her dominant status once more, she dropped her hands to her side. "If Elmer is as upset as you say, I'll just go over to Arroll and spend the night at Pa's. Goldie was going to see us at Barriklow Spring for the Fourth celebration. Mayhap she'll want to come back here and go over with us. Tell the kids I'll be back about nine or ten in the morning," Sylva said firmly, in command again.

"That's a very good idea," Earl said cheerily, not feeling cheery at all. "I'll hit the hay, now. Got a big day ahead." Earl did feel rather relieved that he wouldn't be awakened in the middle of the night with a loud confrontation and argument.

"Oh, yes, you have that big doubleheader in Cabool tomorrow, don't you?" Sylva said. "Did your girl come in like you expected?"

Sometimes Sylva was thoughtful. Earl wondered if he was wrong about her, whose side he should take. Maybe Elmer's mistreatment of Sylva was what had brought this all on. He heard the mantle clock bong the half-hour, ten thirty, he thought and said, "I'll leave a note for Dad where you've gone for the night."

He walked past her and she followed him to the door. She stood watching as he pulled a little note pad from his pocket. He and Elmer always carried one to record sale prices, estimated weights and of types of livestock. Earl wrote out the note and placed it under the bottom of edge of the lamp, winding down the wick, to a lower guttering flame. He picked up the small lamp he had used to show Glen upstairs and departed for his bedroom, also upstairs.

Sylva hurried to the Plymouth and started it up. She was in such a hurry that she spun the tires, hearing the metal ping of stones striking the Model A behind her.

Before she arrived at the junction with the Rolla-West Plains road, Sylva had decided to go north by way of Big Creek, Yukon and Highway 17 to Arroll, rather than south through Clear Springs even though it was somewhat shorter. There were two river crossings. It was night and she could get stuck and be there all night. No! Thanks! She thought to herself. The two crossings on Big Creek would be easier.

Sylva knew her father wouldn't be much surprised to find her in the extra bed now that he had only one child left at home. She had shown up on her parents' doorstep many days, evenings, and nights during her stormy marriage to Elmer. This time it would be different, she would take charge of her future, not be dependent on Elmer's whims anymore. She had a nice little nest egg in her shoe box in the attic, several thousand dollars from over the years. She had plans for that and the big stack of cash she had found in the upstairs office.

Her affair with Lonnie hadn't worked out the way she had planned it. She had intended to just have a little fling, embarrass Elmer and maybe he'd give up all his running around on her. Several things had gone wrong.

Sylva hadn't planned on falling head over heels in love with a mere boy twelve years younger. She just couldn't stay away from him or he from her. On one rendezvous, Lonnie said, "I'm like a moth drawn to a flame, and you're the flame." He was so right and just as the moth dies in the flame now he is in danger and I can do nothing about it, she thought.

Another thing that didn't go the way Sylva wanted: she thought she could be the one to spring it on Elmer. That simpering, mousy, little sister, Pearl had discovered them. Pearl had come for the children because Sylva had to see the doctor for a treatment. Pearl and the children had walked down the road toward the middle of Tyrone. Pearl had forgotten something back at the house and the children had stayed to visit with Aunt Marthie Ann Harrison, who wasn't really an aunt but a second cousin to Elmer, at the Kidd store. Lonnie had walked up out of the woods and was waiting by the big old white oak tree just West of the house on the other side of the small, fenced pasture. She and Lonnie were holding hands, when Lonnie suddenly let go of her and indicated by his look back toward the house she should turn her attention that way.

Pearl was standing on the front porch looking directly at them, Her arms folded, disapprovingly, over her bosom. Since Pearl had already seen them, she had taken Lonnie's hand in hers and led him through the gate, down a path to the junk pile by the woods. The path continued on into the woods and down to the valley glade where they usually met. This time being anxious had cost Lonnie their secret from the Sigler family. The Bailey family knew because she had gone over to their house, brazenly, to see him. They had gone to the barn for privacy.

It was just the next day, Pearl's dowdy little friend, Myrtle Willhite, had come to the house, made sure she was alone with Sylvia and said, "Stay away from Lonnie. You're a married woman. You've no business seeing him." Myrtle and Lonnie had been seeing each other for over a year now. Maybe Lonnie liked older women, because Myrtle was about as old as she was or older. Sylva had taken some perverse pleasure in her discomfort, since she had been engaged to marry Rex Sigler, who had died after he had been drafted in the army in the influenza epidemic of 1918.

Sylva had made it abundantly clear to Myrtle that she would do as she pleased.

Then just a couple of days ago Sarah had collared Sylvia about it. She was respectful to her, because she had always admired her mother-in-law with how she handled her philandering husband, Marcus. Like father, like son, she thought. She remembered how she had fought for Pearl's right to marry whom she wanted, Ira Miller. In more recent months she had been insisting on a settlement of Marcus' estate. Even though she couldn't read or write she was nobody's fool. She had come to their house to ask that Elmer get the estate settled, not just for her but for Pearl's sake. The farm, Marcus had allowed Ira and Pearl to rent, was still being rented from the estate. Sarah felt the farm should just be given to her daughter and son-in-law, even though she didn't much like Ira either.

Just a couple of weeks ago a more serious problem had arisen, Elmer told her they were nearly broke. He had gotten a couple of big bills for clothing and dental work. She had been buying clothes for herself and Lonnie, so he could dress better when they went to nearby towns together. She had also been having the dentist do his teeth. Both were left as outstanding bills. Elmer had a tizzy over the bills. He said he had to borrow money to buy her car and had to borrow more to pay bills. With the drop in livestock prices and farmers' income down generally, they were going into debt they never had in the past. Their margin of profit on their livestock business was shrinking. Elmer knew it wasn't exactly true.

To top it off Elmer had told her that the Bank of Elk Creek where they held majority ownership was in trouble. He had transferred some of their cash reserves from the Raymondville Bank to keep the doors open in Elk Creek. Then came the run on the bank last week and they closed the doors in Elk Creek for the last time. Farmers in that bank had been using up their savings more and more. Few deposits were coming in. Many of them had stopped making payments on their farm mortgages.

Sylva had married for love. She had been enamored with the handsome man she had met in Summersville on the town square. She had loved him too soon, she was already showing with a child when they were married on that summer day in 1918. She aborted a few days later. The next was a happy year but a sad year, too. They had sent Rex's body home for burial in October. Then Lucille was born in December.

Sylva had married for money, too. She had reveled in her status, that she could buy just about anything she wanted or any time she wanted. Now that was over, at least for the time being. Elmer had visited all the places she had charged purchases or services and told them they should only accept cash in the future.

Lonnie had read in the newspaper about the state of Nevada allowing open gambling and commercial casinos. Nevada had also liberalized their divorce laws. Sylva and Lonnie had discussed going away together to Nevada to open a gambling establishment and Sylva could pursue a divorce. It was a little ironic that she and Lonnie had discussed divorce in such a cavalier manner when eight and four years ago she had begged to continue her marriage to Elmer.

Sylva and Lonnie had made a pact to leave the next day. Could she go through with it? Would her children suffer too much without her. Then she recalled that her little sister had been a preteen before her mother had left and Golda had stayed on with her father. She didn't seem to have been hurt by it. She thought she could do it.

The revelation earlier in the week that they had lost all their money in the Bank of Elk Creek failure made the decision easier. She could be reduced to living like all the other poor folks of southern Missouri.

As she drove along, Sylva began to sniffle and she wiped away a tear that trickled down her cheek. She muttered aloud to herself, "I wasn't even old enough to be married. I never had a chance to grow up. To have a life."

Just as she arrived at her father's house, her mood began to brighten considerably as she had convinced herself that her decision to leave with Lonnie tomorrow was the right thing to do.

She had gotten cash from Elmer to go shopping for years, stashed it away in her attic hiding place, then charged about everything. Elmer had paid all the bills and never noticed. Before Earl had brought the children home she had gotten out her treasure trove, placed it in a soft sided valise. She went out by the light of the moon to the Plymouth and put it in the rumble seat compartment. Sylva had no idea of exactly how much she had squirreled away. A couple of years ago when she and Elmer had a big fuss, she had pulled out her shoebox full of money. To her annoyance some of the bills had been chewed on by mice. She had heard that mothballs would keep them out so she had put them in the box after she had counted it all and replaced the bills in better order. It had added up to over three thousand dollars. She hadn't the time or inclination to count it again but it didn't matter. It would be enough, she thought.

Her father's house was dark. She got out of the car and slammed the door hard. She reached in the open window of the car for her purse. By the time she reached the top step of the porch, a brightening lamp glow was illuminating her father's bedroom window. When she opened the door her father was just coming out of the bedroom door. She was happy she didn't have to fumble around in the dark for matches and a lamp, thus the slammed car door.

"Hi, Pa," Sylva said.

With his tousled hair, round face, little droopy mustache, button-like nose and large protruding ears, her father lived up to his nickname of Monkey Jim Smith. Even Sylva had to suppress a sly little smile as she thought about it. She was sure glad she got her looks from her mother.

"Hi, Sylvia. You and Elmer at it again," he said.

Sylva nodded. "Something like that. Thought I'd best stay the night over here, if that's okay."

"Sure thing," her father replied, "It's always good to see one of my girls. The bed's still made from the last time you was here about two weeks ago."

"Thanks, Pa." Sylva turned to the dining table opened the box of matches and lit a small lamp. By the time the flame was burning, Monkey Jim had gone back to his bedroom and closed the door.

In the other downstairs bedroom, she stripped to her underpants, making no effort to pull the shades figuring she'd give any peepers a last chance since it would be their very last. She checked to make sure she didn't need a fresh napkin, blew out the lamp and tumbled into bed. She was quickly asleep.

On Saturday morning she awoke early as it was customary for a country wife. Even though she did no early morning chores now that her son and daughter were old enough to do most of them without supervision, she still had to get up to make sure they were done. By seven o'clock she had breakfast on the table for three. She had awakened Golda and her dad a few minutes before so they could get ready to eat.

The little family chatted some over breakfast, avoiding discussing Sylva's most recent rift with Elmer.

Finally, Sylva said, "I'd better get back. I have things to do today. I can't come to Summersville for the Fourth today, Goldie."

"That's too bad, Sylvia," Golda replied. "I'll try to get over to visit this week sometime."

"Okay," Sylva said and got up to leave. She figured she would be back by nine thirty. She would tell her kids goodbye and be ready to meet Lonnie by noon over by the Tyrone cemetery.

Chapter 5 -

Elmer

Elmer started the large Ford truck he had bought a year ago in East Saint Louis. He paid cash for it but times were getting worse. He sat and thought for a few seconds about his cash problems. He then put the truck in gear, starting down the road toward the West Plains-Rolla Road. He felt disaster looming.

During the two miles before he turned north toward Big Creek, he became pensive. His marriage was a disaster. His management of the family finances was in shambles. He'd lost one bank and most of his interest in Raymondville Bank. Their income was shrinking due to the market conditions related to the national economic decline, which many were already dubbing a depression. What should he do to heal his marriage, should he just call it off? The financial problems were not insoluble, he thought. They would just have to tighten their belt and live more frugally. The cattle drive he had proposed to Earl would give them a little monetary boost. The missing cattle drive money weighed heavily on his mind.

By the time he came to the turn to go east to Jack McKinney's place he had made some resolutions. This time he would really go for a divorce, no backing off. They would become more like most of the hill folk and live as a subsistence type of household. He would have the garden bigger. His children were old enough they could pitch in. He would hire a teenage girl to come in, clean, wash and can fruit, vegetables and meat. His mother could move back in the house in the back bedroom downstairs to oversee things. It would work.

When Elmer pulled the truck up in front of the house, Jack came ambling out the door. He was a big, raw-boned man nearing sixty-five hard. He and Elmer's father, Marcus, had been very close friends. They played poker regularly in the grist mill office. Jack's face, beetle browed, tanned, was split in a snaggletooth grin. The few teeth he had left were tobacco stained, with a streak of tobacco juice from the corner of his mouth. By the time Elmer was out of the truck and going around the front, Jack was by the front gate.

"Hey thar, Elmer," Jack said. "I'd 'bout give up on yeh. It's purt near dark."

"I'm sorry about that, Jack," Elmer replied. "Had some personal problems come up that I had to take care of before I came."

"That's okay. The pigs'r all in the pen by the loadin' chute. We can have'em loaded in ten minutes."

Elmer reentered the truck and drove around the yard to a fenced corral and backed the truck to the loading chute.

Jack's shout, "At's good," was Elmer's signal to go back very slow until he felt the truck touch the chute.

A few minutes later Elmer and Jack were leaning on the top board of the fence looking at the pen full of shoats, an equal mix of gilts and boars. At first opportunity he and Earl would need to mark the boars and have a mountain oyster feast. Barrows fattened better and brought a premium price.

"You've got a nice little herd of young hogs here, Jack," Elmer said. "What are you wanting for them?"

"You given me a dollar sixty-five for the last batch. How 'bout we do the same?" Jack replied.

"Can't do that. Your pigs'll average about twenty-nine and a half pounds. Last load I sold at a five and a half cents. I could give you one sixty," Elmer said. He knew he would settle two or three cents higher.

"Tell you what I'll do, Elmer. I want to go to Hampshires. I hear they sell better. If you could find me a Hamp boar and a couple of gilts ready to breed, I'll let these go for one fifty."

Elmer chuckled and said, "You've got yourself a deal. One of the Grogans found a wild Hamp boar and sent me a post card wanting to know if I'd pick it up. Earl and Dillard Lay went down in Ira's pickup truck. Earl lassoed it and hog tied it and they brought it all trussed up to the home place. We have some Hampshire sows and he found himself really happy with those old girls. The old boar I was going to send off to market soon so I'll let you have him and three gilts. How's that."

"Cain't beat that with a stick," Jack said. "Let's load 'em up."

"You'll get a couple of seasons out of that old boar," Elmer added.

After they loaded the pigs and Elmer wrote a check to Jack, he was on his way to Raymondville. He would take the pigs to Jana to feed in her pen.

Jana was a cousin of Belle Jones's husband. Belle was Elmer's second cousin. Jana had married at eighteen to Joseph Arthur. He was eight years older and had a hundred and eighty acre farm just East of Raymondville. Joe was only married to Jana five years when a young stallion he had bought from Elmer kicked Joe square in the side of the head and killed him instantly. Just a freak accident.

Two years before, about a week after the funeral, Elmer stopped by to offer to sell the horse for her so he loaded the horse on the truck to take back to Tyrone. She asked him to buy her herd of beef cattle and bring her a couple of Jersey cows. A neighbor offered the use of a bull when it was time. That way she would have milk and beef from the occasional calf. She already had three or four dozen chickens. Elmer convinced Ray Miles to take Jana on at the bank. She had a ten acre fenced area by the barn for her cows and calves. The neighbor offered to rent the other hundred seventy acres for two bits an acre. The rent income, the eggs and cream she sold and her forty-five cents a day at the bank let her and her son get by quite well. She sold her small truck, work horses and most farm equipment and bought a used Model A

He backed the truck carefully to the loading chute and unloaded the pigs. Jana came walking out to the truck, waiting for Elmer to come out of the pen.

"You've got more work for me I see," a smiling Jana said.

"That's right. Ten cents a head for each month you feed them," Elmer said.

"I can stand the extra cash. Thanks, Elmer."

They stood silent for a few seconds before Jana continued, "I can whip up something to eat."

"Thanks but I ate at my mother's about an hour ago." He looked searchingly at Jana and said, "I need to go back in town to see Ray about something of a personal nature. All right if I come back in a little while?"

"I'd be pleased to see you later, Elmer"

Elmer got in the truck and started back into town. It was getting dark, now. He sat in front of Ray and Sadie's house, thinking of Jana. About a year ago, he had approached Jana about using her hog pen to feed out some pigs for a couple of months before he took them to market. She had invited him in for a cup of coffee and they started talking about Joe and his death. She spoke of how in love they were and how devastating it was when he was killed. She began to weep and Elmer reached across the table for her hand. The next thing he knew he was around the table holding her in his arms, stroking her hair, kissing her eyes and then her lips. Her son was visiting his grandparents in town which allowed them to spend the night together the first time. Each time he came to or through Raymondville he stopped by for a visit and an occasional overnight. He always arose about four to five o'clock so he could be gone long before Ritchie, Jana's son, was awake.

Elmer emerged from the truck reluctantly, trudging slowly up the steps to the front porch. He knocked softly. Sadie opened the door. Sadie Miles was the rock of her family. She and Ray had two young children eight and six, a boy and a girl. Sadie waited expectantly.

"I need to see Ray about a personal matter. Both of you," Elmer said softly.

"Sit here on the porch. I'll get Ray," she replied.

There was a long high-backed bench and two chairs. Elmer sat on a chair.

After a couple of minutes, Ray and Sadie came and sat on the bench holding hands. Elmer noticed and had some pangs of regret. Why couldn't he have that kind of marriage. Could it be a lot my fault, he thought.

Ray miles was thirty-one years old, about half way between Elmer and Earl, his two good friends. He was friends with Elmer through the bank because they both had owned most of the interest in the Raymondville Bank. Ray's father and Marcus started the bank during the big European War, as it was sometimes called. He was a teenager, just out of high school. Ray's dad had started him off as janitor and general flunky. He had worked in every position in the bank until his father had gone off to start another bank in Licking just up the road. That was about five years ago so he was bank president at the tender age of twenty-six.

Ray was a friend of Earl through baseball. He remembered their first meeting on the field:

* * * * * * * * * *

The Raymondville team was playing a double-header with the Clear Springs team. Earl had pitched for their team in his early teens while he still was living with his mother and step-father. Gould McCallister, a side wheeler, who almost threw under handed, was the pitcher in the first game. The two teams had gone scoreless for eight and a half innings. In the bottom of their ninth the first and second hitters were on with a single and walk. The second place hitter knocked them in with a double. Gould had walked the third place batter and Ray was ready to bat when the Clear Springs manager called for Earl to come in relief. After warming up a few pitches, Earl's first pitch came in at Ray's knees, the second right behind his head and the third, a slow curve ball, caught him in the middle of the back. Ray had glared at Earl for several seconds, threw his bat skidding across the dirt toward the mound causing Earl to have to jump up to let it go under his feet, Earl smiling impishly. Earl struck out the next three batters with nine hard fastballs.

In the second game Earl had hit a home run with two runners on. In the second inning the second place hitter had gotten on base with a ground ball single off the second baseman's glove. Ray came up batting cleanup and had the first pitch go behind his back. He thought to himself, here we go again. The next pitch was a fastball thigh high and Ray parked it over the fence. Ray took a very slow trot around the bases looking at Earl all the way around with Earl glaring at him. That was all the runs the Raymondville team got the rest of the game, no hits, no walks and one on base by error. Earl hit another home run.

After the game Earl walked across the diamond directly at Ray. Earl stopped an arms-length away and said, "Sorry about that pitch. It just got away from me."

"Sure," Ray replied, "and my grandmother was a jackrabbit."

"I just want you to know I didn't mean any harm," Earl said.

Ray nodded, "I know. If you wanted to hurt someone it would have been your smoking fastball." He hesitated for a few seconds and continued. "Why don't you grab your girlfriend and go over to the restaraunt for supper with Sadie and me."

Ray had known Ruth Evans' family in Elk Creek through the Miles' and Sigler's interest in the Elk Creek Bank. They were a nice family and Ruth was a pretty young girl.

Earl had met Ruth when he had delivered a large cash deposit to the Bank. He said, "Let me go over and ask Ruth if she wants to do that."

It was early Fall and it was getting a chill this late in the day. Earl and Ruth had accompanied the Miles' to the restaurant. In the course of eating Ray had encouraged Earl to talk to Elmer about selling the stocks he had invested in after Marcus Sigler's death. He could foresee troubling signs in the stock market. Earl had done that but Elmer hung on to his stock too long then had to sell some for a substantial loss a week after the Great Stock Market crash.

* * * * * * * * * * * *

Elmer's jaw muscles bunched as he tried to control his emotions, now. "I've got terrible troubles in my marriage, Ray," he said.

Ray nodded and Sadie was quietly sympathetic.

"I just don't know what to do," Elmer continued.

Sadie spoke first, "Why don't you tell us about it. Maybe we can suggest something."

"Well. Sylvia has been having a hot affair with Lonnie Bailey."

Ray's face showed surprise, "He's only nineteen, isn't he?"

"Yes. But she leads him around by the nose, like a young bull with a nose ring." He looked at Sadie, and said, "or by another way." He noted Sadie's distaste for his vulgarity.

Sadie squinted her eyes as she spoke, "You must be trying to tell us that this is an adulterous affair. Am I right?"

"Yes. It is all over Tyrone. I'm probably the last one to find out."

Ray said, "Does everyone in Tyrone know of your relationship to Jana Arthur? Everyone in Raymondville does."

Elmer looked at Ray in surprise. He thought Ray had a lot of nerve to say something like that.

"Why are you baffled by what I've said. It's the truth." Ray said.

"I know it's the truth but it's different."

"No its not and you know it," Ray said. "Adultery is what it is. Unless you give up Jana, there's no hope for your marriage."

Sadie spoke, "God loves you and wants the best for you in your marriage. I would suggest to you that you turn to him for help to get your life in order"

"That's what Pearlie says to me all the time." Elmer said.

"Your sister is a good woman, she knows what she's talking about. Again, I would suggest that you ask God's forgiveness, accept Jesus' sacrifice. Then ask Sylvia's forgiveness. Let's hope she accepts it and wants to resume a normal husband and wife relationship," Sadie said.

Elmer was thoughtful for a while before he spoke, "I just don't know if I can do that."

"Sadie's right," Ray said, "unless you do ask for forgiveness, you might as well give up your marriage. With your kids in the picture, it's the right thing to do."

Pensive, beleaguered, Elmer nodded and said a few seconds later, "I'll try. I promise"

Sadie said, "Let's pray about it." Both men bowed their heads. "Oh God, hear our prayer, Lord of Hosts, Lord of life, forgive Elmer his sin and help him heal his marriage. In the name of Jesus. Amen."

The power of this simple prayer rocked Elmer but he just couldn't bring himself to ask forgiveness on his own behalf. His mother had gone regularly to the Baptist Church at Big Creek. His younger brother had accepted Jesus as his savior and had become a preacher of the Gospel. But what had it got him! He had died from the big influenza epidemic after he had been drafted in the army. Elmer had been drafted a month earlier but had not contracted the flu. Elmer had been allowed to muster out the month the war was over.

That year and a half had been one of great turmoil. He married Sylva in May and she aborted in June after a four month pregnancy. She had aborted again early in 1918. When he was drafted in the army in July 1918 she was pregnant again. Then Rex was drafted in August and died less than two months later.

After these thoughts rocketed through his mind, Elmer mumbled quietly, "I will try. I will," as if the repetition would make it really happen.

"I hope you will, Elmer," Ray said.

"I best be going if I want to get back for a good night's sleep."

"Come back on Monday and we'll talk about that cash advance for the big herd to trail to Rolla," Ray said firmly. "You're still overdrawn from the last one though."

"Have you talked to Jake Miles about it? Would your father approve?"

"I didn't have to but, as it happened, he was over this afternoon and I told him I was going to propose this to you. He thought it was a good idea."

Elmer nodded, rose to his feet and proceeded to the truck. When Elmer turned to go East, they knew where he was going. Sadie shook her head with a look of sadness and Ray pensively nodded.

It was near full dark now, with a bank of heavy clouds on the horizon, as he parked the truck by the front gate to the yard surrounding the house and garden area. As he got out Jana appeared in the doorway. Elmer moved slowly up the steps and on the front porch. Before he could speak she was in his arms, pressing her lips to his. His resolve wavered.

When she leaned away from him, he said, "Jana, I need to talk to you."

He told her all that had happened that afternoon and evening and ended by saying, "I have to think that the only solution is to ask Sylvia to forgive me and take a new try at our marriage."

They had gradually moved toward the padded porch swing and sat down. Elmer felt so comfortable with Jana. She said, "I'll not give you up without a fight. Sylvia has run off twice. You've almost divorced her twice. You told me she begged you to take her back when she was pregnant with Vivian. And the second time you just didn't show up for the hearing. Now she's having an affair."

"Are we doing any better, Jana?"

"Well, no. But I truly love you and you've told me the same. Do you love Sylvia, still."

Elmer was thoughtful for a while. He and Sylva had not been intimate for months. Elmer shook his head and said, "No."

"I know you think it's the right thing to do. And I agree. Go back and try once more but if you fail come back to me." Elmer could see the tears streaking her cheeks from the lamplight from the front window.

Jana was leaning into him, her hand on his chest. Her palm was like fire consuming him. He put his arms around her, he thought for the last time. Her lips were on his and he was returning her kiss with passion.

She whispered in his ear, "Remember our first night together. I sent Richie to visit the grandparents. Let's have one last night."

Elmer nodded slowly. They entered the house quickly.

The next morning Elmer arose at daylight. The skies were clear, a good day to mend fences. Marriage fences, he thought.

He drove more slowly than usual, thinking about how he would handle it. He rubbed his face three days of stubble was like sandpaper. He resolved to get Ira out of bed. A half mile before he came to Tyrone, he turned south on the field road to where Pearl and Ira lived. When he arrived there was no smoke coming from the chimney. He was not surprised they were not up and about. Ira was lazy and liked to sleep late and was cranky if Pearl rose too early and awakened him. She did most of the daily chores beside the cooking and housekeeping.

Elmer knocked loudly. Pearl appeared at the door in her night cap and nightgown.

"Ask Ira if he could come in to the barber shop, today."

"Sure, Elmer." She turned away.

Elmer extracted his pocket watch and looked at it. It was nearly six.

Pearl was back quickly, "Ira says he was planning to open the shop at eight as usual, even though it's a holiday. We could use a little extra. I 'spect he'll close early so we can go to the Fourth celebration with the rest of the family."

When Elmer came to his house, he pulled the truck nose in to the front gate. He noticed that the new green Plymouth was gone and the Model A, too. He opened the gate, leaving it open, walking to the porch and into the house. He looked into his and Sylvia's bedroom. The bed was made. He looked in the back bedroom and saw Lucille and Vivian sleeping. Back at the dining room table, he now noticed the note left by Earl telling him Sylva had gone over to Arroll and Earl off for Eva and the baseball games in Cabool.

He walked down the street and back alley to his mother's house. Smoke was rising into the air almost straight up since there was very little breeze. It could be a hot day, he thought. He entered the house without knocking and into the kitchen. His mother turned from the stove with a coffee pot in her hand.

"I thought that was you, son. I could always recognize Marcus' step when he came in. You're bigger than your father but your footsteps are a lot alike," Sarah said.

"Hi, Mother." Elmer always used the more formal address even though his children had picked up the more modern "Mom" and "Dad."

"Have a cup, dear?"

"Sure. Would you mind if the children and I have breakfast with you. Sylvia has gone over to Arroll."

"That's would be a joy," she replied. Sarah poured coffee in his father's big cup and handed it to Elmer. "Here, you can sip this on the way to the house."

"Thanks, mother. I'll be back in a jiffy."

Elmer left the house and walked briskly to his home atop the hill. He found the girls still asleep. "Get up and dressed. We're going to your grandmother's for breakfast."

As he passed the dining room table he removed the note from Earl and put it in the kitchen stove. He went up and the steps to the upper story and found Glen asleep in Earl's bed. He shook him gently awake and gave him the same message as his daughters.

Less than ten minutes later they were back at Sarah's. When they walked in Elmer glanced at the clock across the room. It was almost seven fifteen. Plenty of time.

As all four trooped in and sat at the kitchen table, Sarah turned from the stove. "What good timing. Everything's all ready but the biscuits and they should be ready after all of you have washed up and we've said the prayer."

Elmer and the children looked at each other and sheepishly returned to be back porch to the bucket and wash basin.

When they returned to the table Sarah said, "Two months ago you came forward at church, Lucille. Are you ready to say the prayer?"

Lucille nodded and bowed her head. "Thank you Lord,..............." The remainder of the prayer was nearly inaudible until she said, "Amen."

Elmer looked pleased and began putting pork sausage on his plate.

Everyone helped themselves to fried eggs with fried potatoes, while Sarah opened the oven and brought wonderfully odorous biscuits.

There was an uncomfortable silence between mother and son.

Elmer was thankful that Sarah asked him no questions. When the clock struck half past seven, Elmer said, "I want to go down to Ira's shop and get a haircut and shave. I would like to look good for the Fourth celebration."

"I would have thought Ira would be closed today," Sarah said.

"Bet you got them out of bed," Glenn said. "He's lazy as an old mule."

"Shush, now, Glenn," Sarah said.

"That's what Grandpa used to say," Glenn replied.

"Maybe he did but it don't make it right," Sarah said.

Elmer felt guilty. He had said some worse things about Ira in front of his children. He said brusquely, "Sorry Ma."

Sarah was perturbed but fought not to show it because that is what Marcus would say to her when they disagreed on a point and he wanted to stifle any more comment from her.

Elmer continued, "I have a lot to do to get ready." He glanced at the clock on the wall, it was quarter till eight. "Best be going. You kids get some clothing together at the house to dress for the afternoon. I'll have Ira come by to pick you up and go over to the farm. Pearlie can get them cleaned up and dressed for the holiday spree."

Walking East two blocks he passed the house the Morgan's owned. When he was twenty of thirty paces from the house Aunt Annie, as Earl called her, was sitting on the front porch mending. When she spotted Elmer she quickly ducked inside the house. Weeden Morgan was hoeing in the garden. Weed, as most people called him, looked up and turned his back on Elmer.

The animosity ran deep in the Morgan's since Elmer had divorced Mary, his niece.

* * * * * * * * * *

Weed was an interesting man. He worked out West on a ranch. He had met Teddy Roosevelt out there. When the Spanish-American War broke out he signed on with the "Rough Riders" and had fought at Teddy's side at San Juan Hill. He was severely wounded. Weed was a saver and when the war was over he took his mustering out pay and headed back home to Missouri. He found a piece of ground available to homestead near Yukon. He built a two room house on it.

Weeden had a big forehead, beady black eyes sunken far back behind his brows and a sharp weak chin with a long slit of a droopy mouth. He was well past forty years of age and he thought he was destined to be a bachelor.

Until that fateful evening when Weed was fifty-eight years of age. He made a decision that would change his life for the better. He decided to go to a pie supper at the school. Pie suppers were held a few times a year. It was a way to raise funds for the school. Most of the time a beau would buy his Sweetheart's pie or sometimes a cake. The husband would "buy" his wife's pie or cake. It was an auction and there would be some smart aleck who would bid on a wife's or sweetie's creation. It escalated the price. The school was happy for this to happen as it brought in more money for the school.

This young woman, at least young to him, showed up with this great looking apple pie. It was autumn and apples were in season. She was less than five foot tall, willowy and sharp faced, with light brown hair, almost blond. At thirty-eight she was not considered a spinster but she was certainly an "old maid." He bid on her pie. A dollar. Too high. Unprecedented. There were no other bids. She had brought two forks and dessert saucers. They each ate a piece. He was smitten. Thus came a courtship of twenty months. He finally got the courage to ask her to marry him. He was nearing sixty and she near forty when they married. A year later a daughter, Naomi, was born.

That same year he received a letter from Washington D. C. from the United States Army. A letter inside informed him that he was eligible for a pension at sixty because he had been severely wounded in the battles in Puerto Rico. His left arm had mended poorly and was quite weak. Fortunately, he was righthanded. It gave the amount he was eligible for and a form to be filled out, dated and signed. He completed the form and mailed it the same day.

A couple of months later he got his first check. It was just about enough to live on if there was no other income. There were some automobiles around, mostly model Ts but they couldn't think of buying one. They got around just fine in the buckboard wagon, which doubled as the hay wagon on the farm.

That winter he came down with a severe case of arthritis and his injured arm throbbed unmercifully. He took to his bed in January and February. Neighbors came in to help feed the livestock and milk the two cows. They had sold milk to the store in Yukon and the neighbor men continued the delivery. By springtime he was somewhat recovered but he knew it was time to give up the farm. He knew of a small half quarter section that had a house, small barn and chicken house he could rent from a semi retired farmer just south of Tyrone for a small amount of his government check. He sold his farm by June and they moved soon after. He led two milk cows behind the buckboard, taking a half day to travel to their new home. The house and barn needed some work but not more than he could handle. The really nice part about their new place was a year round spring and a cave where they could store canned goods, potatoes and other garden produce that they could have over the winter

Although it was June, they quickly planted a garden that would provide canned vegetables and root crops. The eighty acres was mostly woods but there was a large pasture on the East end of the farm. He could fence some of it for hay in winter. By late summer he had the house, barn in shape and fence up around the house and garden which took in the entrance to the cave. He designed a cover for the entry to the cave with a door and built terraces to hold the canned goods and root crop.

Weed built a small two wheeled barrow that allowed him to deliver milk and eggs to sell each day. It was only a mile from their new home. He had brought five hens and a rooster. Two hens he allowed to nest and hatch chicks. From the first hatch he had twenty chicks for next year's eggs and meat from excess roosters. A big problem arose the next Spring when water came gushing out of the cave after snow melt and rains seeped into the underground aquifers. The river of water washed out the cave entrance cover and some of their canned goods.

Tyrone school had an annual picnic on the school grounds. Weed and Annie thought it would be a good thing to invite the teacher and students to have their annual pot-luck in their spacious front yard in front of the cave. The children would be invited to explore the cave if the Spring spate of flood from the cave mouth subsided. So the second year they lived there it became an annual tradition to go to Morgan's Cave for the picnic.

This paradise was not perfect. During the summer after Naomi's first grade, the old farmer they rented the place from died suddenly. By mid June the farm was bought by Marcus Sigler. Even though Marcus offered to continue renting, Weed wouldn't think of it in light of the divorce by Elmer from Mary.

A house on the back street behind the "beer joint" was for sale. It had five acres, a small shed that he could use as a place to milk his cows and a small chicken house. He could continue selling milk and eggs to supplement his pension. He delved into his savings from the sale of his farm in Yukon and bought the place. Not much needed to be done to the house or buildings. By the end of the month of June he was moved. Annie said she would take in ironing from ladies in town who could afford to pay. That summer, the house and buildings by Morgan Cave mysteriously burned. Marcus, a believer in insurance, had collected for the loss.

* * * * * * * * * * * *

When Elmer entered the barbershop Red Fronk was in the chair. Ira said, "Give me a few minutes, Elmer."

Elmer waited patiently, rationally considering his options. When Ira was finished. Red inquired, "Could you loan me a rifle. There's a wild dog that has been hanging around my place and I think it has been into my sheep."

"Stop by the house after I get my trim and I'll give you my little twenty-two single shot," Elmer offered.

After Elmer got his haircut and shave he walked briskly back to the house. Sylva still had not come home. Elmer actually felt some relief. He wasn't sure he was ready to face what he had promised the Miles' he would do.

When Elmer came to the house, Red Fronk was sitting on the front porch. Elmer nodded to him and said, "Give me a couple of minutes." Elmer walked through to the pantry and opened the cupboard door and took the little twenty-two rifle off the top shelf. When he came back to the porch he told Red, "I hope you can get that dog. Once they've got the taste of killing sheep, they can't be cured."

"Truer words were never spoke. I'll finish him off. Might even get a squirrel or two if you don't mind. I'll try to have the gun back later today. Thanks for the loan of the gun."

" No never mind. Whenever you can, Red," Elmer replied.

After Red turned to leave Elmer heard the lowing of the milking cows. He looked out the kitchen window and the cows were waiting at the barn door. Usually Sylvia and Lucille milked the cows. Glenn tried to help but was still a little young to be much help. They sent him off to bring feed for the chickens and let them out for the day. They didn't feed them a lot. They feasted on bugs and other crawling creatures around the yard and into the fields.

Elmer went to the back porch. He got a bucket, the strainer and a ten gallon milk can, carrying all three to the back yard gate. He left the milk can and strainer there. They had three good milk cows. They produced about five gallons of milk a day above what they used for the house. As he walked by the attached chicken house to the milk parlor, he lifted the chicken door and latched it open. He opened the barn door and the three cows filed in, always in the same order. Even cows have pecking order, he thought.

Elmer took a cup of feed and put it in the trough in front of three stanchions. When the cows were in place he closed and fastened each stanchion. He put more feed in front of the cow he was going to milk first so she wouldn't fidget around. He sat on the milk stool with his head in the cow's side, pushing gently until he could move her right rear leg back then he was ready to begin milking. Old Boo was the oldest and gave the most milk, her udder was swollen with milk and was dripping from her teats. He washed her well and began milking, he then realized that the dripping milk was a sign that the cows had missed a milking. With all the furor of the preceding evening the children and Sylva had not done the chores. If cows were neglected they would stop giving milk. The neglect of the chores by Sylva caused him a flash of anger because he knew she had come back late from being in Houston or Cabool, likely with Lonnie.

Elmer finished milking, put the ten gallon can in a wash tub, carried water from the well down the street, filling it near the top to cool the milk. Nick McKinney would pick up and deliver it to Cabool to the milk plant. He put out feed for the chickens. He took the slop bucket to mix with bran for the pigs. Elmer heaved a couple of pitchfork loads of hay over the fence for the horses and cows since the grazing wasn't as plentiful in the heat of summer.

He decided to walk to his mother's house to bathe since there was only cold water in the wood stove reservoir at his house. He took some clean everyday pants, underwear and shirt with him.

When he walked in the front door his mother was sitting in her rocker working on some crochet. She looked up with surprise on her face, "Hello, son. The children left with Ira a little bit ago."

"Didn't surprise me that he closed early with the holiday," he said. "I thought I heard his truck while I was doing chores."

Sarah raised her eyebrows.

"Yes, Sylvia didn't come back to see about the chores and didn't come back to see to them last night either." Elmer informed her, with an edge of anger in his voice.

Sarah nodded.

"I'd like to have a hot or at least warm bath," Elmer continued, "I imagine there's still some water that's not cold in your reservoir."

"Help yourself, Son. You know where the towels and soap are."

Elmer bathed quickly and put on his clean clothes. When he returned to the living room, he said, "I think I'll go over to Pearl and Ira's and pick up the children. They may have plans of their own for today."

"Well, I'm stayin' put today, do my celebratin' here."

A few minutes later Sarah heard the truck start and go east. The clock struck twelve. She rose, going to the kitchen. There was a nice crispy hard-fried egg in the food warmer above the stove left over from breakfast. She cut two slices of bread and put the egg between for her favorite lunch. She took her sandwich and a glass of water to the front porch to eat. She had an old box crate by her rocking chair that she used like a table. As she sat eating she saw the dark green Plymouth go up the hill, into the drive at Elmer and Sylva's. "Well, she's back," Sarah muttered to herself.

Lucille came back with Elmer and the two younger children wanted stay with their Aunt Pearl.

Chapter 6 -

Early Independence Day

On the ride back from his visit at Lonnie Bailey's family home, Earl rode Pidge in front of the white two-story house where his family lived. He noted that neither the Plymouth car nor the truck were in front of the house. His thoughts were so much on the family problems that he hadn't even noticed it. But now he noted that the little pine sprout, that he had planted just West of the entrance to the drive, had put out some new shoots. It looked like it would survive, but would this household come out intact.

When he returned to the barn, he unbridled Pidge quickly and trotted back to the house. He opened the screen carefully, entering the kitchen. The clock on the shelf in the kitchen showed it was a quarter after six. He quickly ascended the stairs, took clean pants and shirt from the closet. He retrieved socks and underwear from the drawer of the dresser and took his baseball cleats and glove off the top. He hurried downstairs and out the front door. His plan for the morning was coursing through his mind as he approached the Model A. Earl put the car in neutral, adjusting the choke and throttle. Then he walked to the front and twirled the hand crank hard. The engine caught on the first try.

Earl knew he had to be at the Weiler's by ten to make the start of the doubleheader at eleven in Cabool. He wanted to be on time for warm up. His plan was to stop by Charlie's and his mother's house in time for breakfast. He turned off the West Plains-Rolla Road between Beltz's and Granny Hostetter's place. He was glad it was dry because the road was treacherous in wet weather. Now he had to go slow because of the hard rutted road. He opened the gate that was devised, by Charlie, with an ingenious self-shutting mechanism. It had a large rock, rope and pulleys. He allowed the car to coast the short distance from the gate to the front of the little three room house.

There was a single car garage east of the circular drive, a large barn farther down the valley, that Charlie had built the first year back from Colorado. There was an old chicken coop and feed shed between the house and barn. Behind the house was a smoke house set on top of a cellar. Charlie had surrounded the house with a white picket fence. The house had a big porch all across the back of the house. A few steps outside the back porch stair was a deep well and down in the West ravine was an outhouse.

Earl's mother heard the car approach and came outside the screen door. When Earl came close, he held out his arms to embrace her. Without phones in the Ozarks this was not uncommon for visitors to just show up. Even so, there had been a look of surprise on Mary's face.

"Hi, Mama," Earl said when they were separated.

"Hello, son. Come on in." She turned and held the screen door open.

When he entered the house, Earl could hear Charlie moving around in the kitchen. He turned to his right and into the smallest room in the house. He looked up at Charlie, a strongly built but rangy six and a half feet. Charlie had a mixing bowl that looked tiny in his big hands.

"Hello, Charlie"

The quizzical look on Charlie's face melted into pleasure. "Hello, Earl. Looks like you're just in time for breakfast." Charlie was a well spoken man, from his years in the West and working around people with much better education. He hadn't started first grade until he was seven and his education ended about halfway through second grade. His mother had died about a year after his younger brother, Richmond, was born. She had severe bleeding and infection after the birth and just never really recovered. He was given the task of household cleaning, cooking, washing clothes, ironing. He became Richmond's and his twin brothers' (Jim and John) mother. George his older brother helped his father, John, on the farm.

"I sure could stand a good breakfast," Earl said. "Looks like you're whipping up some of your great batter bread." He heard the clock strike seven.

"Yep. Just need to pour it in this greased skillet and put it in the oven."

"Charlie, I need to talk to you about something personal." Earl turned to look at his mother and back at his step-father. "Just me and you."

He turned back to his mother, smiling to try to blunt her disappointment.

"Mama," he continued, "I need some disinterested advice. That's all. Charlie can tell you about it later."

Charlie put the batter in an extra large cast iron skillet and placed it in the hot oven. "Let's take a walk while the bread's baking."

"You men go ahead. I'll finish the meat and eggs," Mary's voice quivered with disappointment.

Charlie, donning his ever present hat, led the way out of the house to the feed house. "Talk to me, Earl. I can listen while I get out some chicken feed."

They walked side by side toward the chicken house as Earl told Charlie about the affair with his friend Lonnie, Elmer's infidelity and his intimate involvement. Charlie listened without interruption. When they came to the back gate, Charlie leaned on the gate post in an effort to get more at eye level. "I'd just stay out of it now," Charlie said. "You've done all you can. Let them work it out."

Earl thought for several seconds, maybe a half minute, and said, "Thanks, Charlie. I've always respected your opinion. I….." Earl hesitated for a very long time. "….I've never said I was sorry for the things I said to you five years ago. I was wrong."

"Everybody goes through their teen years chomping at the bit. When my father remarried the year I was sixteen, I was hard to live with," Charlie looked at the ground as he spoke. "I took off for Montana. me and a friend. Wanted to see the Wild West before it got tamed. All I got was hard labor making hay on a big ranch East of Great Falls. Near got blowed away by that tornado."

Now Earl understood the many trips to the cellar the two years he had lived here on the farm. Earl smiled. "I am truly sorry."

Charlie said, "Your mother and I were really upset over the Brewer girl. Here she was five months pregnant and barely fifteen and you just seventeen. What were we to do?"

Earl grimaced and said nothing.

"When you went to Elmer, he did the right thing, paying for the girl to go off to Kansas City to have the child and adopt it out," Charlie said. "We didn't have that kind of money."

Earl nodded, looking sheepish.

"We best go in for breakfast, Earl."

Earl nodded again. Charlie opened the gate and closed it behind them.

As Earl started up the porch steps but stopped on the bottom step as he was startled by what Charlie said. "I forgave you a long time ago. I knew this day would sometime come when you'd make your amends."

Earl, not normally an emotional man, stopped dead still, tears welling in his eyes. He brushed at them roughly with the back of his hand. He said, "Thanks, Charlie. You're a good husband for my mother."

They returned to the table set on the screened-in portion of the back porch. Mary was already seated. When Earl and Charlie were seated, Mary spoke softly to her God, giving her thanks for the food, Earl's visit and the good weather.

Mary had established a family traditional of Bible reading after the breakfast. She read the eighth chapter of Romans.

After the reading they chatted amiably. Earl had visited at least once a month in the four years, since he left, when he felt the raw feelings were somewhat healed. After his conversation with Charlie, Earl felt comfortable in the house for the very first time.

When the clock with the warships steaming on the front struck eight, Earl said, "Could you let me us a towel and soap. I need a quick bath."

Mary said, "You know where the towels and soap are and the water's free," giving him smile at her joke.

Earl got the soap and towel and went to the car for his clean clothes. He walked around the West side of the house, down the hill and across the pasture to the creek. The Bradford "bathtub" was of smoothed rock, knee deep, water hole in the year round creek. Spring fed, it was cold even in mid-summer.

When Earl returned to the back porch, Charlie and Mary were still seated at the table. Two basins of steaming water, one soapy and the other clear on an enamel top table. The clear hot water with a dipper to rinse soap off the cleaned dishes. The dishes and silverware were on an end to drain on a towel.

Earl announced, "I best be going. I have to pick up Eva by ten to get over to Cabool for a doubleheader."

Mary said, "Are you pitching today."

"Yep. Second game. What are you up to today."

Charlie said, "We're weeding garden this morning and going up to Henry and Effie's for lunch. They're planning to crank some ice cream. I believe John Dunivan will be coming, too."

"That sounds fun," Earl said.

"The men are going to finish off the stalls in the new barn, stanchions for the dairy cows and flooring for the hayloft," Mary chimed in.

Charlie's voice rumbled to life, "Henry wants to take little Tommie over to Willow for fireworks this evening. We're going to eat at the Horton Hotel, too."

Earl knew cash was scarce with the nation in crisis. He could hear the pride in Charlie's voice that they were going to do something special.

Earl rose and said, "Thanks for breakfast. Charlie, your batter bread and molasses were terrific, as usual." He heard the clock strike the half hour. He knew he would be there with time to spare.

Soon he was on the West Plains-Rolla Road. He waved at Granny Hostetter sitting on her front porch with her son, Johnny, who lived in the house across from hers.

They both waved back.

Several miles later Earl turned off the drive on his right, and up the hill to the two-story house with a single story kitchen on the back. The Weilers' rented the farm from a retired couple as they could not afford to rebuild the house, that had been too damaged to live in by a tornado, on their original farm.

* * * * * * * * * * * *

Eva awoke to noises coming from the kitchen. She was sleeping in the bed with her younger sister who was snoring softly. Normally, Eva as the older sister had a bed to herself upstairs in the second story and the three brothers were in the other upstairs room but Esther had complained so much about Joyce's snoring that Eva agreed to sleep in the living room that held a bed and a sofa and easy chair. Her mother and father had the East bedroom on the ground floor.

She opened her eyes and rolled to her right so she could peer through the doorway into the kitchen. It was her oldest brother, Clyde. She got up and walked to the door in her nightgown. Clyde was stuffing dried grass or hay into the top of the stove with smaller sticks on top to start a fire. He took a big wood match out of a box, struck it on the side and applied the flame to the grass. He put the stove top covers back except for the last round one which he banged loudly back in place.

"What's with all the noise," Eva said.

Clyde turned and looked at her suspiciously. "I'm the alarm clock around here now that you're not around."

Eva knew he was right because she had always been first up. "Someone has to keep up my tradition, Clyde." She glanced at the wall clock. It was after six and the sun was well up. She had always been up at first light every day.

"Besides, I'm hungry. I'm a growing boy," he complained.

Eva looked at him again. He had certainly grown, nearing six feet tall, husky now, a sophomore in high school this year, looking more like his mother's side of the family in build. "You've not been starved to death," she said, chuckling.

Clyde got some larger sticks of wood and shoved them in the front opening to the firebox. He looked at Eva and said, "I'll get the hog jowl out of the icebox if you'll start the biscuits."

Eva knew her way around the kitchen and soon had dough ready to go onto the floured cutting board as her brother was busy cutting off slices of jowl to fry. Eva looked at the oven's temperature gauge, not hot enough yet. She took out the biscuit cutter and started cutting. By the time she was done Clyde had the jowl sizzling in the biggest fry pan.

Eva heard the bedroom door open and her father emerged first, pulling a gallous over his left shoulder and her mother right behind him in her house dress. As they entered the kitchen, Eva said, "Good morning, Mama, Papa."

"Morning, Eva. Looks like you're settling back in your old ways," her father said with a twinkle in his one good eye. He had lost his right eye in a freak hunting incident. His twenty-two had backfired because a mud dauber had filled it with dirt. Wayne Weiler was very slender man, less than average height. Eva knew, however, that he had whipsaw strength and could work tirelessly all day long.

"Aw, Papa, I was up first," Clyde interceded.

"I know, son. You've been up before anyone for over a year now," his father said consolingly.

Rena Weiler, Eva's mother, spoke for the first time, "Hello, Eva." Her voice was surprisingly melodious coming from a short, strongly built woman. Her graying hair framed a round pleasant face with startlingly blue eyes. The hard years as a farm wife lay heavily on a woman near forty.

"Hello, Mama," Eva said. Moving quickly to embrace her, by passing her father. She knew her father was not one to be giving out hugs and kisses to his children. She remembered that he did enjoy playing with his children. He would get down on his hands and knees and play games. He just had a different way to show his affection.

"Looks as if you and Clyde have breakfast well under control," Rena said.

Eva said, "I'd better get the biscuits in the oven, though. Clyde will have the eggs fried before they're done."

Rena took charge of her kitchen. "Wayne would you go pump some fresh water for coffee. Eva and I will set the table and get the butter and preserves out."

Coffee. It would be a rare extravagance for her homecoming, Eva thought. Usually they had herbal or sassafras tea. Chicory was usually a substitute for coffee in the Weiler household. When her mother knew she was coming home she must have bought it. How nice. How thoughtful.

When the table was set, Rena said, "Eva, why don't you get the other children up. Just don't let them bite you." She gave a cute little chuckle.

Eva shook Joyce awake first and then went to the room on the left upstairs, the smaller room where her sister Esther was sleeping to awaken her. Her three brothers slept just across the upstairs landing. When Eva entered the room Wayne B, as he was called to differentiate him from his father, was already awake. Ralph was sleeping on a small cot. Eva sat on the cot and pulled Ralph to her lap and cuddled the three and a half year old brother. He reveled in it.

Wayne stood up in his oversized pajamas that he had inherited from Clyde. He was very short and slender for his age. Eva thought he would be about the size of his father.

"Let's go eat breakfast, boys." Eva said.

When Ralph stood up in one of his sister's inherited nightgowns, he was near three fourths as tall as his nine year old brother.

Esther, Ralph and Wayne B trailed behind Eva, as they came into the kitchen. Eva noticed that Esther was nearly tall and slender as she was, but with darker hair and dark grey eyes. Everyone hurried to their accustomed place around the table and Eva took the chair left for her. Everyone bowed their heads.

"Almighty God, you are a loving and caring Creator......" Wayne intoned and Eva listened raptly to a magnificent prayer that she could only agree with. The prayer was long and probed all facets of thankfulness. She had never heard any individual give such breathtakingly beautiful prayers. ".....in Jesus' precious name. Amen."

Rena rose after the prayer to attend to the last of the hard-fried eggs in the skillet. She then took the little coffeepot from the stove and poured a cup for Wayne, Eva and herself. It was pretty weak but smelled great. Eva knew she would perk the same grounds later for Wayne and herself. Never, never, waste such a precious commodity.

"Mama! Don't I get a cup?" Clyde complained.

"When you're eighteen like your sis," Rena replied. "Drink your milk."

"But I'm all growed up." Clyde said.

Wayne said, "It's grown not growed. Drink your milk. Grow some more."

Clyde ducked his head and obediently picked up his glass of milk.

Eva's mind drifted away to other things as conversation went on around her:

* * * * * * * * * *

Wayne and Rena both read everything they could get their hands on. They both were well spoken and intelligent without the usual hill accent. When Eva told them she wanted to go to the teachers college in Springfield, they were delighted but told her they had no extra money to help her.

The summer before at a family reunion she had met Uncle Harry from back East. He had gone to The University of Pennsylvania and was in the banking business. She had confided in him that she would like to, also, go to college. He had told her if she need financial help to write him. They had written letters back and forth.

When her family moved from the log house to their present residence over two years ago, Eva could not walk six miles each way and continue in school. Her first two years she had walked nearly four miles to Willow every day to school. Even that was hard to do. Most of her classmates didn't go to high school for that very reason. Her cousin, Mable Roberts, convinced her mother, Rena's sister, that they should let her come stay with them her Junior and Senior years. The two cousins had visited back and forth for years and were as close as sisters. When Mable's older sister got married it was a propitious time. A bedroom was unused. Mable's father had a well-paying job with the highway department.

So it was agreed that Mable's father would bring her home Friday afternoon. Then, Eva would go with her family to the Church of God in Willow and stay the rest of the week at the Roberts'.

During their senior year Mable began dating Kenneth Ogle. It became a very serious courtship. Kenneth was teaching at a local high school but had taken a position in Springfield at a better salary. By February they were talking about a wedding the Saturday after graduation and had a place to live.

That was an eventful Winter season. Eva had confided in Mable the uncle's offer of financial aid for her college. Mable said, "What are you waiting for? You can offer to pay him back when you get a teaching job."

That is exactly what Eva did. She enquired about tuition at school and asked Harry to loan her that amount. He sent a check for her tuition money and included some spending money as well. She sent a thank you note and told him she would cash it at SMS in late May when the summer term began. Mable offered an extra bedroom in her and Kenneth's new residence, so her Summer was set.

That same winter Eva had met Earl, too. She came home for a weekend from her teaching job. She had heard of a pie supper at Pine Creek school, the first school district north in Texas County. Their family farm bordered Texas County and the Pine Creek School district. It was a Friday night in February. Clyde had offered to hitch up the horse to a buggy and go over with her. Their family had friends who lived in the school district and a pie supper was a way to raise funds for the school. Eva baked a custard pie since they produced the eggs and milk needed for the ingredients except the sugar, spices and crust.

When Eva got there an exceptionally handsome man immediately caught her attention because he couldn't take his eyes off her. It was like she sensed that she could feel his eyes on her. She blushed slightly as she realized what was going on. During the auction, Clyde bid on a cake that he got for seventy-five cents. Her father had given him a dollar and said that was the limit. The young man who was so attentive to her bid a pie up to three dollars. Her pie sold for ninety cents. When she went to pick up her pie and wait for her bidder, an older gentleman wearing a wedding band, came to claim her pie.

She took her pie plates, forks and pie to go and have pie with her bidder. They each had a piece.

He said, "You're Wayne Weiler's daughter aren't you?"

"Yes, I am. If you know where we live you can drop the pie pan by their house sometime you're going into Willow."

It was customary to allow the uneaten portion to go home with the bidder and return the pan or dish later.

"I'll do just that, when I go to Willow some Saturday," he said. "The pie was delicious."

"Thank you."

Eva rose to go. As she was ready to leave the young man who had been so attentive approached.

"Wait. Don't go just yet," he said. "I thought I was bidding on your pie. Someone fooled me and then ran the price up."

"Oh, really. How amusing."

"I didn't think it was so funny," he said. "I'd like to get to know you better. How about I take you home?"

"I can't. I have to take my younger brother home." To her he was incredibly handsome.

"Oh. Too bad." He really looked very sorry, then brightened. "How about a movie in Willow tomorrow?"

"I can't do that," Eva replied. She noted his intense brown eyes.

"Why not? " he seemed puzzled. He gazed raptly into her grey-green eyes.

"I don't even know your name." He had nice brown hair, wisps falling over his forehead.

"Oh, that. You're right. My name is Earl Sigler" She had a lovely complexion, he noticed.

"That's better. I'm Eva. Eva Weiler. Yes"

Earl, again, seemed puzzled. "Yes, what."

"I'll go to the picture show." She knew she shouldn't knowing how her parents felt about movies.

She gave him the Roberts' address in Willow and they set a time for him to come.

* * * * * * * * * *

Suddenly Eva's mind came back to the present. "Eva, you've hardly eaten anything," Rena said.

"Oh, sorry. I was thinking of other things."

"Finish up Eva," Rena said. "The rest of you get to the chores. Esther, you gather the eggs. If there are any in the barn, keep them separate for our use. Joyce, you feed the chickens and start weeding the garden. The potatoes first. Wayne and Clyde can help with the cows."

Wayne appreciated his wife organizing the chores but he said, "I need Wayne B to get water from the field well. The well with the pump is dry as a bone. I got a couple of quarts of water and that was all."

It was setting in to be a dry year with enough light rains to grow grass and hay but not enough to replenish the underground aquifers. The field well was a dug well and it was fed by a strong spring below the water table.

"Papa, it's so far to lug water," Wayne B complained.

"I know, son. It will be just one day. When I go in to work at the lumber yard today, I'll pick up a barrel with a top so we can haul water in the wagon."

Surprised, Eva exclaimed, "Work! I didn't know you had a job."

"Eva, I was lucky to find part-time work with so much unemployment. I started right after you went off to school in Springfield," her father replied. "Most are looking for full time."

Eva nodded. "I see."

"We've needed to buy an automobile. I've put down some money on a car and I should have enough together to buy it in a couple of weeks. They gave me a month. It's a used Chevrolet coupe with a rumble seat." Wayne's pride in this new venture was apparent. He continued, "God has really blessed us with this part-time job. I'll continue with it as long as they'll have me."

As Eva contemplated this revelation she said, "Mama, if you can get along without me cleaning up after breakfast, I can help Wayne."

The pleasure leaped from Wayne B's face.

Rena said, "That's fine by me. Wayne, go find some buckets and take them on down to the well. I want to talk to talk to Eva alone for a few minutes. Clear out, all of you."

Esther snagged the egg basket and left with Joyce in tow.

When everyone had cleared the kitchen, Eva's mother looked across the table and said with great gravity, "I need to let you know that I oppose your relationship with Earl Sigler."

Eva was stunned.

Rena, not waiting for a response, continued, "He has had a child before he married the first time."

As tears sprang to her eyes, Eva stammered, "M-m-married!"

"Yes. Married. He has a child adopted out and one living with his wife.

We heard from some people in Willow that Earl had a terrible reputation with women. Wayne didn't want me to tell you about it but I find it is too serious a matter. Last weekend, rather than relying on rumor, I asked Earl's mother about it. I met Mary going into the MFA grocery store. She confirmed everything we had heard second hand."

Eva swallowed, tears beginning to course down her cheeks. "Mama, I believe you but I need to speak to Earl about it after his ball games today. I don't want to absolutely ruin his day. Maybe I do have to break it off."

"Yes. I think you do," Rena said emphatically.

"Earl's coming at ten and I will go with him but I promise, Mama, that I'll talk to him about it. I'd better get busy helping carry water if I'm to be ready on time."

"One last thing, Eva. Mary said she wasn't sure and neither was Earl that the child was really his. But he married the woman to give the child a name so it wouldn't be branded as a bastard."

"Maybe that was a good thing," Eva said hesitatingly. "But I am very in love with Earl. I don't think he would be going out with another woman if he was still married."

"Perhaps not, Eva. I just don't want my oldest child to get off to a bad start in life."

Eva nodded.

"And I would not like to see you deceived by a married man," Rena continued. "Now, go help Wayne B."

Eva changed into a well worn work dress and, as she trudged the quarter mile to the well, she thought about the situation. Had Earl really deceived her? In the intensity of their attraction to each other, had he just not thought to tell her of his past? She knew that she would have to jump this hurdle in their relationship or make up her mind to give it up. Could she do that with the powerful emotional attachment she had with him? It was a genuine dilemma, the first really difficult situation in her life.

Wayne B had found two serviceable buckets. The well bucket was upside down on the well cover. They lowered it nearly one hundred feet into the well. When the two buckets were full they detached the well bucket from the rope. Eva took two buckets and Wayne B one bucket. After four trips they had ten buckets to cool the milk, one for the chickens and one for the house.

When Eva reentered the kitchen, her mother had dressed in a man's shirt and overalls.

Rena said, "I'll put the two girls and Wayne B to work in the garden. I'll leave Ralph outside the garden gate if you'll peek out in the yard at him once in a while. I know you have to get ready."

Eva went to the living room to retrieve a folded dress from her valise, clean socks, underwear and sensible shoes to take into the kitchen. She latched all three doors into the kitchen since it served as a bathing place in the Weiler house. She dipped water from the stove reservoir into a wash basin. After removing her clothing she took a quick sponge bath with a wash cloth. This and a little perfume would do for the day, she thought to herself. She glanced at the clock. Nine forty. Eva saw Ralph with a bouquet of daffodils. She heard the Model A coming up the hill to the house. She donned her apparel quickly and brushed her hair. Unlatching all the kitchen doors she hurried to the living room, taking a seat on the divan. Earl stopped the car in the driveway. He left the car in neutral to idle. He opened the door and took two pieces of two by four wood from behind the driver's seat and put them behind and in front of the back wheel tire so it wouldn't roll away. As he rounded the front of the car, he noticed Eva's mother and three of her siblings working in the garden. Eva's father and Clyde were walking from the barn with buckets of milk. When they came to where the milk cans were immersed in cold water, they removed a lid from one of the two cans and began pouring milk through a strainer. Clyde waved at Earl and he returned the salutation. Wayne's weathered face was shrouded in shadow from his hat but he gave a slight nod in Earl's direction. Earl nodded in return, his new fashionable straw hat at a rakish angle.

Earl strode toward the front porch steps. He noticed Ralph peeking around the corner of the house. "Hello, Ralph," he said. Ralph withdrew his head suddenly without an acknowledgement. Earl continued up the steps and rapped on the door sharply.

Earl heard Eva say "Come in."

Earl opened the screen door and went in the house. When he saw Eva sitting on the divan, he crossed the room and sat beside her. He put his arm around her and he leaned toward her but she leaned away from him and did not offer her lips for a kiss. In fact she moved perceptibly away from him. What was wrong, he thought.

Eva stood abruptly. "We need to get going, Earl. You told me last night that you would like to get there in time for a good warm up."

Earl stood as well.

Eva moved toward the door and waited for Earl to precede her from the house.

Earl was aware, now, of a perceptible coldness toward him.

Earl removed the chocks and jumped in the car quickly before it could roll. Earl kept his foot on the brake and asked, "What's the matter, darling?"

"It's nothing, Earl. Let's just go enjoy the day."

"But there is something wrong," Earl insisted.

"It's just…..," Eva hesitated. "It's just that I had a very unsettling discussion with my mother. We'll talk about it after the ballgame. Okay?"

Earl nodded and put the car in gear. They rode in silence to Willow and on to Cabool on the new U. S. highway. Even though the highway was graded fairly often it was still a rough ride.

CHAPTER 7 -

Late Morning

Sylva's intention was to return earlier but she stopped by her best friend Elizabeth's house. Beth had married a local man when she was seventeen, too. He was foreman at the sawmill in Arroll.

When Sylvia knocked on the door her friend answered the door.

"What a surprise," Beth said.

"I was over at Pop's. I'm headin' home," Sylva said. "I came over last evenin' and it was so late I decided to stay over."

Sylvia glanced around the living room and said, "Where's Ed?"

"Oh, he went to look at some timber that a man wants to sell. Price of lumber is down with hard times. I don't even know if they will buy it right away."

"Oh, I know about that. Elmer's been complainin' about beef and hog prices bein' down, too," Sylvia said.

The two old friends chatted on amiably for two hours, Sylvia without a thought for the passage of time and her intended schedule. When Sylva noticed it was well after eleven o'clock, she said, "My! My! Beth, I must get goin'."

"Well, Sylvia, you must stop by again soon," Beth said. "All we get is a couple of minutes when we happen to see each other in town."

Sylva had so much wanted to confide in her oldest and best friend about her plans with Lonnie but she thought it was better left unsaid. "I must go. I have a lot to do today."

When Sylva rounded the S curve east of Tyrone and was coming up the hill she saw Elmer turn on the field road toward Pearl and Ira's farm. She wondered why he would be going over there at this time of day. She continued on into Tyrone and pulled into the driveway in front of her house.

Sylva stalked into the house ready see her children for the last time. When she walked into the dining area she shouted, "Hi, kids. I'm home."

A gloomy silence replied to her shout. Then a glimmer of understanding invaded Sylva's consciousness. "He took my children over to Pearl's," she muttered under her breath, thinking Earl had.

Sylva, seething with rage against her young sister-in-law, viewed Pearl as a rival for her children's affection along with Earl. Pearl loved children and had not been able to have any of her own.

The rumor had gone around the town that Marcus had made sure that Pearl would never have children with Ira. Pearl and Ira had approached Marcus about marriage when she was eighteen, right before her youngest surviving brother, Rex, had died in the influenza epidemic at Camp McArthur. Marcus made it perfectly clear that he opposed the marriage. Then, with Rex's death, Ira and Pearl had put off the wedding for a more appropriate time. So in the early spring of 1919 they had told Marcus that they would marry that June. In mid April Pearl fell very ill. Marcus loaded Sarah and Pearl in the back seat of the Model T, with his daughter lying down with her head cradled in her mother's lap. It was an excruciating trip for Pearl over the rough country roads. It took over an hour. When they got to the doctor's office in Houston he diagnosed her with acute appendicitis and recommended immediate surgery. Marcus asked the doctor, as the rumored story went, to made sure she was sterile. Purportedly, a significant amount of money was exchanged and the deed was done.

As the years passed, Pearl and Ira were not blessed with children for over a decade, the rumored legend got legs. It was passed down to the next generation. She was nearing thirty-two.

The jealous rage Sylva had for Pearl did not deter her from noticing the clock on the shelf showing it was well past noon. Whirling around, Sylvia dashed for the car because she had told Lonnie to meet her at the Tyrone cemetery. She started the car and was at the appointed spot a couple of minutes later. Lonnie was waiting with a small suitcase at his feet. He had pointedly ignored Earl's warning.

When Sylva stopped the car, Lonnie rushed over with his suitcase in his hand. "I can't go yet, I got back late and I'm not packed," she said. "I'd also like to see my children before I go."

"Okay," Lonnie replied. "I can go down to Palstrings'. Clarence sent a note over that he had some work for me." Lonnie worked for several farmers nearby for a dollar a day and sometimes less. He liked working with Earl better because the Sigler pay was better and more reliable. Lonnie was so infatuated that it didn't occur to him to question how Sylva could go off and leave her children, and how disloyal he was to his best friend, Earl.

"I'll just tell him that I am leaving the area and won't be able to help him out anymore," Lonnie continued.

"How about I meet you back here around two o'clock," Sylva said

Lonnie nodded his agreement.

Sylva turned the car around quickly and returned to the house. When she arrived the Ford truck was sitting in front of the gate. She wheeled around the back of the truck and into the shade of the big black oak that sat in the middle of the half-circle drive. Walking up the foot path on the flagstones she saw Lucille sitting on the lawn chair where Earl had sat last evening. It was getting hot and the house would be even hotter, she thought.

As she approached the steps to the porch, Lucille bounded to her feet and said, "Hi, Mom."

"Hi, sweetheart," Sylva cooed.

"I wondered where you were."

"I had to go up to Winslow's for something," Sylva lied.

"Oh, I see."

"Where's Elmer. The truck is here." Sylva's voice changed to a cold accusatory tone.

A puzzled expression creased her young brow as she said, "Dad went down to round up Sam. He wants to take him to Barricklow Spring to the picnic. He said they are going to have an informal horse show."

Sylva remembered the recent days when Elmer brought the young horse, only a year and half old into the front yard of the house, teaching him tricks for show.

Sylva frowned in concentration, "I need to get some things pressed to wear today and I'll press Elmer's favorite riding pants while I'm at it. Could you make a fire in the stove and I'll put some irons on the stove to heat up to do some ironing."

Mother and daughter entered the house and into the kitchen together. Sylva went into the pantry and brought out the folding ironing board and set it up in front of the west window that looked out on the back porch. Sylvia walked quickly to the back most bedroom where there was a large closet under the stairs to find a dress to wear for the first day away and a shirt and pants for Elmer. She felt that it was the best thing she could do as a parting gift, as a wife, to iron Elmer a shirt and his favorite riding pants.

When Sylva returned to the kitchen, the stove was heating up well.

"Lucille, why don't you open the South window and I'll open the door and the West window to let out some of the heat," Sylva said, bustling around the kitchen and putting the irons on the stove to heat.

After Lucille had propped the window open, she waited expectantly for more instructions.

"There are some pork chops your father brought back from Willow yesterday from the lockers," Sylva explained. The Sigler family rented a freezer locker space since they only had an icebox. "Go get the package from the box and I'll fry them up with some potatoes. While you're there get the fresh green beans Glenn picked Thursday from the garden. They're cooked and we can heat them up." Sylva went to the pantry and got two skillets and put on the stove. She put a large spoonful of lard in the smaller pan. She placed four pork chops in the larger skillet and moved the smaller skillet to the back of the stove as the lard was nearly melted.

Without being asked Lucille went to the pantry and got three potatoes. They were large red potatoes just dug on Thursday, too. She liked it when they washed them up and sliced them with the skins on and fried them. She washed them and rinsed them off with fresh water, removed a paring knife from the drawer of the enamel topped table and began slicing them on the top.

Sylvia got a large platter and slid the potatoes off the table top and onto it. She emptied the platter of potatoes into the hot grease of the pan. She put lids on both skillets.

"Honey, if you would watch the chops and potatoes and turn them when they're needing it, I'll do some ironing and packing," Sylva said.

Lucille looked at Sylva rather strangely, "Packing?"

"Yes. I'm going over to my mother's she lives over South of Kansas City. I'm going to stay with her a while. I'll send for you to come visit as soon as I can. Where are Glenn and Vivian?"

"They're at Aunt Pearl's. They'll all come and meet us at Barriklow Spring," Lucille replied.

Disappoint marked Sylva's face as she said, "Oh! I wanted so to see all of you and give you hugs and kisses before I visit your Granny. I can't go to Barriklow so you give them hugs and kisses for me. Promise!"

"I promise, Mom. I will! It just won't be the same this Fourth without you," Lucille said sadly.

Sylvia took a hot iron from the stove and began sprinkling water on the cotton dress she would wear on her trip and began ironing. When she was finished with the dress she left for the bedroom. She laid the dress on top of the bed and began putting underclothing, stockings, perfume, hair brush and other essentials in a large suitcase. She folded dresses that were not ironed on top. She got the hat box with her favorite hat in it. Silva put the stack of cash under the dresses. She returned to the kitchen to see how dinner was progressing.

Sylva looked at the pork chops and potatoes. They were ready so she moved the skillets to the back of the stove to keep warm. She heard the sound of a horse snorting. With a glance she saw Elmer tying the horse to the back gate post. "Lucille, tell your father that dinner is ready."

* * * * * * * * * * * * *

When Elmer left Ira and Pearl's house. Glenn and Vivian were so involved in a game of hop scotch, they declined to go back to Tyrone. Pearl assured him they would see him at Barriklow.

As the truck jostled along the bumpy lane back to the main road that led west into Tyrone, Elmer glanced to his right at his oldest daughter. She was showing signs, even at thirteen that she would be an extremely attractive woman, blond and blue eyed, taller than her mother. That's good, he thought because Sylva was very short.

Elmer sensed a sullen silence in his daughter, because she was usually very much the chatter box. He stopped as he was going turn west. "Is something troubling you, Lucille."

Lucille turned her luminous blue eyes toward him, tears forming in the corners. "Is Mom going to leave us again like four years ago? I can hardly bear the thought," she said.

"It's going to be all right. We'll do all we can so we're not separated again.

"After you left with Earl, then Pearl and Grandma following you out after supper, I know something bad is going on," Lucille said querulously.

"Sweetheart, it will be okay. I assure you."

A tear trickled down Lucille's left cheek and then another followed on the right. "I'm old enough to know what is going on," she said with some vehemence.

"It's something your mother and I have to work out. When we get it done, I'll tell you all about it. I promise." Elmer took his foot from the clutch and pressed down on the gas pedal. Father and daughter, caught up in the vortex of family discord, lapsed into silence.

Elmer waved at several people as he drove through the heart of Tyrone and into the driveway to his house. He left the truck in first gear, the keys dangling in the ignition. He and Lucille walked to the empty house. They entered in the dining area of the large front room. Elmer noticed Sylva's purse on the table. Puzzled now, he went to the bedroom to change into some work clothes. There was a suitcase lying on the bed. He opened it. It was empty. What was going on? Was she planning an escape with Lonnie after all? Well, he thought, I'll deal with that later.

He changed clothes quickly and returned to the front porch. Lucille was sitting on a lawn chair, paging through a magazine.

"Lucille, I'm going down to the barn and call up the horses. I'm going to take Sam to Barriklow Spring for the picnic and informal horse show."

Lucille nodded as she continued looking through the pictures, stories and articles.

Elmer continued, "Sylvia has been here since I went over to pick you up. Her purse is on the table. If she comes back while I'm down there. Tell her I'd like to be on the way by one thirty. Pearl said she'd bring enough for everybody for the pot luck supper."

The "Okay," was spoken so softly by Lucille that Elmer sensed her trepidation.

Elmer walked quickly to the barn. As he approached the corral fence, he was reminded that the hogs he had bought in West Plains would need water with the heat. He entered the west gate and moved over to the northeast corner of the corral to a smaller gate that allowed access to a much larger fenced lot and to the mill pond. This enclosure was not as secure as the corral but would give the animals access to the pond and water. The hogs would be able to shelter in the underside of the old mill and in loading area. He didn't want to deal with hogs suffering from heat exposure and it was certainly building up to be a very hot day. He reentered the corral and drove the animals through the opened gate and allowed them to find their own way to the shallow mill pond.

Because the pond was shallow it froze very quickly on an extended cold spell and was used by the town children for skating and running up to and sliding across the ice. There was a bare spot on the North bank where a bonfire had been lit the winter before.

When Elmer reentered the corral and walked into the welcoming shade of the breezeway between the part of the barn where hay was stored and the granary and tack room. He opened the door to find a saddle and bridle. He started to leave and then realized he would need a rope for young Sam. So he reentered the tack room and came back with a lasso on a fairly short rope. Elmer exited the west gate of the corral. He knew the cows and horses wouldn't be wandering too far from the spring on a hot day. He was right. The cattle were grazing on the south knoll of the pasture and the horses and team of mules were standing under the trees on the south knoll a short distance away. Elmer gave a shrill whistle and Pidge's ears came up. The older mare trotted toward the corral and Elmer. Pidge was sure she was going to get more attention after her early morning adventure. The other horses came up behind her. There were three other saddle horses besides Pidge and Sam. The mules came walking slowly behind them. When they were close enough Pidge noticed there was no bucket. She shook her head and snorted. Elmer held out his hand and she came up for a sniff.

Sam edged closer. When he was close enough Elmer took his hand from behind his back very slowly with the hidden lasso. He made a quick, practiced throw with the rope and the loop settled over Sam's head. He shied away but Elmer quickly pulled on the rope and it tightened. The young gelding stood quietly, then. Elmer backed up a couple of steps and took the bridle from the fence post.

Elmer returned to the granary for a bucket half-full of feed to reward Sam for such good behavior. When Elmer came back to the small herd of horses, Sam was still standing in the same spot with the reins hanging to the ground. Elmer nodded ever so slightly in satisfaction that Sam had learned that reins on the ground was the same as being tethered to it. Sam had learned his lessons well.

Elmer backed away slightly, Sam eyed the bucket longingly but still did not move. He had a chance to examine his prize pupil. Sam was a big horse over fifteen hands and might grow some more since he was only a year and a half old. Someone had intimated that his mother was part Belgian. That may have accounted for his somewhat larger size than the average saddle horse. Elmer walked back to Sam and put the saddle on. He grasped the reins and led him through the northwest gate of the pasture, up past the combination dairy and chicken house and into the yard by the back gate.

He took off the bridle, slipping he noose of the lasso over Sam's head at the same time, putting the bucket down in front of him and looped the rope around a fence post. He heard the backdoor screen open and slam shut from the tension of the spring.

He heard Lucille's trilling voice, "Dinner's ready, Dad."

She was now standing on the stone steps by the back screen door of the porch. Just last year he had screened in the porch with a waist high boarded enclosure. That wasn't what caught his attention. Lucille was so lovely, looking much like her mother although taller and slimmer.

"All right, honey," Elmer said as he moved toward the steps which were not mortared but consisted of large rather flat stones stacked in layers.

When he entered the house, Sylva was taking pork chops out of the skillet with a spatula onto a Platter. She removed the lid from another skilled and scraped browned potatoes onto the same platter. Sylvia held the platter by the edge with a heat pad and said, "Lucille, put this on the table while I put the green beans in a bowl."

Elmer glanced to his left and noticed the ironing board with his favorite riding pants. His first thought was: well, Sylvia is acting like a wife really should. He said, with feeling, "Hello, dear." He turned to his right to the wash stand. "I need to wash up," he continued. He moved to the wash stand. He grabbed the wash basin full of soapy water. He threw the water through the open window and through the screen. Elmer dipped water into the basin, immersing his hands in the water. He soaped his hands, vigorously scrubbing. He then swirled his hands in the clean water. Elmer pulled a towel from a bar by the wash stand and dried his hands. By that time Lucille and Sylva was in the dining area.

Elmer moved to the head of the table, his usual spot facing the West window, with Lucille on his right and Sylva on his left. Three cold glasses of lemonade were by each plate, moisture beading on the sides. He reached for the platter of meat and potatoes.

The platter stopped in midair as Lucille said, "Dad, I can pray."

Lucille knew that it hadn't been their practice to pray before meals in her household but she thought she might be able to change that now.

Both Elmer and Sylva bowed their heads as Lucille said a quiet, sincere prayer of blessing.

After the meal was over, Elmer turned to Lucille, "Would you go out and gather the eggs. I didn't have time to do it this morning."

Lucille went to the back porch to get the two large, cloth lined egg baskets.

When Elmer heard the back porch door slam shut, he spoke, "Sylvia, I want to ask your forgiveness for my being unfaithful to you. I spoke to my best friends, Ray and Sadie, about this and they gave me some counsel of what I should say to you."

Sylva was taken aback with this turn of events. She was silent for some time.

Elmer frowned, why was Sylva hesitating. "Well, Sylvia, what about you?"

"Yes, what about me?" Sylvia said.

"What do you have to say for yourself?"

"You mean about Lonnie and me?"

"Yes! Lonnie and you." Elmer's face was starting to turn an angry crimson. Sylva had experienced his violent rages before.

"Okay, Elmer, this is a good start. I know you know about me and Lonnie. I'm sorry, too, but……"

Elmer interrupted, "But! What? But. But, what? What do you mean, but?" his face reddening even more.

"If you gave me a chance to explain, I would."

"Okay," Elmer sat back and crossed his arms.

"I just decided a few weeks ago to give you some of your own medicine." Sylva saw the muscles of Elmer's jaw bulge. She continued, "You've done this to me for near a dozen years with different women around here. Jana

Arthur is the most recent. Before, when I got fed up with your philandering I would just leave for a while.

"I see." Elmer let his hands and arms fall to his lap, his face losing some of its color. "What now? What else?" Elmer continued.

"This may be a good start. Why don't you take Lucille with you in the truck and I'll go pick up Glenn and Vivian at Pearlie's. I'll see you at Barriklow."

Elmer nodded. "That's not exactly what I meant. What do you have to say for yourself?"

"Oh, you mean am I sorry. Yes, I'm sorry, but……"

Elmer interrupted vehemently again, "But. Here we go again with the buts." He rose from the table and stalked toward the bedroom. When he entered and looked at the bed, he saw the pressed cotton print dress and the suitcase beside it. He flipped open the hat box, her favorite hat nestled inside. He raised the lid of the suitcase and sifted through underclothing, the scent of her toiletries assailing his nostrils. Seething with rage he approached the table.

Sylva saw him approach, his face once more crimsoned.

"Well, Sylvia. Looks like you were ready to go off with Lonnie after all," Elmer said a strangled noise in his throat.

Sylvia didn't have far to search for a lie. She had already told Lucille that she was going over to visit her mother at Moundville, Missouri. "I thought I would go over to visit Mama for a few days."

"You know what, Sylvia?"

"No. What?" Sylvia said.

"I don't believe you for a second. You had planned to go off with Lonnie."

Sylvia's eyes flitted to the side and Elmer knew he had caught her in the lie.

Elmer said, "I should knock that smirky little smile right off your face. I've never hit a woman in my life and don't think I'll start now."

Sylva started to fuel some anger herself, as she perceived this as unfair treatment, said, "Since you're so unforgiving and so disbelieving maybe I'll go off with Lonnie after all. You'd pretty much…….."

Elmer cut her off, "I'll go kill that little son of a whore after all. You damned whore….." He stopped when he heard the screen door slam shut.

* * * * * * * * * * *

When Lucille left the house she detoured to the outhouse for a brief stop. She, then, went to the chicken house and filled both baskets nearly to the top. She counted over fifteen dozen she thought. As she gathered the eggs she had hummed a little popular tune she had heard sung in a musical she had seen in Houston at the picture show with her mother, sister and brother early in June.

On the way back to the house, she stopped to pet the young dogs, a rangy bird dog and three herding dogs.

Lucille felt better about her family situation all of a sudden. Maybe her mother and father were feeling more reconciled after a pleasant meal together. In the past couple of days she had felt more tension between them but she knew things could change suddenly.

She mounted the back steps and opened the back screen door. She moved away from the door as it swung shut. But before it slammed she heard the angry shout by Elmer.

She hesitated to enter the house but she knew that she must. She opened the back screen door to the kitchen and moved to the doorway to the dining area. She found them both stiff with anger and hate for each other. Her father was standing with his arms akimbo, fists on his hips, his face crimsoned in anger.

Elmer spoke first as Sylva turned to look at her, "Lucille, take the eggs to the store. They'll give us credit for eggs against last month's grocery bill."

Lucille knew that was how it worked with the store keeping a running tally of credits and debits. She knew she was to take the eggs to the McKinney store, once known as the Kidd Store. William Kidd had opened the store before the turn of the century.

"Okay, Dad." She started toward the front door but stopped when her father spoke.

"Drop off the eggs and then go to my mother's house until I come pick you up. Your mother and I have a couple of things to clear up."

She nodded her understanding and left the house. Her spirit which had soared just a couple of minutes earlier were now a pit of despair.

* * * * * * * * * * * *

Elmer went to the pantry and reached to the top shelf in the pantry closet. The double barreled twelve gauge was in the case where Earl had put it the evening before, but there were only a few shells of bird shot. He needed double aught buckshot.

When Elmer returned to the dining area, Sylva was sobbing softly, her head lying on her arms on the table top.

Elmer said in a very calm voice now, "I need to go down to the store for a couple of things." He left the house and strode down the street purposefully. When he came to the double doors to the westernmost part of the store, he could see Lucille on her knees placing eggs in a wood crate. He stopped to help finish the eggs.

"Dad we have fifteen dozen eggs," Lucille said. "Myrtle told me to come back and tell her how many we had."

"I'll tell her, sweetheart," Elmer said softly. "You go on down to your grandmothers and stay until I come to get you."

Elmer glanced in the last basket. There were five eggs left, as the store only paid for an even dozen. "You can take the left over eggs to Mother," Elmer added.

Tears sprang to his daughter's eyes for a second time that day in less than two hours. "Oh. Dad. I just know you're going to do something awful."

Elmer averted his eyes and said, "Just know this. I love you and your sister and brother more than you can ever know. It is my hope and prayer that nothing can ever hurt you again."

"Okay, dad. I'll see you in a little while." Lucille ran across between the other store and the deserted beer joint on the north side of the street and into the back street toward her grandmothers.

Elmer watched her, walking to the middle of the street to watch her go. A couple of retired men sat on the whittlers' bench, talking and spitting long, brown spouts of tobacco juice. Elmer smiled and nodded to them. He removed his hat and mopped at his forehead with sleeve of his shirt.

When he turned he looked at the store front adorned with a sign advertising Star Brand Shoes. On the left front was a sign black lettered on a white background: Coffins and Caskets for sale by Wm. E Kidd, Tyrone, MO. It brought a wry smile to Elmer's face and he muttered, "Someone may be needing one, today."

Elmer walked into the cooler interior of the main store. Myrtle was sitting on a high stool behind the counter.

"We had fifteen dozen eggs," Elmer said quietly and smiled. "I need a pack of Luckies and a box of double aught twelve gauge shells."

"Little early for huntin' season ain't it?" Myrtle queried.

"No. It's for a fox or some other varmint coming into my hen house at night." Elmer replied.

Myrtle reached behind her and took out a package of Lucky Strike cigarettes. She sat them on the counter and said, "I'll have to go look for the shells."

"They're back in the far right corner. I saw where Nick got them the last time I was here," Elmer volunteered.

Elmer heard the door open and he turned to see Mae Martin enter. She blinked her eyes to help adjust to the darker interior.

"Hello, May," Elmer greeted her jovially.

"Elmer. Good to see you," she responded.

"How's John these days."

"Complainin' how hot tis."

"Yes it is at that," Elmer agreed. "Doing anything special today?"

"We're goin' over to Cabool for the day."

"Maybe you'll see Earl. He's pitching and playing in a double header."

"Maybe so. John would enjoy that," she rejoined.

Myrtle returned and put the box of shells by the cigarettes. "Will that be all?

"Yes. That's it. Thanks." Elmer tipped his hat to both ladies and departed the store. As he walked up the street, he waved at Callie Kidd sitting on her front porch and saluted Ike miller, who fancied himself a veteran of the Spanish American War. Marjorie Lay and Wilma Dean McKinney were sitting in the shade of a tree on the West side of Kidd's house.

* * * * * * * * * *

When Lucille came to her grandmother's house, she started to open the door but she heard soft snoring. She cupped her hands on either side of her eyes and peered through the screen. Sure enough, Sarah was having a little snooze on the day bed.

Lucille sat on the front porch in her grandmother's rocker. She saw her father walking up the street to their house. A feeling of dread overcame her impelling her to jump to her feet. She followed her father to the house. She felt that if she got there she could stop their arguing by her presence. Maybe it would be the very thing to start them toward getting ready to go to Barriklow.

Chapter 8 -

The Double Header

As Earl and Eva drove along toward Willow Springs there was an eerie, ominous silence coming from Eva, usually so effusive, who sat mute. The unease within Earl mounted. He was accustomed to wild boars, mean bulls trying to gore him and skittish horses that tried to buck him off but this was becoming intolerable. Earl could stand it no longer, he pulled to the side of the street as they entered Willow. "Eva, I can't abide this anymore. You usually keep me busy listening. What's wrong?"

Eva was quiet for a long time. Then she said, "Earl, this is a problem for me to work out myself. You've been really good to me. I have no complaints in that regard."

"That's well and good for you to say but I can tell you're really upset, Eva. If you haven't figured it out yet, you must know that I am crazy in love with you." Earl removed his flat crowned white straw hat, took a handkerchief from his hip pocket, and mopped the perspiration from his forehead.

"I know that, dear, I feel the same about you." Eva, not being one to show a great deal of emotion, for the second time that morning had tears welling in her eyes.

Earl spoke slowly and emphatically, "Then we both care for each other and we should be able to talk about just anything. Why don't you go ahead and speak your mind."

"I won't, Earl. Let it rest until after the game when we have more time to discuss it."

Earl nodded, putting the Model A in gear. He turned right on U. S. Highway 60 to go west to Cabool. In less than a half hour they were at the ball field and Earl was warming up to pitch the first game of the double header.

Eva enjoyed coming to the Cabool ball field because it was a very nice one. Many of the ball fields she had gone to with Earl the past spring and summer were just open pastures with a bare infield. Cabool's was well laid out with grass on the infield instead of all dirt and had a backstop with seats behind it. Most of the time Eva had to bring a blanket and sat on the ground to watch. This time she would sit on wooden bleachers.

Eva sat in the car during warm up. She needed time to herself to decide how to approach the matter of Earl's marital status. After she thought about it a while she decided she would go find a seat and enjoy the game. The first two rows were taken so she went up on the third row to find a seat as near behind home plate as she could. She watched as the grounds keepers moved the chalk dispenser along the first and third base lines. She had only been sitting for a couple of minutes when an older gentleman sat about three or four feet to her right.

A few seconds later the home plate umpire called "Play Ball". Eva knew enough about the game now to know that Earl's team would bat first. She looked at the new wood outfield fence that had been put up since she had been here last. It was about six to seven feet tall and had some advertising. It encompassed the outfield from the left foul line to the right one. The fence was dark green and there were some open green spaces still available for future advertising signs.

The first batter was, Paul Mckinney, from Tyrone that Earl had recruited for the Clear Springs team since Tyrone had no ball team of their own. He was fairly short and played second base. Because of his height the kid walked a lot, Earl had told her. This time he got a hit between the infielder's. The next fellow was one of her cousin's husband. His name was Guy McAllister, a farmer who lived east of Clear Springs. He struck out on four pitches. Earl came striding toward the plate.

One of the older men on Earl's bench yelled out, "Hit one over that new fence."

Earl nodded his head and yelled over his shoulder, "Yep. That's exactly what I'm gonna try to do." On the third pitch he did exactly that over the centerfield fence four hundred feet away.

The score of two to nothing lasted into the seventh inning. Eva noticed that the man sitting to her right had a large notepad and was writing down notes as the game went along. She knew somehow or the other that he was paying special attention to Earl. He was wearing a nice short-sleeved shirt, khaki pants and had on a ball cap with a light brown top and a much darker brown brim.

In the bottom of the seventh Cabool's pitcher, a left hand batter got a sharply hit line drive to left field and the next batter hit a ball to the outfield on the ground between shortstop and third with no one out. Earl struck out the next batter and got a pop up to the catcher. The fifth batter hit a ball to third and he threw it over the first baseman's head. The runner scored from second. The next batter struck out.

Eva had been so curious about the man on her right that she moved about half the distance between them and said, "What are you jotting down on your note pad, sir?"

He looked at her quizzically. "I hoped no one was even noticing me." He hesitated momentarily and continued, "I've been sent by a professional ball club to observe the young man who is pitching for the visiting team."

"Oh. You mean the Clear Springs team and Earl Sigler."

The man nodded. "Yes, that's right."

"Wouldn't you know. I came to the game with Earl."

The man smiled broadly and said, "How lucky can I get? The man's girlfriend even. I'm Joe Black, a scout for the St. Louis Browns."

Eva frowned. She didn't know about the St. Louis Browns. She didn't know too much about big city baseball teams in general. She remembered Earl saying he had gone to see the St. Louis Cardinals play when he had taken cattle to East Saint Louis but she had never heard of the Browns. She did know about the New York Yankees and Babe Ruth, didn't everybody? Then she noticed the hat.

"That's the reason for the cap," she said, pointing at her own head.

"Exactly. I didn't wear one with the STL script on the front so I wouldn't stand out like a sore thumb. After the game why don't you take me over and introduce me to Earl."

Eva nodded. "I can do that."

Joe looked down at his notes, as play on the field went on. "You have a very remarkable young man here, unless what *I* wrote is in error, Earl has recorded fourteen strike outs, two ground outs and five pop up flies including two to the outfield. Two men got hits and one got on by an error. Except for the error the Cabool team would have no runs."

Eva looked at him wide-eyed and thought to herself that Joe Black was very thorough. She moved back to her place.

After the last out was recorded, Eva Stood and waited for a few people to move before she started down the seats to the ground level. She looked behind her and Joe Black was following close behind her. As they walked toward the Clear Springs bench Earl was already coming toward them, removing a bandana from his hip pocket to mop perspiration from his face, pushing his ball cap back off his forehead, high and white in contrast to his lower suntanned face.

When they were within a stride of them Earl held out his left hand and Eva took it in her right hand. Eva looked behind her and said, "This gentleman wanted to meet you. Joe Black this is my friend Earl Sigler. Joe is with the Saint Louis Browns."

Earl appeared puzzled at first and gave a one-sided smile and said, "I don't know for the life of me why you'd like to meet me."

Joe said very straightforwardly, "Word's got around that you're a pretty good pitcher. I saw today that you hit the ball pretty well, too."

Earl became more serious now, "Thanks for the compliment."

"You know, Earl, that the Cardinals have already beat us out for the Dean brothers, Dizzy and Paul. We would like to get to you first."

Earl said, "That's interesting. Where do we go from here?"

Eva, smelling the odor of sizzling meat, said, "How about a hamburger. Breakfast was a long time ago." In Cabool, she knew, there was an understood agreement that there would be a half hour break for lunch by both teams.

Joe said, "I had to leave at three o'clock this morning and haven't eaten yet myself. I'll buy."

Earl shook his head. "No that wouldn't be fair. You are the guest here."

"It's okay. The Browns pay my expenses," Joe replied.

"All right," Earl said, "let's eat."

"I want two burgers, my stomach says it's after one o'clock," Eva chimed in.

"We'll all have two," Joe said. "How do you want them?"

"Mustard and onion on mine," Eva replied and looked at Earl.

Earl thought a few seconds and said, "If they have lettuce, tomato and mayonnaise, I'd like that."

"So will I," Joe said, "I'll go get them. Find a seat and I'll join you."

Eva and Earl walked to the Clear Springs visitor's bench along the third base side. When Joe returned, they sat with the hamburgers wrapped in brown paper on their knees, Earl sitting between Joe and Eva. Joe had even thought to bring back three bottles of soda pop.

After a couple of bites of burger, Joe spoke first, "The Browns' President and Manager said to ask you to come to a tryout camp two Saturdays from now in the morning before our afternoon game against the Tigers if I thought you had some promise. So I am asking you. It's at nine o'clock in the morning and all the participants can go to the game at one. How about it?"

Earl finished chewing and looked at Eva, "You're not planning to come home that weekend are you?"

Eva shook her head and kept chewing slowly, having taken one bite of burger to Earl and Joe's three or four bites.

"I can probably work that out. Joe, I'm a working man, my father and I were planning a large cattle drive this week from West Plains to Rolla that should end up in Rolla sometime on Friday. I can catch the train to St. Louis with the cattle. I'll be there."

They ate in silence for several minutes until Joe stood up and looked at his wristwatch. It was an oddity in the Ozarks. Eva had not seen one until she went to Springfield to college. Most of the men in the hills only had pocket watches if any at all.

"I'll go back to my seat now. See you that Saturday, Earl," Joe said. Earl shook his hand.

As Joe moved away Rolla Patterson, the unofficial manager of the Clear Springs team came and sat beside Eva. Rol was the youngest brother of the wife of John Bradford, Charlie's brother. He put his arm across her shoulders. "How's my favorite girl?"

"I'm not your girl. Favorite? No woman would have you. Even your folks can't stand you, I heard they kicked you out of the house last year." Eva said. It was an old joke by now.

"Yes, but I'm a man of means, living with Mama and Papa all those years, carrying the mail, working at the sawmill and helping on the Farm. I now own that hundred and sixty acres south of Hostetter's. I've even started a house on that first sharp curve."

Eva leaned forward to look at Earl, "You didn't tell me about this."

"You didn't ask, Eva," Earl said.

Rol chuckled and said, "Look how important I am. You could do worse, Eva. And I'm even the manager of the baseball team."

Earl said testily, "Leave her alone, Rol, she's mine. You wouldn't even be manager except you have that nice new pickup. Gould tells us what to do."

"You're right, Earl. But my truck comes in handy taking the team to games and since I'm right next to the ball field I go out and drag the infield to keep it in shape."

"That is a good thing, Rol," Earl said, "Maybe you have a good claim after all."

"Thanks, Earl. You best get out on the field and get warmed up."

"I'll wait until Gould tells us," Earl grinned.

Rol removed his arm and poked Eva in the ribs with his elbow, "See how long my manager stint lasted?"

Eva stood up with one burger still wrapped and the last bite of her first burger in her hand. "I'll go back to my seat in the stands," she said.

Gould McAllister strode up to the bench, a tall gangly fellow. He would pitch the second game. He said, "All right guys, take a few warm up throws and get ready to bat."

Earl started to walk away but Gould caught him by the arm. Gould said, "Do you think Lynch is ready to play?"

"He could handle first base or left field," Earl replied. "Are you going to try George one of these days?"

Gould looked thoughtful and said, "Earl he's pretty green yet. Maybe we can try him out agaist the Plato-Roby team. They're not very good. "I'm gettin' too old to play both games of a double header like this anymore."

Earl snorted, "Why you sound like you thought you were fifty."

"I'm nearer than you realize and I'm near out of steam. I can pitch some innings but you may have to come in and spell me along at the end of the game," Gould said emphatically.

"I can handle that."

Earl and Gould heard the call, "Play ball."

As the team returned to the bench. Gould said, "Spud will play first, Earl on Third, Bill go to left field since you won't be playing third and Lucas will be first off the bench, everyone else the same. Let's go knock the ball around, give me lots of runs."

Spud Lynch, smiling happily, asked, "Where do I bat?"

"You'll take Lucas's place in the lineup." Gould replied, then stopped them from taking the field with an upheld hand, "One more thing. George, would you take the lineup over to the scorekeeper?"

George Baker, Earl's first cousin from Sargent had been practicing with the team for a couple of months, looked very disappointed. He had been practicing with the team since April but hadn't played a game. Earl had been teaching him to pitch and had been getting better with his curve ball. He had thought for sure he was going to get to play after all. He got up and walked to where they kept the batting up lineup pad and began filling out the new lineup. He had practiced playing left field. He thought he was ready.

Back in the stands, Eva was sitting a lot closer to Joe Martin now. She finished her sandwich and watched as the Clear Springs team begin batting. The first batter got on with a bunt hit and the second went out on a fly ball. Earl hit a double that brought in a run. An out on a fly ball and two infield errors loaded the bases. Spud, the seventh hitter, came up and, promptly, on the first pitch, hit a windblown fly ball to right field. It barely cleared the fence in right field.

Spud was so excited he hopped and skipped all around the bases. When he got back to the bench he got handshakes all around until he came to Gould who said, "You were just supposed to get on base so I could hit the grand."

"Sorry, I'll know better next time." Spud grinned.

In the stands Joe Martin stood and looked down at Eva, "Quite a young man you've got there."

"You're leaving?" The questioning tone in her voice caused Joe to sit back down. "The inning isn't over."

"It's over for me. I've seen all I need to see. I need to get back and get a better night's sleep than I had last night."

Eva said, "Why would anyone want to go play ball in a big city instead of these small town teams. It's just as much fun?"

"There's pretty good money in it. Babe Ruth is the highest paid player. He makes close to forty thousand dollars a year."

The figure staggered her, a small farmer in the Ozarks might work his land and not make that much in a lifetime. A one room school might pay you for forty years and you make less than half.

"In that case," Eva said, "I'll encourage him to pay you a visit in two weeks."

Joe looked at his watch again, "Here it a quarter after one and I had intended leaving at one. Oh well, it was worth it meeting you and Earl."

"Thank you," Eva said.

"Your man had quite a day, a two hit game that could have been a shutout. Three hits in five times up with a single, double and homerun. Can't beat that with a stick."

He stood and worked his way down out of the bleachers. Eva watch as Joe made his way to his automobile, a shiny new car, with a gleaming

Indian head ornament. He drove away and Eva wondered if she would ever see him again.

The next five innings went by rather slowly because there were lots of hits, walks and errors on both sides. Clear Springs had scored four more runs and Cabool had six on the boards.

At the beginning of the bottom half of the seventh inning, Gould approached the umpire and asked for a change in the lineup. The two went back to the backstop to confer with the official scorekeeper. They had an official scorekeeper because there was a Texas county league that consisted of the two teams playing plus Houston, Success, Raymondville, Plato-Roby, Licking and Summersville. The scorekeeper turned in his score sheet to the news papers and an unofficial league standings were printed in the local weekly newspapers. When they arrived at the backstop Gould said, "I'll be leaving the game and Earl Sigler will pitch the last three innings, Virgil Lynch will go to left field, Bill Roberts will move back to third and Lucas Hosington will play first and I'll go to the bench."

As Earl was throwing a few warm up pitches, Eva heard the screeching of tires and the backfire of an engine. She peered through the people on the bleachers and saw Dillard Lay running toward the Clear Springs bench. When he saw Earl on the pitcher's mound he ran toward Earl.

Dillard, huffing and puffing, said, "Earl I....." He stopped for breath and by that time Gould arrived at the mound and the umpire was coming up behind. "You've got to come home" He sucked in some more air and continued, "Your stepmother, Sylva has been shot and we think she's dead."

Earl's face blanched to the point that his suntan seemed to fade, "Where's my father, Dillard"

Dillard replied, "We don't know, Earl. We just don't know."

"Go home, Earl." Gould looked at Paul McKinney. "You're in here pitching" Turning to the bench he yelled, "George, you're in left field."

As the infielders gathered around Gould said, "Tell Spud he'll be at third. Bill at short."

Earl heard these instructions as he headed to the bench, a coldness gripped his person that even the July sun couldn't warm. He reached under the plank bench for his boots and began taking off his spikes.

Eva sensing something was amiss came to the bench as Earl was pulling on his boots.

Dillard was still standing and waiting by Earl.

"What's going on, Earl?" Eva said.

"Oh my, Eva, something awful has happened," Earl replied, "I thought it was all over but it wasn't I've got to go to Tyrone. I've got to get there fast and I know how fast I can drive safely in the Model A. Could you drive the Plymouth home. It's got a starter on it and you've been practicing driving with me. Can you do it? I need Dillard to go with me."

"Yes I think I can." She nodded.

Dillard said, "The keys are in the ignition."

Eva followed behind Earl and Dillard on the U. S. highway to the smaller road that led through Elk Creek, Stultz and on to Tyrone. She was able to keep the Model A in sight but fell behind as they neared Big Creek because of the hills and curves.

Eva knew that something must be desperately wrong but hadn't wanted to delay their departure with unnecessary questions. As she rode along, she wondered how and when she would get a chance to talk to Earl about the impending rift in their relationship. As she thought about the situation it helped make the time go by more quickly. She knew she must stop seeing Earl but how she could do it was the real problem.

She stopped the car in front of the drive and got out when she saw Sarah and Lucille standing off to the side by the Model A Ford. The driveway was filled with cars, the marked sheriff's car, the Ford truck, a hearse, and another black car.

Sarah, when Eva was close enough moved toward her and enveloped her with a bear-like hug and Lucille came and clutched both. Eva could feel Lucille's fingers digging into her side. Both were sobbing quietly. Eva put one arm around each and let them vent their feelings. Eva's shoulders were both wet with tears when they separated.

Eva said, "Why don't we go down to your house, Sarah. There's nothing we can do here." The first time Eva had met Sarah, Eva had called her Missus Sigler. Sarah had made it clear that she would like Eva not to be so formal and should address her as "Sarah".

The three walked back down the dusty, hot street, all three holding hands with Lucille in the middle. Eva glanced to her left and noticed Lucille was now taller than her grandmother, soon to be a woman, Eva thought. Glancing to her right she saw the old mill building, the windows looking like empty eyes of a dead time, long gone. The panes of glass dusty and covered by cobwebs. They turned north through the alley between the harness shop and the Kidd house. They still called it the Kidd house although Nick Mckinney and his wife Myrtle and their family lived there with Missus Kidd, the wife of William Kidd who had died seven years earlier. By the time they got to Sarah's house Lucille had stopped sniffling.

Sarah walked straight to her rocker and sat down. "Lucille, go in and get Eva a chair and then go back to get one for yourself," Sarah said. While Lucille got the first chair she continued, "Let me tell you about it. I don't think Lucille can."

Eva nodded her assent as Lucille came back with the first chair. When Lucille came back to the porch with the second chair, Sarah said, "Right here beside me, Lucille." pointing to her right. Lucille sat as close as she could with an elbow on the rocker arm and her hand on Sarah's shoulder.

Eva moved her chair so she was facing the grandmother and her granddaughter.

Sarah sat for a few minutes, her mouth quivering and then began, "Not long after two o'clock I heard a scream, I know it was that time because the clock had struck that time and woke me. I could hear it all the way down here. Actually there were two screams and a shotgun going off between the two screams. I think the first scream was Sylvia and the second Lucille."

Sarah glanced at Lucille and the girl's head nodded slightly.

Sarah continued, "I saw her running down the street from the front porch here. About every three or four steps she would scream again. By the time she got halfway here I was up off the porch and halfway up to the harness shop when she met me. She fell into my arms and sobbed, 'My daddy shot my mama.' I told her to wait where she was and I hurried to Dillard and Dana's. Dana was standing on the front porch. I said she should ask Dillard to go to Elk Creek to phone the Sheriff that Elmer had shot Sylvia. Dana took off in a run to the store. Dillard came back running with Dana right behind her. I told him to take the Plymouth and go call the Sheriff and then go on over to Cabool to get Earl. And, now, here you are."

"I'm so sorry, Sarah!" Eva said attempting to project empathy and understanding.

"It's okay, my dear. Nothing to do now but wait."

They sat in silence for several minutes.

In a quiet quavering voice Lucille spoke, "I want to tell Eva what happened, she needs to know and I need to tell it, get it off my mind."

"Oh, honey, you don't need to do that," Sarah said softly.

"But I do. I must. I will," Lucille said firmly a young woman now, having to grow up too soon.

Sarah nodded her assent.

"Dad sent me down to the store to take the eggs when I came back from gathering them. When I came back from the chicken house, I heard them arguing and Dad used some really bad curse words to my mom. I think they both knew I heard it. Anyway, I took the eggs to the store and Dad followed close behind. I hadn't finished counting out the eggs and Dad came and helped me finish. He told me to come on down here, which I did. When I got here Grandma was taking her nap. I didn't want to wake her so I sat on the front porch to wait. I heard the clock chime for two o'clock and then I saw Dad walking up the street to the house. About the time he got to the house I decided to follow him up there. I thought maybe if I was there they wouldn't argue any more. When I got to the house I went in the East door off the front porch into the living room area. I could hear them shouting back and forth at each other. Then Dad said, 'Stand still woman I'm going to shoot you.' That's when Mom screamed and the shotgun went off, at least it sounded like a shotgun. I screamed then, too, and ran from the house back here. That's it. That's what I know"

Eva said, "That is so awful. No daughter should hear or see such things. My heart is breaking for you."

Sarah shifted uncomfortably in her chair and said, "Eva, my grandchildren are going to go through some rough times. Earl has made some really serious mistakes and gone through some bad things in his life. You are the best thing that has happened to him."

"Thank you Sarah, that's so nice of you to say," Eva said with some trepidation. "I should go back up there and wait for someone to take me home. I have to catch the train back to Springfield this evening."

Eva rose and leaned over to embrace Sarah. Lucille jumped to her feet and hugged Eva so hard it made her bones hurt. Clinging and trembling, whispering in Eva's ear, "Thank you for listening."

Eva held Lucille at arm's length and looked her in the eyes lovingly, "You're God's child, now. He will take care of you. As it says in the scriptures 'be still and know that I am God.'"

Lucille nodded. "I know I am safe in his salvation. And I know that 'God is Love.' He loves me."

"And the Psalms say 'I knew you before the world was made.'" Sarah said, surprising Eva, that she was so knowledgeable about scripture because Earl had told her that his grandmother did not read.

Eva stepped off the porch and started walking back toward the house and to Earl.

* * * * * * * * * *

When Earl arrived at the house, he drove the Plymouth right up behind the Sheriff's car.

When Earl exited the car, Dillard decided to follow. Earl strode purposefully toward the Sheriff. He knew Sheriff Kelly, he had met him in Houston when he had stopped there with his father.

Kelly extended his hand to Earl and they shook, "I'm Harry Kelly."

Earl said, "I remember Harry. Met you a couple of months ago."

"I saw your father yesterday morning in Houston," Kelly said. "He seemed in such a good mood. Never dreamed we'd be called over here with this kind of trouble."

"What kind of trouble, Sheriff?" Earl asked.

"We don't know. We just don't know," Kelly said.

The Sheriff inclined his head toward the house. "We don't know for certain what we've got in here. A man by the name of Red Fronk came up to us when we got here and said your stepmother was lying on the kitchen floor with blood all over the place. He had brought back a twenty-two rifle he had borrowed to kill a dog that was killing his sheep and for squirrel hunting. He had just got it this morning. He lives somewhere over South of here and when he came to the house, he knocked on the front door. No one answered so he went around to the back, thinking he'd leave it on the back porch. When he looked in the kitchen window, he saw Sylvia on the floor. When he went down to the store he found out that Dillard Lay went to call me and go get you. Red didn't know Sylvia was dead but he did see blood on the floor."

Earl nodded and said, "He would come up from the back. They're tenant farmers back behind our South forty. They have no way in or out that's handy unless they go through our fields."

"That's exactly what he told me," Kelly said. "He also told us she didn't appear to be breathing and assumed she was dead. When Dillard called us I called Elliot, since he acts as our coroner and because Tyrone has no phone service as we might need him."

Earl looked at the undertaker. He remembered him from when he had handled his grandfather's funeral back in 1928. He turned his attention back to Sheriff Kelly.

Kelly continued, "We don't know where your father is. He could be gone or he could be in the house. If you want to know the honest-to-God truth we want to search the house but we're afraid to. We don't want to go in there and have a big shoot out. Understand me?"

Earl nodded his head again. "You want me to go in because you think my father won't shoot me. That it?"

"You've got it exactly right," Sheriff Kelly said.

"Well. Okay. I'd better get to it," Earl said grimly.

He walked several steps toward the house, turned and retraced his steps. And said, "In case I don't come back alive, Dillard, tell Eva I love her more than she'll ever know." Turning to the undertaker he continued, "And you'll do the funeral no matter what. Understand?"

The undertaker nodded.

Earl turned on his heel and strode resolutely toward the house. When he came to the West door to the dining area, he breathed deeply a couple of times and said, "Dad, are you in there. It's Earl." When there was no answer he shouted the same words very loudly. When there was no reply to the second query, He grasped the handle on the screen door and opened it. When he entered the dining area he could see Sylva sprawled on the kitchen floor, her face a bloody mess. He went to her and knelt close by, and saw a large hole in her side, her face nearly blown away. He rose and retreated through the dining and living area into the front bedroom. He saw the suitcase and then to the back bedroom. There was no sign that his father was there. Returning to the kitchen Earl stepped over Sylva legs.

He stopped to think. Would his Dad have gone to the barns? His truck was at home. Would he ride off on a horse? He glanced out the window and saw a saddled horse tied by the back gate. No! He hadn't left with a horse tied like that. Turning to the pantry, he looked in, the door to the upstairs was open. Earl went to the bottom of the stairs and said loudly, "Dad are you up there. It's Earl."

He went up slowly in case Elmer was still up there. He said, "Dad." Still no reply when he was about halfway up he glanced to his left into Glenn's room. No one in there. The door to his room on the northwest side of the house was open. His bedroom was empty, too. The door to the long east room was closed. It was used mostly for storage. There was an extra bed on the South side of the room a disassembled table and a few chairs, a dresser with a mirror. In the center front of the house was the office with a desk and a file cabinet. When he entered the long room the office was off to the left. The door opened right to left. He saw the unused furniture. "Dad, you here." Then the smell assailed his nostrils. He knew the smell of burnt gun powder and blood. He looked around the door to his right.

"My dear God!" It was not a prayer, an exclamation. Earl moved toward his father, who had apparently sat on the bed, leaned over the barrels of the shotgun and pushed the trigger. Earl moved closer and saw his father's face, the eyes open, unseeing. He had toppled to his right and the gun to his left. Earl retreated from the room, down the stairs and out toward the gathered men.

When Earl moved toward the front gate, Sheriff Kelly moved toward the gate from the group of Men. Dillard came behind the Sheriff.

"You can go in now. They're both dead," Earl's voice very low, his lips quivering with emotion.

Dillard spoke first, "Earl, I'm so sorry."

"Okay, Vic," the sheriff said, speaking to Elliot, "let's go have a look."

"Wait!" Earl spoke with some command in his voice. "Sylvia's in the kitchen and Dad is in the east room upstairs."

Vic Elliot turned to follow the Sheriff.

Earl said, "Wait, Mr. Elliot, will you do both funerals?"

"You can call me Vic," Elliot said. "My advertising says Gaylord V Elliott but I go by my middle name, Victor. Will Monday be all right?"

Earl replied, "Monday's fine. Would two o'clock work." Earl hesitated slightly and continued, "Vic, do you need anything else from me? I need to go tell Grandma and my Aunt," Dillard came to stand by Earl. Earl turned toward the Model A.

Dillard, still by his side as they approached the little Ford, said, "Anything I can do Earl?"

"Yes, take care of the horse tied by the back gate. I just need to go see Grandma and Pearl."

Earl stopped as he was walking around the front of the car. "There is something else you can do." Earl pulled his ever-present notebook from his pocket. He extracted the note Elmer had handed him the evening before with the name and address of the West Plains farmer. He jotted names and directions to the other farmers Earl personally knew who also were involved. "If you would drive down sometime tomorrow and tell these men that the drive we're going to make will have to be put off at least a week or two but that we'll let them know enough in advance. Drive the truck down. Thanks, Dillard."

"It's as sure as done," Dillard said.

Earl moved toward Dillard to hand him the slip of paper with his right hand, with his left he grasped Dillard right wrist. "You have been a really good friend to me and Dad. Thanks." Earl almost had urge to hug him but knew that wasn't acceptable behavior between two grown men. "See that someone gets word to Monkey Jim today, too," Earl continued.

Dillard nodded and Earl rounded the Ford and readied the car to be cranked. He twirled the crank and the car fired to life. Earl backed out. When Earl came to the harness shop he turned down the narrow alley and stopped in front of his grandmother's house. Eva and Lucille were seated on each side of Sarah.

As Earl approached the porch, Eva moved to stand by Lucille with her left hand lightly on Lucille's right shoulder. Earl went in front of his sister and grandmother and knelt so he could look more directly at them. He said, "Grandma, I'm sorry."

The only sign of emotion, now, from Sarah was a trembling around the corners of her mouth. She said, "He killed Sylvia and then himself."

Earl nodded. Lucille sobbed quietly.

When Earl spoke next, tears streamed down his face, "I failed. I failed you all. I thought I had it taken care of but I failed. Forgive me Grandma!"

"Earl, you didn't fail," Sarah said firmly, "This has been coming on for a long, long time and you had nothing to do with it."

Earl shaking his head stood up.

"I need to be by myself now," Sarah said firmly, "Take Lucille over to Pearl and Ira's. Tell them to come back here for supper around six and they can stay the night here. We can comfort each other."

"I need to take Eva to the train station. I'll stay at my mother's and Charlie's," Earl said.

"Yes," Sarah said, "And they can be a comfort to you."

"I'll see you tomorrow, Grandma," Earl turned to go down the steps with Eva and Lucille behind him closely.

Chapter 9 -

Aftermath

When Earl, Eva and Lucille departed Tyrone, the three of them sat in the front seat with Lucille in the middle. When they got in the car, Earl hugged Lucille to him with his right arm. She was still sobbing softly.

It was a little over a mile to Pearl and Ira's farmhouse. Only the sound of the engine was heard..

Earl's thoughts were not on his grief over the loss of his father but an oppressive guilt for his failure to circumvent the events of this day.

Eva's musings were less on the tragedy but how it affected what she should do about Earl's perceived deception. Was it deception or just neglectfulness? A fecklessness? No, not that harsh. Anyway, she thought that this was not the day to approach the matter. She would just go back to Springfield. When she came back they would have it out. There was no need to compound Earl's present dilemma.

Lucille was grief stricken. Her thoughts were on what had she done. Was it her fault? No. There was nothing she could think of. What could she say to her brother and sister? Glenn would be devastated with the double death. Little carefree Vivian would not be free of this for a long time to come. None of them would.

Pearl and Ira were sitting in the shade in the front yard on a couple of chairs. Glenn and Vivian were sitting on a blanket putting together tinker toys. They were all ready for the picnic.

Earl said, "You two stay here until I wave you over. I need to talk to Aunt Pearl by herself."

When Earl got out of the car and started toward the four, Glenn came running with Vivian close behind. Glenn jumped up in his arms and Earl hugged him tighter than he ever remembered. Earl released him and leaned over to pick up Vivian, hugging her as well. He carried his little sister toward Pearl and Ira. He stopped in front of them, not exchanging a word with the two children.

Pearl rose to her feet as Earl approached. Ira, seated, aimed a brown spout of spittle at a tin can half full of tobacco juice. Ira said, "You 'bout ready to head off to Bariklow?"

"No, Ira," still not able to bring the word Uncle to his lips, "I need to speak to Aunt Pearl about something private but you can listen in." Earl said. Turning to the children, he commanded, "You can continue your game."

Glenn and Vivian complied without complaint adults often shunted them aside so they could talk about things.

Earl walked far enough toward the back yard so the children could not hear, stopped and turned. His Aunt was there and waiting when he turned, with Ira coming up behind.

"I have some just horrid news, Aunt Pearl. My Dad, your brother Elmer, killed Sylvia and then himself this afternoon," Earl said softly, tears forming in his eyes. "I wish I could have softened it somehow but there it is."

Pearl and Ira now knew why Lucille, Sylva and Elmer had not come sooner. It was getting on to late afternoon. Pearl said, tears streaming, her mouth quivering, "That little tart. She brought this all on."

Ira now said, "Now, Pearlie, there's plenty of blame to go 'round."

Earl cut in, "It's my fault. I thought I took care of it but I didn't"

"Oh, Earl, you mustn't think that," Pearl interceded, "Ira's right there's plenty of blame to go around. We'll just have to carry on somehow."

"Let's go around and tell the children, then I'll head on down to Mama's and Charlie's." Earl said.

Pearl said, wiping at her eyes with a handkerchief, "Earl, I can tell them. You've been through enough already. Mary and I became the best of friends when she married my big brother. I was ten, then. She was like the big sister I never had. Minnie died before I was born. Another died as a baby."

"Okay. I'll head off then. I still have to get Eva down to Willow to catch a train," Earl, said, relieved. "Grandma says you should go over to her house for supper and stay the night."

When Earl returned to the car, he helped Lucille come out the driver's side. "Aunt Pearl says she wants to tell Glenn and Vivian about your Mom and Dad." Lucille clung to Earl in a lengthy hug then turned with back held straight and head high toward her aunt and uncle.

Earl had left the motor idling so he put the car in gear and made a circle turn and back out to the main road. He and Eva rode in silence until they came to Nagle. Earl pulled off beside the cemetery and little white church. He leaned forward with his forehead against the steering wheel, the movement pushed the flat crowned straw hat back on his head. He said, "I just don't know how it will go from here." He leaned back and looked at Eva, his eyes reddened but not teary, "The only thing that I know that is right in the world is you. I'll always love you until the last breath I take and I'll never fight with you."

Eva, speechless, knew she couldn't broach the subject of Earl's deception. Not now. Not after this tragedy. When she came back next from Springfield, they would resolve it. As Eva looked at him, her lips pressed together in a straight line, Earl put the car in gear and continued on the way to his mother and stepfather's house.

Earl stopped the Model A in front of the house. He glanced at the garage. The old Chevy sedan was not there. He had forgotten that they told him they were going to Skaggs' house. He said, "They're at Aunt Effie and Uncle Henry's. I forgot."

"I can understand forgetting."

Earl didn't answer. He put the car in gear and drove the five or so miles to the Skaggs' house on a ridge looking over the valleys to the south and west. They pulled in behind the Chevrolet. Earl parked and said, "Okay, walk with me up to the house, Eva," Earl said.

"No. No, you need to see your mother by yourself. I'll wait here and you can come back and we'll go get my things together and go to Willow."

Earl got out of the car, walked to and opened the front gate of the yard. He trudged, disconsolately up the hill toward the house. As he got closer to the house he heard voices coming from the north side of the house. He veered to his right. The back porch was screened in and Earl could see Charlie and Henry seated at a work table. His Uncle, Henry was cranking an ice cream freezer which was sitting in a large metal pan to catch the overflow of salt water. Earl hesitated for a couple of minutes until Henry followed Charlie's gaze to him.

Henry smiled and said, "Come on in, Earl. This is a surprise."

Earl opened the screen door, stepping up onto the low porch. "Hello, Henry," Earl said. He had never called him Uncle because they were so near the same age. Henry had seemed uncomfortable with the title the first time he used it. "It is unexpected. I need to talk to Mother. Charlie, I'll let Mama tell you about it."

Charlie said, "Okay, Son." Earl looked at him in surprise. It was the first time he had called him Son. Maybe it had something to do with what had happened and was said earlier that day. It seemed an eternity had passed since early morning.

"The ladies are in the kitchen," Henry said, inclining his head toward the kitchen door.

Earl glanced to his right. He had heard Tommie making car noises. Tommie was on a mound of dirt, moving play cars around on the mound. Earl turned and moved to the kitchen door.

Aunt Effie and his mother were standing near the hot kitchen stove. They both looked at him in surprise. Effie said, "Got here just in time for supper and ice cream."

"I wish I could stay but I can't," Earl replied and turned his attention to his mother. "Mama, I need to talk to you about something." Earl continued on through the room to the south door and outside.

Earl continued walking until he was near the smoke house and in the shade of a Catalpa tree. When he stopped Mary approached him expectantly.

"Mama, I don't know how to tell you this." Earl hesitated.

As the seconds passed, Mary wondered what news he had that brought him by so unexpectedly, was it his new found love in Eva? Was he marrying again?

"Something awful has happened. My father is dead. He killed Sylvia and then himself."

Mary was too stunned to weep. Elmer had been her first love. First love. Something one never escapes. She had tried to forget and to love the man she lived with but it always seemed second best.

"I am so sorry, Earl. Elmer was really a good man in many ways. And, oh my God, how I loved him. We were teenagers, I fifteen, he nineteen. It was like magic. Love was like a torch, lighting us aflame." Mary paused for a long time, Earl understanding that the "oh my God" was not an oath but a way to emote. She drew several heavy breaths and continued, "He just couldn't stop chasing other women. It was like an obsession. I finally gave him an ultimatum. And that was it."

"I hated bringing this news but I knew you would want to know. You can tell Charlie."

Mary nodded and Earl took her in his arms and hugged her hard for the first time in several years. Maybe, in death, a breach was healed in their relationship. He released her and stepped back. Her eyelashes were wet. Earl spoke softly, "I need to get on my way, take Eva to meet her train. I'll ask Charlie if It 's okay if I spend the night."

Earl turned and headed back through the kitchen giving his aunt a quick hug, stating, "I can't stay for supper. Really, Auntie. Sorry."

When Earl came to the back porch he looked at Charlie, "Mama will explain why I came by. I have to get Eva over to Willow to catch her train. If you don't mind, I'll come by and stay the night."

"You know you can, Earl. Any time," Charlie's deep bass rumbled.

Earl turned and tipped his hat to Henry. "See you."

"Maybe we'll see you at the fireworks, Earl," Henry said.

"Thanks but I think I'll pass on it. I kind of need some time to myself," Earl replied.

He opened the screen door and Tommie spotted him and he came running. Earl caught him under the arms and swung him around several times, with Tommie yipping in delight.

"Gotta go, Tommie. See you next time," Earl turned away quickly with Tommie skipping alongside him down the hill to the front gate. It always delighted Earl to see his young cousin Tom. He swung the gate open and closed it waving to Tommie.

As usual, Earl had left the little Ford to idle. He smiled at Eva and put the car in gear. They were soon back on the main road by the Clear Springs ball field and headed South to the Weiler farm

When Earl pulled up beside the house, Eva said, "Let me explain what happened. It'll be easier than if you did it."

Relief overwhelmed him. He nodded. He would not have known what to say.

Earl watched Eva enter the west door of the kitchen. Earl was always confused by the directions with all the curves back and forth. West seemed like south to him. Eva emerged from the kitchen with her father in tow.

Eva talked and gestured but Earl was glad he couldn't hear the explanation over the idling motor of the car. Eva's father turned his head to glance Earl's way and looked back at his daughter. He spoke at some length. Eva motioned for him to come to the house. Earl turned off the engine and placed the chocks under the tires.

As Earl approached the back door, Eva waited. "Thanks, Eva. I don't know what I would have said," Earl whispered.

"Papa said he'd tell Mama and the children. He thought they should know," Eva whispered back. "Just act like normal. We're invited to supper," she said in normal voice.

The kitchen was stifling hot but with all windows and doors open it was bearable. Eva's mother, Rena said, "We've already prayed."

Two of the better chairs were vacant with two empty plates. Wayne B and Clyde were seated on the backless bench they had brought in from the front porch.

Clyde, sitting across from Earl asked, "How did the game go?"

"We won the first one and were ahead in the second one before I had to leave," Earl replied.

Earl took a bite of cornbread to avert further questions. Eva spooned pinto beans and a good portion of early potatoes and peas in a cream sauce on his plate. She poured him a glass of milk from a pitcher. It was a simple, filling, nourishing meal.

Eva ate more quickly than he had ever seen her.

Rena said, "Don't interrupt Eva and Earl's eating. Eva has to catch her train at eight o'clock."

Eva glanced up at the kitchen clock on the shelf. It was already after seven. When she noticed the time she ate even faster. She finished every morsel and jumped up.

The others continued to eat in silence. Clyde, when his glass of milk was half full crumbled cornbread into it and put some sugar on top. He began to eat the soaked bread. It looked like a good idea and Earl tried it. It was really good. A nice, inexpensive dessert, a breakfast.

Before Earl finished his milk and cornbread Eva was back with her valise in her hand.

After some handshakes and brief hugs among the women and girls, they went to the car. Earl cranked it, removed the chocks and put them behind the front seat. They waved until they were out of sight around the curve and down in the ravine drive to the main road.

Eva was a little more perky now. She chatted about her classes and her new bedroom in her cousin's residence. Earl suspected that it was an attempt to take his mind off the horrific events of the day. Her best efforts didn't succeed. They arrived at the train depot with fifteen minutes to spare.

"How about we go to the Horton and have an ice cream sundae while we wait?" Earl asked, pulling into a space in front of the depot and across the street from the hotel.

They got out of the little Ford and walked across the street hand in hand. They ordered their ice cream dessert, Eva a pineapple and Earl chocolate. Earl said, "Tell me what was troubling you earlier in the day."

"Earl, there's neither the time nor is this the place to discuss what my concerns are. Let's think about that when I get back in August."

"Okay. I have your address, maybe we can cover some of it in our letters back and forth."

Eva looked at him and returned her attention to the sundae. They ate in silence until they heard the train whistle about a mile away. They rose from the stools, Earl leaving a dollar on the counter, and hurried over the street to get Eva's valise from the rumble seat. Earl closed the cover to the seat and hurried to the depot to be ready in case there was no layover. Apparently there was to be none, after passengers were off the conductor called, "all aboard."

Eva gave Earl a rather perfunctory hug and no kiss goodbye. Both were constrained by a knowledge that, in that time and place, there was no acceptance for public displays of affection.

However, when Eva was inside the coach, Eva opened a window and leaned out, kissing her palm and blowing him a "kiss." Earl returned the gesture. They gazed at each other lovingly with their own thoughts of the day. Eva, speculating on what or if there would be a resumption of their relationship. "I'll pray for you, Earl. Goodbye." Eva shouted as the train pulled away. She loved Earl passionately.

"Thanks. I love you." Earl's thoughts were more densely fogged in a morose darkness. His guilt at his perceived failure riding on his back like a heavy burden. When the train pulled out of sight, he felt he must find some solace and he knew where to get it. He thought briefly of going to the school's football field where the fireworks were to be set off but rejected it. He couldn't face family right now.

Earl was desperate for relief of his guilty funk. It was Prohibition and he knew exactly where to go. With an abundance of wood in the Ozarks, many small-time farmers became big-time distillers of illegal whiskey, many dubbed it white lighting because their whiskey lacked color since no tannin was added. Some called it moonshine because it moved around at night.

Just beyond Pine Creek he turned down toward Liberty school off the main road. He went about two miles and back up a small valley. When he came to the house, a man came out with a shotgun in the crook of his elbow.

When Earl got out of the car, he left it idling on a flat spot. The man recognized Earl. Elmer had brought him here the first time and Earl had come back on his own over the last couple of years.

"Hello, Abe. Have you got a couple of quarts of your best?" Earl enquired.

"Y hello, Earl. Come sit down a spell." Abe said leaning the gun against the porch wall.

"Can't do it. Need to just buy and get down the road. I'm going over to Charlie's and they won't be at home yet. I hate fumbling around the house in the dark finding a match to strike a light."

"Understand. Get you two quarts right quick." Abe offered.

Earl mounted the porch. Abe came back with two corked bottles of clear liquid. Earl knew it was strong, as near as possible to all alcohol. Abe handed the bottles to him.

"Dollar and a quarter," Abe said. "You got here just in time. A truck should be coming by any minute to load up. They want to be in St. Louis before daylight."

"Thanks, Abe. Costs eighty or ninety cents in town."

"You and your dad are good people. Your dad taught me at Liberty School down the valley."

Earl nodded, knew the school. His mother's family went there and where Mary met Elmer. "I'll see you next time, Abe."

"I got 'nother batch cookin' upta hill a quarter a mile. Come back anytime, Earl."

Earl stepped from the porch and went to the car. He waved as he turned back to the road. He got back to his mother's and Charlie's just before dark. He had several pulls from the bottle before he got there. He was feeling the strong effects as he pulled off to the side of the drive so he wouldn't block the driveway.

Earl lifted the bottle to his mouth and took another long swallow. He went into the living room and on into the kitchen to find a match. He came back, scratched the match to flame under the table that held the lamp. He lifted the glass chimney and touched the wick, adjusting the flame. He had difficulty replacing the glass to its place. He was beginning to sway now. He walk unsteadily to the front door and off into the yard to relieve his bladder. He returned to the living room and turned on the radio he had bought for his mother and Charlie for a Christmas present. He had bought it at a Saint Louis liquidation auction where they bought furniture on demand and brought some back that they sold out of the old grain mill office.

Charlie had hooked up a car battery to the radio and strung a long antennae outside the house. He got a lot of stations hundreds of miles away. Earl tuned in the Grand Ole Opry out of Nashville.

First Earl sat in Charlie's rocker. He drank some more, looked at the bottle. Only a couple of more good drinks left. He got up and went over to the day bed that converted to a narrow double bed. He sat down unsteadily, thinking he should return the bottle to the car. He was so tired he decided he would just lie down and relax a minute before he took the bottle out. He put it on the floor beside him. Earl immediately went to sleep with his feet on the floor beside the bed.

The clock struck ten as Earl went to sleep. It struck eleven as Mary and Charlie came back. Mary came in first while Charlie put the car away. She saw the bottle first, a frown creasing between her eyes. She picked up the bottle and took it to a small storage closet behind where the heating stove usually sat, removed for the summer to give more space. When Mary went to turn off the radio, Charlie came in the door. A strange odor assailed his nostrils but he just couldn't quite place it. "Go on to bed, Charlie. You have to get up earlier than I do to get the chores done. I'll take off Earl's shoes and get him settled for the night. He's had a rough day."

Charlie didn't object. He slept on a small bed on the back porch and rose at first light. He was used to being in bed near nine o'clock every night. He was bushed after working on Henry's barn most of the day and up so late.

Mary pulled off Earl's boots and placed each foot and leg gently on the day bed. She turned the wick down to a very low flame. It would allow the kerosene to last until Charlie got up.

Earl was up first. It was barely light when he had to rush from the house. He doubled over in the front yard wanting to vomit but only gagged up some bile and spittle. The long-haired dog, a mongrel with a lot of collie and shepherd bloodlines stood on its hind legs with his nose in Earl's face. "Okay, Pal. Good dog," he mumbled quietly, "let's go get the cows." The dog ran around the house. Earl followed him. Pal had his paws on the back yard gate. The white picket fence glowing in the early morning light. When Earl opened the gate the dog ran down the valley.

Earl knew that the dog would find the cow herd and single out the three cows to be milked. He would give them a couple of soft barks. If they didn't separate themselves from the herd he would go to the offending cow or cows and nudge them with his nose. If that didn't work a soft nip at a back leg would work without fail.

As Earl neared the barn, he heard the screen door on the back porch slam closed. He knew Charlie never used an alarm to waken. It just happened. Earl walked over to the little creek, dipping handfuls of water, washing his face thoroughly. When he returned to the barn, Charlie was there with two three gallon milk pails in one hand and a bucket of feed in the other.

Charlie opened the barn door and let the cows file in according to seniority. Bessie first, soon to be replaced by a younger cow, next Daisy, the big producer, and Pet last, her first year.

"You're up early, Earl. Used to have to drag you out of bed," Charlie chuckled.

Earl smiled, "But I could always out milk you. Which one do I get. The one with the little teats."

"Yep. You take Bessie. I always hated those little teats."

Earl finished, stripping Bessie dry and moved to Pet. He put the kickers on Pet since she was young. He milked her and was stripping her as Charlie rose from milking Daisy. Earl's bucket was nearly overflowing.

Charlie looked at the bucket in his hand, "I never get that milk from those two. You should come by more often," his eyes crinkled at the corners good-naturedly.

"You've got to hum a song, Charlie. Let me carry the milk," Earl asked. "Remember, you taught me how to walk without bouncing up and down. I spilled some milk before I learned right."

Earl followed Charlie up the hill from the barn, walking smoothly. Not a drop spilled. Charlie could walk faster unencumbered with milk. He was waiting by an open can immersed in water, the filter in place. Mary came out of the house with a bowl for milk. When most of the milk was filtered Charlie took the bowl and lifted the filter and let about a quart of milk fall into the bowl. Earl took the bowl into the house and placed it in the icebox.

When Earl came back out, Charlie was moving the milk can to an empty tub. Charlie asked, "Would you like to fill the tub with fresh cold water?"

"Sure," Earl replied. He took the two milk pails, rinsed them in the tub of water. He walked to the little three sided well house, with the long water bucket, removed the cover from the well and allowed the bucket to fall into the well, slowing the fall by holding onto the rope loosely.

His hand burned. He had forgotten to put on the gloves on the shelf. He stopped the bucket and put on the gloves that fit poorly because they were for Charlie's much larger hands. He drew the long narrow bucket from the well and held it over a bucket and let out water until the bucket was full and started filling the other. He had to let the water bucket back down for a refill to fill the second bucket. He took four buckets of water to the tub before it was full to the top. Satisfied, he entered the house.

A water bucket with a wash basin was on the enameled top table. Earl took the wash basin to the kitchen, dipped out two steaming dippers full of hot water. He returned to the table and took soap to his hands. He soaped his hands and wrists, rinsed and wiped dry. He threw the soapy water out the screen to the back yard, rinsed the wash basin with cold water and threw it out as well.

Charlie came out of the kitchen with a steaming pan of biscuits and Mary behind him with a covered pan. "Earl, could you get the butter and something sweet to put on the biscuits?" Mary asked. " unless you'd like something from your bottle instead." she added with a frown.

Earl's face flamed in shame. "No, Mama. Your peach butter is world famous," Earl said holding a jar aloft in one hand and the butter dish in the other.

Charlie had returned to the kitchen and Earl was glad Charlie hadn't heard the exchange. He held a coffee pot in one hand, poured himself coffee in his oversized white cup and in smaller cups for Earl and his mother.

When they were seated, Mary spoke grace. She then removed the lid of the pan and scooped out generous helpings of oatmeal and placed a bowl full in the middle of a plate in front of each place. Earl took a hot biscuit and slathered a generous helping of butter on it. He passed the butter to Charlie. Charlie was busy putting molasses into his oatmeal. He handed the jar of molasses to Earl and took the butter with the other. Earl put molasses in his oatmeal and handed it on to Mary. Earl opened the peach butter and spooned out a big dollop on each side of his biscuits. He was almost ready to eat. Charlie poured thick cream into his oatmeal and some in his coffee and passed the cream to Earl. He put cream in his oatmeal, too, but kept his coffee black.

Earl remembered that this was their usual Sunday morning breakfast. Good memories.

They ate slowly, amiably, now. Silent until they are finished.

Mary said, "Your bottle is in the stove cupboard in the living room, Earl." Then more crossly, "You know I don't approve that behavior. You were raised better."

Earl rose without rejoinder and said, "I have to get back to Tyrone. There'll be things to take care of." He left the room, removed the partial bottle of homemade liquor, went to the car, started it and set out. He knew his mother was right. He had become a Christian and been baptized seven years ago.

When the car started, Charlie said, scolding, "Mary, that was unkind. Earl is suffering right now."

Mary not one to never reply, said, "He knows better."

Charlie ducked his head. "I've got to shave and go to the creek to bathe."

"If Elmer had stayed married to me, this would never have happened."

"Well, he didn't. You're married to me," he replied. "You'd best stop that kind of dad gum talk." The battle was on once again.

Chapter 10 -

Tyrone

S arah woke at first light as she had when she was a young bride. As she reflected on her life she remembered when Marcus had brought her to the two room house he had built.

* * * * * * * * * *

Sarah Henry met Marcus Sigler at Big Creek Baptist Church. Hers and Marcus' families had gone there nearly back to its founding. His grandfather John Sigler had brought his family from Kentucky during the turmoil just before the great Civil War, families split over loyalties for North or South. John had come to Texas County, Missouri, with two young sons and a young girl three years old, Peggy Jane. An older son Sanford had stayed behind with his wife Mary. Sanford elected to do battle for the North, while many of his cousins joined the South. After the war was over Sanford had moved north of Tyrone near his fathers farm. The Bosters attended the same church. Marcus's mother brought him into the world without the benefit of marriage. She married Thomas Jefferson Boster two years later. Marcus would forge a life-long friendship with his

130

half-brother Amos. By the time Marcus was fourteen he left home to make his mark in the world. It would be a wide swath. He was frugal, built a two room squatters house two miles south of Tyrone. By the time he was nineteen he had saved a lot of money in the Raymondville Bank.

When Marcus began to notice her Sarah was fifteen. As a skinny thirteen year old she had her eye on Marcus. A year of courtship began with Marcus, now a muscular, heavy shouldered man. His build came from a grueling seven years of arduous labor.

They married when Sarah was sixteen and Marcus twenty-one. The two room house was adequate for them. It was a pretty white house, with steps leading up to a landing in front of the entry door. It was built across from a reliable water source, a spring. The room you entered was a spacious living, dining, kitchen combination and a bedroom on the North side. A back door led to an outhouse and smoke house.

Marcus had worked in a local sawmill for over six years where he had gotten the lumber to build his house on government land. He had cleared about 10 acres and fenced it, across a little periodic stream where he had enlarged a watering hole. He sold logs off the ten acres to the sawmill and used smaller trees for a split rail fence. He had chickens in a small coop and a milk cow and her calf. He had four heavy duty work horses that he had used to haul logs on a dray to the sawmill. He had subsisted on wild game, wild greens, brown beans, molasses and cornbread. Marcus had hoped to liven his eating with a new wife and wanted a family.

Sarah did not disappoint Marcus. She asked for a plot to be plowed and fenced for a garden. They had married in the Spring and within a couple of weeks had a garden sprouting with vegetables.

Sarah took up a lot of the burden of upkeep around the house and ten acres. Marcus was a genuinely adept money-maker. With Sarah's help, it gave him time to accumulate even more. In addition to working at the mill and hauling logs he had hunted wild pigs: boars, sows, gilts, shoats, any size any age. He dressed wild game and brought the meat to town to sell. He smoked meat for himself and sold what was left.

Marcus had some fits and starts in land ownership because of his lack of knowledge of the homestead patents available through federal legislation. He was schooled in land ownership by his banker and James Hart, an attorney in Houston, the county seat of Texas County.

Over the forty years of Sarah's marriage to Marcus he had arranged the homesteading of the original eighty acres and had accumulated ownership of over five hundred acres of land. He built a grain mill. When it burned, he rebuilt a better one. He opened and owned a bank in Elk Creek, a town West of Tyrone six miles. He owned near half interest in the Raymondville Bank. He was one of the richer men in southcentral Texas County by the time had passed from life on earth.

Sarah, who had no formal education, knew she was well-cared for. She couldn't read but she had learned to sign her name in cursive although she couldn't write a sentence. She had mastered sums up to ten dollars in her household duties. If she thought about it she could not remember when she had made any purchases beyond that amount.

* * * * * * * * * *

Sarah smiled to herself at many of the pleasant memories over the past forty-four years since she had met Marcus. Certainly there had been bad times with deaths of four young children, then Rex and now Elmer. But she still had Pearl and her four grandchildren to enjoy and comfort her.

It was time to get up, it was nearing five o'clock she was sure. She could read a clock, but her internal clock served her almost as well as a mechanical one.

Sarah rose quietly so she wouldn't awaken Vivian. She was sleeping quietly with her face toward the wall. Sarah opened a dresser and took out some socks. She sat on a chair and slipped them on her feet. She looked in the mirror and straightened her night cap. She walked quietly from the bedroom and by her sleeping grandson. She had spread a sheet over a day bed in the living room. Glenn had a pillow and a sheet for cover. Glenn was so peaceful and quiet now. The time of grieving the evening before now was past. Frowning slightly, she knew that she must remain cheerful, for the children's sake, even though her heart was burdened by grief. She put on some low-heeled shoes.

Sarah closed the door between the living room and kitchen softly. She continued on out to the back porch carrying the night pot by the bail. She emptied the pot in the grass off the walkway to the out-house. She took care of her business there, bringing the pot to the back porch. She poured water in the pot and rinsed it out and set it by the back door. She took her drinking cup off a nail above the water bucket and filled it with the dipper. She returned to the kitchen and sat at the table sipping water.

As Sarah sat, she thought of Elmer. He had been a willful child, with many spankings and whippings. He was a direct contrast to Rex. Rex had been easy to raise. He had studied hard in school and succeeded beyond his abilities. Elmer may have been smarter but took his studies lightly. He did well despite a lackadaisical attitude. Rex was not an ugly young man but his ears stuck out boldly to the side which kept him from being handsome. Elmer, however, was extremely handsome, well shaped face, bright blue eyes and strong, cleft chin. Was Cain and Abel like this, she thought. Rex had come to recognize his need for salvation through Jesus Christ just before he was ten. It was a year for celebration and a year of grieving.

Virdie had been born in January. Their beloved pastor John Lee Jones had preached a powerful sermon on the Sunday of Jesus' resurrection. Rex had come forward to the mourner's bench and rose to a new life in Jesus. He had been baptized the next Sunday in a waist deep hole of water at the Big Creek crossing South of the church. It was a wonderful Summer. Little four year old Pearl and her big brother, Rex, played in the grass in front of their new Tyrone house. Elmer, now a teenager, was too grown up for such childish things. Virdie was crawling around and beginning to pull herself up on things and stood, wobbling, on two legs.

Sarah thought God sometimes didn't want you to be too happy. Was that a sacrilegious thing to think. It wasn't even a word in her vocabulary but she thought it anyway. It was the third year of the twentieth century.

Elmer had begun his first year of high school in Houston. They had arranged a place for him to live, board and room. The twelfth day of September was his fourteenth birthday. It was also to be a day of tragedy. On the tenth day of the month, Virdie had become feverish, coughing. Two days later she took her last breath in Tyrone. Marcus had a neighbor ride one of his horses into Houston to bring Elmer home. They buried her the next day in the Big Creek cemetery across from the little Baptist church.

John Lee Jones gave a rousing sermon of salvation. He promised that little Virdie, "was too young to know sin," and "was with God in Heaven."

The next Sunday Elmer made his decision for the Lord Jesus Christ and was baptized in the same hole of water as had his younger brother.

Sarah thought how different paths her two sons took. The older, following in his father's steps into the family business of farming and milling. Elmer, two years before Marcus died, had insisted on closing the mill. Elmer took up livestock trading, furthering the reach of the Sigler business acumen. Now Earl was becoming very involved in livestock trading, following in Elmer's footsteps. Rex followed in the footsteps of Jesus' Apostles, a purveyor of the Gospel message. A stab of sorrow gored at Sarah's thought of Rex and his untimely death.

For the second time she reflected that she still had Pearl, Earl, Lucille, Glenn and Vivian. A little sigh of happiness escaped her lips at the thought. Then the pallor of sadness returned.

She wondered if God would forgive Elmer for his sin, his murder, his self-murder. Did he find God's forgiveness before he pulled the trigger that ended his life? It was unknowable, a mystery that would only be answered another time. She thought back to the night before.

* * * * * * * * * *

Sarah had been true to her word. She wanted to be alone with her thoughts that July fourth evening. How should she handle the time with her grandchildren and her daughter? She prayed about it a long time and in the end had peace in her heart with what to do. She turned her rocker so she could face the couch and the little day bed. She brought a sheet and spread over the little bed and placed a pillow with a clean case on the end with another sheet.

When all was ready she went to the ice box. She got a tomato, the first of the year from her little garden, a slice of baloney and a slice of cheese. This sandwich which she made in her kitchen held a lot of nostalgia for her. It was the sandwich she ate with Marcus on their first picnic together. She poured herself A cup of tepid coffee from the pot. She had done that before a few times. She went and sat in her rocker, with her sandwich on a small plate and the cup of coffee. She sipped and ate while she awaited the arrival of Pearl, Ira and the children.

When she was done she took her glass and plate back to the table in the kitchen. She would save them to do with the morning dishes. Sarah would need to arrange it so the family was ready for church the next day. She wasn't looking forward to going in Ira's Chevy pickup, the three grownups crowded in front with the children in the back. She would take along some pillows for them to sit on. It would be nice if they didn't have to eat dust all the way over there.

She had returned to her rocker only a few minutes when she heard Ira's pickup turn into the lane by the harness shop. Dillard made a few dollars handling harness for farmers, even though the lighter harnesses were not much in use anymore with the advent of the automobile. She heard the brakes screech. She rose and went to the door as the children were jumping out of the back. Ira and Pearl emerged from the cab. She opened the door as the children trooped disconsolately toward the house with the two adults coming behind.

Sarah said, attempting to exude a positive mood, "Hello children. Pearl. Ira. Come on in. I have a plan."

"Hello grandma," Vivian said, skipping toward the porch. Glen looked so, so sad. Lucille looked grim but walked with her head held high.

"Go sit on the day bed, children. Pearl you and Ira can sit on my new couch," Sarah was in command of the situation.

Pearl walked up the steps and onto the porch, tears streaming down her cheeks. "Oh, Mama," she said, "What are we going to do?"

"We're going to pray and talk," Sarah replied. "That's what we're going to do."

Ira opened the screen door and held it for the women. He removed his hat, holding it in his hand as he entered the living room, and went to sit by Pearl on the sofa. What is this, Sarah thought, Ira's showing some manners?

"Let's go before the Lord in prayer. You can sit or you can kneel," Sarah said.

Pearl knelt and put her head on the seat of the sofa and the children knelt by the day bed. Sarah kept her seat in the rocker, not sure she could get up without help. Ira remained in his seat.

Sarah continued, "We have suffered a great loss today, my little ones. O God, you are our comfort and our shield. Heal our broken hearts as we face this awful tragedy. Be with these children. show them your compassion, you have to be their father and their mother. Both, now that theirs have been taken away. Comfort this young sister, my daughter, keep her strong in her faith. I ask this in the precious name of Jesus, your Son, whom you had to turn your face away from as he died that most cruel death for us. We are truly your children. Amen."

Pearl prayed quietly, not even audible.

Lucille prayed next, "Dear God, what did I do to deserve this? Did I get there too late? Is this all my fault? Forgive me, Lord, if it is. Be with my Mom and Dad wherever they are. In Jesus name. Amen."

Glen sobbed, "Oh God," and fell silent.

Vivian wailed pathetically.

Sarah said, "Come here children," and then said, "no, I'll come there." She rose from the rocker and sat on the day bed between Lucille on her right and Glen to her left with Vivian on her lap. Pearl came to sit by Lucille with her arm around her with her left hand resting on her mother's shoulder.

They all wept some more and hugged each other. Ira sat silently on the couch.

After a while, Pearl said, "Mama, you're a rock. I don't know what we would do without you."

"My days are numbered less and less. We need to be strong for each other," Sarah said.

Sarah was thoughtful for a while, she faced Lucille and continued, "My darling granddaughter, you mustn't think for a minute that you did anything wrong."

"We will be strong, Mama," Pearl agreed. "We'll take good care of these little ones."

"We've got to be practical, though," Sarah said. "We've got the chores to do." She looked at the big clock with the pendulum swinging back and forth. It's almost eight o'clock. Pearl, take Lucille up and do the chores at the house she knows what to do. Don't go in the house. Everything you need is on the porch or in the barn. Nick will have clean milk cans there.

I'll go over and show Ira where the feed is for the pigs. Earl and Elmer brought a load back with them. They have plenty of water from the pond by the mill."

Everyone started getting up.

"Wait," Sarah commanded, "I'm not done yet. Tomorrow and for the next few days. You'll stay here at the house. Pearl, there's not room enough at yours. Pearl will help Lucille with the chores here in Tyrone and Ira can go home morning and evening to do your chores, then come back here."

Everyone started toward the door but Glen spoke up, "I can go help Ira milk their cows. Earl showed me how and I'm pretty good at it."

Ira said, "That's mighty nice of you, Glen."

Glen looked pleased with himself.

Ira spoke again, "I've got a nice surprise for you kids when we get done."

A look of anticipation came across the children's faces.

Vivian came back from the barn with Sarah. They hurried back, Ira and Glen first. Ira went behind the house and Sarah heard him in the trash pile back of the barn. Sarah sat on her rocker on the front porch. Vivian brought a straight chair out and sat on it. When Ira came back he had a gunny sack full of clanking cans. Sarah was puzzled. Ira went to the pickup and took a large paper sack from behind the seat and set it by the gunny sack. Ira came and sat on the edge of the porch by Glen.

When Pearl and Lucille came back their curiosity was fully aroused. Ira said, "Just sit and watch."

He walked to the bags and took a can from the sack, shielding what he was doing with his body. He took a large firecracker from the paper sack. He put the little explosive under the can with the wick sticking out. He pulled a match from his bib pocket, struck it on the edge of the can and lit the wick. He backed up quickly. When the firecracker exploded with a loud crack, the can flew thirty or forty feet in the air. When it came down it was misshapen, torn apart at the seams.

Glen jumped off the porch. "Let me do it. Let me do it, Ira," he shouted.

Ira showed Glen how to do it and instructed him to get away quickly. It worked, but Sarah was worried that it might be dangerous to do it again, even though it had worked well. Sarah said sternly, "You do it Ira. It might be dangerous for the children."

Ira did several more himself, even though he fell on his backside hurrying away on one of them. Later, Ira pulled out several strings of small firecrackers and set them off with multiple pops. As it was starting to get dark, Ira gave the children and Pearl sparklers and lit them. Vivian and Glenn raced around the yard, their sparkling wands held high, waving them excitedly. Lucille and Pearl sat on the porch and waved theirs. After those were used up, Ira went to the gunny sack and pulled out a couple of bottles. He placed them upright and put rockets in them and set them off.

When the last firework was lit, Ira said, "That's it. That's my surprise."

All five spectators clapped. Some other children had made an appearance during the demonstration and they clapped as well.

Ira said, "Time for bed, now."

Sarah said, "Say thank you to your Uncle Ira."

All three said as a chorus, "Thanks, Uncle Ira."

Ira beamed because that was the first time they had used his familial title.

Sarah said, "We have an early day tomorrow. Off to bed." She put her hand on Vivian's shoulder. "You'll sleep with me downstairs, Glenn on the day bed. Lucille can sleep on the single bed upstairs and Ira and Pearl on the double bed. Goodnight, sleep well."

The first sounds of life, were soft footsteps coming down the stairs. The clock struck five-thirty. Lucille came quietly in the kitchen.

"Good morning, my dear little one," Sarah said.

Lucille gave a little frown, "Grandma, I'm not a baby anymore. I'm pretty near grown up."

"I'm sorry. You sure are. But when you prayed last night I was disturbed that you thought you had any blame for this terrible tragedy. You didn't. Please stop thinking you did."

Lucille replied, "I'll try not to think that anymore, Grandma"

"I need to get a fire going. I have plenty of split wood here in the kitchen. Lucille, if you'd get some kindling out of the old fruit basket on the back porch it would be a help."

Lucille went to the back porch and Sarah rose stiffly, found the brown paper sack from Ira's fireworks, balled it loosely and put in the top of the stove into the firebox. When Lucille returned she put the kindling on top and some smaller pieces of split wood. Sarah took a match from the tin holder, scratched it alight on the stove and lit the paper.

"I'll start coffee, Lucille, if you'll get eight eggs and the sliced bacon out of the icebox," Sarah directed. She took a coffee can from a shelf and spooned coffee into the percolator top and replaced the lid. She, then, brought two large skillets to the stove and put them right over the firebox to start heating up with the six cup percolator on the back where it would be the hottest.

Lucille watched her grandmother intently and said, "Anything else I can do?"

"Yes, go rouse Pearl and Ira. We need to hustle around to get the chores done and leave by nine-thirty. We can let Glen and Vivian sleep for a little while longer."

Sarah knew that it would take well over an hour to get the chores done and nearly that long for everyone to get bathed and on their way. By the time Pearl came down, Sarah had the bacon sizzling. Pearl insisted that she take over finishing the breakfast cooking. Rather than do biscuits, Sarah sliced bread to put on the table. She took molasses off the shelf. After breakfast was eaten, Pearl and Lucille headed up to the house on top of the hill to do chores and then came back to the barn to tend the hogs. Ira and Glenn left in the pickup. Sarah got the big round wash tub and took hot water from the heating basin on the wood stove for Vivian and her bath.

* * * * * * * * * * *

Earl drove slowly from his mother's and Charlie's house. He wondered how long the new argument would last and how heated it would become. Arguing and bickering was a way of life in their house. He was determined that would never happen when he married. That would be one of the ironclad rules he would impose on himself and his wife.

Other more pressing matters forced those thoughts from his mind. He sort of ticked them off in his head. First he would stop in Tyrone to see the family at his grandmother's house. Secondly, he would go to Elk Creek to call the funeral home, the Sheriff and the family attorney. He would, then, go to Big Creek for Sunday morning service so he could talk to the preacher.

After he forded the North Jacks Fork and got up on the ridge past Nagle the road was straight and fairly flat, he took out his pocket watch. It was close to eight o'clock. He made a mental note that it would be difficult to get everything done. When he pulled up in front of his grandmother's he was concerned than there was no one at home. Ira's pickup was not there and no one was on the porch. The rocker was empty and that was Sarah's favorite place to sit.

Earl strode toward the porch and up to the front door. He was ready

141

to shout that he was there but he heard dishes rattling in the kitchen. Earl entered the living room and walked back to the kitchen. Sarah was washing the dishes and Vivian was rinsing and drying the dishes.

When Sarah saw Earl she said, "The children need some clean clothes from their house. I don't want them going in there yet."

"I agree with that, Grandma," Earl said. "You got something I can put them in."

Vivian came over to give Earl an embrace. He leaned, down and picked her up his arms, holding her tightly. Her arms clung to his neck. No words were exchanged but there was a powerful exchange of feelings.

"Yes, Earl," Sarah said, "There are some pokes on the shelf behind you."

Earl turned and took down two large paper bags. "These will do. I need to get some things for myself, too."

Earl walked back to the Model A, cranked the engine and drove to the house where his father and stepmother lived. When he drove past the mill he saw his aunt and Lucille scattering dried corn on the cob around the pen by the pond. He was relieved that they had thought to feed the hogs. He would ask Dillard to take care of that chore, he mused.

Earl entered the house through the East door and went to the back bedroom, found underwear and socks and put them in a paper sack. He brought dresses on hangers and the bag to the car and put the sack on the floor in the rumble seat enclosure and the dresses laid across the seat. He took dirty clothes out of the downstairs bedrooms, carrying them outside, rather than tracking through the blood on the kitchen floor, then around to the back porch to the hamper for soiled clothing. He went up to get some things for Glenn which he placed in the second paper sack. He took a large suitcase from the closet and filled it with clothing he would need. Earl didn't want stay in the house for a while. He took his and Glenn's things to the car putting them on the passenger side of the front seat.

When he came to Dillard and Dana's, he saw Dillard sitting on the front porch. He pulled the little car in front of their fence and left it idling as he got out. Dillard met him by his front gate.

"Dillard, could you feed the hogs until I can get them up to market," Earl said. "I'll give you a portion of the profit. I may even ask you to take them up to East Saint Louis. I'm going to be away for a few days, I just need to get away and get my head on straight."

"It's good as done, Earl. Anything else?" Dillard asked.

"If you run out of corn and there's not any here at the store, just take the truck over to Cabool and buy some more." Earl took out his billfold and gave Dillard a twenty dollar bill. "This should cover it," he continued, "There's plenty of gas in the truck. We filled up on Friday. The key's in it use it as you want."

Earl started to turn away but turned back and looked at Dillard, "One more thing. Could you get someone in the kitchen and East bedroom upstairs to clean up the mess and make any repairs to the house. There's a pellet hole in the kitchen window and there's some woodwork and wall damage from the buckshot. If there's anything else, just go ahead and do it."

Dillard nodded and Earl went to the little Ford, got in and drove to his grandmother's.

Earl took Glenn's bag of clothing and put it on the porch. He went back to the car and carried the bag in one arm and the dresses on hangers in the other hand. When he returned to the porch, he asked, "Where should I hang the dresses, Grandma?"

"There are wall hooks in the downstairs bedroom." To Vivian, who was back on the porch, she said, "Help your brother take Glenn's clothing back in the bedroom, too."

Vivian picked up the bag in both hands. Put it down by the screen door, opened it and held it open. Earl held it open while Vivian picked up the bag and they both went to the bedroom. Earl hung up the dresses and put the bags against the wall under them.

When Earl and his little sister returned to the porch, Sarah said, "Earl, don't go in the kitchen Pearl and Lucille are bathing."

"I don't need to go back in," he said, watching as Vivian sat on the edge of the porch. "I need to go over to Elk Creek to use a phone. I need to call Elliot, the sheriff and Dad's lawyer. I'll try my best to get back to Big Creek for church."

"That would be nice," Sarah said quietly, "We haven't seen you there in a while."

Earl choked back his shame and hoped that his grandmother didn't notice his face turning red as it felt hot enough to give him away. "I'll hurry, Grandma. I'll bathe and change here and see you there." He turned to leave.

"Before you go. Why don't you leave the Ford here and take the green Plymouth to Elk Creek. We'll let Pearl and Ira keep the Model A. When you feel ready to go back to work, the Plymouth can be here. Lucille can drive it if she needs to since it has a starter."

"That's a great idea, Grandma. We won't need three vehicles parked in the driveway anymore." Earl turned and strode up the back street up toward the family residence. When he got there he found the keys in the ignition where they always were left. He turned on the key, pressing the starter on the floor board and pressing the gas pedal just slightly. It started right away. Earl thought, boy is this terrific, no cranking.

The Plymouth was much more responsive to the foot throttle and once he got used to the handling of the car, Earl made very good time. He went to the former bank president's house. The man who ran his father's bank before it failed. He now worked in Raymondville as head teller.

When Farley Mason answered the door, he smiled broadly and then became very serious, "Earl, I'm so sorry for your loss." Bad news traveled fast, Earl thought.

"Thanks, Farley. I need to use a phone. As you know Tyrone has no phones. Is the one at the bank still working? I have a key Dad gave me."

"No, it's been taken out," Farley replied, "but you can use the one here at the house."

"Thanks. It won't take too long. I must call Elliot to set a time for the funeral, call and check in with the sheriff and call my Dad's attorney."

Farley led him to the living room and pointed out the phone. He left the room, closing the door.

The call to the Sheriff was perfunctory. The sheriff did not want to be disturbed at home, his dispatcher said. He told Earl that there would be a Coroner's Inquest on Tuesday at ten in the morning. Earl said he would be there and would bring Elmer's mother and Elmer's sister. The Sheriff's deputy asked if Earl would inform James Smith, Sylva's father. Earl knew he would see him at the funeral.

Earl's conversation with Vic Elliot was over even more quickly. He asked Vic if they could do the funeral at two on Monday afternoon. They agreed it would be held then unless Vic should hear otherwise.

The call to James Hart was somewhat disturbing and mysterious. Earl had called his home phone because he knew he wouldn't be having office hours on Sunday.

Hart's wife, Edith, answered the phone.

"Hello, is this Edith?" Earl said, "This is Earl Sigler, could you ask Jim to come to the phone?"

"Earl, I'm so sorry for your loss. I'll call him to the phone."

"Thank you, Edith."

Earl had to wait only a few seconds. He heard Jim Hart's stentorian voice. "Hello, Earl, I hardly know how to convey my deep sorrow. Elmer has been a lifelong friend as well as your Grandfather, Marcus."

Earl said, "Thanks. The simple fact is: I hardly know where to begin with this situation, Jim, but I probably need to see you."

"Earl, you certainly do," The seriousness of Jim Hart's reply conveyed itself over the phone wire, "Your father came to my office early last Friday morning and had me execute a rather strange document. He signed and I notarized it. He took it with him. You need to find that document and bring it with you."

"What kind of document are we talking about, Jim?" Earl asked. He remembered that last Friday, before they were to go to West Plains to the livestock sale barn. Elmer had left the breakfast table, hurriedly. He had said he needed to go to Houston and would be back in time to make the sale.

"The document will be in an envelope with my name on it. It is not something we need to talk about over the phone," Holt said emphatically. "Just find it and bring it with you."

Earl remembered then. When Earl heard the green Plymouth return, He had walked out on the front porch and sat down on a chair. Elmer had gotten out of the car with an envelope in his hand. He had gone to the passenger side of the truck. When he shut the truck door the envelope was no longer in his hand. "I know right where it is, I'm certain," Earl said.

"That's good to know," Jim said, "Why don't you get it and bring it over today?"

"I need to go to Big Creek to church and arrange for the funeral with our preacher, Dan Montgomery, for two Monday afternoon." Earl replied and asked, "When can we get together."

"How about this afternoon? You can buy dinner here in town and come to my office at two. I cannot emphasize how important it is that I see you !"

"If it's that important, I'll bring Grandma and Aunt Pearl along." Earl replied.

"That's probably a good idea for them to hear what I have to say, Earl."

"Okay. Goodbye, Jim."

"Goodbye, Earl."

CHAPTER 11 -

Big Creek to Houston

Even though Earl made better time coming back to Tyrone, he knew time was precious and slipping away. He pulled the Plymouth up beside the passenger side of the truck. He opened the passenger door and looked in the lipped, open compartment under the dash. Beneath bills of sale, for the hogs from West Plains and Jack McKinney, he found the envelope with the attorney's name and address printed on the upper left corner and Elmer Sigler written in cursive on the middle front. Earl removed the document and discovered it was a Quit Claim Deed in favor of Sarah Sigler. It was dated just the day before yesterday. Earl didn't know about deeds, especially a Quit Claim Deed. He did understand, from the wording, that his grandmother was to be the beneficiary. The questions that flooded his mind would only be answered with the meeting with Jim Hart.

Earl, now in more of a hurry, went to Sarah's house. He entered the house and went directly to the kitchen. His grandmother had left him a clean, empty wash tub. He quickly ladled water from the stove reservoir. The water was tepid but it was better than a cold bath. He had brought clothing appropriate for church. After dressing he went to the living room. Earl glanced at the big clock on the shelf as he passed through, noticing it was almost eleven o'clock. He would be late.

At the church Earl heard hymn singing. He was glad he could come in during singing, most people would be standing and reading the words and not noticing someone coming late. He sat on the end of a back bench. He joined in the singing of the familiar hymn. He was heartened that he remembered all the lyric. The rest of the service was a blur of familiarity but his thoughts were on other things. He had not truly worshipped as he should for a long time.

After the service, old friends and acquaintances gathered around him to offer their condolences. His attention was not even on this solicitude. He noticed that Pearl and Sarah had groups around them, too. His two sisters and brothers were standing in a little clump to themselves with other children a step or two away, not knowing what to say to their peers. Earl sifted through his well-wishers to his grandmother.

Earl got Sarah's attention and asked, "Have you spoken to Dan Montgomery about a time for the funeral tomorrow?"

"No I haven't, Earl."

"Grandma, I told Elliott two in the afternoon. That okay?"

"That will be fine," Sarah replied.

Earl saw Herbert Daniel Montgomery near the front of the church and moved toward him. Earl was aware that he must call him "Reverend" even though he had been brought up in his early years not to use that title. He approached Dan Montgomery. When Montgomery noticed Earl he separated himself and met Earl. Dan Montgomery was a man nearing fifty years old with dark hair and brilliant green eyes. He thrust his hand toward Earl and said, "I'm so glad you came, today. What an awful tragedy."

"Thanks, Reverend Montgomery," Earl said uncomfortably.

"Earl, just call me Dan. Everyone else does."

"Thanks, Dan. I wanted to ask if you could do the funeral tomorrow at two in the afternoon?"

"It would be a privilege to be asked and I'll do it," Dan replied.

"I'll ask some of the men to dig a grave, then." Earl said.

"No, Earl, I can take care of that. You've got plenty to do."

"How right you are. Thanks!"

Earl went outside to look for his family. He saw them clustered near the Model A. He walked toward them. He spoke to his grandmother first, "Grandma, I need you to go to Houston with me today to see the family attorney." He turned and looked at Pearl. "Aunt Pearl you should come, too."

Earl looked around carefully and continued, "I'd hoped to see Monkey Jim here today. But he's not."

Sarah and Pearl still looked puzzled. Pearl asked, "What's going on, Earl?"

"I'm not exactly sure myself. I hope Jim Hart can sort it out for us," Earl replied, turning his attention to Ira, "Ira, would you take the children over to Jim Smith and let them be together for a while. Ask him if two tomorrow afternoon will be all right for the funeral. Tell him we'll stop by late this afternoon to pick up the kids."

"Sure, Earl," Ira replied, "By the way I really like how that little Model A drives."

"Yep. It's a top," Earl replied, "I'm hoping we get back to Tyrone by six."

Ira said, "If you're not back by six, I'll go on over to the farm and start the chores."

Earl took out his billfold and gave Ira ten dollars. "Stop in Summersville at the restaurant and buy dinner. There should be enough for gas if you run low."

Earl turned to Lucille, Glenn and Vivian. "Do you mind going over to your grandfather's for the afternoon?" he asked.

Vivian said, "Can all three of us ride in the rumble seat?"

Earl turned to Ira. Ira assented with a nod.

The three children raced to the car and Vivian was relegated to the middle of the seat.

Sarah said loudly, "Take turns. Vivian in the middle to Summersville, then Glen to Arroll and Lucille back home.?

All three heads bobbed simultaneously. There had been no fuss over who sat in the middle before.

Earl said, "Okay, ladies. Let's head off, too."

* * * * * * * * * * *

After stopping in Summersville to eat and put in a couple of gallons of gasoline, Ira and the children struck out for Arroll. Glen sat without complaint in the middle of the rumble seat.

When they arrived, Monkey Jim Smith was sitting on the front porch. The three children clambered from the seat and ran to the porch. They surrounded their grandfather, all giving him hugs. The girls gave kisses but Glen was not having any of that girl behavior.

Ira was slow to approach the porch, hardly knowing what to say. When he put a foot on the first riser to the porch, Jim smith yelled, "Miller, stop right there!"

Ira removed his foot.

Jim Smith's simian-like eyes were reddened. Even now there were tears in his eyes as he continued, "Miller, I don't want you on my porch. Your fambly kilt my daughter."

Ira puzzled by this unfair accusation against him, replied, "I didn't have anything to with it Mon… …….Jim. Pearl didn't either."

"Mebbe you didn't but Sylvia said your wife was a meddlesome busybody, always stickin' her nose in her bizness."

Ira was dumbfounded by these accusations.

Lucille said, "Grandpa, that's unfair."

Monkey Jim stood and shouted, "Get off my property, Miller!"

"The funeral's at two tomorrow afternoon," Ira said over his shoulder, as he retreated to the car. He took the back roads through to Nagle and on to Tyrone.

When Ira was gone, Jim Smith looked at his grandchildren fondly. "Have you et yet?"

Vivian spoke first, "Ira took us to the restaurant in Summersville."

"Okay, then. Let's go to the river to swim."

* * * * * * * * * *

At the restaurant in Raymondville Earl brought in the envelope with him. He gave it to Pearl to read because he knew his grandmother couldn't.

Pearl read it through. She recognized her brother's signature. She looked at Earl, "I don't get it. It seems like Elmer is leaving some land to Mama."

Earl said, "It appears that Jim Hart wrote this from some other document. I suspect it is all the land owned by the Sigler family. We'll know for sure what all this means when we meet with Jim. He has been the family attorney way back. Did you notice that it was signed on Friday."

"You're right, Earl," Pearl said, "He and Papa go back to before he was married. He got the Patent on the original homestead. He's handled all our affairs from forty years back.

The waiter came to take their order. When the order was taken, Earl said, "Let's cover some other things. I don't know where any of the other papers are that Elmer had. Do you know anything about where he would keep a will or other important papers?" He looked first at Sarah and then at Pearl.

Both women shook their heads.

Ray and Sadie miles entered the restaurant. They both came directly toward them when they saws Earl. Ray spoke first, "We're so sorry for your loss. Elmer came to visit me Friday night and I thought he was ready to make amends with Sylvia."

Sarah spoke for the three, "Thank you Ray. You've been a good friend for a long time."

Sadie said, "Is there anything we can do?"

Earl said, "Thanks, Sadie. We've set the funeral for two in the afternoon tomorrow."

"We'll be there. I'll close the bank early," Ray said.

Pearl said, "We need the support from our friends."

Ray said quietly, "We'll leave you to your meal. It's such a great tragedy!" He started to turn away and then turned back. "Earl, you might want to bring the ladies and take a look in your safe deposit box."

"That might answer some of our questions," Earl said, "But I didn't even know about a safe deposit box. How about we come by first thing tomorrow morning. Do you think he might have had one in Elk Creek, too?"

Ray shook his head, "I don't know but I'll ask Farley when he comes in tomorrow."

This time Ray made his way to the table Sadie had selected.

The Siglers' meal arrived and they began eating. Sarah stopped and said, "Earl, there's going to be a lot of responsibility thrown in your lap"

"I know, Grandma, but I'll need a few days away from it all."

"I kind of figured that," Sarah replied, "so I've got it all organized how we'll do things in Tyrone at least through Friday. And we can carry on a little longer if we need to."

When the meal was finished, Earl said, "We need to be leaving to make our appointment." He pulled out his pocket watch. "We'll be early but I don't want to be late either."

Earl paid his bill at the cash register and left fifty cents on the table. He took his time driving to Houston because he knew his grandmother got nervous on the many curves between Raymondville and Houston. When they came to Jim Hart's office, the doors and windows were all open. As Sarah, Pearl and Earl entered, Jim Hart was sitting at a desk in the large front room with a sofa and a couple of overstuffed Chairs in the waiting area.

Hart rose from his seat, "Hello folks," he said, "I've met Sarah many years ago and Earl has come to the office on a couple of occasions with Elmer," then looking at Pearl, "I assume you're Pearl, Elmer's sister."

"You're right, I'm Pearl,"

"Have a seat folks," Looking back at Earl, Jim continued, "I'm sure glad you brought the women of the family, Earl. The Quit Claim Deed that Elmer insisted I prepare last week disturbed me somewhat. Did you find the original, Earl?"

"Yes. It was in the truck's compartment on the right side. I looked it over and I didn't really understand what it was about."

Jim Hart placed his hand on a thick file. "These are the documents or copies of documents that have been produced on behalf of the Sigler family. First Marcus, then Elmer trusted me with your affairs in legal matters. I appreciate your continued confidence in me."

Sarah said, "I couldn't read the paper Earl found. We don't really understand it."

"Well, that's part of my job is explaining," Jim said, "It isn't too complicated. Elmer came to me last Friday with some suspicions of his wife's fidelity and her intention to seek a divorce. She had accused him of having an affair and told him she was going 'to take him to the cleaners.'

The Quit Claim Deed was a means to protect his land assets. After Marcus died without a will, his estate went through what is called 'probate.' If you remember, Sarah, you appeared with Elmer and said that you were not able to continue running the family business and the judge transferred ownership of the land to Elmer and he promised to support you. Is that correct?"

"It's exactly as you described it," Sarah answered, "I was there."

Jim looked at Earl, "Would you give me the Quit Claim Deed?"

Earl took the envelope from his shirt pocket, rose and went to hand it to him. Jim opened the envelope and looked at with a puzzled look on his face.

"This hasn't been recorded yet." Jim said with some ferocity, "It is really worthless." Elmer's estate will have to go through probate as well. As far as I know he had no will. At least I didn't prepare one for him."

"Well. Where do we go from here, Jim?" Earl asked.

"I would suggest that you go through all his papers at home," Jim said. "It is possible that he might have signed a will without me."

Earl said, "I'm going over to the bank tomorrow morning to go through the safe box in Raymondville. I may have a key to the Elk Creek bank building and I'll see if I find anything there."

"I'll see you at the funeral," Jim said. "We can go over anything you might find then if you want."

"Sounds fair to me," Earl replied.

"You do know about the Coroner's Inquest in front of Judge Unger."

Sarah and Pearl shook their heads.

Earl said, "I forgot to tell you. Sorry, so much has happened so fast."

Jim spoke, "No one has to come but I'd like to see one of you show up."

Sarah looked at Pearl, who shook her head. Sarah said to Earl, "I think we would like for you to go if you would?"

Earl nodded.

Sarah said, "We depend on Earl, now, to keep the family afloat. He's pretty young to be saddled with so much responsibility. After Marcus died, Elmer let Pearl and Ira farm where they are now and Elmer has given me fifty dollars a month for my expenses. I never use it all and some months I give it back. Can Earl just keep on running the ranch and business and give me money to live on?"

"I'll prepare a motion to take to the Probate Judge for him to issue an order to that effect, until the probate hearing," Jim assured them. "I may even be able to have it for you by tomorrow."

Earl stood and strode to the attorney, extending his hand, "Thank you so much, Jim. You've relieved my mind and I hope my grandmother's and aunt's."

Sarah added, "I know you'll do right by us, Mr. Hart."

"Jim. Please, just Jim."

As they were about to go through the door, Jim added, "Earl, hold on to that Quit Claim Deed, since it wasn't recorded it doesn't have any force in law but it might be valuable for the Probate Court. You might want to put it in the safe box. Just a suggestion!"

When all three were seated in the front of the Plymouth, with Pearl in the middle again, Earl started the car and he drove toward Arroll.

They pulled up in front of Jim Smith's house. There was too much quiet for the children to be there. Earl walked to the door and knocked loudly. Then yelled, "Jim, you at home!" He saw a woman in the yard next door looking at him. He walked over close to her and asked, "I guess Jim took off someplace?"

The woman said, "You're Earl, right?"

Earl nodded, "Yes. I remember meeting you a couple or years ago. You know where they are ma'am?"

"Matter of fact I think I do," she answered, "the boy came yipping and hollering out of the house when I was out cutting weeds along the fence. 'Let's go Pappy. I want to get in the river.' He got in Monkey Jim's old car. After a while Jim come out with the two girls. They went off toward the forks."

"Thank you. Grace, isn't it?"

She nodded and seemed pleased Earl remembered her name.

Earl went back to the car and told the women, "Monkey Jim took them down to the forks." Earl started the car and they set off to Jacks Fork river where it separated into the South and North forks. There was a low water bridge that had a nice, safe swimming hole for young people.

When they came to the bridge, Earl guided the car off onto a gravel bar and parked. He saw Jim Smith sitting on a blanket up near the usual swimming place. Earl got out and walked toward his siblings' grandfather. When he got close, he saw a bottle of moonshine on the blanket by Jim. When Jim Smith heard Earl's footsteps close behind him, he turned to face Earl while still seated.

Jim Smith jumped to his feet, Earl noting how agile, he was for a man fifty or more. He swore at Earl and continued vehemently, "Whachoo doin' here."

"I've come to pick up the children," Earl answered politely.

"They're not your chilluns. Get outta here." Jim Smith swore again.

Earl said, patiently, "Jim, it was good of you to bring the children swimming."

Jim looked at Earl with his rheumy eyes, swaying on his feet, stepping toward Earl. He swung his fist at Earl but Earl stepped aside and gave Monkey Jim a little shove. He sat back, involuntarily, on the seat of his pants to the blanket knocking the bottle over. Jim Smith scrambled after it. Earl walked away where Lucille, Glen and Vivian were paddling around in the water with a large number of people.

Earl hoped they hadn't witnessed the exchange between him and their grandfather.

When his sisters and brother saw Earl they came running, splashing through the water, the girls giving him wet hugs. He put his arm around his little brother. He said, "I noticed you paddling around like a dog, Glen, and you, too, Lucille. You can make a lot more headway with the crawl stroke. Earl demonstrated what was known as the Australian Crawl. Try it. See if you like it. Remember to kick your feet, too. I'll give you ten more minutes, then we'd best go."

All three dashed for the water and Earl watched them and walked back toward Jim Smith. He stood looking down at him. Earl said, "I'm sorry about the little push."

Jim Smith squinted up at him. "Them kids take to yer but that don't mean yer daddy had any right to kill my little girl." Tears sprang to his eyes.

"No he didn't, Jim," Earl replied. "We've all suffered a great loss."

Monkey Jim drew his knees up and leaned his arms and head there. He began to sob. Earl walked slowly back to the Plymouth.

A few minutes later his sisters and brothers came back toward the car Glen running ahead and Vivian trying to keep up. Lucille walked back sedately, her head held high, water dripping from her hair, a little water nymph. The car doors were open on both sides to allow more air to pass through. When all three were by the driver's side door, Earl looked at them carefully. Glen and Vivian had been swimming in their underwear and Vivian had on an ill-fitting swim suit. "Get changed kids and we'll head home."

Glen, it seemed, ran everywhere. He went loping to Jim's old sedan, with Vivian coming along behind. They took dry clothing from the car and went into a stand of weeds and brush to change.

Earl turned to the women and said, "You'll have to check them for ticks and chiggers before they go to bed tonight."

The women nodded.

Earl sat back with his head leaned back an emotional weariness setting in.

They sat in silence for a while each to their own sad thoughts.

Sarah broke the silence, "What was that all about, you shoving Monkey Jim on his backside?"

"He was just drunk," Earl replied, "He took a swing and I just gave him a little push. I'm just glad we came in time to keep him from driving home with the children."

Pearl said, "Yes. That was a good thing."

Glen came out of the copse of weeds and brush first, running.

"It's my turn on the outside." he shouted.

Earl got out of the car and Glen clambered into the rumble seat. When Glenn began shoving a valise off to the side. Earl looked at it and said, "Is that in your way?"

"Nope, Bud, "Glenn answered, "We can put it under Vivian's feet. They don't even reach the floor anyway."

Earl hadn't noticed the valise because Lucille had opened the hatch to the seat. He had a suspicion that it had some things belonging to Sylva. He made a note to look at it later.

Earl walked around the car and pulled the valise up against the side where Vivian would sit. As he walked back to the driver's side, Vivian emerged from their "dressing room" with Lucille right behind her.

When the girls were settled in their seats, Earl started the car. Sarah and Pearl chatted about what would need to be done during the week, meals, washing, a little of the town gossip, avoiding talk about more disquieting things. Earl mused over what he would do with his week. After they crossed the ford at North Jacks Fork, Sarah leaned forward to speak to Earl, "You can stay at the house with us tonight. I can make a pallet for Glenn or Vivian. You can sleep upstairs on the single bed."

"Let's worry about that later. I'll go up and help Lucille with chores at the house, there's something I need to do up there when we get done. You two can put something together for supper."

They rode in silence the rest of the way to Tyrone. When Earl brought the Plymouth to a stop in front of Sarah's house, Ira was sitting in Sarah's rocking chair with his tin can spittoon in his hand. He emptied his mouth of spittle and cud of tobacco.

The children were out of the car much more quickly than the adults.

Sarah said loudly, "Glen and Lucille get on some old work clothes."

Earl went to the back of the car and shut the lid on the rumble seat. He wanted to check later if Sylva had packed for a trip. He suspected that she and Lonnie had set something up and Lonnie had ignored his warning. So much for friendship, Earl thought.

When Earl came up to the porch, Ira was standing and Sarah was sinking into her rocker, with a look of exasperation on her face as she looked at Ira's back.

"You came back in one piece, Earl," Ira said.

Pearl asked, "Whatever do you mean, Ira?"

"If Monkey Jim had had his shotgun handy......"

Pearl interrupted, "Ira, I've asked you over and over not to call Jim Smith that."

"Fergot. Sorry."

Earl said, "He probably had one too many," as he glanced toward Vivian who was busy playing with one of Sarah's young cats. Earl continued, "He wanted to punch me, not too successfully."

"He run me off but that's okay. I sure did enjoy drivin' the little Model A. Beats my pickup."

"As far as I'm concerned you can keep it," Earl said, "How about it, Grandma?" turning toward his grandmother.

Sarah shook her head, "It's not up to me. Your're the man of the family now, Earl. Whatever you say goes."

"It's yours and Pearl's now," Earl said emphatically.

"I'm ready to go, Ira," Glen said as he emerged from the screen door.

Sarah said, "Glen."

Glen looked at his grandmother and then back at his uncle. "I'm ready to go Uncle Ira."

"That's better," Sarah said.

Glen looked pleased with himself and Ira seemed happy with it.

Ira said, "I'm ready, too." He went to the Chevy pickup and Glen jumped into the passenger side as Ira cranked it to life. It sputtered and backfired but kept running. Ira turned in a circle on the back street and started up toward where Morgan's lived and through by the beer joint.

Earl got another chair out of the house to go with the other straight chair that was already there. He said, "Aunt Pearl, please sit down and let's talk. We've been on the run all day and haven't really had a good chance to talk."

Earl moved one straight chair around so it was facing his grandmother and aunt. He was ready to say something when Lucille came out dressed in overalls over an old faded blouse. Earl said, "Why don't you go on up and get started and I'll be right behind you."

Lucille nodded, stepped off the porch and walked rapidly up the little lane toward the main road.

Earl turned his head back to look at Sarah and Pearl. Sarah said, "This puts a heavy burden on you, Earl, and you so young."

"How's that, Grandma?"

"You're the only adult Sigler man," Sarah said emphatically. "We're going to depend on you to keep the family running, keeping the business going. Making decisions for us."

"These are modern times, Grandma," Earl rejoined, "Women have the vote now and full rights under the law."

Sarah said, "I can't speak for Pearl but I can't run the business, the farms, the ranch. The last couple of years Elmer has depended more and more on you to help run the stock trading business."

"I'm not going to be able to do what Elmer and you have done," Pearl said, "I have enough on my hands with the farm Elmer has allowed us to live on and use."

Earl shrugged his shoulders, "I'll have to talk more to our lawyer. He mentioned Probate Court and I don't understand what that's all about. Maybe I'll go back over and see him after the funeral tomorrow." The unsaid message from Pearl was her lack of inclusion in Marcus' legacy.

"Earl you know I can neither read nor write. You just take care of everything." Sarah turned to look at Pearl. "Don't you think so, Pearl?"

"No doubt about that, Mama."

Earl rose and said, "Best be going up to help Lucille do chores. I don't want her to think I'm some sort of lazy laggard."

Earl got into the Plymouth to drive to the top of the hill. When came to the back porch he could see Lucille in the back forty bringing in the cows. The kitchen had been scrubbed clean and he assumed the upstairs was done as well. He went upstairs to change to work clothes and went to the barn. Earl told Lucille to gather the eggs and put out some chicken feed and he would do the milking. When she came back into the barn she had the baskets both nearly full of eggs. Earl allowed Lucille to go back to her grandmother's with the two baskets of eggs. Earl finished the milking, carried water to cool it, making a mental note to remind Lucille and his aunt to carry water in the morning again to cool the milk. He went to the icebox on the back porch. The ice was mostly melted. He put anything that might spoil into a gunny sack to take to his grandmothers. He changed out of his work clothes.

As he was changing, a morbid thought intruded his consciousness. Had his Father planned all this in advance. The Quit Claim Deed was giving some validity to that possibility. He shook his head and tried to think of something else.

CHAPTER 12 -

THE CASH STASH

Earl went to the front bedroom where Elmer and Sylva slept. The suitcase was there. Earl went through it thoroughly. In a side pocket he found two sheaves of money. When he went back to the Plymouth he put the money behind the seat without examining it. He drove back down to the barn and fed the hogs.

When Earl came back to his grandmother's, Sarah and Pearl were sitting on the front porch.

Earl set the gunny sack on the porch, Sarah gave an impish smile and said, "What you got in the sack, Earl? A dead possum. I already cooked up some sausage and fried potatoes and there's corn bread in the oven."

Earl smiled at Sarah's little joke and replied, "I don't much like baked or fried or roasted possum myself, Grandma." It felt good to have a little fun.

Luicille and Vivian were marking out a hop scotch game in the dirt of the street in front of Sarah's house, so Earl sat with his grandmother and aunt to watch the game progress. As the game evolved Vivian's jumps were not as good as Lucille's but Lucille missed sometimes when she shouldn't have to keep the game competitive. Earl admired Lucille's grace and her ability to be fair to her sister.

"I'd better put these things in your icebox, Grandma. The ice was about all melted up on the hill You'll be eating down here, might as well have it here." Earl said.

When Earl started to get up, Pearl said, "No you don't, Earl. You'll just put it in all in a jumble. Let me do it."

Earl sat back down. "I'm not hard to convince. You're probably right, but let me carry it around back for you."

Earl got up again. He picked up the sack, went down the front porch steps and around to the back porch with Pearl following along.

Pearl said, "Why don't you take things out and I'll put them away." When they were done Earl looked to see how the ice was holding up.

"You're going to need ice tomorrow," Earl observed.

"What you did was thoughtful, Earl," Pearl said, "I should have thought to ask Ira to bring back the things that would spoil from our ice box at home. Oh. I'll just have him do it in the morning when they go over to do chores."

Ira drove up and parked in front of the house as Earl and Pearl walked back around the house.

Sarah called to the girls, "Come on in and eat Lucille, Vivian. It's been in the warming oven. It's going to be hot eating by the stove but we've got all the windows and doors open. It won't be too bad hot."

Pearl prayed. There was less raw emotion than there had been the evening before. There was no mention of the violent deaths nor the impending funeral.

As the simple meal wound down, Earl said, "I'm going to have some milk and cornbread for dessert. " He went to the back porch for the milk pitcher from the icebox. He returned to the kitchen dining table and poured a glass half full of milk. He crumbled cornbread into the milk and put a couple of spoons of sugar on top and proceeded to eat. All three children wanted to try this new thing. They soon had their glasses of cornbread and milk. Earl wiped his mouth with a cloth napkin.

Sarah said, "How was it kids?" All three nodded their heads, smiling, with their mouths full.

Earl said firmly, "I think I'll go back to Mama's. There's no need to disturb your sleeping arrangements, Grandma." Earl looked at Lucille, "Remember to carry fresh cold water to cool the milk, tomorrow. We don't want to be sending spoiled milk to Cabool."

"I won't forget, Bud," Lucille replied.

Earl said, "I'll be off then. I'll go the Raymondville Bank at nine in the morning when they open. If you and Pearl want to go I'll stop by."

"You can let us know if there's anything of interest," Sarah said.

Pearl nodded, "You handle it, Earl. You handle all the family affairs, now."

Earl rose to leave. He got hugs and kisses from the women and girls, a handshake from Ira. Glen walked to the little green Plymouth. Earl's arm and hand hung down and across Glen's shoulders. When Earl was seated in the car he waved at everyone on the porch and said, "Take good care of everyone, Glen. They need us."

Glen beamed proudly, "See you later, Bud."

Earl waved and went the back street to the beer joint and to the main road east. When he got to the West Plains-Rolla Road, he turned south. He stopped the car in an unused driveway to a deserted house. He went to the rumble seat compartment and opened it, removing the valise. Earl's suspicion was right, it was filled with Sarah's clothing and cosmetics. In the bottom was a brown paper sack. It was sort of a square bundle, tied firmly shut with coarse string.

Earl removed his pocket knife and cut the string. When it was opened, Earl gazed in amazmnt at its contents. He took the sack into car and set out bunles of cash tied around with finer string on the car seat. There were bundles of one dollar bills, fives, tens and twenties. Earl marveled at the amount of cash. Sylva must have been accumulating money for years that Elmer had given to her for household expenses. As he began to count, he realized that there were literally thousands of dollars. He stopped counting when it reached four thousand and knew she had at least a thousand more. Now came the questions. What should he do about it? With it? One larger stash of cash and a smaller one.

He opened the car door and reached behind the seat. He took out the two sheaves of money with a wide band of paper binding it. On the top of each was a note in small writing: cattle drive June 25. Earl remembered how it happened. Earl, Dillard and Lonnie had moved a small mixed herd of steers, heifers, cows and bulls they bought at the Thayer sale barn. Elmer had bought nearly two hundred cattle at the West Plains and Willow Springs sale barns. John Bradford and John Dunivan joined the drive in Willow. Elmer bought cattle from farmers between Willow Springs and Licking. They bedded the herd down in a field east of Tyrone. Elmer hired Paul McKinney and Mack Hall for the drive to Rolla. They drove the herd on to Dow Clayton's farm on Tuesday south of Licking. Elmer bought more cattle at the sale barn in Licking on Wednesday and they moved the herd toward Rolla with one last overnight just south of town.

Cattle drives of this sort during the Great Depression, and before, in South Missouri were not that unusual. Many farmers were driven to desperation by bank closings that took away their savings. Assets of closed banks were sold to other banks who called in mortgages farmers' could not repay. The sale of small herds of beef cattle was common. These farmers used the proceeds to satisfy some or all of the debt. They became subsistence farmers, raising chickens for meat and eggs. Many farmers had a few dairy cattle they milked, sold eggs and chickens for a small income. Many let their dairy cows and hogs run free on the open range. They hunted, trapped or caught wild hogs just as you would wild game. They smoked and cured pork. They canned fruit, vegetables, pork sausage, and some beef. They ate a lot of chicken. They subsisted on what they grew and depended on little else for cash. Many had some part-time work outside farming.

A buyer from the National Stock Yards came to where the herd was grazing. The buyer had the drovers cut out the steers first and herd them out of the field, then the heifers, next the cows and bulls last. he counted each group, made a quick calculation and offered Elmer twenty-five dollars a head. Elmer Settled for twenty-eight and the buyer gave him a bank draft. Elmer, not trusting a stranger and his check, had taken it directly to a Rolla bank and cashed it. Earl knew his father must give most of it to his bank to cover the checks he had written for the purchase of the herd.

Earl remembered now the exact amount the herd of four hundred and five brought, Eleven Thousand Three Hundred and Forty Dollars. The little stash had just become the big stash. This was much easier to count since most of the bills were hundreds. He guessed Elmer had put the money somewhere in the house. It had been only a little over a week. His father must have forgotten that he needed to get it to the bank. In the meantime, Sylva must have found it. Did Sylva really know she had over eleven thousand dollars and most of it wasn't really Elmer's? Why hadn't Elmer taken the money to the bank? Had Elmer discovered the money was missing? Did he think Sylvia had taken it? Questions within questions, Earl thought.

Earl replaced the cash in the paper sack, folding it over in roughly the same shape as Sylva had it, putting the clothing back in the valise and the bag of cash on top. He put the two bundles of bills behind the seat of the car.

Earl knew just who to ask. His stepfather wasn't too book smart but he had a lot of wisdom.

Earl started the car and arrived at Charlie and his mother's house while they were still awake. When he got out of the car, he could see his mother peering out the window into the gloom of the evening.

When Earl came to the door his mother was already opening the screen door. "Come in, Earl. We would have been in bed a long time ago," Mary said, "but we've been up at Skaggs. Jenny, Morgan, George and Howard came over to go to church with them. All of them showed up at Clear Springs school for church. Effie invited us all over for dinner after church. Jenny and Morgan had heard the awful news and invited you to come over if you needed someplace else to land for a couple of days."

"Mary, let Earl come in and sit," Charlie said.

Earl had decided not to bring in the cattle money, that was another matter and something he knew how to handle. It must go to the bank.

Earl held up the little valise. "Would you believe about five thousand dollars are in here?"

Mary's eyes widened in surprise but Charlie showed nothing, he possibly puffed his pipe a couple of extra times.

Earl set the valise down on the floor. He took out the paper bag full of money. He opened it and put it on the round dining room table. He picked up the lamp and put it in the middle of the table. He said, "Help me count it. Sylvia had saved up cash and hid it someplace. I found it in this valise."

Earl's mother and step-father came to the table. Earl counted the ones because it was the larger stack, his mother the fives, and Charlie the tens and twenties. When it was all added up it came to Five Thousand Eight Hundred and Eighty Three Dollars.

"Well, Earl," Charlie said, chewing on a burnt end matchstick, "you've got yourself a pile of cash. I never in my life saw this much at one time."

"Charlie, now comes the hard part," Earl said. "You were the only one I could think of to ask what to do with this money. What about it?"

Charlie pondered for a couple of minutes. "It's family money, yours, your sisters' and brother's, your grandmother Sigler's and Pearl's."

"But then what, Charlie? How to divide it up? What about probate?"

"The most obvious is a division among Elmer's children," Charlie said. "But if I was you I'd call a family conference among the adults. You don't want to burden children with decisions a parent has made that might not be up to snuff."

"Charlie, sounds like good advice. Now I'm going to give you a real bomb."

Charlie interrupted Earl, "About probate. I wouldn't take up the issue of this money with a court or attorney's. They'll try to figure some way to siphon some off."

"I would never have thought of that, Charlie. Now for the big one. I found over Eleven Thousand Dollars in a suitcase Sylvia had packed, laid out on the bed in the downstairs bedroom."

"My merciful God........." Mary hesitated, thinking she had done a swear word, then continued, "What was that woman thinking."

"It was the proceeds from that last cattle drive. You remember that don't you?" Earl asked.

Charlie Nodded. Mary said, "Yes."

"Dad, Elmer, must have left it in the house someplace and Sylvia must have found it. Not a dollar of it was missing. I counted it and it was exactly what the National Stock Yard buyer gave my Dad a check for. He cashed it right there in Rolla, said he didn't trust a stranger's check. It was a Thursday and we got back after the bank closed."

Charlie and his mother were quiet for a long time before Charlie said, "I wonder if that was the root of what set Elmer off to do something so drastic."

Earl said, "That's probably something we'll never know for sure. I am quite sure about something. Sylvia was taking off with all this cash in her baggage. And something else I'm fairly certain of. I think she planned to go off with Lonnie Bailey. And I don't have a clue of where they were going.

"I thought Lonnie was one of your best friends," Mary said.

"I thought he was my best friend and I am putting emphasis on was," Earl replied.

"Don't be too hard on him, Earl," Charlie said, "he's suffering from the lure of the loins as many young men do."

"If anyone should know that, I should," Earl said, "a two time loser."

"You men!" Mary said, "I'm not going to sit around and listen to this kind of talk." She left the room and came back with a pillow and sheets for the day bed. "I'm going to bed," she announced. Mary had never accepted that Earl had really fathered two children. It seems she thought you had to be married to have children, forgetting what happened nearly twenty-two years before.

Earl looked up at the clock with the warships on front, "I think I'll get ready for bed myself. That clock's going to strike ten before I can hit the hay."

"Yep. Four thirty's going to seem mighty early, Earl," Charlie said.

"Be sure and wake me. I'll help with the chores before I jump in the bathtub." The bathtub was their little family joke for the creek in the summertime bathing ritual.

Like clockwork, Earl heard Charlie stirring on his porch bed. Earl placed his feet on the floor and levered himself upright. He slipped on boots and pants. He went to the car and took out some work clothes and changed quickly. He was dressed by the time Charlie arrived by the back gate of the yard.

Earl hurried to join Charlie. Although Charlie was a head taller, Earl felt lighter for unburdening himself the night before, feeling like he could walk shoulder to shoulder. When they came to the barn, the cows followed them from the small west pasture. Earl opened the door to the milking area while Charlie got the feed. The familiarity of this ritual was comforting in its own way.

While Charlie let the cows out in the east pastures, Pal nipping at their heels to move them along, Earl took the manure fork and mucked out the milking stalls to the manure pile outside the barn window. Pal was the best Cattle Dog Earl had ever known. Charlie had the gates rigged so that Pal could open and close them. All Charlie had to say to Pal was "go get the cows" and off he would go opening and closing gates as he went. It was amazing to behold.

Charlie was not one to chat, so the milking ritual was not broken by conversation. He and Earl had done this so many years the routine needed no direction or talk.

On the way back up the hill Charlie broke the silence, "This money thing is quite a tale. Silvia must been setting aside small amounts of money for years, so Elmer would not suspect anything."

"That'd be my guess, too, Charlie. But the money from the cattle drive really amounted to outright theft." Earl took out a packet of Lucky Strikes and shook out a smoke and offered one to Charlie. He took one which surprised Earl, he was so accustomed to seeing Charlie with his pipe or chaw. They stopped while Earl scratched a match alight on a stone. The cigarette looked tiny in Charlie's big fingers. They both began walking again, puffing in silence. When they entered the yard and began filtering the milk, Charlie took the cigarette from his mouth and threw it away.

"I best get to the bathtub, Charlie."

"Go right ahead. I need to let the chickens out and give them a little feed. I'm fattening up some young roosters to take to town to sell this Saturday."

Earl said, "I'll draw the water to cool the milk first."

Charlie said, "Okay," and strode off toward the chicken house.

Earl cooled the milk and went to the car to get fresh clothes, on his way back through the house, he poked his head into the kitchen, sniffing at the frying sausage. "Smells good, Mama. I'm going to get a bath."

"You know where the towels and soap are."

Earl nodded and got a towel from a small cupboard and soap from the wash stand. He went out the back gate west of the smoke house and cellar, down the hill and through the fence to the creek. When he was through with his ablutions he dressed quickly. When Earl entered the porch, Charlie was sitting at the table puffing on his pipe, now.

Mary came to the porch table with hard fried eggs and sausage. She said, "Put that smelly thing away, Charlie. It's time to eat. Earl, "She said, barking commands, "go get the biscuits and gravy while I get out the cream, butter, jam and sorghum."

Earl jumped as if shot and hurried into the kitchen for the biscuits and Mary's wonderful gravy. It was like old times, being bossed around by his mother in the house.

When they were seated Mary prayed. "Dear God, our merciful father, bless this food. Today, we want to remember the Sigler family in their travail. Be especially close to them and comfort them with your Spirit as only you know how, especially those little ones orphaned so young. In Jesus precious name. Amen."

Earl had the urge to say "Amen" aloud as well but stifled it. He reached for two biscuits, broke one in pieces and split one and put butter on both halves. The sausage and eggs were passed and then the gravy. Earl ladled gravy over the broken up biscuit. They ate in silence until Earl spoke, "Thanks for that nice prayer, Mama."

Earl, close to cleaning off his plate, turned to Charlie, "I just don't know what to do about Lonnie. He and I have been pals for the last five years. I've tried to get him interested in playing ball but he's doesn't think he'd like it. He goes and watches me play sometimes. We go fishing and swimming together."

They ate in silence but Earl knew that Charlie would have an answer eventually. Finally Charlie said, "I'd just let it alone. Lonnie will come around and make his amends. He's a good kid."

Earl put sorghum on one half of his biscuit and blackberry jam on the other half. He said, "I imagine the Baileys will all be there. Maybe Lonnie will have something to say."

The impending funeral was now, suddenly, weighing heavy, the day, the enormity of his new responsibilities as head of a family thrust upon him.

Mary said, "We'll be coming."

"Mama, that's so nice of both of you." Earl knew that Mary had never given up her love for Elmer, her first love and Charlie had a residual jealousy of that.

Charlie said, "Death changes everything."

"You said a mouthful there, Charlie," Earl said, "You don't know the half of it."

"I think I understand more than you know. I became mother and housewife to my three younger brothers and sister when my Mama died when I was ten."

It was at this moment that Earl knew that Charlie had lots of empathy for him in his situation.

"You know Earl, that just about everyone in my family will be there. About the only ones won't be there are Reeves from Kansas and my Brother Jims' from Denver." Mary said, stopped and thought for a minute. "You're welcome to come back as often as you want in the coming days but the Bakers said you could come over and visit there. Morgan and Jenny were pretty emphatic about it and George would really like for you to come over. He says there's some good fishing holes he'd like to take you to."

With the lack of telephone service in the middle of the county, Earl had just shown up at his Aunt Jenny's and Uncle Morgan Baker's many times. George Baker was a first cousin but also a great friend.

"I'll probably take them up on it. I think I would like to spend another night here. It's almost childish, but I feel safe here," Earl said.

Earl felt a lump rising in his throat. He was afraid he was going to break down and cry. He cleared his throat, and continued, "I'd best be going. I've got to go to Raymondville bank with this money. I need to confer with my grandmother and Aunt Pearl." He rose quickly and went to the day bed and picked up the valise and went to the Plymouth.

By the time he got to car, tears were streaming down his cheeks, an oppressive, black sorrow, an enormous guilt and dread was engulfing him. The boom of the shot gun blasts echoed in his ears. Had he failed his Father? Could he have done more to avert this? His family was so suddenly torn asunder, his sisters and brothers bereft of parents. How would it all turn out for them? Could he become the bread-winner for a broken family? Could he be a parent as well as a brother to Lucille, Glen and Vivian? How would that turn out?

He drove up to the top of the hill, stopped the car and felt behind the seat. The two bottles were there. He opened the door and reached behind the seat, taking out both bottles. He finished the inch of liquor in one bottle in a long swallow, throwing it into the trees. He had the second bottle of moonshine open almost before he heard the tinkling crash of the shattering bottle on a tree or a rock. He drank half the bottle in several long pulls.

By the time he got to the ford at North Jacks Fork, he was feeling the effects of the liquor. Along the top of the hill in the more flat area, his vision was blurring and he was weaving perceptibly. He nearly hit an oncoming car. At the turn to go west to Tyrone, he opened the bottle and had a couple of more swallows.

In Tyrone he saw Dillard sitting on the whittling bench in front of the Kidd store. Earl parked across the street and walked unsteadily toward his older friend. He stopped a couple of feet from Dillard and said, "Thanks for getting the mess cleaned up in the house. Who do I owe for that?"

"Dana took care of it," Dillard replied. "Looks like you've had one too many, Earl."

Earl ignored the remark. He took out his billfold and took out a five dollar bill and handed it to Dillard.

When Dillard didn't take it, Earl looked puzzled.

"It's too much, Earl. It took less than half an hour."

"Let's just call it a down payment, then. You and Dana are probably our best friends here in town, Earl said, swaying, "I bet I'll be calling on you and her a lot to help me out in the days to come."

Dillard stood and held out his hand, "I'll give it to her but it won't be enough to help."

"What do you mean, Dillard?"

"We're losing our house, Earl," Dillard replied, "We had our mortgage at the Elk Creek bank. The bank that bought our mortgage wants it paid off in full."

"Anything I can do to help. I could probably come up with enough."

Dillard made a wry face. "Don't bother. The house is worth half what it was worth when I bought it if that much. We've been offered a farm house to live in. The farmer moved to town, we'll pay rent and share crop. You could graze some cattle there once in a while. There's some pens for some hogs, too. We'll get by. Elmer and you've kept me in enough cash money, trail riding and driving truck."

Earl smiled, "I can always use extra pasture and a place to put a few pigs." He turned back toward the car. When Earl opened the door, Dillard leaned around him and grabbed the bottle of moonshine off the seat.

"And I could use a drink. You sure don't need any more, Earl."

Earl made a grab at the bottle but Dillard held it behind his back. As Dillard backed away, Earl said, "You win, Dillard. You're right, I don't need anymore."

"I promise you. I'll finish this off and never have a drink again, Earl."

Earl smiled, "I'll hold you to it."

"At least until tomorrow," Dillard smiled impishly. "See you at Big Creek."

Earl tipped his hat to Dillard and got into the Plymouth. He drove to the lane just past the Kidd house and turned north to his grandmother's. He parked the car in front of the house. Pearl was sitting in a straight back chair with Earl's sisters and brother sitting at her feet and Sarah in her rocking chair. As Earl approached the porch, the children started getting up.

"Not yet, kids, we're not done reading the Second Chapter of Romans," Pearl said sternly.

Earl's sisters and brother resumed their seats. Earl stood at the bottom of the steps and listened. After Pearl finished reading, Earl walked up on the porch. He went to kiss his grandmother on her cheek. When the buss finished, she wrinkled her nose and said, "Earl, not today of all days."

Pearl waved her hand in front of her face. "Go brush your teeth. You smell like a sewer."

"I'll do just that, Aunt Pearl." Earl retreated to the car and got his toothbrush and his dry tooth powder. He went to the back porch, wet the brush and poured a generous amount of the powder on the brush. He brushed his teeth vigorously and rinsed his mouth with fresh water.

When he returned to the front porch, Earl said, "Where's Ira?"

"He thought he ought to go to the barbershop," Pearl said. "The funeral has caused big demand for haircuts."

Lucille said, "I got all the chores done except the eggs. The store wasn't open when we went up the first time and the baskets were full of eggs still."

"Why don't all three of you take the eggs down to the store," Earl said, "and I'll give you a quarter to buy treats for all three of you. Then all of you go on up and get the rest of the eggs."

Glen shouted, "Yippee. Let's go. Let's go."

Earl said, "Glen go get the eggs and walk slow. No broken eggs. Lucille you decide on the treats." He handed her the quarter.

Earl went in the house and brought another straight chair and sat it facing his Aunt Pearl and Grandma Sigler. He told them in as straightforward a manner as he could about the money.

Sarah sighed heavily and Pearl waited on her mother to speak. "I kind of understand her setting aside money from household expense but the outright theft attempt really gets to me. Surely she didn't think she could get by with it. The police would have been after her. With cash as tight as it is it could have absolutely ruined the family."

Pearl said, "How could she have done it? You recon Elmer found out she stole the cattle drive money and that's what set him off?"

Sarah look intently at her daughter, "It won't change anything with questions. What's done is done and we can't undo it."

Earl nodded his head.

"When Elmer began stock trading right after the war," Sarah continued, "He ordered the St. Louis daily paper and studied the markets and began buying based on what he called the 'trends.' He used to talk to Marcus about it and I was the little mouse. I'm a lot smarter than they give me credit for. But Elmer was real smart and made a good living at it for his family. As roads got better and cars and trucks got better, the grist mill lost more and more business. We finally shut it down about five years ago. Marcus was never the same up to when he died three years ago."

Pearl kept on after Sarah seemed out of breath, "Your dad bought his first truck when they finished that new highway 66 into St. Louis. He and Dillard took a load of cattle up to East St. Louis about once a month and brought back a truckload of furniture that they sold. They took turns going up with hogs or cattle. They did a lot of small cattle drives to Rolla, they could get more animals to market that way and began to concentrate on hauling just pigs. Sylvia once said they were just rolling in cash. No wonder she started squirreling it away with all the ups and downs in their marriage."

Finally Earl interrupted, "I know what to do with the cattle drive money, it has to go to the bank to cover Dad's checks to buy the cattle. What I need to discuss with you is the money Sylvia accumulated."

Earl looked at his aunt and grandmother. They both shrugged their shoulders.

"I asked Charlie about it. I thought I needed an outside opinion. He thought we might want to divide it up among the six of us. What do you think?"

Sarah spoke first, "You're going to need to put money back into the family business. We're depending on you to keep things going. I don't need any of that money."

"We're getting along just fine on the farm Elmer let us use after Papa died," Pearl said, leaving unsaid the festering dissatisfaction with being left out of the Marcus' inheritance. "Besides, you let us have the Model A."

Earl said, "How about I set up a thousand dollar savings for each of my sisters and brother that they can collect when they are eighteen or if they get married. Girls lots of times get married sooner." The rest we'll put back in the business. When we get Elmer's estate settled, I'll make sure you're taken care of properly, Aunt Pearl."

"Earl, that seems a dandy solution," Pearl said.

Earl stood, "I best be going. I'll let you know what's in the safe box." He turned and went to the car. He waved at Sarah and Pearl as he drove the back street toward the beer joint. He saw Aunt Annie and Uncle Weed sitting on their front porch. He waved and they waved back.

As Earl drove along toward Raymondville he became more sober but a deadly gloom still gripped him, like a vise. When he pulled up in front of the bank Ray Miles was just opening the door with Farley waiting to follow him in. He saw Jana rounding the corner, coming from her house on the edge of town.

Earl dragged the valise across the seat, reached behind the seat and brought out the cattle drive money in the packets. He followed the two men and Jana into the bank. When Earl entered the bank Ray saw him and walked toward his office, motioning Earl to follow. Ray went to his desk and sat down and invited Earl to a seat.

When Earl was seated, he said, "I came upon the cattle drive money from about nine days ago. I guess it slipped my Dad's mind to get it over here."

Earl placed the two packets of cash on Ray's desk. Ray got up and put his head out the door and called to Farley, "Far, I need your help and get one of the other ladies to bring in the Sigler safe box."

A few seconds later Farley came into the room. Ray said, "bring up a chair and help me count this cash."

Earl said, "There should be exactly Eleven Thousand Three Hundred and Forty Dollars."

Ray and Farley, being professional bankers, had the money counted quickly. Ray looked up and said, "I got what you just told us. How about you, Far."

Farley nodded, "Me, too."

Ray opened his desk drawer and pulled out a large card. He said, "Sarah was a signatory on Elmer's account, you sign this signature card and have her sign it and you can write checks on that account. Farley, go deposit it in that account."

"Ray, Farley, I have an idea of what to do with this cash. Take enough to cover any overdrafts. Leave Five Hundred in Elmer's account, make it Sarah's. I'm assuming the account was overdrawn."

Farley said, "Yes, maybe a Thousand dollars overdrawn."

Earl said, "I keep a checking account here. Put the balance of the money in it. I'll be handling the family affairs from here on out. I'll need a substantial checking account."

Ray objected, "Earl you can't do that. It's Elmer's money and it should go in his account."

Earl interrupted, "My father's dead. He can't use the money. The family needs it to keep operating on an even keel. I can take the cash to another bank and open an account there."

Ray's face reddened, "You can't do that. Your family owns part interest in this bank."

Jana knocked on the door jamb and Ray motioned her in with the safe box. When Jana left, Earl said, "I just don't want you telling me what can be done with the family's money. If you want me to I can bring my Aunt Pearl and my Grandmother Sarah to tell you what they just told me about a half hour ago."

"All right, Earl. Farley, deposit the residual in Earl's account," Ray said.

"We're not done here," Earl said, "I've got another batch of cash." He took the brown paper sack of money from the valise and put it on Miles' desk.

Ray leaned over and opened the sack. Farley sat back in his chair. Ray gave a shrill little whistle as he removed the bundles of cash.

Earl said, "There's Five Thousand Eight Hundred Eighty-three Dollars."

"What's this, Earl, you dig up Marcus' tobacco tins of cash he buried in his backyard?" Ray said.

"You don't really want to know and I'm not going to tell you where it came from. It is honestly earned money of the Sigler family," Earl gave a lopsided smile, "Suffice it to say that it's none of your business."

Ray and Far began removing the strings from each stack.

"Here's what I want you to do with this money," Earl continued, "Set up three savings accounts of One Thousand dollars for each of my sisters and brother, Lucille, Vivian and Glen Sigler. They will be allowed to take the money when they are eighteen or when they marry, whichever is first. The balance will go into my working checking account. Hold out Five Hundred in small bills. I need to pay the drovers and funeral expenses."

Ray said, "Far, go take care of it." He shook his head as he looked at Earl. "You really know how to take charge. You'll do all right."

"Wait a second, Far," Earl interjected, "Would you bring me balances from any family accounts."

Farley hesitated and said, "There's a savings account in Elmer's name."

Earl looked at Ray and asked, "Can that be put in my name and my grandmother's?"

Ray looked at Farley. "Go do it, Far." Looking back at Earl he stated, "I don't imagine that you have a key to this box. We gave it to Marcus years ago and I know that he passed it on to Elmer because Elmer put a couple of things in the box."

"Ray, I don't have a key.

Miles opened his desk drawer and held up a screwdriver. "I know how to take care of this little problem." He inserted the edge of the screwdriver in a crevice and twisted. The box popped open with a some loud protest. Ray pushed the opened box toward Earl.

On top was a stack of Stock Certificates. "What are these, Ray?"

"Marcus and my father got together about ten years ago and started buying some stock in some companies," Ray replied. "Dad cashed his in about six years ago. I'm kind of glad he did. Marcus didn't. I don't know if they are worth anything but I can give you the name, address and phone number of the stock broker in St. Louis they dealt with. Maybe you can take a list of the names and number of stocks owned to them and they can tell you if they have any value." Ray pulled out a sheet of paper and wrote on it.

Earl found several promissory notes from various individuals to Marcus and a couple in favor of Elmer. Many of the names were people he knew, a couple he didn't. He put them in his pocket, deciding to consult Jim Hart about them.

In the bottom was a small gold ring. Earl held it up and looked at. It appeared to be a wedding band. He was puzzled.

Ray said, "Marcus came over to put something in the box and I was in this room. He held up the ring just as you are now and said, 'I bought this for my mother when I had my first job because Thomas Jefferson was too poor to buy her one.' He was referring to his stepfather, Tom Boster. Then he said, 'I took it off her finger when she died. Thomas Jefferson wasn't getting it. He was anxious to leave for Arkansas with his new woman.'"

"You're telling me that my grandfather's step-father was courting a woman before my great grandmother passed. "

"Yes, he said he went over the day she died and took it off her finger. He didn't want Tom Boster to have it. He said old Tom Boster took off with the other woman while his mother was still warm."

Farley returned with the balances of all the Sigler accounts. His account was now nearly Twelve Thousand Dollars. Elmer's checking account now had exactly Five Hundred Dollars. The savings account that was in Elmer's name was over Seven Thousand. There were three deposits in his siblings names for a Thousand Dollars each.

"One last thing, if it's not too much to ask." Earl said, "would you write down the amounts of the checks my father wrote to buy all the cattle for the cattle drive. I would like to know how we came out on it. We talked about doing an even bigger drive, but, of course, we had to cancel. I may put it together myself."

"Sure thing, Earl," Farley said and left the office again.

"Elmer mentioned that he was thinking of trying to put together a drive of a thousand to fifteen hundred cattle this summer," Ray said. "I think you can do it Earl. Elmer had a lot of confidence in your ability to gauge the market and buy right. It would take a lot of money to put together that kind of drive. We would back you on it."

Earl, smiling, said, "Thanks for the boost in my confidence. I may just try it. I need a little time to myself, to mend, to think."

"I can understand that, with what you've been through," Ray empathized.

Farley returned with the list of checks. He handed Earl a signature card for his bank account. "This for anyone you might want to put on to be able to sign checks for your working account."

"I can't think of anyone appropriate right now, Farley." Earl stood and said, "I need to get along. See you next time." He tipped his hat as he left the room.

Earl walked to where Jana was working. He looked her squarely in the eye, "Whatever arrangement you had with Elmer with the pigs are the same if you want them to be. Do you have enough money for feed?"

"Earl, you don't look like Elmer but you have ways so much alike. It's almost like I'm talking to him," Jana said, and added, "No I don't need money for feed. Elmer took care of that for quite a while."

"I'll see you in the bank off and on, Jana."

"Or I can drop you a penny postcard if I'm running short."

"Thanks, Jana. See you later."

"Yes. Later."

Earl strode from the bank. He opened the door and looked at the list of checks. He did some quick calculations in his head. They had made a substantial profit from the cattle drive. He made up his mind on the spot about something he felt he must do. He started the car and drove in the direction of Licking.

When he got to Dow Clayton's, he pulled up by the front gate of the yard. Ray Dow, four years old, was playing in the yard. Dow emerged from the house and met Earl at the front gate. Dow was a little shorter than Earl so he leaned on the gate to get to eye level.

"What are you doing off over here, Earl?"

"I had to stop by the bank to take care of some money matters," Earl replied. "Elmer bought some cattle from you to take up to Rolla. How many was that?"

"Seventeen steers and four heifers."

"I remember now," Earl said, "those were prime beef. We came out so well I'm giving money back." He pulled his check book from his pocket. "There was a neighbor farmer Elmer bought from, too. How many did he have?"

"Fifteen.":

Earl wrote out a check for Forty-five Dollars and handed it to Dow. "Would you give him fifteen dollars for me. I'd appreciate it."

"Whoa. If you want me to give him fifteen, you gave me nine too much," Dow protested.

"Dow, I told you your cattle were prime. My Dad, Elmer, bargained hard for the price he got and I'm determined to give some back in his memory."

Dow stuck out his hand. "If this is how you do business, you'll get a lot more." Earl shook his hand.

"I've got to run. Lots to do today." Earl said.

"See you at Big Creek, Earl."

Earl loped to the car. He stopped by two other farmer's houses and gave back fifteen more dollars which was well received.

Earl was back in Tyrone before eleven o'clock. Elliott Funeral Home had sent a car through Tyrone on the way to Big Creek to make sure everything was just right in the church and in the cemetery. They stopped by to see his grandmother and told Sarah they would be in front of the Kidd store at one o'clock if we want to convoy over with the hearse.

"Do you think it is a good idea for the kids to go to the funeral?" Earl asked, "especially for Vivian and Glen."

"You might be right, Earl," Sarah replied, "But death is as much about life as birth, and everyday living. You're right, Earl. Who could keep them."

"I could ask Dana. Vivian and Glen might enjoy being around some of the town kids while we are gone. I'll talk to them about it when they get back. I need to go up to the house and dress in my light weight summer suit. It's a dark blue and will be appropriate."

Chapter 13 -

The Wages of Sin

Earl had walked to Dillard and Dana's house and left Glen and Vivian there to play with their daughters, and other children of the town. Now all five of the remaining Sigler clan were assembled on Sarah's front porch. Earl looked at Lucille and said, "Are you sure you want to go to the funeral."

Lucille nodded.

"Okay then, Grandma and Aunt Pearl sit up front with me. Lucille and Uncle Ira in the rumble seat. Let's go," Earl said.

On the way to the car Lucille held Earl by the coat sleeve. Earl stopped and Lucille, standing on her tiptoes, whispered in his ear. "Let me sit by you, Ira tries to put his hand up my dress when he gets a chance."

Earl's face darkened. He took control of his emotions, "I'll watch him from now on."

When they got to the car, Earl stopped his aunt from getting in the front. "Aunt Pearl do you mind sitting with Ira. Lucille is feeling really vulnerable now and she wants to lean on Grandma's shoulder."

Ira was busy opening the rumble seat hatch and heard the exchange.

He gave his wife a hand up as they got into the rumble seat. The little green car was just entering the lane south from the house to the main street when the first hearse was rounding the curve at the top of the hill. Earl pulled into the road right behind the second long black vehicle. The word had gone around the village of Tyrone about the convoy and several cars were waiting on the street before the store. Vic Elliott got out of the second hearse. He handed Earl a bag with Elmer's personal effects. Earl placed it behind the front seat behind him.

The convoy moved slowly toward the West Plains-Rolla Road and on north to Big Creek Church. It was a small white wood structure on the east side of the road across from a small cemetery. The burial ground had a nice maple tree and several cedar trees and many flowering plants. It was an attractive, well-manicured cemetery with a lot of character. There were only two cars in the lot when they arrived. Earl stopped the car and got out. Across the road he saw two mounds of red dirt marking the burial spot on the northernmost part of the fenced graveyard. Their burial would be some distance away from where his Grandfather Marcus and Rex were buried with Rex's five very young brothers and sisters.

Vic Elliott approached Earl. He stopped close to him and asked, "Do you want to open the casket. We feel uncomfortable about opening Sylvia's. We just couldn't do much with her face."

"I'll speak to my grandmother and aunt about it," Earl replied, "As for Sylvia, it might be best to ask Jim Smith, he's Sylvia's father."

Earl inclined his hat and head toward Monkey Jim Smith's old black sedan. He was sitting in the front seat tipping up a bottle of bootleg. "Be careful if he's drunk, he might take a swing at you."

"Thanks for the warning. I'll keep my distance." Vic strode away toward Jim Smith.

Earl walked around the car to corral his aunt and grandmother to ask their opinion about an open casket. "Vic Elliott was asking if we wanted to open Elmer's casket after the service is over. Sylvia's face is such a mess he didn't really want hers open. He's over to talk to Jim Smith about it, now," he asked, "What do you think?"

Pearl spoke first, "It doesn't matter to me. I'd like to remember him as he was when he was alive. He was a smart, handsome man. He was respected and admired. He was a great provider for his family."

Sarah had a different take, "I'd like to see him one last time. He was my first born. It's tradition around here for before burial viewing."

Earl looked at Pearl and she said, "You're the tie breaker, Earl. What do you say"

"My opinion is: we should defer to seniority, go Grandma's way."

The three heard shouting coming from the direction of Jim Smith's car. His wife had shown up with her new husband from western Missouri. Monkey Jim Smith was shouting at his ex-wife the most profane language anyone would ever hear. Swaying drunkenly, Jim saw Earl and came running toward him.

Earl shouted, "Grandma, Aunt, go in the church now. I mean now." He turned toward Monkey Jim as he heard the little man shouting curses at him.

When Smith was about ten feet away he started pulling a pistol from his big old fashioned thigh length dress coat over overalls.

Earl reacted by nearly sprinting the few steps between them and grasped the pistol and the smaller man's fingers in his left hand, gripping so hard Monkey Jim howled in pain. "Drop the gun or I'll break your fingers right on this gun. Don't think I can't!" The two men were standing chest to chest as nearly as possible given their size differential. "Drop it!"

Jim Smith nodded. Earl began releasing his grip and the gun fell harmlessly to the ground. Earl stooped swiftly and picked it up. As Earl was rising up he knew Monkey Jim would try to take a swing at him. Earl crowded right up against him and said, "Monkey Jim, go in the church before you get hurt. I'll give the sheriff your gun. You can get it back from him."

No sooner had Smith entered the church, than Sheriff Kelly drove into the parking area and parked by the Plymouth. Earl walked over to give the gun to him. "Sheriff, Monkey Jim pulled this on me and I took it away from him."

The Sheriff took the gun to his car and threw it in the window. He came back to stand by Earl and said, "I'll be with Monkey Jim from the time he comes out of the church for burial. After the internment I'll have him up against that back fence. I'll put the fear of God in him."

Earl nodded and went in. He walked to the front of the Church and sat by Lucille. Sarah was between Lucille and Pearl and Ira on the far end of the pew.

It was surprisingly cool in the church for as hot as it was outside. However, Earl knew from experience that the heat would build in a hurry with the room full of people. One of the men was busy opening windows, using props to keep them open. The hard wood benches now had backs to lean against. Earl remembered it was a little over a year ago his Aunt Pearl telling him about the new backs.

Ray and Sadie Miles were one of the first to come. Jana came with them. Sitting directly behind Earl, Ray put his hand on Earl's shoulder and whispered, "Stop and see me this week when you can."

Earl looked over his shoulder at Sadie, who was wearing a beautiful red, broad brimmed hat. It was as red as fresh blood. Earl nodded his assent.

He turned his attention back to the front as the pall bearers, six for each casket, came in and placed the caskets on their biers. Sprays of flowers allowed a sweet, cloying scent to emanate through the front of the room. As people began to fill the little church, the scent of the flowers fought with the smell of sweat and tobacco odors that had not been cleared well from many men's mouths. Women's perfumes contended with the fouler odors.

After the clock on the wall struck two times the pianist played a sad, dirge-like piece. Dan Montgomery came to the pulpit. He looked around several seconds and began, "The church is full. Men and women are standing outside the windows and doors. The Sigler and Smith families want to thank you for coming to give them comfort in this time of terrible loss."

A loud wail from Sylvia's mother, hushed the murmur of voices after Dan Montgomery's opening statement. The wail subsided to sobs.

Dan Montgomery continued, "A dear friend and preacher, Sadie Miles, is here and will offer an opening prayer."

Sadie, her clothing rustling, stood and prayed, "Magnificent Creator, the men, women and children here present are a living testament to your goodness. Across the road is the City of the Dead, peopled by the saved and unsaved. I have been told that these two about to join the City across the road have at one time professed to salvation through the shed blood of Jesus. We all fervently pray that you, in your infinent mercy, will welcome their souls to your omniscient presence. We pray this in the precious name of Jesus. Amen"

Sibilant low echoes of "amen" swirled around the room and a loud "Amen" from Dan Montgomery. A loud wail came once more from across the aisle but Dan Montgomery, boomed over it, "We will sing a couple of favorites of the deceased and the church quartet will sing. First we will hear a reading of the obituary notice sent to the local papers. Sylvia's will be read by Esther Hall and Elmer's will be read by Roe Hall.

After the readings, Dan Montgomery announced that the hymns "In the Garden" and "Amazing Grace" would be sung with only a short pause in between for those who wanted to find them in the hymn book. Then the quartet would sing "In the Sweet Bye and Bye". During the hymn "In the Garden" Sarah and Pearl wept quietly. Earl was so choked by emotion he was unable to sing. During "Amazing Grace" an incessant wail arose across the aisle.

After the singing, Dan Montgomery rose and walked softly to the Pulpit. Clearing his throat he began, "Our Christian Brother King James wrote the Bible in English so we can read a particular verse from the book to the Romans, chapter six, verse twenty-three." Dan raised his hand and slapped it on the pulpit so hard it sounded like a cannon shot had been fired in the confines of the room. "'The wages of sin is death.'"

The wailing stopped. The preacher now had their attention: "Yes my friends. Today we see those wages come to fruition in this life but that is not what the Apostle Paul was speaking of. He was referring to the eternal death that the unrepentant, unbeliever will suffer in Hell. Then Paul tempers this judgment with a magnificent promise. The second part of that verse says, 'but the gift of God is eternal life in Jesus Christ.'"

"If you read that verse carefully, the word 'is' is in there twice. Both are in italics which is a way to emphasize that little word. It makes it more definite what is going to happen.

"When Jesus was asked if a little girl was dead, he said, 'she is only asleep.' I stand here today and tell you these two are 'only asleep.' On the great judgment day these two young people will rise to meet their savior, Jesus in the air.

"Do you doubt that. Then let me tell you this. Both Sylvia and Elmer made professions of their faith in their savior Jesus Christ in this very church building. What does it say in the second part of the verse we just read: 'the gift of God is eternal life.' I tell you my God does not give gifts lightly. Nor do I think he takes them back.

"Once we were dirt and to dirt we will return. These two sleeping souls will join the others, my dear Sister in Christ has described as the 'City of the Dead', in that lonely City, to the bowels of the earth that gave them earthly life.

"For those of you who are dead in your sinful life take this opportunity today, to make your life right with the Lord. I'll be around for a while after the burial. See me. Seize this opportunity now. Jesus stands at the door of your heart and is knocking right now.

"We will close this service with the singing of the hymn 'Living for Jesus.' The people in front directly behind the bereaved families will be allowed to view the body of Elmer Sigler and go out through the side door toward the cemetery. Then, those outside will be invited to come through. Finally, The Sigler family will view Elmer's body last. The Sigler family will exit the back door and go to the right and the Smith family will exit the back door and stand to the left. Elmer's casket will depart the church first and the Sigler family is invited to follow to the burial site. Then Sylvia's casket will exit the church and the Smith family will follow to the burial site. No one should be at the burial site before the families."

When everyone was surrounding the burial pits, Dan Montgomery recited from memory the Twenty Third Psalm. After this he intoned, "Ashes to ashes, dust to dust shalt thou return. Thus, saith the Lord of Hosts. Amen. You are dismissed."

The crowd was quietly weeping, women openly and men were wiping tears from their cheeks with large bandanas. The bright blue sky and fluffy white clouds became a counterpoint to grief.

The large crowd of many scores of people began to drift away toward their cars and trucks and a few horse-drawn carriages or buckboards.

As they walked back, Earl said, "Grandma, wait in the church for me. It'll be awfully hot in the car. I need to see Mr. Elliott about the funeral expenses."

Earl noticed Dan Montgomery approaching the church and moved to intercept the preacher. Earl stopped a pace away and pulled his wallet from his hip pocket. He removed thirty dollars and handed it to Dan.

Dan's eyes widened in surprise. "This is most generous," he said.

"It is what is deserved for a difficult funeral. My grandmother and aunt and sister and myself took great comfort from your words. We thank you as shepherd of this church for so many years,"

Earl's and the preacher's attention was drawn to the shouting, cursing Monkey Jim Smith. The Sheriff had the small man in an vise-like grip on his arm just about the elbow. Smith was hopping along with pain squeezing his eyes into a squint. Golda was trailing along behind. When they got to the car, Monkey Jim was taken to the passenger side of his automobile. The Sheriff released him and turned to Golda, "I presume you're Jim's daughter. Can you drive?"

"Yes, I'm Goldie. I've been driving for years," she replied.

"Get him home and get him sober. You tell him I don't want him anywhere near Tyrone. If he even gets as close as two miles he will be in danger of going to jail for a long time. Understand me?" Sheriff Kelly said emphatically.

Golda nodded and got in the car. She waited patiently while her father fell into the passenger seat and closed himself in. She started the car and drove north on the West Plains-Rolla road.

Dan put his hand on Earl's arm and asked, "What was that all about?"

"You missed out on that little side play. Monkey Jim tried to pull a pistol out his pocket and I took it away from him before the service started. I think he was looking for revenge," Earl replied.

Dan Montgomery shook his head and turned toward the church.

Earl said to his back, "Tell Sarah and Pearl we'll leave in a couple of minutes."

Dan raised his hand in understanding.

Earl turned to look for Vic Elliott. He saw the undertaker working his way toward the gate of the fenced cemetery. Earl walked to meet him. They met at the East edge of the road.

Earl asked, "How much for the funeral?"

"Elmer's or both." Vic replied.

"Both."

"Two Hundred and Forty," Vic said.

Earl took twelve twenties off the roll of bills he had been given that morning at the bank. He looked at Vic as he handed him the cash and asked, "You sure this is enough."

"It's plenty," Vic hesitated a long time. "I would never overcharge for a Sigler funeral. You'd be surprised at how many dozens of funerals your grandfather and father paid for."

Earl's look of surprise was momentary as he said, "Let's continue that family policy. Drop me a penny post card for any funeral that you don't get paid for along with the price."

"Looks like you're just a chip off the old blocks, Earl. Thanks."

Earl noticed his family moving toward the Plymouth. He said, "See you later, Vic," and turned on his heel toward the car. Lucille, once more sat in the middle of the front seat.

The return to Tyrone was in dreary silence. Earl was thinking of what he should do next. He was certain that he must go to Houston to see Jim Hart. He had not seen him at the funeral. Something must have come up to prevent his being at the funeral. Earl mulled over what he would do with the rest of this week. He knew he couldn't just jump back into work. The close business association he and his father had enjoyed over the last two or three months would make it much easier for him to do stock trading. He hadn't had a chance to visit with his mother's side of the family with all that went on before and after the funeral. He made up his mind to go to Houston to visit Jim Hart. He would call the Baker's and accept their invitation to visit Sargent.

Lucille's thoughts were sad but were also of a practical nature. She thought of an idea to help distract the three of them, herself, her sister and brother. She would organize a "summer school" for the next four days. She had also heard that Grandview Baptist Church was having a "vacation Bible school" the two weeks following this one. Lucille vowed, in her mind, to get Glenn and Vivian dressed each day. She was determined that the three of them would go to Grandview even if they had to walk. As it turned out, occasionally they walked and were drenched in sweat from the three mile walk in the heat of the day. They would take cold baths without the benefit of soap to wash away the perspiration and cool off.

As for Sarah, her thoughts were of the eight children she had borne. Only one was left, Pearl. Her dear little Pearl, married to a man no one in the family really liked. However, her main concern was to give herself time to rest from the emotional storm that had engulfed her family. They needed time for healing and reconciliation. She resolved to take a good, healthy nap every afternoon.

Pearl had the most practical thoughts. She was wondering how she could help her nephew cope with being thrust into such a difficult role at such a young age. However, she knew how smart Earl was. Elmer had so much confidence in his abilities so she also instinctively knew that he would succeed in providing for the family. The more serious problem was how to help her younger nieces and nephew cope with being orphaned so suddenly. Pearl knew she and Ira would get along fine. They would subsist mostly on what they grew. Ira would continue working as a barber as long as he had business. He would have to take time away for haying. They would continue to sell cream and eggs for additional spending money. The new little Ford would make life a little better. They would sell four or five calves every year and an old cow on occasion.

When they got home, Sarah seated herself on her rocker on the front porch. Earl said to Lucille, "Would you mind going up to Lays and get your sister and brother?"

"Sure, Earl."

When Lucille was well up the lane, Earl said, "I'm sure you're curious about what went on with Monkey Jim Smith. He was pulling a gun out of his pocket before the service. I was lucky to get to him before he was able to use it. I took it away from him."

"Oh. That horrid little man," Sarah said, "I'm ashamed for my grandchildren that their maternal grandfather is such a stooge."

"If you think you need some protection here at your house you can go up to Dad's house and get a gun, " Earl said.

Ira spoke up, "I have a dandy little four ten with buckshot to keep the foxes out of our chicken house. I'll bring it over."

"Thanks, Ira, for taking that on. I appreciate your jumping in and taking things in hand here in Tyrone. But I need to talk to you about a private matter." Earl walked down the steps toward the Plymouth and stopped. Ira came up and stopped beside him with a puzzled look. "Ira I'm going to tell you something one time. I want you to keep your hands off my sisters. If I hear of it happening again, I'm going to whup you two weeks from Sunday. Do I make myself clear?"

Ira's face turned beet red. Earl waited.

"You're clear," Ira choked out.

Earl shouted to the ladies, "I'm going over to Jim Hart's. I'll be back by six. Would you get word to Dillard to meet me on the porch at six at the house? If I get there before he does I'll wait for him."

Earl drove west to the Tyrone Road that ran north past the cemetery, past the Sevege house. He drove north until he met the road that connected Yukon with Houston. He turned west and was soon in town.

Jim Hart's office was only a block from the courthouse.

The office was still open. A secretary was seated at the desk when he came in. She looked up with a smile. "What can I do for you?"

"I'm Earl Sigler. I'd like to see Jim."

"Mr. Hart has been most anxious to see you, too. Come on back," the young woman rose and led Earl down a hall and into Jim's regular office.

When Earl came in, Jim Hart leapt to his feet, "I'm so happy you came in. I want to apologize profusely for not getting over to the funeral. A judge pulled me into his court over a case I had pending. A serious matter arose that I can't even discuss outside the courtroom."

"That's okay. I know these things just come up," Earl said. "Besides that, we don't have any telephone out in the middle of the County. Speaking of phone, I need you to connect me to Morgan Baker in Sargent. They have a phone because the line runs right along the train tracks."

Jim went to the door and spoke down the hall, "Susan, get Morgan Baker's house on the phone so Earl can talk to them. Let us know when they are on."

Jim returned to his chair as Earl said, "I brought something from the safe box in Raymondville." Earl pulled the promissory notes from his pocket. He sorted through them and handed the ones he knew to Jim. The attorney took them and looked at the pieces of paper.

"It appears your father and grandfather was pretty generous and may have made no effort to collect."

Earl nodded, "I thought I would approach them and see if they would like to begin to pay us back. I know it's hard times but I'd like to set up some way for them to pay us back a little at a time, even if it's a dollar a month. If they miss a payment now and then I want it made clear that I'm not going to have the Sheriff down on them."

"What else have you got there?" Jim asked.

Earl handed him the other two promissory notes, "These are two I don't know."

"I'll look them up on the tax rolls and find where they live. I'll have Sue take care of it for me."

Sue put her head in the door and said, "Jennie Baker is on the line."

Jim picked up the phone receiver and handed it to Earl. Earl said, "Hello Aunt Jennie, this is Earl. Mama said you wouldn't mind if I came over for a day or two." Earl listened to his aunt, then continued, "I'm going over to Mama's tonight. I'll show up over at your place about ten o'clock tomorrow." He listened some more and said, "Bye, Aunt Jennie."

Earl handed the phone to the lawyer and said, "I'm going over to my cousin's house for a couple days. He wants to do some fishing. I bought a new rod and reel and a couple of bass lures and I haven't even had time to try them out."

"It will be good for you to get away from work for a couple of days, Earl," Hart empathized. "I'll make up a simple contract that you can fill in the amounts and when they will be paid. Both the person who made the promissory note and you can sign it."

Earl said, "I added them up and they came to more than three thousand dollars." He hesitated and then continued, "Sounds good to me, Jim. It just seems to be a good idea when someone borrows money that they should have some way in mind to repay it, even a little at a time. I don't want to be charging interest like a bank," Earl said.

"You're a fair man, Earl, but more practical than your father or grandfather. They were generous but with a fault"

"Why don't you make out a couple of those little sheets without a name but a blank so I can fill it in if I feel I should make a loan someday. This way it will be done up right from the beginning," Earl mused aloud.

"I'll have this all in order by Wednesday when you come over for the Coroner's Inquest at ten o'clock."

Earl said, "I'll see you then."

"Word got back to me that Monkey Jim pulled a gun on you," Hart enquired.

"You got it exactly right. I'm hoping the Sheriff has a handle on it." Earl rose to leave.

"Be very careful with that man. You may not know it but he shot a man about ten years ago. Some people say he fancies himself a 'wild west' gunman." Hart warned. "He used to tote a gun around in an open holster."

Earl nodded and left the room. He thanked Susan for her help on the way out. He assured her she could call him at Baker's if anything should come up.

When Earl pulled into the driveway, past the little pine tree, the afternoon sun glared off the silvery metal roof of the Sigler home. He got out of the Plymouth and pulled his hat a little lower over his eyes to help fend off the glare. The shade of the front porch was inviting after the heat of the day. The call of duty was stronger, he walked around the house to the back. His aunt was coming out of the chicken house with two baskets full of eggs. Earl noted the empty tub for cooling milk and the two buckets set aside to carry water. Earl picked them up and went down the hill to fill the buckets with fresh, cold water to start the chilling of the milk. When he was leaving the little three-sided shed where the well was, he saw Dillard emerge from his gate and start up the street. Dillard caught Earl as he was walking up the hill because he had to walk slower to keep from losing some of the water.

When Dillard caught up he said, "It's been a busy couple of days."

"You said it, Dillard. It seems like I've been meeting myself coming and going," Earl agreed.

Earl went to the back of the house and emptied the water into the tub. He put the buckets down and walked back to the front porch. He mounted the porch and slouched into one of the chairs. Dillard sat in the other one.

"Boy, does it seem good to just sit down and rest. I've been on the go since four thirty this morning," Earl sighed in relief.

The two men sat in silence for several minutes.

"You deserve to sit just a bit," Dillard broke the silence.

"What I wanted to talk to you about. Grandma and Pearl have decided that I should carry on the family business, ranching, farming, stock trading just like my Dad did."

Dillard nodded, "I kind of figgered that it would be that way."

"Dillard I need your help. My Dad depended on me a lot over the last several months. I really believe he would have had a hard time getting along without someone backing him up. That's where you come in," Earl paused to take a breath.

"I'll do whatever I can. Elmer always was generous."

"I want to hire you on as foreman of the farming and ranching end so I can concentrate on the stock trading. Would seventy-five a month be enough? And I'd pay you the usual on any cattle drives over and above your regular pay." Earl enquired.

Dillard's eyes widened in surprise, "Earl, that's more than generous. Sure I'll do it"

"There's more to it. Do you think Dana would mind doing washing for me a while for as long as she wants. We have a gas powered washer. It kick starts a little like a motorcycle. You can do your washing up here, too. Ask her to sort through my Dad's and Sylvia's things and lay them out in the living room and dining room and we'll go through them and box up what we can't use. There's a hamper full of dirty clothes on the back porch."

"I'll ask her, Earl."

"Let me know what she thinks is fair," Earl added.

"When do I start?"

"Right now. Here's pay for the cattle drive," Earl took off three twenties and handed it to Dillard.

Dillard said, "This is too much. I hired on for the drive at two dollars a day."

"I'm giving everyone a bonus, double-pay," Earl replied, "We made a very tidy profit on the drive so I'm doubling for everybody. Here's forty dollars for Lonnie. He worked ten days at two a day. Here's twenty for Paul. He worked five days. And the same for Mack Hall. Part of your job will be paymaster."

Dillard took the money and put it in his pocket.

Pearl and Lucille appeared with the baskets of eggs. Pearl said, "I wondered how water got into the tub, Earl. Thanks."

Earl waited while his aunt and sister started down the street.

"Of course, you know, you should treat our property as if it was yours," Earl said, "Ride our horses, use our vehicles, speaking of which. You don't have a car, do you?"

Dillard shook his head, "I use Kidd's old car when we need to go to town."

"I gave Pearl and Ira the Model A. We don't need two cars sitting here in front of the house. If I'd thought of it in time, you could have had the Model A," Earl smiled wryly. "Ira can't use both at the same time, just stop by and ask which one he'll not need that day. You use the other one. Sometime this week I'll find a car that will be just for you to use."

"Don't get too generous. I want yeh making money and not goin' broke," Dillard commiserated.

"Don't you worry. I told you this morning that I'd be leaning heavily on you and Dana. You should be paid accordingly," Earl said emphatically.

"Anything else, Earl"

"Yes. I want you to check all the fences down on the home place at Grogan. I checked the ones here last month. Check the ones on Pearl and Ira's place. I'd like to get their permission to run twenty or thirty more cows on their place. I'll give them a share of what they get at market or pay so much a head. I'll let them know what you're doing over there. If you need help to find the fence lines the share croppers down at Grogan can help you. I'm losing one renter next year out on the home place. I think I know who I can get to go in there," Earl said drawing a large breath, "I've never given such a long speech."

"Mebbe yeh could become a politician," Dillard chuckled.

Earl squinted at him suspiciously and realized Dillard was joking. Earl started, chuckling as well. Earl rose, "I'd better get down to see Grandma and the rest. I'm going down to my mother's tonight and I'm going over tomorrow to visit my cousin and loaf and do some fishing."

Dillard standing now, "I don't blame yeh a bit to rest up a couple days. You've got a lot ridin' on yeh now. Yeh know, yeh're the youngest boss I ever had."

"Just don't start taking advantage of my youth and inexperience," Earl smiled impishly.

"I don't think there's too much danger of that, Earl. Friends don't do that to friends."

"A couple more things when you see Lonnie, tell him to meet me here at the house by seven o'clock on Friday. He's going with me to West Plains. I'm going to start the ball rolling for a really big cattle drive. I want to move over a thousand head up to Rolla. I want at least one more rider to leave with us from here. Two would be better. I also need to ask George Bailey to sell me a couple more horses."

"I'll work on it, Earl."

Earl got up and started walking toward the Plymouth. When the two men got to the gate, Earl opened it and said, "Get in and I'll take you down to your house. I'm going to stop at the store on the way to Grandma's."

Earl stopped in front of Dillard's house. Before Dillard got out Earl said, "Help yourself to anything in the garden up at our place. I'll tell Grandma and Pearl that you'll be taking things out."

"One last thing Dillard," Earl pulled out his little notebook, "I'd like to see you get one of these. I write the name and address of every person I see, every phone number, the number of livestock I buy and every dollar I spend. You can keep track of what you do and what you spend for the ranch."

Earl stopped in front of the store. He went in and bought seven bottles of cold Pepsi Cola and asked for a cloth sack to put them in. He drove the back street and parked in front of his Grandmother's. Ira was back and was sitting on the front porch in a straight back chair. His sisters were playing with a kitten and Glen had a yo-yo going up and down a string.

Pearl came to door as Earl was walking toward the porch. "I heard you come up. Supper's ready," she said.

Everyone walked toward the back porch to wash up before eating. Earl waited to last so he wouldn't have to sit in the heat of the kitchen as long. He set out the bottles of Pepsi on the kitchen table.

After a supper of pork chops, mashed potatoes, gravy and green beans Earl told his family he was going to his mother's and then would visit his cousin George Baker and his family. Pearl had made homemade bread earlier and it came out of the oven, hot and aromatic.

It was a little before seven o'clock when Earl left for Charlie's and his mother's house. When he opened the gate, Earl saw Charlie's tall figure in the garden. Earl stopped at the bottom of the hill and walked up to the garden. When he came to the garden gate he saw his mother down on her hands and knees picking green beans. Charlie was hilling up the potatoes so the skins wouldn't be green when they dug them later in the fall. Charlie's shirt and overalls top were drenched with sweat.

Charlie saw Earl before his mother did. He said, "Grab a hoe if you'd like to help."

Mary looked up and said, "Hello, son. Charlie's pulling you leg. We're 'bout done."

"I'll go on down to the house and go through my Dad's personal effects from his pockets." Earl turned and went back down to the Plymouth. He got the bag of Elmer's things from behind the seat. Earl went to the back door to the porch and went to the table. He opened the bag and allowed everything to just slide out on the table top. He sorted everything the usual pocket change, comb, pocket knife, stub of a pencil that had been sharpened with a knife. Earl picked up the billfold and looked at the bills, riffling through them he discovered a little over three hundred dollars. The last thing he wanted to examine was his father's notebook. Earl replaced everything in the bag but the notebook.

The notebook was small enough to fit into a front pocket. Each one had one hundred pages, so it would last three months. Written on top of each page was a date, day, month and year. It was like a business diary. Earl leafed back to June Twenty-fifth. That was the day they sold the herd of four hundred and five cattle. Elmer had written: sold 405 head of cattle at $28. Cashed check in Rolla. Bank closed. Cash, middle desk drawer. Check on pigs at Jana's. Ready to go.

Earl thought, it happened just as I guessed, he got back too late to take the cash to the bank and put it in his middle desk drawer. Earl remembered taking the hogs from Jana's to market.

Earl looked at next entry. Saturday June 26th: up early go to Willow sale. Look at cows by Pine Creek. No deal. Too much. Bought pigs. Avg. wt. 30 ½ lb. Double deck back to home place.

Remembrance was clear on that day. Earl had stood by his father's side as he talked to the farmer by the crossing at Pine Creek. He had twenty-two prime steers about eight hundred pounds each. The farmer had wanted way too much. He had offered to haul them to market for a half cent a pound. The farmer had agreed. Earl had picked up eleven the following Monday evening and delivered them that night to East St. Louis. On Tuesday evening he had picked up and delivered the other eleven. Each time he had slept a few hours and was at an auction house buying furniture that he delivered to stores in Houston and Licking. They had made a small profit on each load of furniture.

Sunday June 27th: marked 53 pigs, home place. Picked peaches and plums. Corn looks good. Bought two horses from John Tom.

That was a particularly nice day. They castrated the pigs and had a half bucket for the tenant and a half bucket for later in the day. They went down and bought two horses. Earl rode one and led the other back. Earl found Elmer picking peaches and putting them in a gunny sack. Elmer handed Earl a gunny sack and asked him to get some plums. As Earl rode home he noticed that the corn in the long field had tasseled already. It would be a good crop.

Monday June 29th: Dentist in Cabool. Looked at sheep. Didn't buy. Looked at steers and heifers at Sigman's. Want too much.

Tuesday June 30th: Summersville sale. Bought 31 large hogs. Ship to St.L Wed or Th Looked at large herd of cows East of Summersville (2 bulls, 92 cows, 50 steers, 53 heifers) made deal. $5,023.50. Herd over on Thur.

Wednesday July 1st: Hardy, Ark. to sale barn. Stop to visit uncle in Mammoth. Didn't buy anything wanted to see prices. Made contacts. Three names and addresses were listed.

Earl remembered Wednesday well. He took the furniture to Houston, then went to Tyrone. When he found Elmer gone, he took his swimsuit and a thick blanket. He went to the Lay hole (some called it the blue hole) down by where Lon Lay lived on South Jacks Fork. He swam and napped on his blanket for nearly two hours. It had been a long time since he'd been able to relax. Elmer had left a note for him to get up early on Thursday and get two people to move the herd from Summersville to the home place. He drove the little Model A by his mother's for a quick visit. Charlie was out helping to build a shed for Gould McAllister. When Earl got back to

Tyrone it was near eight o'clock. He had stopped at Dillard's and went over to Bailey's. Earl told both to be in the saddle by five o'clock next morning. Since it was a long day, Earl offered Dillard and Lonnie three dollars. When he got back to the house he draped his wet swim suit over the clothes line in back. Earl got some work boots, his old sweat stained hat, worn jeans, long sleeved cotton shirt, fresh underwear and socks. He was ready to leave when Sylva stopped him.

"Now where do you think you're going," Sylva said in her most bossy tone. His sisters and brother had already seen him when he came in and they were studiously ignoring the byplay.

"I have to get up about four o'clock and I thought I'd go down to Grandma's. She gets up early and I didn't want to disturb the house," Earl replied.

"Where's Elmer?" Sylva said curtly.

"He went to Hardy, Arkansas, to a sale barn," Earl said and added, "I expect he'll get back late."

"Why you getting up so early, anyway?" Sylva queried.

"Dillard, Lonnie and I are riding over to Summerville to bring over a herd of cattle to the home place." Sylva looked distinctly displeased at this news Earl had given her.

"Why Lonnie? Get someone else," Sylva was really steamed up now.

"Sylvia, it's already done and it's too late to change it," Earl put his hat on and walked out the door. As he was walking toward the front gate, Sylva caught him.

She actually ran around in front of him and said, "Don't you dare just walk away from me when I've got something else to say."

Earl said curtly, "You're not my mother. I do what Elmer asks me to do. He's my father and I work for him."

Earl started around Sylva and she got in front of him again. "You can't disrespect me like this Earl. I won't have it."

Earl gently pushed her aside, walked through the gate and fastened it behind him.

Sylva cursed at him roundly while Earl was cranking the Model A. He drove down the hill to his grandmothers. She gave him a baloney and cheese sandwich for supper. Earl asked if she had peanut butter and jelly to make six sandwiches the next day. She did and Earl helped her put them together for their lunch next day.

Elmer's next entry was Thursday, July 2nd, Went to Thayer sale barn. Bought 12 nice heifers, Hereford. $23. each Pasture heifers with John Tom he has good bull.

Thursday had gone well. Earl was pleased that Lonnie and Dillard had remembered to bring canteens as there would be a long stretch without water until they got near Nagle. They rode cross country and were at the farm a little after nine o'clock and had the cattle to the home place by seven in the evening. Elmer had met them and they had moved the heifers to Ira and Pearl's. They let them in the gate by the Morgan Cave.

Friday, July 3rd; Go to West Plains. Office a mess, money gone. Need be in bank. Go see Hart. Did Sylvia? Two sofas. One day bed. Bedroom suite (bed, chest, dresser). Picked up pigs at Jack's Took to Jana. $50. for feed Bought pigs. $302.90

Elmer had folded four penny post cards with the orders for furniture in the page after Friday.

Earl removed them and inserted them in his notebook. He would write them a note on a penny post card to assure them that he would honor their order for furniture.

Saturday, July 4th; Barriklow this afternoon. Ask Sylvia $. Only answer. Lonnie?

Earl was fairly certain that Sylva's plan to leave and the money had coincided with a deadly effect. He replaced everything in the bag. He made up his mind to take the business diary on Wednesday to the Coroner's hearing.

His mother and Charlie came in the house. Mary stood on the back porch and said, "I'm going to the bathtub." She took a towel from the cupboard and the soap dish and headed out the back gate to the creek. Charlie sat, aromatic with sweat across the table from Earl.

"Charlie, you don't know how much it meant to me to have you and Mama at the funeral," Earl said with all the earnestness he could muster. "I saw you there and so much of Mama's family. The only ones I got to say hello to was Uncle Ray and Aunt Lula. I guess Calvin and Tommie must have stayed with someone."

"They stayed with Johnny and Alice Hostetter. They haven't been able to have any children and they really enjoyed having those two little boys around," Charlie said.

Earl thought for a while. "All the beef we bought here in Clear Springs was prime. My Dad, Elmer, bargained hard for a good price so I'm giving them more for their beef. A dollar and a half more. I'm also going to give you money to give to those local farmers and to John Dunivan and John Bradford. They'll say it's too much but I'm giving a bonus for a good drive. We didn't lose one animal."

Earl filled out a list with the amounts to be given to the various people. "When you see John Bradford or John Dunivan tell them to be ready in about ten or twelve days for a much bigger cattle drive Elmer had planned. I'm going to try to put it together from his notes." After counting out the money to give to Charlie, he added, "Tell them to find a couple of more riders, three dollars a day if they provide their own mount and feed. Two dollars otherwise, I'll provide a horse."

"You know, Earl," Charlie said, "I think Johnny Hostetter and Ray Peabody would jump at having a little extra cash in their pocket. I know for a fact they both have fine mounts."

"Would you mind asking them for me, Charlie," Earl had a grateful ring to his voice. "I'm going over to Baker's, take them up on their invitation."

"George'll be tickled to see you," Charlie glanced up as he was speaking. Mary was entering the back porch, her hair still wet from the creek water. "Guess it's my turn in the tub." Charlie took a towel and he knew Mary would leave the soap down there. He took fresh dry clothes with him.

When Charlie was out of earshot, Mary said, "It was a sad day but the preacher made it bearable. I got a seat inside with my sisters. The men all stood outside."

"Mama, you don't know how much it meant to me to have you all there. Even Weed Morgan and Aunt Annie and Naomi came. Two Morgan cousins from Stultz I saw there, too. It was a good turn out."

"Charlie said there were more than two hundred people standing outside the church."

"I'm going to bed early and get up early." Earl said, "I need to meet someone in Willow before six thirty, then I'll go on over to Baker's. I told them I'd be there by ten.

CHAPTER 14 -

The Dog Days of Summer

Earl got up when he heard Charlie stirring about four-thirty. He dressed in some of his best every- day clothes, packed up his bag and was ready to head out the door when his mother and Charlie came in to say goodbye and wish him well at Sargent.

The little green Plymouth took Earl efficiently into Willow Springs. It rode well. It had the wood spoke wheels, a carryover from the horseless carriage days. He stopped at the first place that had gasoline and filled up the tank. He arrived at the Horton Hotel before six o'clock. He ordered coffee at the counter and sipped the hot liquid black while he waited. Wade Ferguson, brother of Charles who ran the clothing store, came in and sat at his usual table. He was the auctioneer on Saturdays and a meat cutter for the two grocery stores in town.

Earl went to sit at the auctioneer's table and ordered breakfast. He wanted Ferguson to start spreading the word about his intended cattle drive in a little over a week. He assured Ferguson that he would buy all the beef on hoof that he could a week from Saturday. Earl went south of Willow five miles to return twenty-six dollars to a farmer Elmer had bought some mixed stock from. He was appreciative and, in turn, told him of another farmer that had a small herd for sale. He made up his mind to visit him on Friday. He left for Sargent about eight-thirty. He would be early but that would just give him a head start on the day.

Earl was missing Eva. But he knew it would be near the end of August before she would come home to begin teaching at a little school in the country. He went by and picked up a penny post card at the Willow Springs post office. He wrote a quick note: "Eva, it's over. I don't know how it could have been so awful. My love for you keeps me going. I'm anxious for your first letter. I'm visiting my cousin in Sargent. We'll go fishing and swimming. I do have to go to Houston for the Coroner's Inquest Wed. Only yours, Earl." He put it in the outgoing mail slot and left with a heavy heart for Sargent.

His Aunt Jenny was a person to cheer anyone. George had dug worms by the barn, big ones. They headed North of Cabool along a stretch of Piney River where George was familiar. They caught good stringers full of bass and perch. George even snagged two hog suckers. They had a royal feast of fish that night, fresh vegetables and a blackberry cobbler, fresh picked that day. After supper, George and Harold proposed going swimming. Earl confessed he forgot his swimsuit on the clothesline in Tyrone. George loaned him one. But chores came first.

Earl went with them to do chores at the barn. The sweet smell of silage was enough to make any cow hungry. He witnessed the use of milking machines for the first time in a Grade A dairy parlor. George said they got nearly forty percent more for their Grade A milk.

Over breakfast, Morgan Baker told Earl that he was going to close his sawmill because Frisco was closing the siding where they loaded lumber. They had told him that he wasn't producing enough for them to make the stop anymore. Jenny revealed that the store wasn't doing well either. With the new highway, more and more people were doing their shopping in town instead of at this little country general store.

George decided to go with Earl to the Coroner's Inquest that morning. They could stop on the way back and do some more fishing. They pitched horseshoes down by a new house being constructed for when George married Kate, his fiancée. It was below the hill from Morgan and Jenny's house.

Earl stopped by Jim Hart's office. They conferred briefly. Earl showed Jim Elmer's business diary. Jim felt it was not wise to bring up the diary at the Inquest. It would change nothing. Hart gave Earl the blank contracts and names and locations of the two IOUs that were unknown to Earl.

The Inquest was fairly short. The Sheriff and Coroner both gave statements. Red Fronk who discovered the bodies was questioned. Judge George Unger issued this ruling: "Mrs. Sylva Sigler came to her death at the hands of her husband and that Mr. Elmer Sigler's death was self-inflicted."

It was getting close to lunch. Earl asked Hart where good food was served. He told Earl that Sheriff Kelly's cousin Paul had a nice little café that had a twenty-five cent blue plate specials for lunch. George and Earl ordered the liver and onions, with fresh peas and mashed potatoes. It was filling and delicious. They added peach pie ala mode.

When the two cousins were getting into the Plymouth, Earl said, "Is it okay with you if I go through Tyrone and pick up my mail. I have another stop along the way."

When Earl turned off the road into a rutted track, George asked, "Where you taking me?"

"Wait and see," Earl replied.

Back in a heavily forested area, Earl stopped in front of an old ramshackle cabin. He turned off the motor and waited. A man dressed in filthy overalls and slouch hat came out of the door with a double-barreled shotgun cradled in his arms.

Earl opened the car door and stood up. At first the shotgun centered on his chest and then was lowered. The man said, "Hello, Earl. Din't recognize yeh. Used to seein' yeh in at Model A."

"Hi, Nate. Wanted to buy a case of your best."

"Okay, Earl. Be back." Nate turned on his heel and went into the shack. He emerged with a cardboard case of moonshine.

Earl opened the hatch to the rumble seat. "Just put it in here on the floor," he said.

Nate put the case where Earl indicated. Earl took twenty dollars from his billfold and gave it to Nate. The moonshiner took out a roll of bills and gave Earl some change.

When they were back on the main road, George said, "That was a rough looking place."

"That's the kind of people that you have to deal with if you want to get a good bottle of whiskey these days."

George was silent a while, then ruminated, "We go to a man over North of us. He lives in a nice white house and doesn't look like something out of the civil war. Dad likes a bottle now and then. Since I'm older he lets me have a drink once in a while. He keeps it down in the store and he doesn't want my mom to know."

Earl went to the post office in Tyrone. There was no mail. Earl arranged for a box for himself and told the postmaster in no uncertain terms that all of Elmer's mail should be put in his box and not given out. He went to Sarah's and asked about mail. She handed him all of the mail she had picked up that day. There were several post cards wanting Elmer to look at livestock. There was a large envelope from Raymondville bank. It had a new checkbook for his grandmother's account. An official statement for each account was included and another signature card reminding Earl to include a co-signer. There was no letter from Eva. Earl asked Sarah to sign the bank card. He went back to the post office and wrote a quick reply to those asking for a price on their livestock, assuring them he would stop by the next week.

Earl took George to some fishing holes he knew about on Elk Creek. Earl caught five nice sized bass and George snagged three suckers, two reds and one hog. They went swimming at the swimming hole in the town of Elk Creek. Too many young kids were there so they set off for Sargent. They cleaned the fish for another fish supper. They sat a long time and drank from a quart bottle of bootleg.

After chores, George and Earl pitched horseshoes until dark.

Every few minutes they went to the Plymouth and took a couple of chugs of moonshine. Both were unsteady on their feet when they mounted the stairs to the main house.

When they got in the house, Morgan said, "You boys been drinkin' quite a bit. Just be glad Jenny went to bed early."

George trying to deflect, said, "It's been awful hot the last couple days."

Morgan said, "The radio said last year was the hottest year since back in the eighteen hundreds. And they said it might be worse this year."

Earl said, "Not to change the subject, Uncle Morgan, could you give me some paper and envelope. I'd like to write a letter to Eva." The Bakers were aware of his newest girlfriend.

Morgan went to a desk and took out a box with paper and envelopes together.

"Thanks," Earl said, "I'll get up and write her in the morning I don't think I'm up to it tonight."

"I don't think you are, either," Morgan said.

"Are you able to get the livestock report out of Saint Louis in the mornings?" Earl asked.

"Yep. We listen in most mornings at seven after breakfast," Morgan replied.

"I'm feeling the pressure to get back to work. I've been away from it for a couple of days but my family is depending on me to keep up the business," Earl mused aloud. "Would you mind if I took George away for another day. He's good company. I need to go over the Willow and West Plains area to line up some places to graze a trail herd."

After listening to the market report next morning, he decided to take the hogs from Tyrone to East Saint Louis to market. He would have to double check the closing market on Friday to make sure. Soon afterward he and George headed for Willow. He remembered a farmer in the little valley about a mile North was bringing in his hay last Friday. He stopped at the house and asked if he could bring a herd into his fenced hay fields. The farmer agreed, stating, "The cattle will fertilize my hay crop the next year." He agreed that a penny a head was a fair price for pasture for one day.

The Post Office was now open. Before sealing the letter he read it over:

Tyrone Missouri
7 - 9- 31

My Dearest Eva,

I suppose you think me slow about writing. I haven't an excuse to offer except that, which you already know. As you know its been pretty awful the last few days until I just dident write although I dident forget you in the least. I realy thought I'd be coming that way in a few day's but I hardly think now that I will until later. I was going to make a trip to Kansas City in a day or two with some more fellows and of course I'd have stopped to see you. They have decided to put it off for a while. I haven't been over to Tyrone for awhile but I think I'll go back today. I haven't decided on any thing much yet but suppose I'll have to go back to business in a few days. It's too bad I cant see you every few days it would help so much. You will write every few days of course that will help some. I'll try to write often but if I'm neglectful please forgive me for it for I'll have my hands full. I'm over at Willow Springs this morning. I went fishing yesterday over by Cabool and had good luck. I sure wished for you to be along. I had better go and get this mailed so I must close for this time please write often for you know I'm always glad to hear from you. I'll be looking for you home until you get here. I do hope you'll get all you expect to out of school. I'd be sorry if you diden't. I'm hoping to see you before long.

With Lots of Love
Earl.

Earl addressed the envelope and pasted on a two cent stamp with a profile of George Washington in the middle of it. He licked the flap, closed it and looked around before kissing it. He slid it in the mail slot and returned to his car. It was getting really hot again. George was outside the car to keep cooler.

The two young men chatted amiably as they went to West Plains. Earl stopped at the farm where they had the herd before on an overnight in a fenced pasture. The farmer was fair on his use of pasture for just one night. Earl estimated that he would have between one and two hundred head. Earl gave him a dollar back for each animal they had bought directly from him last time.

Earl was met by bemusement at someone so honest that he would give back money when he thought he had made too much profit. Earl felt it was just good business practice. Earl went by to see the farmer he had received a tip about two days before and bought twenty steers and seventeen older cows.

Both George and Earl wanted to take a swim that afternoon. They stopped back by Willow and had lunch at the Horton Hotel Café.

A train came through from the West, a passenger train. Earl was lovelorn, wishing Eva was on that train. He remembered how excited he was to see Eva less than a week ago. It seemed like a long time ago.

Earl decided to take George over to the Lay Hole on South Jack's fork. Their swim suits were still in the rumble seat compartment. The river was up and kind of murky from silt. Earl remembered seeing lightning off in the distance to the North of Sargent. Earl thought to himself, I bet Charlie spent a good part of the night in the cellar. He smiled.

The two cousins were back for chores and supper by five o'clock. It was steak, mashed potatoes and gravy, fresh corn on the cob, and Jello with bananas.

They listened to the news. Cattle was down, hog were up. The Cardinals had won three to nothing. The young sensational pitcher, Dizzy Dean, had shut out the Cubs.

Earl saw the Cabool weekly on the table in the living room. He picked it up. The headline blared:

TERRIBLE TRAGEDY ENACTED
DEATH COMES ON NATIONAL HOLIDAY
TO MR. AND MRS. ELMER SIGLER
WELL KNOWN CITIZENS OF TYRONE

Earl read it through the last long sentence seared his brain:

Now there are three motherless and four fatherless children, aged mothers and other relatives who mourn the passing of Mr. and Mrs. Elmer Sigler, who are now sleeping that eternal sleep in two new-made graves in Big Creek cemetery.

The Baker house had a lot of modern gadgets. Morgan had rigged a windmill and pumped water from the creek to a five hundred gallon holding tank on stilts about fifteen feet high. It gave enough pressure that they had indoor plumbing to their bathroom. The kitchen had a hand pump for drinking water and kitchen use. A line was run to the barn for flushing out the milk parlor. It was one of the requirements for a Grade A dairy.

Earl helped muck out the barn and put the manure into the wagon with a spreader.

They all cleaned up after coming back to the house and played Pitch until nine o'clock.

Finally, Earl said, "I better hit the sack. I told Lonnie Bailey to meet me at our house at seven tomorrow morning. I want to go down and start buying cattle for the drive my dad planned for next week. I would actually like to be there by six thirty so I can visit my grandmother and see my sisters and brother."

George said, "I know you miss them but it's been fun the last three days. Would you like another hand on your cattle drive. Dad and Harold could handle things around her for a while."

"George, it's hot dirty work. I pay three dollars a day if you provide your own mount. If you really want to go I'll ride over and string along two pack mules. I'll have tin plates pots, skillets, coffee pot, other utensils. You can buy sugar, bacon, canned milk, coffee, pinto beans, corn meal, flour and anything else you can think of here at your store. I'll arrange for you to meet John Bradford and John Dunivan in Willow early Thursday morning next week. I want the three of you in Thayer by one o'clock in the afternoon. You'll have to push hard to make it. There are three or four creeks where you can water the horses between Willow and Thayer. I'll write down the directions of how to get to the sale barn in Thayer." Earl stopped and said, "Phew. That's the biggest speech I've made in months."

"Sounds interesting, Earl. I'm on."

Earl smiled, "It may not be so interesting after you've been in the saddle ten to twelve days. You'll get tired of bacon and eggs every morning and fried egg sandwiches for lunch. Then brown beans and Johnny cakes in the evening. Strong coffee and no women. We'll buy bread in Thayer."

"I'll make it okay," George retorted.

"How about Kate. Can she get along without you for that long," Earl said.

Morgan guffawed and said, "We'd better get to bed."

The next morning Earl rose before sunrise when he heard the clock strike five. Earl washed his face and shaved, took care of other business and was out with his suitcase in the living room. All the Bakers were there to see him off. Jenny handed him a sandwich on a white cloth table napkin. She said, "You must eat something. It's a peanut butter and jelly sandwich. That should last until you get to Tyrone. Tell my Uncle Weed hello for me."

"Thanks so much, Aunt Jenny. It's been a fun three days. It refreshed my mind and took it off a lot of problems and anxiety that I might have had," Earl said thankfully.

Earl could already feel the pall of guilty gloom descend over the loss of his father. He hurried from the room fearful that he would start weeping in front of the Baker family.

George quickly followed Earl down the hill to the Plymouth. Earl opened the rumble seat compartment to put his suitcase in the floor. He saw the case of whiskey and took out a quart and handed it to George. "Do you want two?" Earl asked.

"No. I'll have trouble enough to keep this out of my Mom's sight."

They said their farewells with a vigorous handshake. Earl drove around through Cabool and out to the road through Elk Creek. He stopped in front of the old bank. He looked at his pocket watch, it was a little after five thirty. He felt he had time to make a quick survey inside. He used the key from Elmer's key ring to open the door. He found nothing of interest except a bound book imprinted with Marcus Sigler Milling, Co., Tyrone, Missouri. No checks had been written or removed from the binder. Earl took it with him as a remembrance.

Earl drove on to Tyrone and went straight to Sarah's house. She was sitting on her front porch in her light colored house dress with her night cap still on. Earl got out and went to his grandmother, leaned over and embraced her. When he stood up, there were tears in her eyes.

"You stride around like you own the world, just like Marcus and Elmer did," Sarah said, "I'm so proud of you."

"Thanks, Grandma. Anything new?" Earl asked.

"There's mail on the little table in the living room," Sarah replied.

Earl went in and got the mail, he could see Vivian still sleeping on the downstairs bed. That was good that she could sleep. Earl got a straight back chair and came back to sit by his grandmother to look at the mail. Earl took the little checkbook from his pocket and gave it to his grandmother. "There's five hundred dollars in your own checking account. When you need cash get Pearl to fill one out or someone at the store can and you can sign it and they'll give you cash for the check. I'll put fifty dollars in your account every month. When I have a chance I'll show Pearl how to keep a running balance."

"Well. Isn't this nice, my very own checking account. What is this world coming to?" Sarah actually giggled in delight.

Earl had never heard her like this. He was pleased.

There were more post cards addressed to Elmer asking him to stop by to look at pigs or cattle and one for three horses. He wrote on this last card "George Bailey will come to look at and buy your horses." and signed his name.

There was a letter from the National Stock Yards in East Saint Louis, inquiring if Elmer was planning another cattle drive.

"Well, Grandma. As much as I enjoy your company, I need to be off. I hope to meet Lonnie at the house by seven o'clock and I need to get there early to get some writing paper and an envelope out of the office."

"We'll be eating breakfast in about a half hour."

"I had a peanut butter and jelly sandwich on the way over from Sargent," Earl explained.

"Many days when I am by myself, that's what I have for breakfast. Beats all that cooking."

Earl went to the Plymouth and drove up the hill. He stopped by the front gate. He went in the front door and through the house to the doorway leading upstairs in the pantry. He hesitated on the landing. He saw Aunt Pearl and Lucille coming toward the house. He went on up to the little office facing the front of the house. He opened a desk drawer and found an envelope and paper. The room look as if a twister had gone through it. He went back down to the dining room table and sat to write a letter to the National Stock Yards. He wrote he would be at the same farm by Rolla with cattle and that he hoped it would be over a thousand head. He signed and sealed the letter. He would mail it on his way out of town. He knew this was an ambitious project but one he felt he could handle. He would not ride with the men but he would be with them all the way. Sometimes following in the truck and sometimes ahead.

Dillard and Lonnie were experienced from Thayer on to Rolla. They knew to follow the old West Plains-Rolla road. They'd have to cross the new United States Highway 63 several times between Hardy, Arkansas to West Plains. Earl had a plan for bypassing Pomona and Willow Springs. He would split the herd in Grogan, probably late Saturday evening. He would leave about five hundred head on the home place until Tuesday morning. The rest he would divide up between Ira and Pearl's place, the smaller Tyrone farm and rent some pasture from others around nearby. They would move the herd up the West Plains-Rolla Road Tuesday morning. The hard part would be from Raymondville to Licking because they would have to follow the new U. S. highway 63. On Monday he would go to the Summersville sale barn. It was a small offering there, but he might be able to buy thirty to fifty head and bring them over to Tyrone after the sale. They would overnight at Dow Clayton's Tuesday night. Earl would travel ahead and add to the herd from local farmers along the way. He had a plan to stay off the new highway from Licking to Rolla.

Earl was thinking so hard about the project that he was startled, by the knock on the door. He rose and walked to the door. It was Lonnie. Earl opened the screen door and went out on the porch. Lonnie was standing with his head down, refusing to look Earl straight in the eye.

"Stand up straight, Lonnie," Earl said sternly, "What's done is done. I appreciated your showing up at the funeral with your family. You've been good friends of my family for a long time. Don't let one indiscretion get you down."

Lonnie did stand up straight.

"Sit down and I'll tell you what I have in mind." Earl sat on the lawn chair on the front porch and Lonnie sat in another. Earl continued, "I'm probably going to keep you busy driving truck a lot. I'll pay you two dollars a trip to East Saint Louis. You'll sometimes make two trips in a day up and back. Get a good night sleep Saturday night. You'll leave at five this Sunday evening. I'll write out exact directions on how to get there and what to do when you arrive. You should be back by two Monday morning. I need to send all the hogs I have in the pen down by the barn and mill. We can double deck them and make it in two loads. I'll make a pallet and sleep on the porch of the mill. Wake me up and I'll help you load the second truck load. I'll give you enough cash for two meals and gas for the truck.

Today, you're going to start learning to drive the truck. We're going to West Plains to the sale barn. I want to buy cattle in preparation for a big drive starting next week in Hardy, Arkansas."

Earl got up and Lonnie followed him. "Lonnie, have you driven a truck."

"I haven't driven anything. My Mom has a car but she won't let anyone drive it but her, not even Dad. It's her business car. She delivers and sells her lace and crystal in it"

They went to the truck. Earl showed him how to start the truck. "I'll drive down to Dillard's and to the store. Notice how I coordinated the clutch and shifting gears," Earl said.

As Earl drove down the street to Dillard's, Earl said, "Notice how I double clutch to gear down. The engine will help you slow down going down hills and you won't have to use your brakes so much."

When Earl stopped the truck, Dillard started walking toward the front gate. Earl got out and met Dillard. He brought Dillard up to date on his trip to West Plains and his plans to send Lonnie to East Saint Louis Sunday evening

Earl saw Ira drive in behind the beer joint. He heard the pickup doors open and close and he saw Glen walking the back street toward his grandmother's.

Earl said, "I think Ira is opening his barbershop for something, Dillard. Hop on the running board and we'll go over to see him."

Earl arranged with Ira for the use of one of the two vehicles until Dillard would have his own wheels.

Earl remembered his Aunt's request to say hello to Weed, his great uncle. He walked to their house and passed Jenny's "hello" and his own. Weed told him that he had heard of a teaching job at Stultz. Earl wrote Eva's name and address on a sheet of paper from his business diary. Weed promised to pass it to his Morgan cousin who had mentioned the job.

Earl showed Lonnie where the starter was on the floor board. By the time they got to Willow Springs Lonnie was becoming very confident in his driving. Highway 63 was more of a challenge. Even though it was graded gravel, it had many more cars and trucks on the road.

Earl bought a truck load of steers nearly a half ton each. He cautioned Lonnie to get along slowly until he had the feel of the truck with livestock on board.

They unloaded at Tyrone and put the steers out to pasture behind the barn. Earl left the truck at the chute where he had unloaded.

He walked down toward his grandmother's house. He had made up his mind about something of a change he wanted to talk about this evening.

Thunderheads were building up in the West and the air was perceptibly cooler. Earl thought, a little cooler wouldn't hurt and more rain would be a Godsend.

When Earl entered the living room he could hear the sounds of silverware clinking on plates. When he entered the kitchen, Pearl was first to notice him. She said, "Glen get another chair, Lucille get a plate and silverware and a cup.

When they finished eating, Earl said, "I'm going to sleep at the house tonight. We've got to try to get our lives back to as normal as possible."

"I want to go back home, too," Lucille said.

"Me too," Glen joined in.

Pearl cleared her throat to get their attention, "Ira and I had talked about moving back out to the farm tomorrow night. We should let Mama get her life back to normal as well."

"Is it okay if I sleep with grandma a couple more nights. She snores something awful, but I sure feel comforted by sleeping with her," Vivian implored.

Everyone guffawed at what Vivian had said. She seemed pleased and didn't realize that what she had said could be taken as an insult.

Sarah said firmly trying to keep a straight face, "You can stay here as long as you please. We'll have a grand old time, just the two of us."

Pearl said, "Dana came by and said she had boxed up everything like you asked. She said she had done all the sheets and remade the beds. She's such a dear."

"She is at that," Earl said. "I hired Dillard on as foreman to take my place. Dad was paying me a hundred dollars a month. Probably fifty too much. I really need someone like Dillard to take some pressure off. He'll be coming over to check your fences, Ira. Would I be able to run some cattle on your east eighty now that you have your haying done. I'll pay what I am paying other farmers for pasture. The cattle will be there for about two days."

Ira nodded.

Pearl said, "Sounds like you're jumping back in business in a big way but do you think it's a good idea to take on Lonnie after what he did?"

"I'll talk to you about that privately, later," Earl allowed his eyes to look at his sisters and brothers.

Pearl then knew that she had spoken out of place. She nodded.

"I have a double header down in Clear Springs. I'm going to have Lonnie and Dillard follow me to Willow and I'll look at some of the lots of cattle. Lonnie's going to be doing a lot of truck driving for me. I think Lonnie's learned his lesson besides he's been a friend for a long time.

Earl left the house and got into the Plymouth. Lucille and Glen got in the car with him. He drove to Dillard's. Earl opened the gate and waited while Lucille and Glen followed him to Lay's front porch. He knocked on the door. He told Glen and Lucille to sit on the edge of the porch while he waited for someone to answer the door. Dillard came to the door, wiping his mouth with a napkin. Earl said, "Sorry about messing up your supper."

"Aw. We were done. It's okay." Dillard replied.

Earl said, "I already told Lonnie I wanted him to go to Willow tomorrow. Could you go and make a buy of more cattle?"

"Sure I can go, Earl." Dillard said, "But Monday I have to move out to the farm."

"You know you can use the truck. When you and Lonnie get back tomorrow, or Sunday, take it down to the ford on North Jacks Fork and sluice out the manure and wash it down good so you don't get manure on your furniture. If you need Tuesday to get settled, do it. We need to have four horses and three riders in the truck by sunup Wednesday morning to head off for Arkansas. I'd like to have the horses loaded up in the truck and on the road by five o'clock."

"I'll be ready early Wednesday."

"Tell Dana thanks for doing all she has. She can continue to use the washer as long as she wants to. I have an idea about hiring a live in housekeeper. My aunt. But she doesn't know about it yet. How much do I owe Dana?"

"Forget it. She just appreciates getting to wash our clothes in the washing machine instead of doing them on a scrub board, besides your hiring me has taken a big burden off us."

"Okay," Earl said, "See you tomorrow morning. Eight at the store okay? I told Lonnie to be here by eight."

Dillard nodded.

Earl left the porch with the children behind him. They slept the night. The next morning, Lucille told Earl her plans to go to Vacation Bible School at Grandview. He was glad that Lucille was showing signs of adulthood that had been thrust upon her. Earl's night was filled with excruciatingly vivid, horrid dreams. The old gloomy guilt smothered him like a cold blanket in winter.

Earl had Dillard sign as co-signer on his working account and mailed it back to the bank. He gave a check to Dillard and told him to fill it out and sign it when he bought cattle in Willow. He assured Dillard there would be no problem clearing the check because he would let the clerk in Willow know about it before he left. Earl would look at some lots and Dillard could bid up to but not beyond what Earl thought was a fair price. He wanted him to focus on steers and heifers of eight to ten months. Earl told Dillard he would be at the ball field at Clear Springs. He asked them to stop by to let him know how it went.

When Earl picked up his mail early on Saturday morning, there were the usual post cards asking Elmer to go by to look at stock and two addressed to Earl. The first ones. He was already becoming the face of the family business.

On the way back from Willow to Clear Springs for the double header at eleven, the enormity of the cattle drive and the responsibility of providing for his family began to weigh heavily on him. Before crossing Pine Creek, he leaned his head on his arms on the steering wheel of the Plymouth. He opened the car door and went to the rumble seat hatch and opened it. He reached in and removed a quart of whiskey. Earl took two long swallows. Waited a minute and took two more pulls. He got back in the car and put the bottle on the front seat. The earlier gloom of guilt, an enormous lonely feeling and insularity and sorrow and loss were washed away by the infusion of alcohol.

When Earl got to the ball field. Rol Patterson was there raking up some damp spots on the infield from the rain the night before. Earl parked in the shade of a white oak tree far to the right of home plate. He picked up the bottle and had a couple more slugs at it. When he turned around, Rol was looking at him.

"You're not going to be in any shape to pitch if you keep that up, Earl."

"You forget, Rolla, you're not the manager and don't even play on the team," Earl replied rather cruelly. He was immediately sorry. "I shouldn't have said that Rol."

Rol still looking crestfallen, said, "It's all right, Earl. You're not really yourself today."

Paul Mckinney rode in on his horse. He and Earl began warming up. The game started at eleven as planned. The team from Licking was not very good. Earl pitched a shutout and they won easily. In between games, Earl went to the car and finished the bottle of whiskey. When he came back Gould wanted to let one of the young guys pitch because he wasn't feeling ready. Earl said he could pitch both games, the alcohol was making him feel invincible. During the fifth inning of the second game, his arm started hurting. Before the top of the sixth, Dillard pulled up with a truckload of cattle. Earl asked Gould to give him a couple of minutes break. Dillard told him he bought two truckloads of cattle and would be going back to Willow after they unloaded. Earl told him to put them in the field by his house (he was thinking in those terms already). He returned to pitching. In the seventh inning his arm hurt so badly he was tempted to ask for relief. Instead he finished the game with his arm aching and hurting like nothing else ever had hurt him. Clear Springs had won both games but likely at the expense of a possible major league pitching prospect, even the lowly Saint Louis Browns.

On his way back to Tyrone, Earl had trouble shifting gears on the car. He guided the car with his left hand and let his right arm hang immobile by his side. Sleep that night was pure misery. It kept the nightmares away that had haunted him the previous night.

Earl rose before daylight. He had an idea. He found a large towel, knotted two corners and made a sling. On his way through the pantry, he got a can of wieners and crackers. He put the food in a small poke and filled his canteen with water. Earl walked slowly toward the barn. He cleared the corral of pigs and called up the horses. He put oats in one of the high feeding troughs. Earl had decided to ride Plum, a big rangy roan. He got the bridle and saddle on with difficulty because of his arm. The mules were pretty docile. He was able to put halters on them, eight foot lead rope and pack saddles. Earl tied one mule to Plum's saddle and the other one was hitched behind the first pack horse. He put the pack saddle on both mules. He hung his canteen over the saddle horn and put his poke of food in the saddle bag. By the time he left the sun was coming over the horizon. As he was ready to ride out, Dillard was coming up to the truck.

Dillard seeing the sling, said, "That roan throw you?"

"No. I hurt it yesterday," Earl smiled wryly, not wanting Dillard to know how foolish he had been. "I'm heading over to Sargent. My cousin is going to help on the drive. He'll be bring along our chuck on the pack mules. I'll stop by Baileys' I want to see George and I'll have Lonnie come over to help you clean up the truck. I told Lonnie he would be taking some hogs to St. Louis. That can wait until tomorrow night. I told him to double deck them and make two loads. If you could help him load, I'd appreciate it because of my arm."

"What happened to your right wing?"

"Dillard, I'd rather you hadn't asked. I'm embarrassed about it."

"That's okay. I'll see you later."

Earl thought about what to say, "I may not be back until Monday. I think I'll ride on over to Clear Springs to spend the night. I wanted to stop by and see my young aunt, Fern Odor."

"See you Monday, then."

"One last thing. Glen and Lucille aren't up to do chores yet. Would you let Lucille know she needs to get some Ice in the box up there, since we're setting up housekeeping up there."

"Earl, I can take care of that. I'll go get the tongs and carry fifty pounds up there myself."

"Thanks, Dillard. See you Monday."

When Earl got to Bailey's everyone was asleep but George Bailey was sitting on the front porch. George agreed to look at the three horses and try to strike a deal. He thought he could buy all three for less than sixty dollars. Earl removed sixty dollars and handed it to George. He asked George to send Lonnie over to see Dillard when he got out of bed.

Earl, with his early start, was in Sargent before ten o'clock. George was at home but Jennie had Morgan to take her to church in Cabool at the Christian Church. George had been solicitous over Earl's injured arm but he was clear that it was foolish for him to attempt trying to pitch a double header. George took Earl up to the house and they got into his Aunt Jennie's bread box. He found the peanut butter and jelly and made a sandwich for lunch. Earl had already eaten the crackers and weenies on the way over for his breakfast.

Cutting across country, Earl came out near Liberty School. He rode the township roads to the entry to the Odor homestead. Henry, Tommie and Effie lived with her grandmother and Fern Odor. Fern was only a little over a year older than Earl. He had lived in the same household with her for a couple years so she seemed more like a sister than an aunt. He got there about two in the afternoon. Earl had watered his horse well down in the valley when he crossed the creek. He visited a few minutes and Fern agreed to come and keep house and cook for a few weeks at his house in Tyrone. Life would be bearable with her there.

He headed on toward Clear Springs and down toward Lon Lay's. A farmer about two miles down that road was selling out and heading for California. He introduced himself as Arthur Fleener. Earl had seen him around growing up but did not know him well. He had twenty two good steers, twenty-nine older cows and an overage bull. He told Mr. Fleener that he would send a couple of men to come get the cattle on Saturday morning. The farmer had sold his young heifers and calves to a neighbor. His last sale would be his chickens to be butchered in Willow. Then he would load up a few belongings and leave the farm for the bank to take over. The farmer looked curiously at Earl's arm in the sling, but made no comment.

A half hour later Earl was opening the gate at Charlie's and his mother's place. There was a car parked in front of the house. At first he didn't recognize it and when he got closer he realized it was Ray and Lula Peabody's car. That was good.

Charlie told him Johnny Hostetter would help on the drive and his new Uncle Ray would, too. Ray passed information about a farmer over near him was who selling off some of his beef cattle.

His mother and aunt were busy getting supper together. They ate supper companionably and Earl asked to be excused to ride over to look at the cattle his Uncle Ray had told him about. Charlie suggested he unsaddle Plum and let him rest with the long hard day. He told Earl use their car. It worked out well as Ray and Lula had to go back to do chores and Charlie had his yet to do.

Earl cranked the car left-handed, driving with some difficulty. He made a successful buy of the cattle his uncle had told him about. He told the farmer that Ray and Johnny would come by on Friday to get them. When Earl returned, Mary fussed over his arm and convinced him to let her put cold compresses on his red, swollen arm with cold well water. It was extremely soothing and helpful. The throbbing ache subsided considerably and the swelling seemed to be less.

Earl turned on the radio and listened to the livestock report out of Saint Louis. Cattle prices were down again. He would have to be really careful or he could have a big loss on the cattle drive. He realized that he was being too generous with the individual farmer. He could come out on the cattle he had bought in Willow last Saturday. Next Wednesday, Thursday, Friday and Saturday would be a real test of his ability to be discriminating in his bidding.

When Charlie came back from chores and had finished washing up, they all sat in the living room. Earl said, "I need to saddle up and get back tonight. I've started sleeping back at my house."

Mary noticed Earl's use of "my house". He was already taking possession of Elmer's property

"Lucille and Glenn slept up there with me. I should be there with them."

They both nodded their understanding.

"I asked Fern if she would come up and cook and keep house as long as she felt she could," Earl continued. "I know she and John Dunivan are getting married pretty soon. We have a farmhouse that will be empty in a few days. When John and Fern get married they can live there. I'm going to ask John if he wants to move in there and get it in shape to live in ahead of time."

Mary said, "It's a good thing you're doing for my sister and for John. You need to turn your house into a home for your young sisters and brother."

Earl was grim in his response, "It's for that very reason I must get back this evening. Plum will be rested enough now. I'll saddle up and hurry home. If I put him to a steady trot, water him well at the river. On the flats I'll let him lope. We'll be back with daylight to spare."

Charlie, helped Earl put Plum in the barnyard and get the bridle and saddle on him.

"Thanks, Charlie. I'll be off."

The Dog Days of Summer would wear through the rest of July and well into August. A thunderstorm might relieve the heat and the drought.

CHAPTER 15 -

The Cattle Drive

When Earl rode back into Tyrone late Sunday evening, he was exhausted, his arm in a sling. It ached incessantly. He rode directly to the barn, removing the saddle and bridle with his left hand and arm. He stored them in the tack room and let Plum out to pasture after giving him a couple of mouthfuls of oats.

Earl walked to the house. When he found that Lucille and Glen were not there, he walked on down to his grandmother's house. The whole family was sitting on the front porch in chairs or on the edge. When Sarah saw Earl's arm in a sling, she said, "What's the trouble, Earl?"

"I hurt it pitching yesterday," Earl answered without telling them that he had pitched a double header while drunk. "Glen, Would you, mind getting me a cold bucket of water to soak my arm in. Not the bucket you use for drinking."

"Glen," Sarah commanded, "Get the bucket by the reservoir of the stove."

In a few minutes Glen returned and Earl put the bucket on his lap and immersed his arm in the cold water. Soon, the throbbing pain in his arm began to subside. Everyone watched silently. Finally, Earl spoke, "You don't know how good that feels, Glen. Thanks."

"You're welcome, Bud."

"I've sure learned something. Cold sure helps an injury," Earl said.

Earl took his arm out of the water and put it back in his homemade sling.

Sarah said, "Have you et yet?"

"Yep," Earl replied, "I ate at Mama's"

"You don't mean to tell me," Sarah said rather crossly, "you've been ridin' around all day with your arm in that kind of condition in a sling. I saw you headin' off to the West just about daylight."

"I forget you don't miss much in this town, Grandma," Earl smiled sheepishly. "I needed to see George Bailey about him buying some horses for me. I needed to speak to Lonnie, too, about taking some hogs to East Saint Louis tomorrow."

"Tell us the rest of it, Earl. I saw you leading off those two mules. You stopped at the house for something," Sarah continued her interrogation, "What was that all about?"

Earl proceeded to tell her everything. He explained about stopping at the house for tin plates, knives and forks and cooking ware for the coming cattle drive; his trip to Sargent; the return to see his other grandmother, his two aunts and uncle on the Odor homestead. He told them that he had asked his Aunt Fern to come cook and keep house for him. He told of his stop at Charlie and Mary's and the purchase of some cattle nearby.

Lucille was miffed, "You mean we're going to have someone living in the house we don't know. I don't need anyone to cook and keep house for me."

"I know you like to cook but my Aunt Fern is only little older than I am. She has learned to cook from one of the best cooks in the whole county. She can teach you a lot and she won't be with us a really long time.

We are losing our tenant on the home place. They will be moving out in a couple of weeks. It is my intention to ask John Dunivan to live there. It will be a good place for John to start out his marriage to my Aunt Fern. When they marry she will move out and we'll see where we go from there." Earl stopped and waited.

Glen was first to speak, "I think I kind of like the idea. I don't want Lucille experimenting on me with her cooking. I might crack a tooth on one of her biscuits."

Lucille punched Glen in the shoulder. Glen feigned great pain.

Vivian said, "Where will Fern sleep?"

"Why don't you kids decide?" Earl said.

Glen was quick to reply, "I want my room back. I know Earl and I slept downstairs last night but don't you think we could move back up again. Let the women have the downstairs."

Lucille, left out of deciding, interrupted, "I kind of like sleeping in my own room again. We have our twin beds in the back bedroom. Could your aunt sleep in the front bedroom?"

"I guess you've got it all decided. We'll tell Fern when she gets here." Earl answered, "What about Vacation Bible School, is that still on?"

"Yes it is," Lucille replied.

"You'd best get up to bed then, you'll need to get the chores done before you go."

Vivian wasn't going to be left out, "Is it okay if I go back and sleep at our house, Earl?"

"Why certainly, my little dove." Addressing Lucille, Earl said emphatically, "Leave a lamp lit with the wick turned down for Glen. And leave a lamp lit on the table for me. I need to talk to your Grandmother about some adult matters."

Pearl said, "We're heading off home, too."

After everyone had departed Earl pulled a chair up close by his grandmother's rocker. "You want me to light a lamp for you, too, Grandma. It's getting dark in a hurry."

"No, Son, I mean Earl. I know my way 'round in the dark. I get up most of the time before it's even light out. I just know where everything is."

Earl's heart skipped a beat with that little slip of the tongue. He had graduated from one level to another in his grandmother's mind.

"Grandma, I have to be very truthful with you. I've started the planning for this big cattle drive after the one Dad put together was so successful but I'm really worried about it. The market was down on Thursday and Friday. It was down a half penny last week. I'm going to the bank in the morning and call the buyer for the National Stock Yards. They buy on contract with the meat packing companies. I just need to know how I stand with them. I heard what went on between my Dad and their buyer last time and I know they can kind of wheel and deal with you."

"You'll do fine, Earl. You learned from the best in the business. Elmer always told me 'once in a while you get burned on a buy but in the long haul I always come out ahead.'" Sarah assured him, "You'll do just fine."

Relief flooded Earl. His confidence settled in a better place. He rose and walked up the hill to his house. He was thinking that way now.

When Earl entered the house, his brothers and sisters were already in bed and the last bit of daylight was a slight glimmer on the Western horizon. It had been a long day and he was exhausted. He heard, "Earl," coming quietly from Lucille.

Earl walked to the back bedroom and his sister was sitting up in bed. He sat on the bed beside Lucille. She turned and put her arms around him. She cried quietly on his shoulder as he held her tight.

"It's going to be a tough time for us for quite a while, Sis," Earl said quietly. "I know how independent you are, but you'll really appreciate Fern being here after a while, especially when school starts. It'll take a lot of burden off me and you both. You'll still have chores to do and I need to get back into business again in a serious way. Dad would expect this of both of us, to get on with life. Your mother loved you kids. You'll miss her but we've just got to go on."

Lucille nodded her head on his shoulder, "I love you, Bud. Go get your sleep."

Earl went to the dining room table, blew out the lamp and walked through the kitchen, pantry and up the stairs. He undressed in the dark, falling gingerly into bed to protect his arm, which was beginning to ache again. He could smell himself but he was too tired to get up and take a bath, even a sponge bath. He fell into an exhausted dreamless sleep, for the first time in several days. He awoke a couple of times when he turned onto his right arm.

Earl rose early. He dressed, walked to Glen's room and snuffed the lamp. He walked softly down the stair in his stocking feet with his boots in his left hand. In the kitchen, he put paper and kindling with small sticks on top and lit the wood stove. Earl lit the lamp on the table. He got a spare bucket from the porch and walked down to the well, drew a bucket of water. He went to put some larger sticks in the stove. He went to the front porch. Earl sat with the bucket on his knees and soaked his right elbow some more.

When the sun was just peeking over the top of the trees in the East, Earl roused Lucille and Glen. When the two siblings were dressed they found Earl at the dining room table writing cards to people who were wanting to sell livestock, giving a fairly accurate time of when he would stop by.

"What you doin', Bud." Glen said when he came in.

"Taking care of business," Earl replied.

Lucille came in the room. She said, "Let's get chores done Glen, so I can get breakfast on."

Earl said, "I'll take care of breakfast, since my arm won't let me do much else."

"Boy, that's a scary thought," Lucille said banteringly.

"You're going to get the treat of your life," Earl said, "You're getting chuck wagon supper that we'll eat for ten or eleven days on the cattle drive."

Glen screwed up his face in disgust.

"Just you wait," Earl said encouragingly, "you'll love it."

The two left the house and Earl went to the kitchen and back porch. He got the wash tub and brought it into the kitchen. He put more wood in the stove to keep it going and ladled some warm water into the tub, removed his clothes and took a quick, badly needed bath. When he was done he tossed the water out the back porch door.

He went back upstairs. He changed into clean clothing and returned to the kitchen. He deposited his dirty clothes in the hamper.

Earl returned to the kitchen and found a large skillet and big mixing bowl. He found the flour, corn meal and baking powder. He went to the icebox, noting the big chunk of ice. He brought back two eggs. He combined some flour and corn meal and baking powder. He found salt and put in a small spoonful. Earl took the two eggs, a can of milk and some fresh milk and mixed them together and added it to the flour and cornmeal. It looked about the right consistency. He found the molasses on the shelf and took it and butter to the table. He put more wood in the stove.

Earl went to the back bedroom to rouse Vivian. She came in her nightshirt. "Would you set the table?" Earl asked.

By the time the table was set, Lucille and Glen had come in and were washing their hands. Lucille looked at the dining table. She said, "You forgot glasses and a cup for Earl."

Earl put the skillet on the stove and put a small spoonful of lard in it to melt. He added more wood to the stove. The coffee pot was gurgling and smelling as coffee should when it is about ready. Earl ladled out the Jonny Cake batter into the skillet until the bottom was nearly covered. It sizzled and started to show bubbles coming up through. Earl allowed it to firm up a little and quickly turned it with a spatula. Glen stared at the browned Johnny Cake and said, "What's that Earl?"

"It's evening chuck. Better known as Johnny Cake. You put butter and molasses on it. It is filling and healthy food. It's what we eat every evening, sometimes with brown beans, on a cattle drive," Earl informed him. "Get your plate. You're the first victim."

Earl chuckled and Glen made a face but got himself a plate.

Glen took his plate to the table.

Lucille, standing by the stove, said, "I'll pray." And she did, simple and straightforward.

Earl greased the skillet and spooned more batter in the skillet and said, "Who's next?"

Vivian rushed from the kitchen for a plate.

Earl said, "I forgot milk. Lucille why don't you pour three glasses."

Soon all four had a Johnny cake on their plate. Earl poured himself a cup of coffee. The young siblings were eating heartily. Earl said, "What do you think?"

Glen said, "Could I have a small second one?"

Lucille said, "Me, too."

Vivian who had eaten all of hers said, "I'm full, thanks."

Earl figured this response was good. He finished his cake and did two smaller Jonny Cakes and another full size one for himself.

After they finished eating, Earl said, "You get ready for Bible School and I'll finish cooking up the rest of the batter. When you come back you can either go down and have lunch with Grandma or have milk and Johnny Cake cold for lunch. You decide among the three of you."

Lucille said, "I could tell we had really tired Grandma out this week. We'll come back here. We have baloney and cheese in the box. If we want we can do Johnny Cake or sandwiches. We might go play with some other kids here in town. If not we'll just stay around the house here."

"I'll take you over to Grandview and cut through the country to Raymondville," Earl informed them, "I need to make a call to the stock yards and talk to the banker. I'll be buying some cattle on the way back and collecting some old debts. I expect to be back sometime later this afternoon. Go get ready. When you get dressed, Vivian and Glen can do dishes."

Earl wrote out a couple more penny postcards to do with cattle and hog visits.

When the three siblings came back Earl said, "Lucille, let's take the eggs down to the store. What time do you want to be at the church."

"Ten," Lucille replied.

Earl and his older sister got the eggs from the back porch. Earl flexed his right elbow. He carried the egg basket in his left hand and opened the car door with his right. It hurt to pull the door open. He slid the basket to the middle of the front seat. The two of them counted the eggs together. They took the count of the eggs in even dozen. They kept out the two extras. Nick McKinney was the temporary clerk. He took out the running account and subtracted the amount for the eggs.

"Your balance to date is Ten Dollars and fifteen cents," Nick intoned.

Earl took out a ten and fished in his pocket for change.

Earl said, "Find me two lemons and three Pepsis. These kids need a Pepsi for lunch and we'll make lemonade this evening. You can put those on our July bill."

Nick found the lemons and Earl took out three bottles of Pepsi from the cooler. Nick added the lemons and Pepsis to their bill. Lucille carried all three Pepsis, smiling broadly.

When they got back, Earl opened the hatch to the rumble seat. He noticed the box and called to Lucille's retreating back, "I'm going down to the mill. Be right back."

Earl took the whiskey into the office in the mill and covered the box with some burlap bags. He kept out one bottle and put it behind the driver's seat. He went to the house, checked his pocket watch.

His sisters and brothers got in the car, Lucille in front and Glen and Vivian in back.

"You're going to be early but I need to get moving along," Earl said to Lucille.

"It's better than having to walk." Lucille stopped and then continued, "We can play school until the other kids start getting there. I can quiz Glen on geography. He's kind of weak there. I can have Vivian work on her multiplication table."

Earl smiled. He was proud of his young sister.

*　*　*　*　*　*　*　*　*　*

When Earl got to Raymondville it was after nine-thirty. Earl hoped Fern came over soon, he needed to get around earlier than this.

Ray took him in his office and got the National Stock Yard on the line. Earl inquired if he could speak to Joe Sullivan. Earl quizzed him on what kind of price he could expect from a mixed herd like the last one. Joe asked how many cattle and Earl told him about fifteen hundred. Earl told him of Elmer's death. Joe offered his condolences. The conversation centered on falling prices over the last two weeks. Joe wanted to know a fairly accurate time to meet the herd. Earl told him he would be at the farm where they met the last time at noon a week from Thursday. He told Earl that the last herd was prime, especially the steers and young heifers. He said he would be ready to offer three quarter a cent a pound over market if the quality was about the same.

Earl thought he could plan accordingly. He knew if he could make a quarter of a penny a pound he would have a profitable cattle drive.

When Earl stopped speaking to the buyer, Earl called Ray Miles back into the office. "You didn't have to leave the office while I talked. I have nothing to hide from you."

"It wasn't that, Earl, I had some other things to do. How many cattle are you planning on bringing up this time."

Earl did an approximate count in his mind and said, "I'm hoping for fifteen hundred head."

"You're really trying to outdo Elmer."

"Actually, Ray, it was his idea. I'm just carrying it out," Earl said.

"I told you I would cover you and I will. How much do you think you'll need us to put in your account?" Ray asked.

Earl ran some numbers through his mind and said, "Maybe twelve to fifteen thousand."

"You have almost that much in accounts here in the bank, that'll be no problem," Ray said.

"Make me out a cashier's check for twenty five hundred for the buys I may make in Arkansas. They don't know the Sigler name down there."

"Just go out and ask Jana to do that for you," Ray replied.

Earl went to the teller's cage and got the check from Jana.

Earl visited three people who owed his father and grandfather money. He had them sign the simple contract to make payments on a regular basis. Earl assured them if they missed one time he wouldn't come looking for them. If they fell behind they would have to work out something else, maybe a lesser payment. He also visited four farmers and bought fifty-five steers, thirty-one young heifers, fifteen older cows and one bull. One farmer asked him to find another bull. Earl told him he would bring a bull from his place. If the farmer liked the bull they would agree on a fair price.

He told all of them he would come back in eight days to add them to the herd he was taking to Rolla.

After his last stop, Earl drove a little faster than usual. He hoped to have a letter from Eva for sure.

Earl pulled up in front of the store and walked in quickly. It was hot this afternoon. It felt cool inside the Kidd store. Earl asked for his mail. He sorted through his mail quickly. No letter from Eva. What's going on, he thought. Surely she had gotten his card and letter. He had expected something before now. Nothing to be done about it, he thought. Too premature, he conjectured?

If Earl hadn't set in motion the cattle drive, he would have just driven up to Springfield. Maybe she was so bogged down in her studies that she hadn't had time to write. He remembered she was very troubled about something before she left. What could that have been all about?

Earl was so caught up in his thoughts that he hadn't heard Dana ask him something. He said, "I was thinking of something else. What did you say?"

"We got some fresh beef in today. Would you like some?"

"Sure," Earl replied, "How about four steaks, we'll have it for supper. Give me three potatoes to go with them, I don't know if we have any at the house."

Dana wrapped the steaks in paper and put them in a bag with the potatoes. "We got all moved this morning. Dillard and the girls are working this afternoon getting everything put back in drawers and on shelves. I'll spend all day tomorrow undoing it but they mean well."

"Good for you."

"You have a surprise coming, Earl," Dana smiled, "Your aunt showed up today."

"I better get up there," Earl said quickly, "I didn't expect her so soon. You better give me another steak."

"Better make it two. Her boyfriend is with her."

"Two, then," Earl said, exasperated. When Dana came back she wrapped the additional steaks and added two more potatoes, he hurried from the store and up to the house. When he got there John and Fern were sitting on the lawn furniture. Glen was under the big oak tree in front playing with some toy cars. Lucille was lying on a blanket, a pillow under her head, on the porch reading a book.

Earl stepped up on the porch and John extended his hand. They shook. John was a man of a little less than medium height, dark brown hair and piercing brown eyes. He was borderline skinny but Earl knew he had whiplash strength from their last cattle drive. He was also exceptionally handy with a rope to lasso and bring back a stray.

John said, "Hello, Earl. I brought my woman up."

Earl turned to Fern. She had dark hair and soft brown eyes. Earl was so used to her when she smiled he didn't even notice the protruding front teeth. Fern couldn't completely put her upper and lower lips together over the four offending teeth. Fern would have been the most attractive of his mother's sisters without this deformity. Earl embraced her and said, "I'm so glad you came. I don't know why I had it my head it would be tomorrow but today is wonderful."

Smiling pleasantly, Fern said, "I thought you might need me. When you came by yesterday I thought I detected some urgency."

"It wasn't a life and death emergency but I'm sure glad you're here," Earl responded, "I'm hoping you're ready to jump right in." Earl paused, and continued, "I've even got a job for John this afternoon but first things first."

Earl had noticed his sisters and brother were pointedly aloof from the visitors, Glen playing by the black oak, Vivian in the side yard in the shade of a little hickory playing with a kitten, and Lucille silently reading on the porch. Earl said, "Lucille get your brother and sister to come up here and we'll have a little discussion."

When all three of his siblings came to the porch, Fern rose from her seat in a lawn chair. Earl spoke softly, "This little one is Vivian, the free spirit, the happy-go-lucky one." Vivian smiled engagingly. "This young fellow is Glen. He's my right hand man around here. He's smart as a whip, as are all three. He rides like an Indian." Glen beamed with pride. "Last but not least is Lucille. I just don't know what I could have done without her. She is going to be a great cook and is learning to drive the Plymouth. I want her to show you how to drive, too, Fern."

Fern extended her hand rather gingerly. All his siblings shook her hand as if she was something delicate that might break.

Earl continued, "John is Fern's intended husband. He helped on the last cattle drive. Fern will be our house guest. I emphasize guest and you will treat her like a guest." All three siblings nodded and Earl continued, "She will do some cooking, teach Lucille some tricks to cooking and keep the house from looking like a pig pen. That doesn't mean leaving stuff around and failing to put dirty clothes in the hamper and not making your bed."

Lucille asked, "When do I start teaching Fern how to drive?"

"Tomorrow you'll drive the Plymouth over, half way to show her how and she can drive home. She can pick you up at eleven thirty and you can drive everyone back, Lucille." Earl paused and then continued, "Let's show Fern where her room is." Everyone except John filed into the house and to the downstairs front bedroom.

Earl stood by the door with Glen, "Vivian said, proudly, this is it. We girls will be in the downstairs."

Glen, his chest out proudly, said, "The men will be upstairs."

Fern, her mouth open in surprise, said, "I've never had this much room to myself. Maybe I should be paying to work here rather than the other way 'round. You don't know how crowded were are in that little four room house with four adults and a child."

"We'll let you find your way around the house yourself, Fern. I know the kids will be a lot of help to you in that regard." Earl held up the bag with the meat and potatoes. "This is supper. You kids go back to what you were doing and I'll show Fern the kitchen and the back porch where the ice box is located."

Fern followed Earl into the kitchen. Earl noted that the buckshot holes in the woodwork and plaster had been repaired since morning. When they were on the back porch Earl placed the wrapped steaks into the ice box, turning to Fern he said, "Dana Lay usually comes over on Monday to do her washing. I kind of expect her to come tomorrow since they were moving today. She'll show you how to use the washer it's gas powered."

"Everything is so modern and nice, Earl, it'll be a pleasure to be here," Fern said. "Your brother and sisters are polite and well-behaved. I expect no problems."

Earl said, "I kind of wanted to get you off by yourself to talk about remuneration. I know you're getting married sometime soon, this will give you a chance to save up a little cash to furnish your new home. What do you think would be fair? How about seven dollars a week?

"Let's do five. That's plenty," Fern said emphatically.

"That's acceptable, if you use our running account at the store for any personal items you may need for yourself. Why don't you walk down that way in about fifteen minutes. I'm going to take John on a trip down to Grogan on horseback to buy some cattle" Earl answered.

They left the back porch and Earl spoke to Lucille, "Why don't you show Fern the garden and you to can get some vegetables for supper and plan out the meal together." Earl turned to John, "Can I convince you to go with me to buy and herd some cattle to the home place. You'll get paid for a full day's work."

"Sounds like an interesting' proposition," John responded.

Earl left the porch with John at his side. Earl walked out past the chicken house and to the corral by the old barn. He got a bucket of grain, gave a shrill whistle. "Bang this bucket against a board and those nags will come on the run," Earl said. He busily chased what hogs were in the corral out to the enclosure around the mill and shut the gate. By the time he got back, John had opened the gate and the five horses were in the corral.

"John, pick any of three other than that red horse, we call him Plum or the smaller one, that's Pidge. I'd like for the other three to get used to the saddle a little more for the trail."

John picked out the pinto, a fine strong horse about three years old. She was good size for a mare, nearly fifteen hands. John made a loop and had the lasso on the horse with the first try. Earl thought to himself that John might be a natural born horseman.

Earl used his left arm to use the lasso. He got the rope around the neck of a big dun Stallion. They got the bridles and saddles on efficiently. When John mounted his horse, she hopped around a bit. Earl knew the stallion would put on a show. Earl chased the other horses out of the corral and asked John to leave the corral and wait for him outside. When Earl had his left foot in the stirrup, the stallion shied sideways but Earl was ready for it and he levered himself aboard with his left arm and had his foot in the right stirrup before the horse leapt into the air. The Dun gave six hard bucks before he realized he wouldn't dislodge his passenger. He mince stepped around the corral and allowed Earl to guide him out the gate beside John and the other horse.

John said, "You're pretty good on a buckin' horse. I'd have been off on my rear end or head."

"John, I've had a lot of practice. I've had to break a lot of young colts to the saddle over the past five years."

Earl saw Fern walking toward the store and they followed her down. Earl ground hitched Fred, his horse, and entered the store behind Fern. Dana was still there. He asked her to pass on that Fern would be buying things for the house and anything else she wanted and to put it on the Sigler bill.

Dana told Fern that she would be coming the next day to do wash. Fern said she would be gone for a while about ten o'clock. They both agreed it was a lot better than using a scrub board.

Earl returned to Fred and John and Sue, the horse. They headed to the school house and on south to the original homestead that they called the home place. Earl told John that his tenant on the home place was moving next week and he needed someone to live there and keep it up. Earl said, "Would you be interested, John."

"Boy, would I ever. I think Mama and John would have kicked me out a long time ago if John hadn't been so stove up with rheumatiz for the last ten years. They just kept me around to do the farmin' for them." John Bradford, John Dunivan's stepfather had married his mother when William Dunivan died when John was quite young. John spoke again, "I've lived under the same roof with that grouchy ol' man for nigh on twenty years. It'll be a relief to be out."

"Yeah," Earl said, "George would like for them to move into town and retire there so he could take over the farm. He and Maudie have a growing young family. They've been tending that little store and post office down by the Turkey Ranch for over ten years. Living in that little house."

Earl stopped in front of the house on the home place. "Here it is, John."

John nodded his head and said, "I think I can do somethin' with this. I'd like to raise some turkeys. I'd like a couple of Jerseys, keep one fresh and one bumping a calf." He was referring to the practice of taking a fist and pushing it into the side of a cow to ascertain a pregnancy.

"How about chickens?" Earl asked.

"Those, too. Not too many."

Earl reined his horse around and they left the home place and back on the road again. He stopped by Les Hall's to look at cattle. He had twenty-six nice steers, eleven young heifers and two old canners. Earl told him cattle had been going down about a half penny a week. Earl wrote a check for the cattle.

John and Earl rode down the valley about a mile before they crossed the North Jacks Fork head-waters. They went west past Grogan school house and rode on about two miles up on the ridge between the Elk Creek and Jacks Fork watersheds. Elk Creek fed into the Piney River and ultimately to the Missouri River. Whereas, Jacks Fork fed into the Current River, which eventually went into the Mississippi. Earl rode into a driveway. When John noticed the name on the mailbox, George Morgan, John said, "This a cousin of yours, Earl?"

"No, he's actually a great uncle. I haven't seen much of him for many years. When I was young they used to have a Morgan reunion once in a while and I'd see him then. When we moved to Colorado, I was six. When we got back I saw him once or twice," Earl replied.

When John and Earl dismounted, George Morgan opened the screen door. Using a cane he hobbled slowly to the yard gate. Earl and John ground hitched the horses. George said, "Hello, Earl. Good to see you. Come on up to the porch and we'll talk."

George walked painfully back to the porch. When all three men were settled into a chair on the porch, Isabelle came out to join them. George said, "You remember, Belle."

Earl said, "Hello Aunt Belle."

"We're sellin' out. My son don't want the place. Our grandson wants it. I'm leavin' him five young heifers and five older cows. The cows I want to let go are out in the field back of the house. My grandson separated them. I have twenty-nine steers, twenty-three young heifers and twenty old cows. I kept one young bull and my old bull. I'm tradin' the old bull and the yearlin' bull to a neighbor for another bull for my grandson to use."

John and Earl walked around behind the house. The steers and heifers were prime. The old cows were in very poor condition. He was concerned that they would even make it to Rolla.

Earl was brutally honest about the cows but praised the steers and heifers. Earl proposed a price and George immediately accepted. "We're movin' into the banker's house and payin' rent. I think he's movin' over to Raymondville where he'll be closer to work. I'll put this into savins' and I had some saved up already, between interest and what my grandson pays on the farm, we'll get by."

Earl wrote a check and handed it to him. "I think you'll get by Uncle George. Weren't you and Uncle Weed both in the Spanish War."

"Yep we were. We both get a little veteran's pension. Weed more because he was wounded pretty serious," George responded and then continued, "By the way Weed sent your friend's name and they sent word to her that she was hired if she wants the job."

Earl was so pleased he could hardly stand it. Eva would be teaching about six miles from Tyrone. However, he was hurt and baffled why he hadn't heard from the woman he loved. "Thanks, George. That's good news. Let your grandson know we'll be any help we can to get him started."

George held up the check, "Thanks, Earl."

Earl and John mounted and rode back to the field, opened the gate, drove the cattle out, closed the gate and drove them toward the home place. They added the cattle from Les Hall's. When he got there, he looked at the grass across the road on the West side. It was heavily grazed. Rain would help, just a quarter inch shower some evening. He drove the cattle into the hay field north and east of the farmhouse. Earl figured they wouldn't get any more hay this year as dry as it was. With so many farmers selling off their herds, Earl figured he could even buy some hay.

By the time they got back to Tyrone it was nearing eight. They unsaddled and turned the horses out to pasture. Earl said to John, "That it was a successful trip."

"Good news about Eva," John said.

When the two men entered the back porch door, Fern and Lucille met them at the back door. Fern said, "Lucille figured it might be eight-thirty before you got back. If you want to wash up and sit on the front porch until dinner is ready that will be okay." Fern and Lucille were wet with sweat from working in the heat of the kitchen.

Seated on the front porch, Earl asked John, "Can you stay the night?"

"I think I best be getting back for chores tomorrow mornin'. I asked George if he could send Emmet over to do the chores this evenin' but I didn't ask for tomorrow mornin'."

They ate and John left soon afterward.

By the time the meal was over it was near dark. Earl lit a lamp in the living room. He said, "Time for bed. Fern, I don't expect you to do chores. However, you might want to go out and see what goes on." Earl paused and continued, "Let's have breakfast at seven." Earl knew he leaving with Dillard no later than seven-thirty.

Lucille suddenly said, "There's a thunder bucket under Fern's bed that we girls can use."

Earl was up as usual about five. He wrote penny post card answers to queries about livestock purchases. He put off the hogs until after the cattle drive. He vowed to himself that he would plan four or five trips to East Saint Louis with hogs.

Earl began estimating the herd he was assembling, his estimates added up to over one thousand three hundred fifty head. Was it too overly ambitious? He would either have a nice return for his efforts or a bad loss. He did not want to entertain the latter thought.

By six o'clock he was walking up on his grandmother's porch. She was sitting in her living room rocking chair in her night dress and white cap. He asked if she might have gotten some of his mail by mistake. She took two penny post cards off the table by her chair and handed them to him. Earl was very disappointed that a letter from Eva was not among the mail mistakenly put in his grandmother's box. He took the two cards and walked by his Uncle Weed's place. Weed was sitting on the front porch. Earl went in the yard through the front gate and said "hello" to him from his brother George. Earl thanked him for sending over Eva's name and told Weed they had chosen to hire her. He left and was at the store a little before seven. The store had opened at six-thirty. Earl bought penny post cards and sent notes that he would look at some pigs in two weeks. He mailed the cards.

The card he kept was from the farmer by Pine Creek that had turned down Elmer's offer about a week and a half ago. Earl would visit him late morning and go on down to look at some more cattle down by Willow. As Earl walked by Dillard's old house Dana came out and said Dillard was up at the barn. When Earl came to the barn Dillard was busy feeding the hogs.

"When you get done come up and get the Plymouth and take Dana over to Houston to buy anything you need at your new place," Earl said.

"Okay, Earl, anything else?"

"Yes, could you pick up the kids about eleven thirty at Grandview Baptist Church. They've been going to a Vacation Bible School over there. I'll take Lonnie over to look at some cattle by Elk Creek and take the kids to Grandview on the way. I should get back about noon or a little before. You can take Lonnie down to the home place this afternoon and make steers out of all the little bulls under four months old. Hold back two of the best looking ones. I'm going to go down toward Willow to look at some more cattle. Have Paul and Lonnie at the barn by four thirty tomorrow morning. I want the horses with four saddles on them in the truck by five or before. We'll ride in front. Lonnie and Paul can ride astride the horses in back. They'll have to be careful of low hanging limbs along the way. I'm taking you the way we'll do the drive."

"I'll be waiting on your front porch before noon," Dillard responded.

Earl drove the truck up to the house. When he walked in Fern had a big platter with fried eggs and bacon in her hand. Fern sent Vivian to get the milk out of the ice box. Fern came back with the coffee pot and poured Earl and herself a cup. Fern sat, bowed her head and said grace.

After everyone had a plate full of food, Vivian said, "Lucille prays nice, too."

Glen snickered.

Fern said, "I'll remember that." Looking at Lucille, "We'll take turns."

Earl said, "I let Dillard use the car to go over to Houston. Do you kids want to ride over in the truck? Dillard and Dana will pick you up on their way back and bring you home."

"It's way too early, Earl," Lucille said, "we'll walk."

"I'll walk over with them and visit some of your neighbors out west of here on the way back. If I'm going to be here a while, I'd like to start getting acquainted," Fern volunteered.

When Earl went out the front door, he found Lonnie waiting on the front porch, lounging in a lawn chair. Earl said, "Ready?"

Lonnie nodded.

Earl and Lonnie picked up the cattle in Elk Creek. Earl left Lonnie in Tyrone to wait for Dillard. Later in the day Earl bought the cattle near Pine Creek and Willow to be included in the cattle drive.

Before five the next morning they were on the road. Earl showed them how to leave West Plains, travel township roads through Hutton Valley, past Kings Mountain, then by logging road, connecting with the West Plains-Rolla Road north of Willow. Earl bought one hundred forty-three cattle in Hardy, all steers and young heifers, except for one good young bull. They were able to drive past Thayer to their stopping place before full dark. The pasture was fenced so they went into town to eat.

On Thursday Earl bought forty-nine steers, twenty-eight heifers and two good, bred Jersey cows for John Dunivan. They would drop calves in the Spring. George Baker, John Bradford and John Dunivan met them South of West Plains. Earl was pleased that they had the initiative to come down because the three drovers could use extra help. On Friday Earl bought one hundred seventy-six cattle, again concentrating on steers and young heifers. Earl split his help. Earl and John Bradford rode off together with Earl on the extra horse. They picked up the two small purchases of cattle he had made between West Plains and Willow. They pushed those cattle hard and met the main herd before they went North past King Mountain. Earl rode back to West Plains, loaded his saddled horse on the truck and was at their overnight pastures before supper. He ate Johnny Cake and molasses along with the cow pokes with two cups of hot, strong coffee. He got his bedroll out of the truck an using his saddle as a pillow slept with his men.

The next day Earl went north ahead of the herd with the truck and asked Lonnie to follow the truck at a trot or soft lope to keep up. Earl took him to the farm by Pine Creek and with Lonnie on horseback and Earl, on foot, brought sixteen steers, ten heifers and six older cows to the West Plains-Rolla Road. When they met the herd, Earl told Dillard to take it slow going north.

Earl took Lonnie and Paul, to Willow with him. He bought eighty-three steers and heifers. Earl, Lonnie and Paul took the cattle through the back streets to intersect with the West Plains-Rolla Road. He instructed Lonnie and Paul to push the cattle hard and not stop for watering the herd until they got to South Jacks Fork. Earl was sorry that he didn't have one more drover but there was no help for it now. He drove ahead in the truck. When he caught up with the big herd. He saddled the extra horse and doubled back to help Lonnie and Paul. They were nearing South Jacks fork. Now they had one on point and one on drag and the one on the flanks of the small herd.

When Earl, Lonnie and Paul got to Clear Springs they found the larger herd had already moved north. Earl looked at his pocket watch, they had made good time over the thirteen miles. They pushed the small herd on north and caught up to the larger herd at North Jacks Fork. As soon as all the cattle were watered they moved north. At Nagle Earl had them turn the herd west toward Grogan, where they turned north again. They allowed the herd to drink at the last crossing of the North Jacks Fork, the third time they had crossed it. Earl drove the truck on north and blocked the road with the truck, opened the gate to the hayfield on the original homestead. Earl thought he should have six hundred three head of cattle. He counted and allowed two hundred to enter the field. The sun was low in the sky by now. He drove the truck to Morgan cave a mile South of Tyrone, blocked the road with the truck, opened the gate. When the herd came a few minutes later he funneled the last of the cattle into Ira and Pearl's west eighty.

On Sunday, Clear Springs had a game. Earl sent word by Paul that his arm was in no condition to play at all, pitch or in the field.

On Monday Earl bought thirty-six head of cattle in Summersville. There was still no letter from Eva. Over two weeks now, Earl lamented to himself. Earl had other mail to answer and he sent another card to Eva imploring her to write. He promised he would come visit her in a few days.

Tuesday they left Tyrone with twelve hundred seventy-six cattle, adding one hundred sixteen cattle Earl had bought between Tyrone and Licking. The herd nearly sucked Dow Clayton's spring-fed creek dry. Earl bought seventy-nine steers and heifers at the Licking Sale Barn and added one hundred and six along north of Licking. They watered a herd of fifteen hundred seventy-seven at a small stream that was the upper reaches of the Current River. A cow broke a leg there. They loaded the carcass in the truck after removing enough meat for the men for supper. Earl took the cow to the butcher in Licking. It was not a total loss.

They made a dry camp that night. Earl drove back to Dow's place and got a ten gallon milk can of water. When he got back the steaks were done with fried potatoes and skillet biscuits.

They started the herd moving before six the next morning and they had the cattle in a field South of Rolla with a small stream before ten.

The contract buyer, Joe Sullivan, came about eleven thirty. The cowhands cut out the steers and herded them through a dehorning chute, with the buyer jotting down weights of each animal. Then came the heifers, then the cows and the few bulls were last. Earl had already estimated the weights at a little over seven hundred pounds a head. When Joe finished his tally, he said, "You have fifteen hundred seventy five head and I estimated their weight at seven hundred three pounds per animal."

"I guess we lost one between here and Licking," Earl said, "We'll have to keep an eye out for it on our way back."

"You realize that's over a million one hundred thousand pounds of beef that you have on the way to the stock pens in Rolla by the railroad. I hope they have enough pens there to hold all those cows," Joe said emphatically.

Earl and Joe talked about price until Earl was satisfied. He estimated he would make about a third of a penny a pound on the cattle he had bought the last week and a half. Of course, the two hundred and ten that he and Elmer had raised from calves were his biggest profit. But the other animals had given him a substantial return of over thirty six hundred dollars. On average it wasn't as profitable as the smaller drive in profit per animal but it was still a satisfying return for his efforts. Part of it was because of the falling market. Another factor was the delay from the time of purchase to the time delivery. It was a drag on profit margin. Earl had listened to the farm report at Dow's and cattle had been up almost four tenths of a penny.

When they got to Rolla Earl asked Joe to give him a Cashier's Check for the herd. The Check for over forty-two thousand dollars weighed only a fraction of an ounce but it felt heavy in Earl's pocket as he got in his truck and headed South to Raymondville. He had some regrets that he wouldn't be able to camp out with the riders as they headed back home.

Earl walked into the bank and gave the check to Jana and walked into Ray Miles' office. He sank tiredly into the chair across the desk from Ray.

Jana followed Earl in with a deposit slip.

Ray said, "How'd it go?"

Earl slid the deposit slip across the desk. The banker whistled. "You came out smelling like a rose."

"You know about two hundred and ten head were our own," Earl offered.

"But still you added more than nine thousand to your account."

Earl rose and said, "I need to get home, check my mail and get a bath."

Ray wrinkled his nose, "I know what you mean. Do you have another cattle drive in mind?"

Earl shook his head, "Not soon, it's getting so dry and hot. There's not much water between Big Creek and Rolla. If I do it will be a couple of small herds of two or three hundred head. There's just too much risk with prices falling so fast. We got just over four cents a pound. It just can't go much lower or farmers will be giving away their cows. Joe Sullivan told me that the government has started buying herds up in Iowa, killing them and burying the carcasses."

Earl got up and strode out of the bank. He started to get in the truck and remembered he would need cash in small bills, ones, fives and tens. He reentered the bank and got the cash from Jana.

Earl wanted to go directly to Tyrone and check his mail. He would surely have a letter by now. Yet he knew he couldn't. He had to take money back to Dillard to pay the men who helped on the cattle drive. Also, he had seen a Model A for sale on a car lot in Licking. He had promised to have a vehicle for his foreman, Dillard.

When Earl came to the car lot in Licking, he parked the truck on the street and entered an office. A fan was moving air around but it was still stifling hot. The sign in the window advertised the car for sale for ninety-nine dollars. Earl bought the car for eighty-six, provided it ran well. He proposed that he take it for a drive north toward Maples. He met the cowhands just after he crossed the stream where they had watered the herd the day before. Earl stopped the car.

Earl said to Dillard, "Get off your horse and drive this old rattle trap home. I got a deal on it in Licking." Earl turned to the rest of the men and said, "We're going to pay you now for however many days we been on the trail. I'm also giving out a five dollar bonus to everyone. Also, I don't want you eating camp food the rest of the way back home. I'm giving you a dollar to buy supper in Licking and a dollar to buy breakfast in Raymondville. When you get to Tyrone come to my house and Fern will have dinner ready for all of you unless Mack, Paul, Jess Jones and Jess Story want to eat at home."

Earl handed some cash to Dillard and they paid the men.

Earl called Mack Hall aside and told him, "I'd like to put you in charge of getting these men home in one piece. How would an extra couple of dollars do for that responsibility. You can camp out at Dow Clayton's tonight. I'll have Dillard stop by and clear it with him. If anybody wants to ride back into town for a little refreshment they can do that but I want everyone in the saddle by shortly after five tomorrow morning."

Earl peeled off three more one dollar bills and put it in Mack's hand. He turned to the men standing and waiting for further instructions, "Dillard's been your trail boss up to now but he needs to drive this car back to Tyrone. Mack, here is going to take over. Whatever he says goes."

All the men nodded and remounted.

Earl and Dillard drove back toward Licking. They couldn't get there fast enough to suit Earl but he didn't urge his foreman to drive faster.

Once in the truck Earl drove to Tyrone but didn't get there until it was almost seven in the evening. He pulled up in front of the store, tried the door but it was locked. He decided he wouldn't impose on the McKinney's to open up after hours. He would just wait until six thirty in the morning to see if he had a letter from Eva.

As he drove up the street to his house, Earl saw off in the distance billowing thunderheads. He thought to himself, that it would be wonderful to get a good rain on the pastures that were drying out and his sixty or so acres of corn growing down by the home place. Two more good rains could produce a really good corn crop and refresh his pastureland.

When he stopped the truck he could hear the rumble of thunder off in the distance.

Chapter 16 -

Love Lost

E arl parked the truck in the driveway in front of the Mill building. He got out, walking into the orchard. He stood in the shade of a big apple tree beside the hole where an old cistern had collapsed long before he came to Tyrone the second time. He was born in Tyrone a September day almost twenty-two years ago. The fatigue, the loneliness for the woman he loved, and the despair of his grief combined to lay his spirits low. He remembered his box of liquor in the Mill office. He walked quickly to the office. The box of bottles were intact where he left them under the burlap bags. He took a bottle. Earl walked up the stairs of the porch of the Mill and sat with his legs off the edge. He opened the bottle and tipped it up, taking two long swallows. It burned into his belly. He needed more. He tipped the bottle again and again.

On an empty stomach the liquor worked quickly. His mood lightened. Off in the distance he could see the curtain of rain approaching. He knew he had to get back to the house before he got soaked. He took a long swig, returning to the truck. He put the bottle on the front seat and rolled up the windows. He hurried up to his house. Drops of rain were already falling as he came to the front porch.

Earl entered the house. It was very quiet. He looked to his left and saw that Fern had her Bible open, reading. He walked over and sat down in a rocking chair with a woven string bottom.

Fern said, "The children went down to Sarah's. We heard the truck come as we were finishing eating. I thought you'd come on up."

Earl wondered how he had missed his sisters and brother. He conjectured that they had gone the back street. He said, "I wanted to do something by the Mill and check on the pigs."

"The food's still in the warming oven. If you want I can get it out, if you haven't eaten," Fern said informatively.

Earl heard the rain begin hammering on the metal roof. "I'd better check open windows upstairs if you'd check the ones down here," He said.

Fern jumped to her feet and went to the downstairs bedrooms. Earl checked the kitchen window as he walked through. He closed the west windows in both upstairs bedrooms and wiped up water on the sills and floor with a dry towel he had in his bedroom.

By the time Earl got to the top of the stairs, his ingestion of liquor took hold. He started to sway and became a little fearful about a misstep and fall. He took hold of the rungs in the railing, holding on to them and leaning against the wall, he went carefully to the landing. He grabbed hold of the jamb by the door leading upstairs to steady himself down the last three steps.

Earl found a plate and some eating utensils in the pantry and took them to the dining table. Fern was back on the divan reading.

Earl went back to the kitchen for the food from the warming oven, he was staggering back toward the dining table with pots and pans in both hands. He dropped them heavily on the table and started back toward the kitchen swaying.

Fern jumped from the divan, rushing to Earl's side, "Earl are you okay?"

"Yep. Okay."

Fern wrinkled her nose, "Why, Earl, you're drunk." She gave him a quizzical moue.

"Yep. Drunk."

Fern guided him to his chair. "Let me get your food and coffee." She put a pork chop on Earl's plate, spooned mashed potatoes and green beans on his plate. She ladled gravy into a depression in the potatoes. Earl began cutting up the pork chop awkwardly. Fern returned with the coffee pot and poured some coffee.

Earl shoved food in his mouth, chewing hard. "This is wonderful after eating trail food flavored with cow manure." He picked up the coffee cup and dribbled some off his chin. Fern was thankful that the coffee had cooled considerably.

When Earl had finished his plate, Fern offered him some blackberry pie.

"I'm too full," Earl slurred. "You think it'll still be good in the morning?"

Fern said, "It'll be right here on the table. The kids picked them fresh today."

Earl said, "I think it's bedtime."

Fern was glad to hear him say that even thought it was still daylight. She helped Earl to his feet and guided him to the stairs and allowed him to finish the climb to his bedroom. It was still raining and Fern was glad it was. It would have been terrible for Earl's sisters and brother to see him in such a state.

Earl collapsed into bed with his clothing on.

Downstairs, Fern vowed to have a serious talk to Earl about his drinking.

Lucille, Glen and Vivian came running back through the last of the raindrops from the passing thunderstorm. Vivian went straight back to her bed without urging.

Fern said, "I'm not going to wake you until six. You can have your chores done long before breakfast is on. Besides young people need more sleep than grownups."

Glen said, "Okay," and turned to leave.

"Want Lucille or me to do your lamp for you?" Fern offered.

"Nope. I'm getting to big for that stuff." Glen kept walking away.

Lucille smiled engagingly at Fern. "It has been nice having you here, Fern. Earl was right."

Fern smiled. "Give me a hug. I miss having hugs from my Mom and Sister Effie and Tommie."

Lucille approached Fern and gave Fern a rather tentative embrace. It would be one of many to come.

Earl awakened in the night, removing his clothes and finding the west window. When Earl awoke on Friday morning, his head was aching worse than his arm and he felt queasy. He hurriedly put on his clothes and rushed downstairs and out the back door and tried to vomit but nothing would come out. He went back to the kitchen, dipping water from the bucket and washed his face. When he turned to go into the dining room and living room, Fern was there standing in the door.

"Earl," Fern said, "you were lucky that your sisters and brothers were not here last night. Don't you ever come into this house in that condition again. If you do, I'll be gone the same day."

Earl crimsoned with shame, "I won't do it again," he stammered.

"Do you keep your drink here in the house?"

"It's down at the Mill."

Fern looked at him carefully, "I found liquor in the pantry."

"I didn't put it there," Earl said convincingly. "It must be my father's."

"If you must drink and drink to drunkenness," Fern said firmly, "stay someplace else."

"You have my word on it as your 'little brother,'" Earl replied.

Earl turned abruptly and left the kitchen by the back door, out into the back yard and to the east side of the house. He stood a long time watching the Eastern sky brighten, a lingering thunderhead to the Southeast burned brightly in the surging sun. Earl had the urge to thank God for the good rain but it never came to his lips. Maybe He wouldn't listen to me now, he thought.

After a few minutes, Earl heard footsteps behind him.

"Earl, I…."

Before Fern could go on, Earl said, "I deserved that. I needed a good tongue lashing. You'll never see me come in the house that way again. I promise."

"Thank you for that."

"There's just so much expected of me. I don't think I'm ready for it. I have awful nightmares, my father accusing me," Earl lamented.

Fern said, "Don't use that as an excuse for drunkenness."

"And Eva," Earl continued, "It's been almost three weeks and I haven't heard a peep from her."

"What! You've been seeing her for three, four months now. There are other women. You're young, there's no rush."

"I know. I know! She's the only woman I'll ever love like this," Earl was adamant.

Tears sprang to Fern's eyes, "There's nothing to be done about Eva except to try to go see her and find out why she hasn't written." She tried to purse her lips without success and continued, "You are too talented to fail in business. Your father's death was a terrible shock, a tragedy. Just give this time. God will heal your grief and guilt if you would let him."

"Thanks for the encouragement, Fern. I'll ponder it. In the meantime

I'm going to sit and rest on the front porch until six thirty and I'll go down to see if I have a letter from Eva." Earl sauntered around to the front porch and sat down. Fern followed and sat down on another chair beside him/

Earl took out a Lucky and lit it hoping that it would help his pounding headache. If it did it wasn't noticeable.

Fern said, "I don't think your sisters and brothers have been getting enough sleep. I'm going to start letting them sleep until six. They have plenty of time to do chores before breakfast at seven."

"That sounds like a good idea to me," Earl assented. "Maybe we can do that on into the school year, if you stay that long."

"John and I have talked it over. We want to save up a little. We're thinking of next June."

Relief flooded Earl. That was something that would take something off his mind for a while. The two, aunt and nephew, sat in companionable silence until they heard the clock strike six. Fern rose and went to get Lucille, Earl went upstairs to awaken Glen. When the two brothers returned to the kitchen Lucille was waiting at the kitchen door.

Earl helped Fern get the fire started in the kitchen stove. Fern followed Earl back to the porch and they sat with Fern closest to the dining room door.

"I'm going to let Vivian sleep until she wakes up or get her up a little before seven," Fern said quietly.

Earl nodded and took out another cigarette. "At six thirty I'm walking down to get the mail," he said through billows of smoke.

They said nothing more until Fern left after a few minutes. Earl sat until he heard the clock strike the half hour.

Earl rose quickly and walked to the Kidd Store. When he entered Nick was there. He got the mail for Earl. Earl sifted through the letters and cards quickly. No letter. Suddenly the blackness descended again. He turned quickly and was out the door.

As Earl walked back toward the house, he noticed the little Model A in the drive by the Mill. Earl walked in by the corral and barn. He heard Dillard in the barn. When Dillard emerged from the granary door, he was startled to see Earl. "Sorry for bein' so jumpy," Dillard said.

"Sorry," Earl apologized, " I wanted to see you and tell you I'm going to head up to Springfield. I'll try to get back by Sunday for a double header over in Houston."

"Anything need doin' this week?" Dillard asked.

"You've had a rough week and a half," Earl said, "don't do anything extra. You have some settling in you need to do over at your new place."

"Dana mentioned putting in some late garden. Maybe some turnips, runty onions and some other late vegetables. I think if I got some late sweet tater starts and we have a late frost they might produce some," Dillard said hopefully.

"Load the plow, drag, harness and mules on the truck today and get on it. Lonnie can come over and help you. When he comes back for dinner, I'll tell him to finish his day of work over at your place." Earl stood and looked though his mail again, while Dillard went off to put out feed for the hogs. There was a letter from Jim Hart. Earl opened it. Jim was giving him notice of the Probate Hearing the next Monday at ten. He wanted Earl to bring Sarah and Pearl. Holt also made it clear that Jim Smith would be there as well. There was a note from the Inman's that they had twenty-five pigs that they wanted to sell.

When Dillard came back from feeding, "Anything wrong, Earl?"

"Did I look that upset," Earl asked, "it was just a notice of the Probate Hearing. I knew it would come up eventually, just not this soon."

"I remember what a mess that was with Bill Kidd. He didn't have a will. I guess people think they're going to live forever and don't get around to it." Dillard smiled ruefully.

Earl interrupted, "I better hustle up for breakfast before Fern throws it out. Ask Dana if she could come over and help cook for the men when they come in at noon. I got a note to come over and look at some pigs at Inman's. They raise some good eating chickens. I'll pick up seven. That should be enough to feed everybody," Earl turned away and back around again, "If you want you can go with me over to Houston when I go see my lawyer. You can pick up seed, onion and sweet potato starts."

Earl wheeled and started trotting off toward his house.

After breakfast Earl announced his plans to go to Springfield as soon as soon as he could. He offered to drive his sisters and brothers over and pick them up on his way back. He broke the news to Fern about preparing a meal for ten or twelve men. He told her that Dana would be coming over to help.

"I'm going over to look at some pigs," Earl said as he was getting up from breakfast.

"Can I go along, Earl?" Glen asked.

"Okay," Earl replied, "why don't you help Lucille carry the eggs down to the store. Take eggs back to your grandmother's if she needs some. I'll pick you up in front of the store in a few minutes."

Earl pushed his dishes aside and went to a table in the living room to get the postcards he had received, some addressed to him and still some to Elmer from people who had not heard of his death, mostly from far south outside the county. He brought them to the table and began writing out answers on some penny post cards he had picked up at Kidd's.

During breakfast, Earl had turned on the radio so he could listen to the livestock market. Cattle had fallen a tenth of a cent. Hogs had risen nearly a half penny. He decided when he heard it to send the hogs down by the barn to the National Stock Yards on Sunday night. He would have Lonnie haul them up. He figured he could do it on one double deck load.

Earl sometimes surprised himself how he could think about one thing while he did something else, all at the same time.

After he was finished with addressing the post cards. He looked at Vivian and Fern who had come back in from taking the dirty dishes into the kitchen.

Fern was sipping her coffee. She said, "Ask Lucille to bring back ten pounds of potatoes."

Earl got up from the table and left through the west front door. Earl trotted back down the street and to the truck. The whiskey bottle was sitting on the front seat. He put it behind the front seat. He drove to the store and parked in front. Lucille and Glen had just finished counting the eggs.

Lucille said, "Hi, Bud."

"Hi yourself, Sis. Fern said to bring ten pounds of potatoes. I want you to bring back a dozen lemons for lemonade for dinner, too." Earl hesitated, "Do you think you can carry all that?"

"Easy as pie," Lucille replied, "I carried a twenty-five pound sack of flour up for my Mama just a a few weeks ago." Suddenly her face turned white and tears coursed down her cheeks.

Earl went to her quickly and embraced her as she sobbed. "There'll be times like this, Sis. I've had them, too. We've just got to go on. The good memories will win out, Sweetheart."

Earl released Lucille.

Lucille said, "I'll be okay. You and Glen go look at the pigs."

Earl and Glen went to see the pigs. Earl gave too much for them because the Inman family was so very poor. They loaded them and took them to the corral by the barn.

When the two brothers came back to the house, Dillard and Dana were at the house. Earl had the seven nice fat young roosters in two gunny sacks. Dana took them from him and said, "I'll go murder them. I know where the axe is and the chopping block. Fern looks too delicate for the job."

Fern made a face. "You forget. I grew up on a farm but go have at it," she said.

Earl was pleased at the repartee, indicating a budding friendship. He left with a lighter heart accompanied by Dillard and his siblings for Grandview Church and Houston. He left his sisters and brother too early at the church but he knew Lucille would entertain them.

Dillard was never a big talker, so the two men drove in complete silence until Earl let Dillard off in front of the farm produce store and grain mill. Earl went on to Jim Hart's office. Hart had a client already in the office. An elderly woman departed. Jim came right out. Earl rose and the two shook hands. "Come on back," Jim said.

Earl sat in one of the seats across from Jim. Earl asked, "What do I need to do to get ready for this?" Earl leaned forward expectantly.

"You need to bring your grandmother and aunt. I'll bring a copy of Elmer's Quit Claim Deed. And, of course, my testimony of Elmer's intentions and why he had me prepare the Quit Claim Deed will be crucial. I would suggest that you bring the records of your financial dealings over the last three weeks since Elmer's death."

"I'll get all my cancelled checks and I have deposit slips in a file at home, I'll swing by the bank on my way home. I won't get my monthly statement until after the end of July. I'll bring the deposit slips for the savings accounts that I have set up for my brother and sisters. Should they come?," Earl asked.

Jim shook his head, "They're minors and have no say as yet. You should come prepared to speak of the money you found in Sylvia's luggage."

"I have the bill of sale for the cattle we sold back in June. The deposit of that exact amount that I made the day after their deaths should give some indication that the money was misplaced or unavailable for about nine or ten days," Earl explained.

"As you probably could guess, Monkey Jim and Goldie will, in all likelihood, be there. I've alerted the Sheriff. He said he would be there and frisk Smith before he's allowed in the courtroom," Jim assured Earl.

"Jim what I tell you is in strict confidence," Earl said earnestly, "even financial matters, yes."

Hart nodded, "That's right. I could be disbarred if I broke confidences."

"On these two cattle drives we made over seven thousand dollars before expenses," Earl smiled proudly. "I didn't make as much on this last bigger drive but cattle prices, while I was buying, was falling really fast. The only reason we did as well on the last one is because we got a special deal."

"You can bring up that you did well on the cattle drives, but I wouldn't bring up the amount you made at the hearing," Jim warned.

Earl continued, "I sold all of the steers and some older canners and all the young heifers from the home place and in Tyrone. But I've been busy replenishing the herd by creating some new younger steers and buying better heifer stock to replace the heifer's I sold. As you probably know already, inbreeding can be a problem. I have two good bulls and another young one about ready to start mounting heifers. I just don't want my bulls making calves with their own offspring."

"I understand, Earl."

Earl smiling, said, "I hear Dillard's voice in the outer office. Why don't you call him in, he's my new foreman."

Jim Hart rose and went to his office door and said loud enough for Dillard to hear, "Come on back in the office, Dillard."

By the time Jim was seated, Dillard was entering the office. Earl stood and introduced Dillard, "This is the foreman for the Sigler livestock enterprise, Dillard Lay." Jim stood back up and shook Dillard's hand.

"Pleased to meet you, Dillard," Jim said, "I'm Jim Hart. I've been the Sigler family attorney for over forty years now and working on the third generation." Jim smiled, "That makes me pretty old."

Earl said, "I hired Dillard to do what I used to do and maybe a little bit more. He's been a good friend to me. He taught me the finer points on quail hunting."

Dillard looked pleased and said jokingly, "But I bet I'm paid less."

Earl smiled, "I'm not going to get into that discussion."

"All I can tell you, Mister Hart, is that this job offer come at an awful good time," Dillard said.

"Just call me Jim, Dillard."

"Anyway," Dillard continued, "we just lost our house to the bank. I was only workin' one day, sometimes two at the sawmill with the hard times. I worked some at the Kidd Store and spelled Nick on his milk run ever now and then. It was beginnin' to make it hard to make ends meet."

Earl rose, "If that's all. I better get going if I'm going to dodge by the bank real quick and stop by to pick up my brother and sisters from Vacation Bible School."

Dillard and Earl went to the car quickly and drove to Raymondville to pick up his cancelled checks for the month. They drove south to Yukon and west to Ozark Church and from there they headed south to Grandview Church. Everyone was gone. Earl and Dillard caught up to Lucille, Glen and Vivian a little over a half mile south. When Earl pulled up in front of the house, the cow hands were standing in the shade of the big Black Oak, with their mounts ground tethered.

Earl got out of the car quickly, pulling out his pocket watch. It was a quarter to twelve. "Dillard, we've got time before dinner, let's get these horses down to the barn and get some oats in them. They've worked hard and deserve it."

Earl and George took off the pack saddles. Lucille, Glen and Vivian were watching closely. When Earl noticed, he said to them, "Can you take these pack saddles to the back porch and we'll unpack them later? The dishes need to be cleaned and the food put in the pantry."

Earl mounted one of the pack mules and rode down to the barn behind George who was leading the mules by their tethers.

When Dillard got to the barn, he herded the pigs out of the corral into the pen by the Mill pond.

When all the men got back to the house it was time to eat. Earl was pleased that all had stuck together and all were going to eat dinner: Lonnie, Dillard, Paul, George, Mack, Jess Jones, Jess Lay, Ray, Johnny, John Dunivan and John Bradford, as fine a group of cow hands around.

The men were happy to be able to sit on chairs on the front porch or sit on the edge of the porch after eating meals on the ground on the trail. There was crispy fried chicken, mashed potatoes, gravy, a stewed tomato and green bean dish in creamy sauce. After dinner the men ate all four black berry pies with heaps of freshly churned ice cream on top.

As the men were leaving, Earl put his arm around George's shoulders. "Thanks for coming along, George. I could have gotten someone else but not as good, by far."

"Ask me again and I'll come."

"I wanted you to tell Gould something," Earl said. "I'm hoping to be back for the double header on Sunday, but I won't be able to pitch and I may not be able to play third, maybe first base."

After George left to get his horse and head off for Sargent, Earl walked through the kitchen where Fern and Dana were busy washing and drying dishes. He went upstairs and packed a small valise with two extra shirts, pants, socks, underwear, his glove and spikes. He left his riding boots by his bed.

* * * * * * * * * * * *

Earl stopped to fill his gasoline tank in Mountain Grove. He got to Springfield late in the afternoon. He stopped and asked where he could find South Kimbrough. They gave him good directions. As he drove on

South Kimbrough he watched for 1710. When he found the small house, he parked in front. He walked to the door and knocked. Mabel Ogle came to the door. When she saw who it was a frown of disapproval found its way to her face.

Earl noticed but asked, "Is Eva here?"

"No, Earl. She's at the library doing some research for a paper due this week."

"Where is it? I'll go find her," Earl insisted.

"No you won't. She doesn't need to be disturbed while she's studying. Come back after supper and I'll let her know you're coming."

Earl decided not argue the point since Mable's hostility was so palpable. He turned and retreated to the green Plymouth.

Earl remembered a hotel in the downtown area. He drove back around the block and back north on Jefferson until he came to the middle of the city. He saw the Herr's store and turned back east toward the hotel. He went into the lobby and booked a room for the night. He thought he should ask about staying a second night. The clerk assured him there would be a room available for Saturday night.

Earl went up to his room. It was cooled with newly installed air-conditioning. He laid down on the bed and fell instantly asleep. When he awoke, it was after six o'clock. He anxiously splashed water on his face an combed his hair.

When Earl came out to the car there was a piece of paper under his windshield wiper. Earl plucked it off and put it in his pocket without glancing at it.

He drove south on Kimbrough again to the Ogle's. When he parked in front, Eva opened the door and strode down the walk. Eva, his beautiful Eva. Earl quickly opened the driver's side door, strode around the front, and held the other door open for her. She gracefully sat in the passenger seat and Earl walked around to the driver's side. "Where to?" Earl asked.

He was hoping she would suggest a nice restaurant or small café. He was hungry.

"Earl, we need to talk." Eva said it with a flat unemotional tone.

Earl thought to himself, this is bad.

"I'll direct you how to get to Phelps Grove Park south of the College."

Eva directed him and they came to a nice city park with picnic tables, a play ground with swings, metal slides, teeter totters, and push-go-rounds. Eva had him park by a picnic table and she walked over and sat on the wood seat. Eva pointed to the seat across from her. This was going to be no picnic, Earl thought.

Eva looked him squarely in the eye, "I talked to Mama and Papa about you and what I should do."

"What you should do? I don't understand, Eva."

"They said I should just drop you. Ignore you and it would be over."

"Over. Over? Please, Eva, if you knew how much I love you, you couldn't say it's 'over.'" Earl's voice was quivering with emotion.

"You're a married man, Earl. I cannot see you. I can't have anything to do with you anymore. How could you expect me to feel any other way. You deceived me. You were not truthful with me. I fell so in love with you," Eva's face was ashen, tears coursed down her cheeks.

Earl reached for her hand on the top of the picnic table. When his hand touched hers she snatched it back as if she had burned it.

"Take me back to the Ogles'. Now. I knew I'd cry and I don't cry easy. But I didn't want them to see me cry." Eva rose and walked back to the car and got in the passenger side.

Earl sat in the driver's side but didn't start the car. He said, "You said you love me and I am crazy in love with you. I can't do without you. This is the worst time of my life right now. We've got to work this out."

"Take me back."

"I only stayed with Ruth Evans for one day after we were married. I didn't even sleep with her after we were married. I just didn't want the child not to have its real name. I don't consider myself married but I can take care of that," Earl said emphatically.

"We're going to Ogles' now," Eva was persistent.

Earl said, "I'm pleased that you got the teaching job."

"It's only a half year. I taught last year. Someone on the board has a son who was going to teach this year. Now he'll not finished school 'til December. I'll have to find a job for the last half year."

Earl was more hopeful, now. "That's good. Would you like to go to a movie or something this evening."

"No!" Steel in her voice now, "Take me to Ogles'."

Earl started the car and they drove in silence to 1710 South Kimbrough. Eva alit from the car and literally ran to the house. Mable opened the door and let Eva in.

Earl started to follow Eva up the walk, hoping to talk to her some more. Mabel met him at the door. "I just wanted to say goodbye to Eva."

Mable said savagely, "Come back when you're not married."

* * * * * * * * * * *

Earl drove slowly back to the hotel. He felt there was nothing else to do but go home. He checked out and they told him they couldn't give a refund. He told them he didn't want one since he had taken a nap on their bed and used their water and wash towel. He asked where he could get a good bottle of whiskey. The clerk softly whispered directions to a speakeasy on Sunshine. Earl thought, that's nice, it's right on my way. He stopped and bought two bottles. Earl was really hungry, now, despite the emotional turmoil. He stopped at a small diner and ordered a hamburger with onions and mustard. He wrapped it in a paper napkin and took it with him. Earl ate the burger and nipped on the bottle past Monett. The new highway 60 was fast driving. He made up his mind to stay in Sargent, remembering Fern's warning. The rest of the way he smoked one Lucky after another interspersed with a drink from the bottle. By the time Earl got to Cabool, almost three fourths of a bottle was gone.

By the time he got to Sargent it was right at nine o'clock. When Earl parked in front of the new house under construction there was a light in the window. George came out when he heard the car. Earl got out with the bottle in his hand, swaying perceptibly.

The sun had set with a rosy hue still in the Western sky. It was already heavy dusk down here in the valley. When George got close enough to recognize who it was, he said, "That was a fast trip. Looks like you're a little worse for the wear."

"Don't give me any of your malarkey, George," Earl held out the bottle, "Here have a nip."

George took the bottle, opened it and had a chug. He wiped his mouth with the back of his hand.

Earl held out his hand.

George shook his head, "I think you've had enough for today. The little woman throw you over?"

The words pierced at Earl, "Don't give me anymore of your mouth or your chin will feel it."

"I'm really worried, Earl," George chuckled, "You couldn't hit the broad side of a barn in your condition."

"Yep. You're probably right."

"Let's go up and find a bed for us. We've got to get up and do chores. Five comes mighty early," George complained. "I'll find a place for the bottle before we go up."

They walked up the long steep stairs to the main house. Harold and Morgan were awake, listening to the radio, a mystery of some kind. They shushed them. George motioned Earl to the Kitchen. George went to the refrigerator and took out grape jelly and got peanut butter off the shelf. "You know where the bread box is, Earl. Get us some bread for a sandwich."

When the bread was on the table. George sliced off four slices. Finally, George said, "You didn't even notice."

"Yes, I did," Earl said.

"No you didn't."

"Yes I did. You got rid of your old ice box and got a new one, that white one."

George laughed loudly, "That's no icebox that's a refrigerator. Mom just had to have one and Pop couldn't turn her down."

Earl looked around, "Looks like your dad threw in a new stove, too."

The two young men slathered peanut butter and jelly on their bread. "My Mom sure appreciates it. It's not near so hot cooking here in the kitchen. Plus I don't have to lug ice up the hill or split wood for the stove."

"Now that all these modern things have saved you all this time, how about us going fishing tomorrow?" Earl said.

"That's a swell idea. Let's go talk to Pop about it."

When the radio story was over. Morgan was approached about the idea. He suggested that they go fishing in Jacks Fork and they all get together at Skaggs or Bradford's for a fish supper. Harold wanted to go. So it was set. Morgan would do his chores early and head over to Skaggs if no one was there he would know to go to Charlie and Mary's.

The next morning when Aunt Jennie found out what they were up to she made sandwiches to have for breakfast and lunch on the way and insisted on going along to visit her sisters all day. As it turned out Henry wanted to go fishing, too. They stopped at Earl's folks and walked down the valley with their gear and got John Dunivan to go along. With five men and Harold fishing, the caught a dozen perch in the slough on the elder John Bradford place. There were several nice places to fish on down the valley on North Jacks Fork and another slough. They caught two dozen perch on worms. On Jack's Fork John, George, Earl, Henry, and Harold caught ten large bass. Henry left at two o'clock to go back and do his chores. On the way back John took a bass and a couple of perch for their supper.

When George, Harold and Earl got back to Skaggs' house, Mary, Effie and Hattie were there. Lula was there, too. Ray had brought her over and gone back down to help Charlie cut wood for the winter. Earl had wondered why no one was at the house. Effie said, Ray would go back and do his chores and Charlie would do his and all three brothers-in-law would be there to eat between six thirty and seven. The ladies said they would take care of cleaning the fish if the boys would go to the river for a swim and get rid of their chiggers and ticks. George and Harold had brought a change of clothes, at the insistence of their mother. Earl had a change of clothes in the Plymouth. The three young cousins headed for the Lay Hole and promised to be back in time for supper.

* * * * * * * * * * *

When Eva came back into the house from seeing Earl she went straight into her bedroom. She lay down on the bed with an arm over her eyes.

When Eva came in and Mabel heard Earl's car driving away, Mabel waited a minutes before she went in to see Eva. She knocked lightly on the door frame. Eva said, "Come in Mabel," without removing her arm.

Mabel went in and sat on the edge of the bed. "Come sit in the living room by the fan," Mabel urged, "It'll cool off more in here when you're ready for bed,"

"Mabel, what am I going to do?" Eva lamented.

"Come sit by the fan."

Mabel rose and left the room.

Eva got up slowly as if a great weight was upon her, following slowly into the living room. The fan did make it seem cooler.

Mabel lounged in a corner of the sofa and Eva settled in an overstuffed chair.

"That's a tough question. My answer would be do nothing."

"That's easy for you to say," Eva replied, "You're not desperately in love with that man."

"I know about love a little, but isn't 'desperate' a little strong," Mabel affirmed.

"Would 'acutely' work better, Mabel?"

"I still think doing nothing right now is the only answer." Mabel allowed a more serious note to come out. "You did read the riot act to him. Told him you couldn't be seeing a married man."

Eva said, "Yes I did."

"Then it's his move."

"How do you mean that?" Eva asked.

"Would you want to go forward if he was divorced?" Mabel asked.

"That's a bridge I hadn't thought of crossing. He cannot be unmarried without going through a divorce. I'd sure have to pray on it and talk with my folks if that happened." Eva became very thoughtful for a long time before she continued, "You're right. It really is his move. I'll just have to wait."

"Good girl. Thinking like you've got a brain in that pretty skull of yours. You're the sister I never had. A little bit of sisterly advice sometimes works."

"You're right. I'll concentrate on my studies. I only have a month to go and I do want to get good marks." Eva's voice quivered, "I'm sorry I got a continuation of the job at Stultz it's so close to Tyrone. I'm not happy I got a job at Clear Springs the last half of year. It would have been better if I had a job down far South in Howell County.

Mabel thought it was time for a little humor to lighten things up, "I talked to Kenneth, my sweety, about your problem. He thought a good sharp kick might have been appropriate and not in the shins."

Eva giggled like a teenager. That story had gone around school among the girls years ago of how to hurt the male sex the worst possible way.

Eva left the room and got her book on American History and sat in the chair she had vacated a couple of minutes before.

Mabel was looking through a second-hand Good Housekeeping magazine.

At nine o'clock her farm girl habits overtook Eva. She stood, a slender 5' 7" woman, and headed for bed. She slipped light weight pajamas on and settled in bed. Sleepless. For a while she thought about Earl and wondered if he was thinking of her. Talking to God helped take her mind off her romantic problems and she became drowsy. It was probably fortunate she did not know what Earl was doing to take his mind off his romantic problems.

* * * * * * * * * * *

When Earl and his cousins returned to Skaggs' for supper. They were regaled with a great fried fish supper. When the men went to sit outside after the meal where it was cooler, the mosquitoes drove them back indoors. The conversation was so boring, Earl motioned George to follow him back outside. George followed him to the Plymouth. It was twilight. Earl sat in the driver's side and pulled his whiskey from behind the seat. He opened the bottle and took a long drink. He held the bottle out to George.

George shook his head, "I can't go back in with liquor on my breath and it's not a good idea for you either."

"George," Earl said, "Eva won't see me because I'm married. I don't consider myself married. I haven't lived with Ruth for over two years now."

"You're married?" George questioned, "I thought you were divorced. No wonder. I'd dump you, Too, if I was her."

"Thanks, George. You've given me something to think about."

"You're welcome," George answered.

"I best head on back to Tyrone. Fern asked me to bring her down to Clear Springs tomorrow," Earl said. "I pretty near forgot about it."

George got out of the Plymouth. Earl started the car and drove back home to Tyrone.

CHAPTER 17 -

An Abysmal Fall

The days moved as slowly as molasses from a jug. Except for two unusual occurrences, widely separated, everything was routine. Earl's time was occupied by buying hogs, cattle, horses and occasionally a few sheep from individual farmers. He bought over a hundred heifer's to replace the older cows and young heifers he had included in the cattle drive.

The day Earl took his grandmother and aunt to Houston for the Probate Hearing was momentous. Earl insisted on going to Jim Hart's office early to take care of some personal business. He asked about a divorce. Hart said he would draw up the papers that day and submit them to the court. Jim warned that it might take five or six months, or more, to get on the docket. Earl revealed that he had been faithfully giving Ruth Evans (he still thought of her in that way) forty dollars a month out of what Elmer had paid him for his work. Jim said he would include that figure in the application for the divorce. Earl urged Hart to move the procedure along as fast as he could.

When Earl, Sarah and Pearl came to the courtroom where the Probate Hearing was to be held, Monkey Jim Smith was there already. A Sheriff's deputy was patting Smith down with the Sheriff looking on. Monkey Jim said, "You touch my privates and you'll regret it."

"Shut up, Smith. You can get arrested for making threats to an officer of the law," Sheriff Kelly growled. "You're done. You can go on in."

Earl, Sarah and Pearl followed Jim Smith in. Golda was sitting on the left side and her father sat beside her. The Sigler clan sat on the other side, with Earl by the aisle and just behind Jim Hart.

It started off explosive. After the judge ascertained who was there and asked who would speak first. Jim Hart stood.

"Your honor I submitted some documents to the court on behalf of my Clients, Sarah Sigler, Pearl Miller, Sarah's daughter, and Earl Sigler, the son of Elmer and grandson of Sarah. Sarah and Pearl have asked that Earl work on their behalf to continue to operate the family business of farming, ranching and livestock trading. The Sigler's have also bought and sold furniture. Earl has brought some documents that are original that we will place in front of you to corroborate any testimony Earl should make."

"Bring them forward."

Earl whispered what each of the things he gave him represented.

"This stack of checks represent the activity in the business account in the name of Earl Sigler. There is a savings account of over seven thousand dollars in Sarah Sigler's name. There is a small checking account in the name of Sarah Sigler. There are three savings accounts in the names of Earl's three siblings, Lucille, Glen and Vivian. The bank has not sent out their monthly statement yet but they gave a balance of both checking accounts." Jim Hart stopped for a breath and continued, "Your honor if you have any questions, please ask. After you've had a chance to look this over, I have some explanations and comments About what I've presented to you."

Judge D. L. Johnson riffled through the canceled checks. Looked at the balances in the savings accounts and the two checking accounts. After he saw the balance in Earl's checking account, he looked up at Earl with his eyebrows raised in surprise, "This is an excessive amount in your checking account. It's nearly fifteen thousand dollars. That's more than they pay me in two or three years, young man."

Monkey Jim Smith jumped to his feet. "Half that money's mine," pointing his finger at Earl he shouted, "Him and Elmer kilt my little girl. Maybe all of hit should belong to me." Spittle flew from his mouth.

The Judge was pounding his gavel while this was going on. He said sternly, "You'll have your turn. Another outburst like that in my court, I'll have you evicted, maybe even arrested, and for sure fined. Do I make myself clear."

Earl stood, "Your honor. Let me explain about the large balance. I must keep a fairly large balance on hand to conduct the livestock business. When we made a cattle drive, I bought over one thousand three hundred head of cattle. I had to write checks for about thirty thousand dollars. In less than a month I have added nearly six thousand dollars in profit to the business account."

"Thank you, Earl, for that explanation. I have a comment and a question. You unquestionably are an able young business man. How is it that the bank allows you to spend more than you have in your account?"

Earl stood again, "Thank you for the compliment but a lot of it was my Father's doing. The bank allows me to overdraft because they know I'm always good for it. We also own a portion of the bank."

The Judge said, "That's a good explanation."

Jim Hart stood again, "If you noticed the large deposits that were made early in the month and late in the month. The very large deposit at the end of the month represented the sale of the herd Earl alluded to that he delivered to a buyer in Rolla, Missouri. It took twelve men to deliver the herd. Earl Sigler has employed a full-time foreman to manage the farm and ranch operations. He also employs a young man nearly full time as a driver to deliver livestock to the National Stock Yards in East Saint Louis, Illinois. He employs a full time housekeeper to help with his brother and sisters. He employs many others part-time." Holt took a couple of breaths and continued, "The large deposit on the fifth of July represents the amount of the sale of another herd by Elmer nine days before. The smaller deposit was a little less than six thousand dollars. It was found in Sylvia's luggage by Earl Sigler on the afternoon before the funeral. Apparently, Sylvia was preparing to go someplace with over seventeen thousand dollars of the family's cash resources."

Monkey Jim Smith jumped up again, "Yer honor, you cain't just let this shyster lawyer accuse my dead daughter of stealin'. You shouldn't 'low hit."

The Judge was much more tolerant of Smith's outburst this time, since he was more polite about it. Johnson said, "We're all grieved by the loss of your daughter. You'll have your say. If you interrupt again the Sheriff is hereby instructed to remove you from the room."

Earl whispered to Hart, "Ask the judge to let me explain."

"You honor, my client, Earl Sigler would like to speak to the court." Hart rose as he was speaking.

Earl stood. "This may take a while."

"Go ahead, Mister Sigler."

Earl began, "When we sold the herd back in June, Elmer, my father, got a check and he didn't trust a stranger's check so he took it to the local bank in Rolla and asked for cash. I am quite certain that he got back to Raymondville too late to deposit the money and took it home with him. I am presuming that Sylvia found the money or knew where my father put it. She probably, in her mind, felt that it belonged to her as much as it did him. At any rate, after they died, I did go through Sylvia's luggage and found the cattle drive money. Not a dollar was missing. After I got my father's personal effects from his pocket, his daily business account gave the exact amount he had received. If she had left with the money, it would have devastated this family. Even though large amounts of cash is involved, that money is needed to make a business like ours go on from day to day." Earl paused and took a couple of deep breaths before continuing, "As for the smaller amount, I believe that Sylvia set aside small amounts of cash each week from the money Elmer gave her for food, clothing and other essentials. A sort of rainy day fund. I discovered this in her luggage in a brown paper sack tied up with string. After all the money was counted. I knew that the money from the cattle drive had to go back into the running of the family business. I have since set up a business account in mine and my grandmother's names. The problem, in my mind, was what to do with the smaller amount of cash." Earl paused again for breath, "I consulted with a man whose wisdom I trust. He suggested that the family divide it up among the six surviving family members. I took that suggestion back to my grandmother and aunt and added my own suggestion to set up a thousand dollar savings accounts for my sisters and brother. My aunt and grandmother insisted that we put the balance back into the working account. And that's where we are right now."

The Judge nodded, "Well explained, Mister Sigler. I am impressed with your business acumen and with the way you handle yourself. You're pretty young to be thrown into such a vortex but I think you'll do well by your family."

Earl could see Monkey Jim squirming in his seat across the aisle

Monkey Jim could contain himself no longer, "Yer honor, that cattle money don't belong to me but that other money was Sylvia's and as her father hit should be mine."

The Judge looked menacingly at Monkey Jim, "I told you to be quiet, but I'll ask you questions that you don't need to answer. What about your wife? Your daughter? Your grandchildren by Sylvia? I don't think so. It is Sigler money. I am convinced that Earl, his grandmother and aunt have done exactly the right thing."

Earl said quietly, "May I speak again, your honor?"

Judge Johnson nodded.

"I am willing to give up my share, your honor." Earl said, pulling his checkbook from his pocket, "I'll write a check for a thousand dollars payable to Mister Smith, right now." Earl realized that he should not have goaded Monkey Jim because of his reaction.

Smith was back on his feet again, glaring at Earl, "No siree, Sigler. You're not buyin' me for no measly thousen' dollars. You and your pop kilt my little girl."

Earl jumped to his feet and was turning to go at Smith but found the burly Sheriff Kelly blocking his way. The Sheriff's deputy had a hand gripping Monkey Jim's arm. The Sheriff turned away from Earl and grabbed Monkey Jim Smith's other arm and they crow hopped him down the aisle from the courtroom.

Earl sat back down with the Judge pounding the podium. "I'll have order in this court. Right now."

The murmuring stopped.

Johnson looked at Jim Hart, "Counselor, do you have anything more?"

"Yes, your honor, I do." He turned to Earl and said, "Do you have the original of the Quit Claim Deed?"

Earl handed him a folder with the document in it.

"Your honor, if I may approach the bench, I have a document that I would like for you to see and I will explain its background," Hart said.

Judge Johnson held out his hand and Hart walked quickly up and gave it to the judge. Johnson read it and he turned it over and over twice. Finally he said, "So! It's a signed Quit Claim Deed. It has no recorder's notation on it."

Hart back at his seat now, said, "Yes your honor I know that. Let me explain." He hesitated and the judge nodded. "Elmer Sigler came to my office early on Friday morning of the third of July, the day before he killed his wife and himself, which has been established by a Coroner's Hearing. He asked me to draw up this document handing over his property to his mother. I told him he would need to record it, even though I thought he probably knew that anyway. Earl Sigler called me the morning after the tragic occurrence. I told him it was imperative that he find an important document I had prepared for his father. Earl remembered Elmer's return that Friday and that Elmer had an envelope in his hand that he put in the truck. I asked Earl to bring it with him to an appointment we set for Sunday afternoon. Earl brought his grandmother and aunt with him. I was totally surprised to find the document was not recorded. I sort of guessed at Elmer's purpose. I think he was going to use it as a wedge to try and keep Sylvia from running off again. You know she has done that several times. Elmer had put in papers for divorce three different times but never carried through with it."

Judge Johnson asked, "Is this all of the family's concerns? How about the ladies or Earl?"

All three shook their heads and Hart said, "That's it, your honor."

The judge looked at Golda, "Young lady, you have anything to say before we bring your father back in?"

"Yes sir, your honor. I don't like at all the way this is going. My father had some really legitimate concerns. That man," she pointed her finger at Jim Hart, "and that man," pointing her finger at Earl, "are making my sister to be some kind of thief, that she deserved to die. Maybe Earl Sigler and the rest of them are as much to blame for her death as Elmer was."

Judge Johnson interrupted her before she could continue, "That'll be enough of that. The Corner's Hearing established that Sylva's death was at her husband's hand and no one else was involved. There were several witnesses called and that was established without a doubt. You will not. I repeat, you will not make that accusation again in this room."

"Sheriff, you may bring Mister Smith back in." the judge said, looking from Golda to Kelly.

A few seconds passed before Monkey Jim entered the courtroom flanked by the Sheriff and his deputy. Smith's face was still red from anger or embarrassment. He sat heavily by his younger daughter.

Judge Johnson scowled at Smith and said, "I will not tolerate any more accusations of misbehavior of the Sigler family in regard to Sylva's murder. Now is the time to have your say."

"Yer honor. I came to tell yeh that half that farm and half of the money belong to me and my family. That is the pure truth of the matter," Jim Smith said.

The Judge nodded his head, "That is a good explanation of your position."

Monkey Jim looked pleased and sat back down.

Judge Tolbert continued, "However, under the law as written in the Missouri State Codes, the first heirs are considered the issue, or children, if you will. Do you understand that Mister Smith."

"Hit may be the Code but I dasent have to like hit. Mebbe they's need to have hit taken outen their hides," Smith muttered loud enough for everyone in the room to hear.

Judge Johnson banged his gavel loudly, "I'll not countenance any threats, actual or implied in this Court. Do you understand me Mr. Smith."

James Hart rose quickly, "Your honor, I propose, on behalf of my clients, that Earl Sigler be appointed Executor of the Estate of the late Elmer Sigler and that he be appointed guardian of his sisters Lucille and Vivian and his brother Glen."

The Judge tapped his gavel lightly, "That is a fine proposal. This court hereby orders that Earl Sigler be appointed Executor of the Estate and guardian of Lucille, Glen and Vivian, his siblings."

Jim Smith leapt to his feet, "Yer honor. Yeh jest cain't to this. Earl Sigler knocked up some fifteen year old girl and they sent her off to Kansas City to have hit and give hit away. He knocked up another teenage girl and had to marry her becuz Elmer wouldn't bail him out a second time. He ain't fitten to take care of my little granchilern."

Earl was embarrassed to have his sordid past paraded publicly. He was deeply ashamed. He tugged on Hart's coat hem. Hart leaned over. Earl whispered, "Should I say something."

"I'll take care of it," the attorney whispered.

Hart stood, "I'd like to address this issue. Jim Smith's past is not clean but I won't stoop to specifics. My client's actions over the past several months have been exemplary, especially since the death of his father. They speak for his good character and business acumen."

The Judge tapped his gavel on the bench, "It is the judgment of this court that Earl Sigler, being an adult child of Elmer Sigler, is a capable young man and I hereby appoint him to be guardian of his minor sisters and brother, Lucille, Glen and Vivian Sigler. I hereby appoint him to be Executor of the Elmer Sigler's Estate until the final settlement by this court. I require an accounting of all assets and debits of this estate to be provided to this Court by September first of 1931. I will appoint a four bondsmen for the Estate. Mister Sigler will provide me a list within a week of ten or twelve citizens of the town of Tyrone. I will select four after some inquiries. The Siglers must pay promptly any costs incurred by the court to oversee this matter. This order will be provided to your attorney within two working days in writing. Any questions?"

Jim Smith stood again, "Whar do I come in?"

The Judge said firmly, "You don't."

"I want to be one of the four bondsmen to make sure my granchilern are proper took keer of. And I want someone I know on with me."

Judge Johnson looked at Earl and Hart quizzically, "What do you think of this proposal?"

Earl leaned forward and whispered to Jim Hart. Holt said, "Mister Sigler would like to address the Court."

The Judge nodded and said, "Do so."

Earl stood, speaking slowly, "I really don't have any serious objection to Jim Smith and another Tyrone resident being in oversight. I think it is really important that Mister Smith, as my brother and sisters' grandfather being vitally interested in their welfare and seeing them on a regular basis. My one concern is if he tries to cause mischief in the oversight."

The Judge tapped his gavel, "It is so ordered. Mister Smith can pick one from the names Mister Sigler provides. But I don't think it advisable to have Mister Smith as a bondsman."

Earl quickly wrote down twelve names and Jim Hart took the list forward to the Judge. He read the names aloud and said, "Mister Smith you have a week to pick one."

Monkey Jim said quickly, "I know who I want. Mister Grogan."

Earl was immediately suspicious why Smith would pick so quickly. He might find out later, he thought.

* * * * * * * * * *

Eva was studying hard; she wanted to get good marks in her studies. She had some difficulty with one of the teachers early in the year. Eva felt like she had been singled out for some abuse, that she failed to understand. Eva decided to confide in Mabel about the problem.

A few days later, Eva and Mabel were having lunch at home. Mabel said, "Kenneth is right on top of your problem with this male professor of yours. Kenneth knows him and had classes with him. He's getting up close to fifty now and he hasn't gotten over women's emancipation yet. He's intimidated by smart, pretty young women. He said he saw it happen in this man's classes before. He suggested that you not be too quick to give right answers until he calls on you. Give the right answer when called on and then act a little ditzy about something unimportant, then you'll get a good grade."

It worked like a charm. She gave right answers and brought up something that made her look a little off kilter. The professor nodded when she gave the right answer and looked knowingly back at his class when she did strange things. Her final grade was a whole lot better than her mid-term. An E no less.

Eva had gotten a part-time job at Heers Department Store on the square. The prior year had been one of the hottest in over a century. The ownership had ordered air conditioning installed during the spring of 1931. It was wonderful to work there in the cool. Eva had written to her mother and father and told them about it and encouraged them to come up shopping now that they had an automobile and the extra income from her father's job in town. She had gotten a card back that they were planning to come up the first week in August. Eva looked forward to that.

The ache in her heart, her soul, every fiber of her being called for her to set her pen to paper, to make contact with Earl again. They had telephone in the city but she knew that it was impossible to just call Earl and ask him to come to see her since rural Texas county had no phone service.

The family came on a Saturday, the seventh day of August. They left the chores in Clyde and Esther's hands, promising that the next Summer they could come by themselves. They all had a wonderful time that day. The whole clan came to supper at the Ogles' house. They left by seven in the evening so they would have some daylight to drive by.

Eva tried to keep as busy as possible to take her mind off her lost love, that wouldn't go away in her heart. She yearned for Earl's arms. She wanted to talk to her mother about it, to her father but she didn't want to ruin their day. She would have this conversation when she got home. She knew which of her parents would oppose her in the relationship with Earl if she wanted to continue it.

She wrote a penny post card to CC Morgan and told him she would be there on the evening of the thirtieth of August and be ready to teach the next morning. When Eva had met CC the year before she had asked him what his name was and he said, "Everyone calls me CC, I've never known anything else. He was a forty-two year old bachelor. He had taken a real fancy for her. The school had arranged for her to stay at George and Isabelle Morgan's. The school district paid for her room and board. Her monthly check was free and clear except what she paid for her personal needs. She bought a couple of nice dresses, a warm winter coat and a few nice hats. She particularly liked fancy hats. By the middle of the year she had accumulated a nice wardrobe, nice feminine under things and silk stockings. She began to wear some make-up for the first time. Her savings account in Willow grew and grew.

CC was the head of the school board. He came around quite regularly the first weeks she was teaching and would stay and have lunch with Eva. Eva had only had one serious boyfriend and she was totally unaware that CC was interested in her in a romantic way until the first pie supper. In early October they had the first one to help raise money to pay the cost of keeping the school going. Eva made an apple pie with fruit from one of Belle's trees. Eva offered to chip in for the cost of the flour, sugar, lard and spices it required. Belle said, "Nonsense," just like that. It was when CC bought her pie and tried to sit too close to her and casually put his arm across her shoulders, that she realized that it was his intention to pay her court. She did her best to fend off his attention without offending him too badly. In late February they had another pie supper. She did not prepare anything this time. CC was perturbed that she hadn't. After Eva met Earl she had her opportunity one day when he came by the school and "have lunch" with her.

Eva took him aside and said, "CC I appreciate your interest in me but I think I'm too young for you and beside that I have met a man more my own age that has captured my attention. I do so hope you find a woman who deserves you. You're a fine man." CC was not handsome but rugged and not ugly at all.

"Thank you for your kindness, Eva," CC said sincerely, "I had my hopes up but I'll keep trying."

CC came by to the school only one more time that year. Eva figured out that Earl had his Uncle Weed Morgan be the go between on her behalf. There was no doubt that her rebuff of CC had probably played into her only being offered a half year's employment. The last half year was a God-sent opportunity. The teacher in Clear Springs was planning a December wedding and the school could not continue her employment because of some antiquated laws which redounded to Eva's benefit.

Eva had some misgivings about teaching in the school where Earl went to church in the years after the family returned from Colorado. But, then, a job was a job.

* * * * * * * * * *

His torture was complete. Earl could remember Eva's arms around him, her lips on his but there was nothing he could do. His dreams at night were replete with happy times with the woman he loved. The dark dreams also haunted him. These competing emotions of happiness, despair, guilt, fear of failure led him more and more to the bottle. He became adept at hiding this from those who depended on him and loved him. He spend a night or two away from home in the Horton Hotel and other places.

He knew she would be living and working only minutes from him, that made his misery more complete. The answer came in his work. He played baseball again. He tried pitching but he could only last an inning or two. He played first base which didn't require as much throwing. He was the team's big offensive weapon. He was always good for two or three RBI a game. He came in to pitch sometimes in the middle of the game or the end of the game when he could make a difference, sometimes. Clear Springs lost more often now but they still had a lot of fun. Paul McKinney pitched more and got better and better with Earl's tutelage.

Spud Lynch played on the team and asked Earl several times to be included in the next cattle drive. Spud had a three quarter ton International truck. He frequented the same sale barns as Earl. He had bought about two hundred head of cattle he wanted to drive them to Rolla as Earl had done in July. Earl made it clear that it was more and more difficult to make a profit with cattle prices continuing to drop. However livestock made a strong rebound in early August. He alerted Spud that he intended to start buying for a smaller drive.

On Thursday, Friday and Saturday Earl went to Thayer, West Plains and Willow Springs, accumulating ninety-two steers and fifty-five heifers. Lonnie was kept busy driving truck, hauling the animals and leaving them in Ira and Pearl's east eighty.

Earl listened to the market report every day. Wednesday it was down some but back up on Thursday.

Earl had Lonnie move Ira's bull to the Tyrone pasture to keep him away from the heifers until they moved the herd out on Tuesday morning. He bought a few more cattle by Clear Springs. He had Lonnie, Dillard and John Dunivan move them up to Ira and Pearl's on Monday while Earl went to Summersville and bought more cattle of good quality.

Earl took one load home and sent Lonnie for the rest of the cattle while he went to the bank in Raymondville to phone the contract buyer, Joe Sullivan. Earl wanted an idea of what he could expect. He told Joe that another livestock trader would be coming along and bringing about two hundred head. Joe asked about quality. Earl assured him he had even better than the last time.

Earl dye marked over two hundred head of cattle so they could tell them from Spud's. Earl picked up fifteen more head by Yukon and eleven North of Raymondville on Tuesday. Earl drove the truck ahead to make the purchases and dye mark them. They had five drovers, John Dunivan, Paul McKinney, Lonnie Bailey, Ray Peabody, and Mack Hall not counting

Spud. Earl brought the provisions, bedrolls, cooking ware, eating utensils, extra saddle, bridle and a spare horses in the truck. In Licking Earl added sixteen steers and three heifers. Spud bought some poorer grade cattle.

When the herd arrived South of Rolla on Thursday morning on schedule, Earl was there waiting with Joe Sullivan. They drove the herd in the pasture and separated Earl's cattle from the herd and drove them through the chute so the buyer could get a good look at them, counting them.

When they were all through, Joe said, "I counted two hundred and forty-six. I estimated seven hundred and ten pounds. These are exceptional quality." He quoted a price higher than Earl expected. Earl accepted immediately.

When Spud's cattle went through the chute. Joe offered Spud a price. Spud was severely displeased and let Joe know in no uncertain terms. "You've offered me almost a half of a cent lower than you offered Earl," Spud complained loudly.

Joe pulled Spud aside so the others couldn't hear, "Your cattle are not prime as Earl's are. I am actually giving you more than I ordinarily would just because you are with Earl. You can drive them on up to the pens and put them on the train for East Saint Louis and take your chances in the sale ring."

When they were ready to leave. They loaded all seven horses with their saddles on into the truck With all the cow hands in the saddles. When they got home and were all unloaded Spud complained, "I'm going to lose money on this drive if I pay two cowhands and half the provisions as we agreed."

Earl said, "I'll pay the hands and you can forget about the grub." He resolved not to make another drive with Spud again.

Friday morning Earl drove to Raymondville to deposit his check from Joe Sullivan. He stopped by the store to pick up his mail. He kept hoping

Eva would relent and drop him a penny post card at least. When he came in Nick was minding the store. Nick said, "I thought you might just stay in bed with this bein' Friday the thirteenth."

"It's a lucky day. You don't even know what day of the month it is," Earl said. "I forgot to settle my bill at the end of the month. Let's do it now. From now on you should remind me."

Nick picked out the running account and said, "You owe sixteen dollars and thirty-seven cents."

"Let me see that. I don't believe it," Earl feigned anger.

Nick handed it to Earl. Earl scanned through it and was pleased to note that Fern had bought some things for herself.

Earl pulled his billfold out and gave Nick a twenty. "Looks okay after all. It should be more than that."

Nick said, "You forgot we took off for that butchered hog Dillard brought in."

Earl nodded and said, "Thanks, Nick."

Ray Miles congratulated Earl on another successful cattle drive when he came to deposit the check. Earl had wanted to see how Jana was getting along with feed for the pigs. When Earl inquired about her, Ray told him that he had to cut her back to part-time. Earl decided to go over to see how the feed was holding up. When he got to the house, Jana offered him some lemonade. It sounded good so he went in and sat at the kitchen table.

As she was pouring the lemonade Earl asked, "How's the feed holding out?"

"I probably need to buy some more," Jana replied.

Earl stood and pulled out twenty dollars. "Is this enough?"

"It's probably enough to last quite a while," Jana came around the table and took the bill from him. She did not move to sit down again and Earl thought she was wanting him to leave, so he reached for his glass and drank it down.

"How are the pigs doing?"

"Growing right along. They should be ready for market by October."

It was very quiet in the house. "Is everything going to be all right with you going on part time?"

"That's so nice of you to ask. You're thoughtful like your dad." She moved closer to Earl.

It was so quiet in the house Earl asked, "Your son must like to read, he's so quiet."

Jana said, "He's down at his grandparents."

Earl was becoming uncomfortable with her closeness to him and backed up a step, "Maybe we should go out and check on the pigs," he stated.

Jana stepped even closer to him and suddenly put her arms around his neck and kissed him firmly, wetly on the mouth. Earl responded almost instinctively, putting his arms around her waist and then took them quickly away. He took her arms away from him and placed them back at her side. He backed away to a more safe distance.

She spoke first, "Earl, I'm so sorry. I shouldn't have done that. You remind me so much of Elmer. You know he and I were intimate. I get so lonely. I miss him so much. I really, really loved him. I had hoped that he would divorce that hussy and marry me."

"Let's just forget it ever happened. I am really flattered, however, that you found me attractive. The truth is I'm in love with a woman who won't see me because I am married. I've started the process for divorce," Earl said earnestly.

Jana nodded, "Elmer told me about it. He was sorry later that he forced you to marry because he realized that you really didn't love Ruth like a husband should."

"The most awful part is Eva's going to be teaching school for close to four months just down the road and the last half year down by where my mother lives. I just don't know exactly how to go about approaching her," Earl said miserably.

"The question is: does she love you back?" Jana said.

"She said she did over and over and wrote me love letters that would nearly steam the glue open on the envelopes. Yes I believe she really did. She just said she couldn't be going out with a married man."

"I fell into that trap and it broke my heart, Earl. I would suggest that you continue to pursue her. Let her know you've started toward getting a divorce. A woman wants to be pursued."

Earl moved away another step, "Thanks, Jana, you give me hope. I'll plan to go over and see her as soon as she gets back home."

"Bring her over here. I'll tell her flat out not to let a divorce to stand in the way of love and I'll tell her she can trust your fidelity. I think it's marvelous how you handled me," Jana said sincerely.

"Okay. Let's go look at the pigs," Earl turned and walked out the door trailed by Jana.

Earl leaned on the fence looking in the pen where the pigs were. They were growing but he noticed that Elmer had failed to bring him over to have the little boars marked. "I'll bring some guys over to take care of the boars later today. They're getting pretty big for holding them to get it done. Do you like mountain oysters?"

"Yes we do. If you want to time it right, Earl, I'll treat you and your men to a supper you'll never forget. I'm a really great cook. You'll see what you're missing out on," Jana giggled mischievously.

"You're a lovely woman, Jana. The right man will come along for you, just you wait."

True to her word, Jana fed them some of the greatest pork ribs, baked potatoes, coleslaw and homemade bread. For dessert she served raisin pie. He had never had better pie. In the future he would always look for better raisin pie and never find it.

On the way back to Tyrone Earl met a line of thunderstorms swooping down from Houston, gusts of wind buffeted the green Plymouth. When he went through Yukon the rain pelted down and he hoped he would have no trouble at the ford on Big Creek. The creek was muddy but he was able to get across without incident. He drove through large puddles and by the time he pulled up in front of his house the rain had passed. He was pleased that rain had come to replenish the grass and water his corn crop on the home place. Earl took Lonnie and Paul Mckinney home, with mountain oysters to boot.

* * * * * * * * * *

Eva came home by train on the last Friday in August. She had a nice weekend with her family. She did have an opportunity to talk to her mother before breakfast on Saturday morning. Rena was adamant that Eva should never think of taking back up again with Earl. Eva assured her mother she hadn't read Earl's letters. She didn't tell her that she had kept them. Later on Saturday her father had listened dispassionately to Eva asking what she should do. She poured out her misery over loving a married man. Wayne had opened the door to the possibility of a reconciliation if Earl was divorced. Eva knew her mother would not countenance such a compromise.

They all went to church on Sunday morning. Eva prayed fervently for God's guidance in her life without mentioning her dilemma over Earl. Eva felt that God would know even though she hadn't overtly mentioned her concern. Would He help?

Late Sunday afternoon her father drove up the West Plains-Rolla Road and turned west toward Tyrone. It would be complete agony driving through without a stop to see Earl, Sarah, Pearl, Lucille, Glen and Vivian. Especially Earl, the man she loved with such passion that it was painful. When they drove by Earl's house, the truck was there, the green Plymouth.

He had to be home. She stifled the impulse to ask her father to pull into the drive. She imagined herself alighting from her father's car and dashing toward the house. She could just feel Earl's strong arms. Oh, the pain. It would be an abysmal Fall.

* * * * * * * * * *

Earl knew that Eva would be coming in by train on Friday evening. He went to West Plains to buy hogs. The market has been down quite a bit for four days in a row. He knew when prices were down for several days, there usually was a rebound. Earl bought some good quality hogs. He would have Lonnie take them to the National Stockyards in East Saint Louis. Earl had several people write cards looking for some good Jersey or Guernsey milk cows, preferably ones that were bumping. These farmers who had asked him to deliver these cows lived between Willow and Tyrone or close proximity so Earl had planned to try buying them in Willow or Summersville.

Earl had driven by himself in the Plymouth. Lonnie came down later in the day after delivering a load of Cattle to the stock yards overnight. On his way back through Willow he stopped at the Horton Hotel Café and sat by a window looking over the train platform. He didn't know the schedule for arrivals but he wanted to be there just in case a train arrived and he could get a glimpse of Eva. Could he stand it? That was the question in his mind.

After the waitress came by for the fourth time to ask if he would like dessert, he thought he should give up his table since it was becoming crowded with customers in for an evening meal. He rose reluctantly and stood on the front porch of the hotel. What if Eva did show up?, Earl thought. It could be an embarrassment to Eva and, even, to himself. He hurried to the Plymouth and drove home.

When he pulled up in front of his house, Fern and his sisters and brother were sitting on the front porch enjoying the coming cool of the evening. Fern was reading the newspaper from Saint Louis that Earl had ordered and came by mail. It was a day old by the time it came but Earl wanted it to get some of the news and analysis of livestock trends.

The two younger kids came racing to meet Earl at the front gate. Lucille got up and walked toward him regally, like a princess, Earl thought. Fern looked over the top of the paper and smiled. Earl had taken several jolts from his bottle behind the front seat on the way but had bought a container of Sen Sen to mask the odor so it wouldn't be noticeable to Fern.

When Earl got to the porch, Fern said, "We didn't wait supper but we have leftovers in the warming oven in case you came back hungry."

"No thanks. I ate in Willow." The hurt expression in Fern's eyes cut him to the quick, "I'll explain my folly later, Fern." The hurt was lessened.

Earl hugged his sisters and put his arm across Glen's shoulders comradely. "I'm going to walk down to Grandma's. I need some personal advice. Maybe I'll need some from you, too, Fern. Did John stop by? Last time we were down at the home place the tenant still had not completely moved out."

Fern shook her head, "Haven't seen him."

Earl was so glad to have Fern. He would offer to buy some inexpensive furnishings in St. Louis at an auction, maybe take John and Fern along.

"I'll be back in a bit," Earl said and strode off down the street toward Sarah's house. She was sitting on the front porch waiting for it to cool enough to go to bed. It was still very hot. The summer had recorded many heat records. She was in her night dress and night cap already. When Earl mounted the stairs Sarah smiled broadly.

"Your step is so like Marcus'. Sit down Earl," Sarah commanded softly.

Earl realized that Sarah's eyesight was failing her and she was recognizing him by his steps and not by sight. He wondered if he should offer to buy her some glasses. He decided to wait to broach that subject.

"Grandma, I've got a really thorny problem. I'm paying for the mistakes of my youth in a terrible way. I'm so in love it is almost painful. I had that one child with the Brewer girl and another with Ruth Evans. Now I've found the woman I would want to spend my entire life with and she says she can't see me because I am married," Earl said rather plaintively.

"Son, I don't have a good answer for you. God warns us about having intimate relations before marriage. It's for a good reason," Sarah said and hesitated like she was thinking really hard. "Elmer had much of the same problem you had. He learned it from his father. You were the product of intimate relations before marriage. Thank God, you're here. I don't know what we would do without you."

Earl hardly knew what to say to her answer. He was ashamed and proud at the same time. He was ashamed of his behavior. He was proud that his grandmother had so much confidence in him.

"I'm so desperate. I just don't know what to do. Eva won't answer my letters. I want to see her desperately."

Sarah said slowly, "Earl, do you think Eva loves you like you love her?"

"I think so, Grandma," Earl replied.

"I know what you should do. Talk to Fern. She a wonderful person. I'm so glad you got her to be with my grandchildren while you're out working. She is younger and has a different way of looking at things. I'm too close to it," Sarah said with certainty.

Earl and his grandmother chatted about the family business and how it was going. Sarah asked how Earl was progressing with the report that was due to the court on the next Thursday. Earl assured her that it was all ready and he was planning to deliver it to James Hart on Tuesday morning. He told her that he might try one more big cattle drive in the Fall sometime before it got too cold at night.

When the clock struck eight, Sarah rose and said, "Time for bed."

Earl said, "Good night, grandma. See you tomorrow."

When Earl got back to his house, he was there just in time to tell Vivian, Glen and Lucille good-night. Fern had accomplished adherence to a set bedtime better that Sylva ever had.

Fern joined Earl on the front porch as the last of daylight was beginning to fade into darkness.

Earl said, "Grandma said I should get your advice."

"Is this sister to brother, friend to friend or adult to child," Fern chuckled mischievously.

Earl smiled, "Maybe a little of all three. It's Eva. She came back this weekend and starts teaching at Stultz this Monday. I saw Uncle Weed a couple of days ago, Eva's staying at Uncle George's again this year. She's told me she won't see me as long as I'm married. Jim Hart put in the paperwork like a month ago but he told me that it might be several months before we even have a date for a hearing. I'd like to see her. I am just totally miserable without her. What do I do?"

Fern was thoughtful for a long time, "I would suggest you go over to Stultz just as school is out on Monday. I know you want to go to Summersville for the sale. You take the Plymouth. Lonnie can take the truck. After you make your last buy, head off to Stultz. You should be able to be there for dismissal."

Earl nodded, "I can be there by four."

Earl made up his mind to have Lonnie drive on over to Summersville and he would swing by Jim Hart's office. He would urge Jim to do his best to get a quick reply to his suit for divorce, to get on the docket. Earl bade Fern goodnight and hurried up to bed. He wanted and early start on Saturday morning. He had to look at some hogs before he went to the Willow sale.

"Earl," Fern got her nephew's attention. "Would you mind if the children and I could go with you to Clear Springs for the ballgame on Sunday. It will give me a chance to see John."

"Of course. And thanks for the advice."

The weekend went well. Earl didn't revisit the bottle now that he had a plan to see Eva.

* * * * * * * * * *

When school was out on Monday, Earl was sitting out front in the Plymouth.

The doors opened and the school children were let out by Eva. She stood at the door and watched as they went down the steps, unaware that Earl was there. When Earl opened the car door and stepped out, Eva heard the door open and glanced his way. A smile strode across her lips and as quickly went away.

Earl walked toward the school house. Eva retreated inside as Earl followed her.

She stood in the aisle facing the door when he entered. Tears were brimming in her eyes. Eva swiped the back of her hand across her eyes, dashing the moisture away.

"Earl, what are you doing here?" Eva's voice trembled.

"I came to tell you how desperately I love you," he said simply.

"Oh!" As simple as that.

Earl continued, "I put in the paperwork for divorce. You are the only woman I have truly loved."

"Thank you for that, Earl, but I can't see you until you are free," Eva said. "I talked to Mama and Papa about it."

"I just wanted you to know, Eva," Earl said earnestly.

Eva turned her back to him, "Please leave."

As Earl left the school, he could hear Eva weeping. His heart was breaking but he knew she really loved him, too. The response spoke louder than words.

The weeks winged by into Fall, through September and into October. It was misery for Earl not seeing Eva when she was so close.

CHAPTER 18 -

A Romantic Discontent

The Autumn of 1931 began an onset of the incredibly destructive Dust Bowl years. Murky brown sunsets were common as the soil of the newly plowed and planted wheat fields of the Great Plains blew away across the bone dry skies that had seen no rain since the harvest in June and July. The evidence was also in the sheen of dust that daily accumulated on flat surfaces of the homes downwind from the soil erosion by wind. It would only grow worse.

The insidious drought farther West had affected South Missouri and Texas County.

The corn that Earl's tenant had planted in May flourished with an occasional rain in June through August. The crop that Dillard and a half dozen temporarily hired men cut, shocked and shucked was loaded in the Ford truck and hauled to Houston to grind for feed. It was used in fattening hogs and cattle for market the next year and for the chickens. Earl sent a check to his former tenant.

As livestock prices continued to fall, Earl had more and more difficulty in making a profit on his efforts. He took losses more often than he had successes. Little did Earl know that times could get worse.

A sort of reprieve came on the last day of September by way of Joe Sullivan. His letter was short and to the point. It read: Dear Earl: I have had a request for some more quality beef like you brought us back in June, July and August. Earl picked the letter up on Friday morning and decided to go to Raymondville to call and see what Joe would guarantee him on delivery.

Earl called and was confident that he could have another successful cattle drive. When he came back Earl consulted quickly with Dillard so he could start putting together a group of men and coordinate it.

The evening before, Earl had set down with his accounts and figured up his income and debits for the month of September. It was a substantial loss. He had actually come out ahead about one hundred dollars. But his milling bill from Houston was nearly four hundred dollars. His substantial profit in July had dwindled to a lesser profit in August to a loss on paper in September. He was tempted to submit the report to the oversight panel showing a profit for the three months but he felt that would be dishonest of him since he had started out breaking it down month by month. He knew that he would get back the cost of milling in larger and healthier animals down the road.

Earl kept as busy as possible during September so he wouldn't dwell on the continued estrangement from the woman he loved. The days of melancholia came and he dealt with it by resorting to overuse of bootleg whiskey.

School began in Tyrone the same day it had in Stultz. Fern was the stabilizing force in the cobbled together family. Earl was the surrogate father and Fern served as a sort of nanny for the children if not as a sort of mother figure. Earl's sisters and brother respected and took direction from Fern without question. Only on rare occasions did Earl have to resort to any sort of discipline.

By most measurements Lucille was a model young girl. She had scolded her brother and sister in rare instances. Earl had swatted his youngest sister only once and it seemed to be enough. Glen was another matter. He had several fights at school and was increasingly surly toward Lucille. Earl had threatened to give him a whipping with his belt if there was another fight at school or if he continued to mistreat his older sister. The threat seemed to work for a while. Glen was never impolite or outright defiant with Fern. Earl was thankful for that. Glen seemed to sense that was not a line he wanted to cross.

John Dunivan's mother and step-father (the senior John Bradford) told him they would be moving to town early in September. This set in motion the sale of the farm to George, their oldest son. George would continue to run the grocery store by the Turkey Ranch, serving twenty to thirty families nearby. The family would live both places for the next dozen years.

John Dunivan moved into the house on the Sigler home place. John came by to see Fern more often, predictably, around supper time for a home cooked meal.

Earl had trouble finding someone to move into the house on the Southwest eighty that Marcus had Bought, right after he married. He bought three additional eighties that adjoined his original homestead.

The first time John came up to Tyrone, he told Earl that he had ordered two hundred young turkeys. It was his intention to keep twenty hens and two toms and he would allow the hens to all nest next spring. He figured the two toms and twenty hens would produce four hundred young turkeys each spring and summer.

After supper the adults sat on the front porch watching the fading light. Earl said, "You'll have to clip the wings on those birds or they'll fly off and go wild on you, John."

"I've been studying up on that, Earl," John rejoined, "I've built roosts in that old barn enough to hold five or six hundred birds. I'll get them used to roosting in there before I begin to let them forage. I hope to buy very little feed once they discover bugs are food. They'll even eat acorns, you know."

"You don't say. I never heard that," Fern chimed in.

"Me neither, Fern," Earl added.

"Yep. Those birds have one of the toughest, strongest craws you'd ever imagine," John said.

Earl chuckled, "It just goes to show, you're never too old to learn something new."

Fern said, "It's getting pretty dark, John. You best get back down to Grogan."

Earl stood up and stretched. He knew he should give John and Fern some privacy. "I'd better get up to bed. Early day tomorrow, as usual. See you, John."

John stood up and shook Earl's hand, "See, yeh."

Earl opened the screen door and walked through the house and upstairs. He heard the murmur of voices from the front porch. Then silence until he heard John's horse moving away east to the road down to the home place. He heard the screen door close and heard the squeaking of the springs when Fern lay down for the night.

Earl awoke with a craving for liquor. It had happened with more regularity lately. He rarely drank until absolute drunkenness and he used Sen-Sen as a cover when he knew he was going to be around his mother, grandmother, Pearl or Fern. It was a cover for bad breath, from tobacco or bootleg.

Earl got up quietly and went to the Plymouth and pulled out a bottle nearly half full. He drank it down, got out of the car and walked down toward the mill and barn. He lit a cigarette on the way. He leaned on the fence by the barn looking at the big fat hogs that he would send off on

Sunday evening to the National Stockyards in East Saint Louis. Hogs were up yesterday morning, Friday. He hoped to make a few bucks on this load. It would offset some of the losses he had experienced in recent days.

Earl walked back to the street and walked toward the Kidd Store. He waved to Ike Miller, Ira's father, as he walked by. They gave Ike and his wife some excess eggs. He saw Jim Martin in his back yard splitting wood for the kitchen stove. The store wouldn't be open for a while. Earl pulled out his pocket watch in the early morning light. It was just after six o'clock.

The new house under construction about a block from the store to the East was being built by Virgil Reese. Virgil had sold a sawmill and had come in and bought the store and sawmill from Callie Kidd.

Callie only made rare appearances at the store now that she was sixty-four and had been pretty crippled up by arthritis. Now Myrtle and Nick McKinney did the bulk of work keeping the store going with Dana, who was Callie's daughter, filling in on a fairly regular basis. They would continue operating the store until Virgil was ready to take over.

Earl walked by Parmenter's house; smoke billowed from a chimney. When he passed Uncle Weed and Aunt Annie's, Naomi was in the front yard. Earl stopped to visit for a minute. He took out his little box of Sen-Sen and popped some in his mouth. He leaned on a fence post and said, "Hi, Naomi."

Naomi, much too young for guile, jibed, "Papa told me OC was beatin' your time with your girl. You gonna do anything about it?"

"She's not been giving me much time to be beat out of. You have any suggestions, Naomi."

"If I was you I'd find another girl to put in OC's way so he'd pay attention to them," Naomi said emphatically. Naomi had planted a seed.

"Thanks for the advice, Naomi. I'll see you later." Earl waved goodbye.

Naomi, waved back.

Earl walked on West to his grandmother's. When Earl walked across the porch to the front door, Sarah emerged from the living room. She sat in her rocking chair and Earl in a straight one. "I thought I heard your steps, Earl" she said.

"Grandma, I've got a great idea. Why don't you get yourself ready and we'll all go down to Willow today. I've noticed that you're not seeing too well lately. You can get yourself fitted with some glasses. The kids can ride in the rumble seat and I'll have Lonnie drive the truck down by himself. He was planning to go with me anyway. You can shop while I buy livestock and the young ones can go to a movie."

The four of them hadn't done something like this for long time, Earl thought.

* * * * * * * * * *

Eva tried to forget Earl's visit and the pain it had caused. She had borrowed George's horse and buggy to drive home on Friday night a couple of times in September then back on Sunday afternoon. She always dropped a penny post card in the mail to alert her family to her coming.

Naomi was right. OC had not given up on Eva. He showed up with some regularity at noontime to have lunch with her. She tolerated it but gave him no occasion to think that she was really interested in him. On the other hand, she did nothing to insult him, walking a very fine line.

George and Belle told her along toward the end of September that they were planning a pie supper on the fourth Saturday evening in October to raise money for the school. Belle was very emphatic when she said, "You must prepare a dessert for auction. You missed last Spring and there was some criticism on it."

Eva agreed to it readily. She knew now how to handle OC.

September melted into October, literally. An incredibly hot month passed into history and the early days of October were not much better.

Eva went home the third weekend in October. Through the grapevine Eva heard of the thousands of dollars that Sylva had planned to escape with. She had also heard that Earl had been appointed executor of his father's estate and guardian of his sisters and brother. She ached for a way to be with him, to help him with difficult days ahead. She had also heard that he had hired a relative to be housekeeper. She longed to be able to discuss his troubles, the work he was doing, his pitching, seeing his grandmother, his aunt, his brother and sisters and his mother and step-father. They had become dear to her in the time they had together last Spring and early Summer.

Eva had a particularly gifted young boy in the eighth grade. He had some very poor teaching for a couple of his grades, fifth and sixth. She gave him some special attention and tutoring after school to prepare him for high school in Cabool. The year before Cabool had started a bus service for students from Tyrone, Grandview, Stultz, Elk Creek and other one room schools farther north, west and south. She encouraged him to study hard the last half of the year as she didn't know what kind of teacher would be following her.

Eva sent a post card that she would be coming home on the third weekend of October. George helped her harness a horse and hitch it to the nice little buggy. When Eva got to the Weiler house on the second Friday evening before the third weekend of the month of October, everyone was in bed but her father. Wayne helped her unhitch the horse, take off the harness and let the horse out in the north pasture. It was dark much earlier even though it was only just after eight o'clock.

They had Eva sleeping with Joyce on the double bed in the living room. Eva still got up early so she didn't mind being downstairs to help get the fire started in the kitchen stove. As usual she was up before everyone else. A few minutes later she heard steps on the stairs and Clyde came in the kitchen as Eva was lighting the dried grasses under the kindling in the stove.

Clyde said, "Hi, Sis."

"My you're getting so tall and grown up, Clyde," Eva said. Clyde looked proud.

Eva heard the heavier tread of her mother. "Hello, Mama," Eva said cheerfully.

Rena smiled, wreathing her face with pleasure. "Hello, Eva. Looks like you have bed head yet."

"Oh, I'll get around to combing my hair out as soon as I get a good fire going."

Rena said, "You two go on out on the front porch. Take your comb and sit down. You had a long hard trip last evening."

"Actually, Mama, it wasn't so bad. They have a nice soft rubber tire buggy and the roads were all freshly graded. I made really good time. I thought it might be nine before I got here."

Clyde followed Eva to the front porch and they sat on a couple of old chairs that were pretty rickety. Clyde said, "I heard your boyfriend Earl is bringing a herd of cattle through here this afternoon. He was down at a liquidation sale over between here and Willow. He bought all the best cattle."

"How do you know all about this?" Eva was working at a particularly difficult snarl.

"How could I not know? Earl drove up to the house on Wednesday last week and asked if he could rent pasture for a week. He's paying a penny a day for each cow. Last Saturday he put over four hundred head of cattle in the hayfield on the home place. That adds up near to thirty dollars for a week. Papa, just couldn't turn it down," Clyde said with pride in his voice.

"I understand that but let's get one thing clear. Earl is not my boyfriend," Eva said firmly, "I broke it off with him weeks ago."

"Well! You shouldn't have," Clyde said vehemently. "I know how you felt about him. I know he's married but he can get divorced and then he'd be free to see you again. I heard Mama and Papa talking about it. Mama thinks you shouldn't at all but Papa says maybe it could work out."

Eva's heart gave a little flutter. She thought to herself, Papa thinks it could work out.

Esther came out in her work clothes and said, "I heard what you told Eva. I'm on Mama's side. He's just too big a risk."

Eva's heart weighed heavy again, a rock weighing her down. "Go on you two and start milking. I'll give you a little head start and I'll start carrying water to cool the milk."

As Eva walked down to the well to carry up water she looked up at the early morning sky. It was a kind of muddy brown from the dust storms out west. She drew two buckets of water and carried them up the hill. Her father helped her empty the buckets and went back with four buckets instead of two. Wayne B tagged along behind them. When they had the water up and filled all four buckets, Wayne said, "I heard Clyde out on the front porch telling you about Earl renting pasture. I just couldn't out and out turn him down. He'll pay almost as much for pasture in a week as I can make all month working in town."

"It's all right, Papa. I understand. With the hard times money isn't easy to come by."

They started walking back up the hill with the water. Wayne spoke again, "I want you to drive me into town and come back for the family later when they can get ready. Rena needs to do some shopping and you can look around, too. If Clyde wants to drive, go ahead and let him."

When they were pouring the water in the wash tubs, three buckets to each tub, Eva's youngest sister Joyce was coming back from the chicken house with two baskets full of eggs.

Eva's father turned to Wayne B, "Go help your sister clean eggs and put in the crate. We've got to take them into town. They'll help pay our grocery bill."

Turning back to Eva Wayne continued, "If you let Clyde drive, remind him we're hauling eggs and if any get broken he and I will have a chat. Also buy some real bacon, none of that hog jowl for breakfast."

"I'll tell him to be careful, Papa," Eva said, "Your car sure does look good."

"Yes and it runs well. It's kind of hard to crank. Clyde can do it and he knows how to be careful now after it kicked back on him once. He's lucky he didn't get a broken arm."

They ate breakfast after saying grace and Eva drove Wayne into town to the lumber yard for his job. He worked two days during the week and six hours on Saturday. It brought in enough extra money to help make survival possible with a large family and a poor Ozarks farm.

Eva came back and put on one of her newer dresses and a nice little necklace with paste pearls and applied some light lipstick and a little rouge. After they were all ready, Rena looked at Eva rather critically because of the lipstick and rouge but didn't say anything. They loaded the eggs in the trunk and Eva let Clyde drive after she cautioned him with her father's admonition.

Clyde parked by the MFA store. Eva helped Clyde carry the eggs in for cash payment. Rena took charge of the money and gave each child a nickel to buy treats. Eva would augment with her own money for anything her brothers and sisters wanted. They started walking West along the south side of the street. About a half block away Eva saw Sarah Sigler sitting on a bench in front of Wilbanks store catty-cornered from the Charles Ferguson Clothing store. Sarah was puffing on her little woman's pipe. Sarah said her family had originated from North Carolina and all the Henry women smoked their little woman-sized pipe.

Eva stopped in front of Sarah and said, "Hello, Missus Sigler."

Sarah peered at her and fished in a dress pocket and took out some spectacles and fitted them across her ears and settled the nose piece in place and looked up at her. She smiled broadly, "I thought that was your voice, Eva. I've told you over and over to just call me Sarah. It's so good to see you. If you haven't noticed, I've got new glasses and it sure helps me see better. I can even do sewing now."

"Yes, I noticed, Sarah. Your glasses look good on you," Eva said emphatically.

"I just got so used to going around half blind all the time that I forget to put them on many times." Sarah peered at Eva intently, "I wish you'd take up with Earl again. He's put in for divorce from Ruth, you know. He's just pining away for you. Sometimes I think it will be too much for him to bear."

Eva was thoughtful for a long time before she replied, "There's a difference of opinion between my Mama and my Papa about what I should do. I think I shouldn't do anything until we come to an understanding about which way to go."

Eva's heart was racing again, just thinking of the good times with Earl.

Sarah said, "I'll tell Earl that. Maybe it'll make him feel better."

"I'd rather you didn't. It might get his hopes up again and not do any good." Eva felt her eyes start watering up. She turned away, "I was just taking my brothers and sisters up to the drug store for a treat. She rubbed at her eyes and looked back at Sarah attempting to exude the love she felt for her.

Sarah returned her glasses to her dress pocket as she bid her farewell, "That treat can't wait. I 'd like to see you again. Soon, I hope."

Eva nodded and the crossed the north-south street, that was the West Plains-Rolla Road, quickly, in a break in the traffic. Ralph complained loudly that they were walking too fast. Eva said, "Clyde, pick Ralph up and carry him. They moved rapidly up toward the drug store. It was the only place in town that had installed air conditioning and had a soda fountain.

The six Weiler siblings found the place packed with mostly young people waiting three deep at the fountain. Eva offered to buy them all a sundae the selection was three strawberry, two chocolate and one pineapple. She spotted Lucille, Glen and Vivian at a table near the back and waved at them. They appeared to be sipping milk shakes or malts.

Eva got in her order, ahead of some other people who looked at her angrily. When the college age soda jerk saw Eva, tall and beautiful, he asked for her order. She handed out the sundaes to her brothers and sisters and kept hers and Ralph's. There were four chairs where the Sigler children sat and they saved one for Eva but Eva put Ralph on the chair on his knees so he could be somewhat level with his sundae. Ralph began eating his strawberry sundae, dribbling juice and ice cream down the front. Eva moved around behind Lucille so she could stand with her back to a wall.

Lucille turned her chair around so she could look at Eva. "You're breaking his heart," Lucille said earnestly, "He talks about you all the time but he never sees you. What's going on."

"Well, honey. He's a married man. I can't be going with a married man," Eva replied a little testily.

"I heard him talking to Aunt Pearl once. He's trying to get unmarried. He doesn't live with her or do anything with her." Lucille said sincerely.

Eva took a couple bites of her strawberry sundae. After swallowing she said, "Maybe we'll get it worked out one day."

"Eva, he's drinking bootleg and awful lot. I smell it on him. He's trying to hide it with his Sen-Sen," Lucille said emphatically. "He carries around his little box but I know what's going on. He keeps a bottle of booze behind the seat in the Plymouth and the truck both."

Eva was shocked. She didn't know how to handle this new information. Was it her fault. What could she do?

Lucille opened her mouth to say something more but Eva shook her head, "I don't want to talk about this anymore."

Ralph was playing with his sundae, now. Eva went around the table and took it from him, finishing it off, and took him quickly outside. There was a street water fountain in front of the Post Office next door. Eva took her handkerchief and wet it and cleaned Ralph as best she could. She waited in the shade of an awning in front of the five and ten cent store. Eva and her sisters and brothers saw their mother coming out of Ferguson Clothing. Eva picked up Clyde and caught up with her before they got to the MFA Store.

"I'd kind of like to go home, Mama," Eva said

Rena said, "That's fine by me. I need to do some canning. It's been so warm I haven't even started to think about digging potatoes.

"I can help you with that, Mama," Eva offered

Clyde said, "I'd like to buy a soda for my treat."

All the others echoed that sentiment. Eva said, "Go ahead and I'll drive home. You can't drink your soda and drive both."

Eva helped Rena get her groceries, an empty egg crate and her clothing buys in the trunk of the car. It was a tight fit.

When they got home, Rena reminded them, "Be careful with the bottles, there's a penny return on them."

Eva and Esther helped pick the last of the green beans and cut off heads of cabbage to start making kraut. They pulled beets to make pickled beets. They pulled off all the cucumbers, large and small for sweet and sour pickles. The three of them worked steadily, taking a short break for a baloney sandwich. They sterilized jars, dozens of them, for green beans, pickled beets and pickled cucumbers. The cabbages and cucumbers were all sliced into large three and five gallon glazed containers with salt, sugar and spices as appropriate for what they wanted to produce, sweet, sour or in between.

Clyde returned for Wayne. When they came in the house Clyde said, "The herd is right behind us, we got out of town just in time. Wayne worked from eight in the morning to two in the afternoon. About four o'clock they heard the lowing of the cattle and the rumble of hundreds of hooves coming down the valley. Rena and Wayne could not restrain the younger ones from running down to the road to watch the herd go by. Eva couldn't help following them down. Would she see him? Eva recognized Earl by his hat and the way he held himself in the saddle. Her heart raced faster. He raised his hat high in the air, waving it back and forth. Eva turned away and went back toward the house. She knew she was not over him and probably never would be. Eva remembered the day in the summer of 1927 when she first saw the name Earl Sigler carved into the weathered, wooden gate that led to the Weiler home years before she ever met him.

The weekend flew by but Eva was haunted with the conversation she had with Lucille. Eva left at three o'clock Sunday so she could get back to George and Belle Morgan's before dark.

* * * * * * * * * *

That incident haunted his days as Earl worked with the other wranglers moving the cattle up toward Rolla. Eva's tall, elegant figure imprinted itself on his brain, invading pleasant nighttime dreams. There was just the glimmer of a smile on Eva's lips as she turned away and walked back up the hill. Should that encourage him? Earl thought it should.

During the day and a half layover in the drive north, Earl started calculating the result of his purchases. Based on Joe Sullivan's guarantee, Earl estimated a possible loss. He knew why. Several of the livestock traders had become very jealous of Earl and Elmer's success in driving cattle to Rolla on a road that was difficult to drive by truck from South central Missouri to the railroad that would transport cattle to East Saint Louis and the National Stock Yards. It was, without a doubt, the best place to sell cattle. The approximately one hundred thirty mile cattle drives the Sigler's had begun was the most efficient way to get cattle to market, given the poor roads. Out of spite his competitors began driving up the price Earl had to pay to get a herd together by running up the final bid in the sale ring of the sale barns.

A tidbit of interesting information came to Earl while he was in Tyrone Sunday, Monday and early Tuesday. There was going to be a pie supper at Stultz. That set an idea percolating in Earl's mind.

On Sunday Lonnie developed a boil and couldn't ride. He would drive the truck and Earl took his place.

Earl was more careful in his buying on Monday in Summersville and Wednesday in Licking. When the bidding got too high, Earl allowed his competitors to buy at too high a price. If he did another cattle drive, and he likely would, he would make sure that he bought at a price that would be equitable.

When the herd got to the usual rendezvous point south of Rolla, Joe Sullivan was there to meet them. Bad news was waiting. Another contract buyer had bought a large herd in Oklahoma. It had fulfilled the obligation to a packing company. Joe offered less than he had promised, near a penny a pound less. Earl was looking at a bad loss. He could financially absorb it. He would have smaller capital to work with.

"I'm sorry I can't offer more, Earl," Joe said, "The market has had another drop."

"If you can't do better than that, you'll never do business with me again. You've never been on a cattle drive, how many days it takes, how many men, how dusty, how hot it is. The food tastes like cow manure after a few days on the trail. The comradeship among the men is great but that doesn't pay the bills," Earl said emphatically.

The two wrangled over the price until Earl thought he could at least meet his expenses. He didn't tell Joe Sullivan their relationship was ending. Earl vowed to make the next trip to East Saint Louis with a load of hogs.

The hogs at Jana's was probably ready. He wanted to see her about another matter anyway.

Lonnie's boil had healed. He was able to sit on a horse. They loaded the horses, saddled as usual. The unmarried men rode back home on their own. Earl gave them meal money for Thursday evening and Friday morning. Fern had a large supper ready when they got home. She had a more sumptuous meal Friday noon when John Dunivan came back. Fern went down to the home place to do John's chores while he was gone. Pearl came to help Glenn to do the chores in Tyrone and stayed at her mother's.

When Earl paid the cowhands he had less than fifty dollars to show for all his efforts. It barely covered his other expenses and paid him practically nothing for his own time. It would not happen again, he vowed. Little did he know that the price of cattle and hogs would continue to slide.

Earl's ratiocinating led him to his attorney first and later to see Jana Arnold.

Earl was at the door of his attorney's office before his scheduled opening. He got out of his car and followed Jim Hart inside.

"This is unexpected. What's on your mind?" Jim said. Hart went to the secretary's desk and removed some papers from a file box.

"I won't take much of your time, Jim" Earl related his frustration about the broken promise that Joe Sullivan had made.

"It has a simple solution, Earl." Earl looked puzzled. Jim continued, "Ask for a percentage or a flat amount retainer. You're an independent contractor just as I am. I work on retainer's all the time with new clients. I don't ask you for one because I know you're good for it and your family has given me business over forty years now."

"Do I have to have anything in writing?" Earl asked.

"Not necessarily unless they demand it. If they contact you I would drive a truck load of critters to East Saint Louis and ask for a retainer. They may want a signed agreement. If so, read it carefully, sign it and bring a copy to me."

Earl said, "Thanks, I'll do that. How much for the advice?"

"Ten will be fine."

Jim Hart told him what he was waiting to hear about the divorce hearing.

Earl took a ten dollar bill out of his billfold and handed it to Jim. "I better scat. I've got a lot of errands before I head off for West Plains. Hog prices were up yesterday. I think I'll send Lonnie up to the stockyards with two loads of hogs. I may pay Spud Lynch to take some hogs up on half the profit. They can make two trips Sunday evening and early Monday morning."

Earl stopped a couple minutes in the bank and got sympathy from Ray Miles for getting skinned on the cattle deal. Then he headed over to Jana's to set in motion his scheme to resolve a romantic discontent.

Jana was sitting on the porch with her son. He was playing with a toy. Jana met him outside the yard gate.

"Jana," Earl said, "I just came by to look at the hogs. I think they're probably ready for market."

Jana nodded, "I think so, too."

They walked over to the hog pen and Earl looked in at the hogs. In the nearly four months the feeder pigs Elmer had bought had turned into market size hogs.

"I wanted to ask you to plot something that might interest you." Earl said conspiratorially. "I would like for you to make one of your great raisin pies. I'll pick you up about six Saturday evening and take you to Stultz for a pie supper. We're going to do a grand switch. I'll buy your pie but the auctioneer will award it to a bachelor who might interest you. I think he'll be happy to eat pie with you and your son if you want to bring him along. He will think he bought Eva Weiler's. But the auctioneer will convince him, I hope, that he really bought your pie. If it all goes off as planned I'll have my pie and eat it too."

Jana smiled impishly, "You're on, Earl, but I'll not bring my son. I haven't done something crazy like this my twenty-nine years. I can hardly wait to see Eva's face when you suddenly appear."

"I'll have Lonnie Bailey there as my straw man," Earl continued, "I'll finance him to buy any dessert for himself. I'm sure there'll be some pretty young girls there."

Earl got back to the house just after nine o'clock. Lonnie would be part way to West Plains. Earl let Fern know about the pie supper at Stultz. He suggested that Fern and Lucille make a dessert for the supper. He also suggested that Fern invite John. The five of them could ride over together.

Earl hurried to the Plymouth and made good time since the roads had been freshly graded and no new rain had come to rut it. He got to the sale barn before they began the swine sale. Earl had Lonnie do the bidding to circumvent other stock traders from driving up the price out of their continued spite. Earl would raise an unlit cigarette to his mouth to start Lonnie bidding. When the price got too high he would raise an unlighted cigarette again. When Earl had made his purchases, he and Lonnie got up separately. Earl warned him to be subtle in his bids and show his number for the clerks unobtrusively.

They repeated the same thing in Willow the next day. Earl made up his mind to have Dillard help him next week. He would shift back and forth until his competitors caught on, or ever did.

* * * * * * * * * * *

Eva was looking forward to the pie supper on Saturday. She stayed late on Friday giving her prize eighth grade student additional help in preparation for high school the next year. She felt she had made some progress with him. She knew she wouldn't have him for the last half of the year.

When she got home she was a little late to help Belle with supper. She apologized and told Belle why and what she was doing. Belle thought it was really fine that she had taken the initiative to do it.

Eva, stoked the stove and began mixing the ingredients for a dark chocolate cake. While she was mixing the chocolate icing, Belle suggested she make a little white icing with red coloring in it as a heart centerpiece for the cake. Eva thought it was a good suggestion. It would give her a challenge to make a perfect red heart, almost like Valentine's Day in October.

After she finished her cake, Eva went to the garden and dug their potatoes for them. She put them in gunny sacks and took them to the cellar and spread them out in the potato bin.

The next day she picked the last of the green beans and cut the last heads of cabbage. She sterilized jars for the beans. She cut the beans and set them on the stove to simmer while the jars steamed. She began using the slicing board on the cabbages, always looking for worms. The sliced cabbage was put in big glazed pots, layering with salt and vinegar poured on top. Eva told Belle, "I'll do some Bavarian Sauer Kraut. Do you have some Caraway seed?"

"Why don't you make a small batch, Eva," Belle said, and I'll send George over to Elk creek for the Caraway. He can get some flour and sugar and fresh sausage for breakfast tomorrow morning. He can get some fresh meat for later in the week."

Eva fashioned sort of a square tent with toothpicks and wax paper to put over her cake. George drove her over early at six so she could have the school ready for the auction.

OC was there when Eva got to the school. He helped move things around but Eva knew he had come early to see what she had brought. There was so much dust floating around because of the dust storms out west and the dust from the road, Eva left the wax paper "tent" on her dessert.

Eva looked at the clock. It was seven fifteen. The school was nearly full.

* * * * * * * * * * *

Earl was back at home by two o'clock. He picked up his mail, looking at his post cards. He went across the street to the barbershop. Ira had someone in the seat.

As Earl sat waiting he opened a letter from the Probate Judge. Judge Johnson said one person on the oversight panel was not happy with the September figures. Judge Johnson said he would look carefully at the next quarter before he would make any recommendations.

Earl composed a letter to the Judge in his head. He would explain that the markets had taken a precipitous fall in the first half of the month and it accounted for some of the early losses. In the last half he would concentrate on buying hogs, which had stabilized more than cattle. He would plan to do more trucking on commission or flat rate for farmers rather than purchasing which was more risky. Earl would plan to drive more himself or send Dillard more often which might save ten or more dollars a month.

Earl got in the chair and told Ira he just wanted a little trim around the ears and squaring off the back on his hair cut.

Earl was pleased that Ira paid attention and had done exactly as he asked. "Tell Aunt Pearl hello and tell her to pray for me as I'm going to Stultz for the pie supper."

"Yeh're gonna need some prayin' if yeh're not keerful," Ira admonished.

Earl got up and left as Nick McKinney came in. "Hello, Earl."

"Hello, Nick. Careful of your ears."

Nick chuckled and Ira frowned as Earl walked out the door. He walked back toward his grand-mothers's. He waved to Aunt Annie and Uncle Weed who were sitting on the front porch. Weed yelled, "Good Luck?"

Earl wondered who didn't know about this evening at Stultz in Tyrone.

Sarah was sitting in her rocker, her head leaned back snoring softly. She sensed Earl's approach and sat up straighter. She took her glasses out of her dress pocket and put them on. She was smiling as Earl got closer. "Hi, Son. What brings you by. You want some advice for the lovelorn?"

Earl shook his head, "How much more should I hear about this. First Dana at the store. Then Ira at the barbershop. Then Uncle Weed. Then who's after you?"

"Everyone in town is having a little fun at your expense, Earl. Don't take it too serious."

Earl shrugged his shoulders, "You're right, Granny." He called her that when he wanted to be really syrupy with her. "I brought some fresh meat from the locker in Willow. I didn't want to carry it around with me so just go up and pick some out and bring it home with you."

Earl turned to leave.

"Goodbye, son. Have a good time."

"Goodbye, Grandma."

It was after three o'clock when Earl got back to his house because he helped Lonnie unload. Lonnie couldn't bring all the pigs back in one load so he went back for the last of over two hundred young gilts and barrows they bought. He urged Lonnie to hurry if he wanted to get back in time for the pie supper. Earl promised to buy Lonnie's dessert if he would run up the chocolate cake with the red heart to five Dollars, exactly.

John Dunivan did come to go with them. Fern and Lucille had made apple pies from late apples picked fresh from a tree. Fern made sure that John knew what color plates her pie was set on so he would bid on hers. Lucille hoped that she didn't get some old man who dribbled chewing tobacco juice down his chin. Jana and Lucille rode in front, Lucille in the middle, Lonnie, Fern and John in the back.

Lonnie ran Eva's cake up to exactly five dollars.

Earl watched through a window until the raisin pie that Jana made came up for sale. As soon as the auctioneer picked up the pie, Earl walked into the school and stood where Eva couldn't see him. He ran the price up to five dollars. So the switch was in place. Earl knew the auctioneer well as he worked in both the Licking and Summersville sale barns and he was in on the switch as a lark.

A young nice looking teenage boy had noticed Lucille come in with her pie. His father bought her pie for his son. Lucille was pleased when he came to claim the pie instead of the older man who had been bidding.

John bought Fern's pie. All was well.

The auctioneer called, "OC come on up."

OC stood up with a puzzled look. The auctioneer hadn't picked up the chocolate cake yet to hand to Eva. The auctioneer turned to the table with the desserts on it. Jana was right behind OC. The auctioeer picked up the raisin pie and handed it to Jana.

"I didn't buy this one, Fred." OC complained. He looked at Jana with a startled look on his face.

"You paid five dollars didn't you."

OC nodded and the auctioneer continued, "Then you just paid five dollars for this young widow's pie."

OC held out his hands and smiled at Jana. OC was suddenly pleased with his purchase. OC said, "I guess I did."

Eva was looking puzzled as well.

They left Eva's cake until last. The auctioneer held up the cake and Earl walked forward. When Eva turned around she was looking at the man she loved so dearly. Her lips quivered for a moment and then she smiled. She figured she was the victim of a scam but a nice one.

Eva led them to a far corner and they sat down together.

"Well, Earl. How did you pull this off?"

"Maybe a better question is why," Earl said. "I got good news yesterday. They gave me a date in February. It was a big surprise. My attorney, Jim Hart, said they never give this much notice of a divorce hearing but he just insisted on it."

They both ate a large piece of cake without talking.

Eva said, "The look on OC's face was worth the chicanery."

"I have to admit it was a hoot."

"It gives me something to talk to my folks about," Eva said earnestly.

"That's a good thing." He reached out for her hand and she pulled hers away.

"Let's not get too cozy, just yet."

Eva got up and walked away.

Earl was disappointed. He wondered if all the effort to do this was worth it.

CHAPTER 19 -

A Painful Interlude

The few weeks Eva had left on her tenure at Stultz dragged by slowly. She enjoyed the children and it was pleasant at George and Belle Morgan's. The banker was not going to move to Raymondville until January. Eva was thankful for that. They had been so generous with her. She continued to go home in their buggy. She went the last weekend in October and twice in November. One was for the Thanksgiving four day weekend. She told Rena and Wayne that she would be back the Friday before Christmas.

The memory of the nights of the pie suppers were a tattered remnant of the times together with Earl last Spring and Summer. She longed to recapture that. School in Clear Springs would begin the second day of January.

Earl came by on the second Tuesday afternoon, the fifteenth of November. Eva knew that was the day that Earl took some time off because there were no sales. Many times he'd go fishing or swimming if the weather was warmer. He was there as school was letting out. After all the children had gone home Eva walked back inside without acknowledging he was there. Earl had followed her inside.

"How about going over to Cabool for an ice cream sundae or milkshake? I kind of favor vanilla malts myself," Earl said tentatively.

"That sounds like fun, Earl," Eva replied, "but life's not as much fun anymore."

"It can be again. I've been miserable without you. You know how much I have loved you and will never love another like you again."

Eva's eyes started tearing up and she dashed her wrists across savagely. "Earl, please leave. I just can't do this right now. I haven't had a chance to talk to my folks about it."

Earl took a step toward Eva.

Eva turned and walked back toward the front of the school.

Eva heard Earl's steps retreating from the room. She heard the car start and drive away. She had ached to have his strong arms around her. Why did he have to torture her with these sudden appearances.

The one good thing had came out of the pie supper was the absence of OC. George and Belle told her that their nephew was going over to Raymondville two or three times a week. Jana would go out to dinner with OC and bring the boy along. Once they went to a movie in Houston, just the two of them.

The one time OC came by was the Monday before Thanksgiving and asked if she could continue teaching the rest of the year. The teacher that was supposed to replace her was failing a class and wouldn't be ready until next Summer. So much for nepotism, she thought.

Eva got a little whimsical satisfaction out of their dilemma but her commitment to Clear Springs would have precedence. She had taught the year before when she was only seventeen and had done a really good job of it. She had turned eighteen on the tenth of December that year.

"I've already accepted another teaching position in another school and I can't just up and tell them 'so sorry I can't.' It just wouldn't be right," Eva said, "would it?"

"You're right it wouldn't be," OC replied. "It won't be easy to find someone this late with so little notice."

Eva went home Thanksgiving weekend. On that Saturday, Rena wanted to take the children to visit her brother Ed over by Pine Creek. Eva drove Wayne in to work at the lumber yard. When she got back everyone was ready to go. Clyde and Esther had dug some worms and vowed to have enough fish for supper. Clyde had a Prince Albert pipe tobacco can with hooks, sinkers and four small cork floats. String was wound around the can and fastened in place by the can lid. They could cut willow poles, attached string, bobbers, and weights with hooks on the bottom end.

After Eva had taken her mother and her brothers and sisters to Uncle Ed's house, she returned to load the eggs in the back of the car. Rena had given her a shopping list for groceries. Eva knew she would have time on her hands. She sort of planned out her day in her head. Her first urge was to go to the sale barn.

Eva had gone to sale barns with Earl in the past. It was an exotic, stimulating experience. The activity was so frenetic. Lots of various types animals inhabiting the sale ring, the rhythmical call of the auctioneer. "Going once, going twice, sold to number thirty one" or whatever number. The smell of manure and sweat in the arena was almost as intoxicating as wine.

Eva took the eggs to MFA. She took the cash and did the shopping for groceries first since there were no items that would spoil she left them in the trunk. Eva took the left over egg money to the lumber yard and gave it to her father so it wouldn't mix, inadvertently, with her own money.

"With it being a holiday weekend the owner is sending everyone home at noon," Wayne told Eva.

"Okay, Papa," Eva said, "I'll go do a little shopping on my own and stop by the pharmacy for a treat." Eva went to Ferguson Clothing and bought a nice dress for Sunday and other special occasions. There was a hat she just couldn't resist. Carrying her new purchases, Eva went to the pharmacy. It was much quieter than the last time. She ordered a vanilla malt. She never had a vanilla malt before but Earl had mentioned it and she thought she should try it. It was great. She looked at the clock behind the counter of the soda fountain. It was pretty close to twelve. She finished her drink and hurried down to the car.

She saw Charlie and Mary Bradford entering Wilbanks grocery so Eva hurried along the North side of the street on down past the theater. She heard the picture show in progress, the firing of guns, probably a western. She crossed after she passed the Chevrolet dealer to MFA.

Eva drove home after her father cranked the car to life. She brought in her new purchases and Wayne changed into fresh clothes, overalls and shirt. He wore his usual old slouchy, sweat-stained gray felt hat and clean work boots.

They drove to Ed Swecker's house. Eva and the other four adults sat in the living room and talked until mid-afternoon. Eva wanted to talk to her folks about Earl but she knew she would have to wait until they got home.

"I brought home an extra chunk of ice to make ice cream this afternoon," Ed announced, rising to his feet. "Rena agreed to mix up her own special concoction and it's in the icebox chilling right now. Eva would you go find the children and bring them up so we can start cleaning the fish?"

Eva found her brothers, sisters and cousins. They had a couple of dozen small perch and two good sized bass. Wayne had snagged a hog sucker. Clyde and Esther cleaned the fish and they had a very nice supper together.

When the Weiler family got home, they were finishing chores by lantern light.

Eva was anxious to get her sisters and brothers off to bed so she could have a talk with her parents about her relationship with Earl. She needed to get it resolved. She knew she was in love with Earl but she couldn't just go against her parent's wishes. She thought of herself as an adult now but family was important to her.

After chores were done, the younger children were given a glass of milk and sent off to bed. Eva, Rena, Wayne, Ralph and Esther were still sitting at the table.

Eva said, "Clyde and Esther, do you mind going upstairs, too. I'd like to talk to Mama and Papa by myself."

"I know what you want to talk about," Clyde smirked.

Esther rose, with a knowing look in her eye and silently left with Clyde right behind her.

"Mama and Papa," Eva began slowly, "I want to talk to you about Earl," not shy about hyperbole, "I am still desperately in love with him."

Rena spoke quickly, "He's a married man. He had a child with another girl he never married. Is that the kind of man you want, Eva?"

"Oh, Mama. If you only knew how much I would like to stop loving him," Eva said with passion. "I told you he bought my cake back in October. He got word from his lawyer that his divorce was set for February. They usually don't know more than a couple of months ahead."

Wayne said, "I know how love is. When I saw Rena the first time I thought how pretty she was and I just knew that she was the woman I would marry." Rena looked pleased.

Eva nodded her head, "It's like an unquenchable fire. You pour water on it and it just won't go out."

"It might be something you just have to live with, Eva," Rena said.

"I wish it was that simple, Mama. Earl just keeps showing up. I haven't made any attempt to see him but he just won't give up."

"Maybe he wants to get you in the family way like he did the other two," Rena said tartly.

Wayne intervened, "That's not fair Rena and you know it. Eva, give your mother and me a couple of weeks to hash this out between us. You can come back in a couple of weeks, can't you?"

"I can come back then, Papa," Eva said thankfully, "Mama, please pray about it. I have and I think that if Earl really gets divorced, I'd like to start seeing him again."

Shaking her head, Rena intoned, "I don't even like to talk about it. I will pray on it but I won't promise anything. Your father and I just don't see eye to eye on it."

"Thank you so much, Mama. I covet your prayers," Eva said with sincerity.

Wayne said, "I know what it is to love someone. Look at me and your mother. Your Uncle Jake wrote me after I married Rena. I had us a farm. I had had a life changing encounter with my Lord Jesus Christ in the little Church of God in Willow. Jake wanted me to come back to Pennsylvania and help on the family farm back there. The family was Amish first and later Mennonite. They had stifling religious beliefs. I couldn't ask your mother to go off and leave what we had begun to build together. You were just a tiny baby back then."

"Thank you Mama and Papa. Please pray about it. I just don't know if I can bear this much longer."

* * * * * * * * * * *

Earl had some success in business in October. His big success was on the pigs that Jana had gotten ready for market. Earl was continuing to pay too much for cattle and had actually lost or broken even. He had just about given up on buying cattle for market.

Earl did get a nice surprise. Late in October a check came by mail of three hundred and six dollars from Joe Sullivan's company, twenty cents a head more for the cattle he had delivered. Joe hinted that he needed another large herd. Earl was skeptical. He had heard that the government was talking about buying up cattle and destroying herds wholesale. Last year they had bought excess milk and poured it on the ground. Well, we'll see, he thought. Many farmers were teetering on the brink of failure.

The success with feeding out pigs opened up new avenues. Earl bought feeder pigs. He had five different places he had young pigs being fed to ready for market. The corn he had ground earlier in the Fall was being put to good use. By Spring he could be sending several truck loads to the stock yards.

The news Earl had delivered to Eva hadn't met with success. His dark moods and nightmarish dreams revisited. His reliance on bootleg whisky was not the least diminished.

The one good thing that happened in early October was George Surby. He had lost his job at the lumber mill in Raymondville. Ray Miles had sent him to see Earl.

George lived on a small farm between Yukon and Raymondville. He knew he couldn't keep up payments on the house and land without outside work. He decided to let the bank have the property and become a tenant on the southwest eighty. Earl told George there were plenty of late apples in the orchard. He, also, told George half the potatoes and turnips in the Tyrone garden were his if he wanted them.

Fern was the one constant in the cobbled together family. She made sure Earl's sisters and brother went to the little Methodist Church just a couple of hundred yards west of his house. Glen rebelled. He thought he shouldn't have to go since his brother wasn't going. Earl went occasionally to maintain peace over the issue. The Pentecostal Church between the blacksmith shop/garage and Martins was not of interest to Fern at all. The shouting and weeping was just not her cup of tea.

Earl's management of the estate and claims against it were handled with swift dispatch. There were several demands that were suspicious in nature and one of outright fraud. Elliott sent a bill for the caskets and embalming. Earl had paid Vic Elliot in cash but had no receipt to prove it. He paid Elliot but decided that the funeral home would get no more business from him. The one that really amused Earl was a bill from a medical doctor, W. F. Herron. He billed for forty four visits by Sylvia over just a little more than a year's time and one for the day of her death. Earl knew that the doctor could not have seen his step-mother that day.

Sarah and Pearl had told Earl on several occasions that the relationship between Doctor Herron and Sylvia was much more than patient and physician.

Two outstanding notes from the Elk Creek Bank surfaced. One was for seven hundred fifty dollars on the twenty fifth of March and another on April fourth both just three months prior to his death. Earl questioned why these loans appeared in a demand over four months later. Earl went ahead and paid the notes after he questioned his friend Ray Miles about it. Ray had signed both notes. Ray explained that Elmer had bought a lot of the stock that Earl had found certificates for in the safe box and was short of ready cash. He had taken the first loan to buy the Ford truck and later for the Plymouth. Earl was grateful that he had the truck for business but could have gotten along with the Model A that he had given to Ira and Pearl. Earl remembered how Sylva had pestered Elmer to get her a new car.

The Elk Creek bank had failed in May of 1931 and all its assets had been transferred to the Raymondville bank. All its outstanding debits were allowed to languish.

The last outstanding note was a rather strange one for five hundred dollars appeared on October twenty fourth almost four months after the tragic fourth of July. It was signed, purportedly, on September fourteenth 1929 by Elmer just months after his grandfather Marcus' death. Why it would appear suddenly after three years had passed was very suspicious indeed. The real problem was that one of the four men who were bondsmen and had oversight of the estate was W. L. Lawson. Lawson held the outstanding note. Earl felt compelled to pay off the note even though he had serious reservations about its' authenticity.

There had been no real Autumn. Ninety degree days lasted until Halloween. Nick McKinney threatened to shoot anyone who tried to tip over his outhouse. The boys of the town did it anyway, led by Willard Lynch the primary ringleader. They would have gotten Weed Morgan's but they saw Weed sitting on his back porch smoking his pipe. They tried Jim Martin's but Jim set off a couple of firecrackers he had saved from the Fourth of July. One of the boys had gone inside to make water and got himself all wet trying to get his overalls on too quickly.

The heat and drought brought more muddy brown skies and showers of fine dirt all over every flat surface. Many people wore bandana masks to keep out the choking dirt

It did finally turn cold the second day of November. Earl woke to the first frost.

The cold weather brought some welcome showers. Earl had been concerned that he would have to feed his cattle hay a month or two early. He might have had to buy some hay or have starving cattle on his hands or, worse yet, have to sell part of his prized herd. The rains perked up the grass in his fields.

It warmed up again and it stayed that way for most of November.

Earl invited John Dunivan to come for Thanksgiving dinner and an afternoon of quail hunting. Dillard had a good hunting dog. He was invited for the hunt. They would have taken the dog without Dillard but he insisted the dog wouldn't hunt without him along. Earl and John got a big laugh out of that one.

Earl traded John a young pig for a turkey. He told John to notch the pig's ear and they would butcher together next Spring. Earl set aside a hog to butcher. George Surby was also given the chance to set aside a hog.

There was a smoke house on the home place where they could cure hams and bacon.

When Earl's visit to see Eva in November was met with a cold shoulder, he went on a drinking binge. He took his fishing gear, a tarpaulin to create a makeshift tent, cooking and eating utensils, and a bedroll. Most important of all he bought a case of rot gut for a companion. He caught a lot of fish in the Spring River near Hardy, Arkansas. He fried the fish in bacon grease from his breakfast meals. The binge didn't do anything but give him intense morning headaches and a persistent grinding stomach ache. He left on Wednesday and was so sick by Sunday that he decided to come home. He got back home in time for supper. He had bathed in the river but as the alcohol exited through his pores, he still smelled like a reformed drunk. He stopped at South Jacks Fork and bathed a second time. The water chilled him to the bone. He gobbled Sen-Sen by the handful.

After supper Fern said, "Pearl invited us all over for the beginning of a revival at Big Creek. Do you want to go with us?"

Earl shook his head, "I don't feel up to it. I came home sooner than I intended because I was feeling pretty awful."

"I'm not going either," Glenn said, "I'll stay here with, Bud."

Fern frowned at him, "You're not going to disappoint your Aunt Pearl." She rose from her seat and motioned for Earl to follow her outside.

"What is it, Fern?" Earl asked.

"You're not fooling me, Earl," Fern glared at him, her mouth pursing around her protruding teeth, "I can smell the alcohol on you when you come in. You're not drunk anymore like that one time I threatened to leave if you showed up drunk."

"I didn't come home drunk again," Earl said angrily.

Fern continued as if she hadn't been interrupted, "It's the deceit, now, more than being drunk. You may not be drunk right now, but you're a drunk. That's the plain simple truth of the matter."

Earl's face reddened in shame, "I'm sorry, Fern. I'll try to do better. I went to see Eva last Tuesday afternoon. It wasn't good. I feel like I'm not ready to raise a family, run a business, oversee four farms. Maybe if I'd had more preparation. I have these nightmares. I see my bloodied father and step-mother."

Fern's voice softened, "I know. I hear you at night. But you are ready for the business and you've done the right things in oversight of the farms and business. You're an incredibly talented young man when it comes to stock trading."

"Thanks, Fern," Earl said quietly, "I'll try to do better."

"I'll ask Pearl to put in a prayer petition on your behalf," Fern said.

"I'm not sure God wants to have much to do with me right now," Earl growled deep in his throat.

By mutual, unspoken consent, the two returned to the house. Earl went to the overstuffed chair by the table where Fern left his incoming mail. There was a stack of cards from various farmers offering for him to buy, cattle, horses, pigs, hogs, sheep and goats.

Earl wrote out replies to those wanting to sell livestock. He decided to get assistance from George Bailey for the horses. He got in the Plymouth since Pearl and Ira were taking Fern and the children with them. When Earl got to the Bailey's, George was on the front porch. He gave the penny post cards to George with a note signed by him that George would be working on his behalf.

George said, "give me ten dollars apiece for my four horses and I'll buy these others to go along with 'em. Then I'll take 'em all up to Rolla to take them off to Peoria to the glue factory."

"Okay, George you do that and I'll give you fifty cents apiece to deliver them." Earl took out two hundred dollars to buy horses, "and keep out two more dollars for expenses for grub."

"I'll head off before daylight tomorrow. I'll be back sometime Tuesday or Wednesday." George stuffed the bills in his overalls bib. George liked his hooch but he was dead honest and Earl knew he would account for every dime, every penny. "You know, Earl, that place in Peoria is more than a glue factory. They ship off meat to them Belgians in east Wisconsin and them Dutch in west Michigan. They like that horse meat."

Earl stopped by to see Spud Lynch on the East side of town. He was in the barn milking cows with Willard. When Earl entered the barn, Spud was just finishing up with his last cow. Spud said, "What's going on, Earl?"

"Would you mind helping us take some goats to Rolla and put them on the train for Chicago. A farmer over toward Mountain View has over two hundred and twenty goats he wants to sell. I figure that if we double deck them on my truck and yours we can get them there in two loads. We'll have to tie tarps across the top to keep those critters from jumping out." Earl's reply was longer than he imagined.

"You're on. What are you payin'." Spud inquired.

"Ten cents an animal. If you squeeze forty five goats on you can make nine dollars for a days work. That's not bad," Earl said.

"Yes but I've got expense, gas, wear and tear, tires…….." Spud trailed off.

"Okay. Twelve cents and you've got some work," Exasperated Earl chopped off the words, "I'm going to Raymondville to make a call to East Saint Louis and over to look at the goats. There's a good market for goat among the Italians in Chicago."

"I didn't know that. That's good to know if I have a chance to buy goats in the future. You want me to ride along so I can know how to get there."

The two men got in the Plymouth. Earl stopped at Ray Miles' and made the phone call to East Saint Louis at Joe Sullivan's residence.

Joe told Earl that the Federal Government had set up a program to buy out herds of cattle. He asked Earl if he could deliver a herd to Rolla. Joe would bring the government man to meet them on a Thursday like they had done in the past. Joe would have to arrange for a bulldozer and find a ravine where they could bury the carcasses. Joe said the government was offering twenty eight dollars a head. Earl whistled in surprise.

"That's at least five dollars more than I can get in East Saint Louis," Earl said.

"And that's on a good day," Joe replied.

"How much you giving me, Joe."

"Twenty-seven dollars."

"Twenty-seven and twenty cents," Earl said emphatically.

"How many cattle can you bring me, Earl?" Joe asked.

"Let me ask how many you want?"

"Can you manage four thousand?" Joe replied.

"If you give me until the second Thursday or Friday of December I can probably get you four thousand there."

Joe hesitated and said, "If you can bring that many, I'll give you twenty-seven and ten cents."

"How would it be if I brought five thousand."

Joe said emphatically, "That's as high as I can go. It's going to cost me for the place to bury the carcasses and hire a bulldozer."

"This will be a good thing for a lot of poor farmers in South Missouri and North Arkansas," Earl said, "Any cattle I buy privately, I'll give the farmers twenty-six dollars and ninety cents. I'll make my big profit from the cattle I buy in the sale barns."

"Sounds like a plan, Earl."

"I'll see you about seventeen days." Earl thought to himself, I've got a lot of planning to do. Places to line up pasture along the way.

Earl hired additional wranglers until he had lined up seventeen men. For the first eleven days, except for Thanksgiving, Earl had as many as six horsemen going with him to sale barns and to private purchases. Most days started before six o'clock and didn't end until after eight in the evening, beginning when it was dark and ending in the dark. He bought over three thousand head of cattle in sale barns. Earl did not disguise his buying. Most of his competition left off bidding when it got to twenty five dollars for fear that they would have to take them to market at a loss.

Earl sent Ira to Springfield to buy five four man tents. The tents were a necessity for the advent of colder weather in December. Earl also hired Harold Baker, George's teenage brother to help Ira set up camp and be a gopher for the cook. Earl hired John Martin to come along as the cook.

He hired Ira to haul horses and cowhands everywhere he went to buy cattle or in sale rings. Every day they were driving cattle to assembly areas in Tyrone, by Willow, West Plains and Clear springs. It was daunting, hard work.

Earl let it be known in the nearby towns he would be buying cattle. He took Dillard with a checkbook to a location with three or four cowhands. He would go back to Tyrone to get more horses and at least three cowhands and he would buy more. Earl bought cattle in various locations before ten o'clock in the morning, then he would be off for the sale barns. In twelve working days, including Sundays, he averaged buying over four hundred twenty cattle a day.

When Earl brought back a check of over a hundred forty thousand dollars, Ray Miles was wonderfully surprised.

"You told me I would have to cover you, I didn't know how much it would really be. We have a weekly meeting every Tuesday, on the second Tuesday you were over sixty thousand over and they insisted that I start charging interest," Ray said rather sheepishly. "When it got over a hundred thousand overdraft they thought I'd gone off the deep end. This check will exonerate me." Ray smiled broadly.

"No I don't mind interest for a couple of weeks," Earl said, "How much is that going to be?"

Ray grabbed a pad of paper. He did some figuring and said, "A little over a hundred and fifty."

"It was worth it to make ten thousand profit, Ray."

"Yes it was well worth it. By the way we are making payouts on shares from the Elk Creek bank."

Ray handed Earl a check for three hundred seventy-five dollars. Earl took out his daily business notebook and wrote the amount in it. "Just go ahead and deposit it in my grandmother's savings account. It was really Marcus' money. I'll tell her," Earl said.

A few minutes later Earl left the bank and got in the truck with Ira. Ira needed to take him home and go back to Licking where the cowhands were going to camp out. Dillard and Earl had come home with their gear and all but one extra horse.

Ira stopped at the store to let Dillard out and took Earl on up to his house.

When Earl stepped up on the porch he was surrounded by his sisters and brothers. He got hugs from his sisters and a manly handshake from Glen. Fern came out and watched the outpouring affection for her nephew. Earl noticed Fern, "John will be back with the rest at noon. You think you can feed seventeen or eighteen hungry men tomorrow."

Fern nodded, "Dana has been over helping. We baked pies all day. She will be coming back in the morning and Dillard will be here."

"Good. I'm going down to my folks and stay the weekend. They're making molasses and I can help. I'll bring some back with me."

His sisters wailed painfully, "Oh, Earl," Lucille said, "We've hardly seen you for over two weeks and now you're going away again."

"I tell you what I'll do," Earl said, "I'll take you someplace you choose over the Christmas holiday. Christmas falls on Sunday and you don't have to be in school until January second. I'd like to be around for Christmas so Santa can find us. We'll have eight days after that. You pick a place and that's where we'll go. We can take Fern if she wants."

All three of the young Siglers jumped up and down in excitement. Glen said, "We'll figure out something."

Earl went upstairs with his duffel bag, sorted out his dirty clothes and took a hard sided suitcase for some clothing for the weekend. He put on his best high heel boots and clean clothes. He hoped go get in a hot bath at his mother's and step-father's.

The weekend at his folks was restful. On Saturday morning Earl helped carry canes to squeeze out the juice which was funneled into a cooker. The juice was cooked and flowed from one channel to another, back and forth until it was boiled down into a thick dark syrup, black strap molasses. It was ladled out into quart jars and capped. Just about anybody in the neighborhood could have some. Many supplied labor, a horse or canes to the process.

Many older neighbors who were physically unable to contribute were given jars of molasses for past contributions.

At one o'clock Charlie and Mary got in the front seat of their old Chevrolet with Earl in the back to go to Willow for their weekly shopping. Just before they started for home, Charlie stopped by the ice house to pick up a block of ice. While they were in town, Earl stayed away from the sale barn. He didn't want to look a cow in the eye for weeks. He walked up from MFA to Wilbanks Grocery where the Bradfords preferred to do their shopping. Earl saw Eva across the street looking in the Charles Ferguson Clothing Store window. Earl crossed the street at a diagonal. He walked up to Eva without her noticing.

"Anything I could buy you?" Earl enquired.

Eva whirled around, a smile on her face, "Well, laudy be. Look what the cat drug up."

"I thought a good school marm was supposed to use better English," Earl said, smiling back.

"I think I should practice on taking up with an old hillbilly cowboy like you."

Earl's heart beat a lot faster. He said, "I guess you and your folks had your discussion."

"Yes. Night before last."

"That's absolutely terrific," Earl said quickly, "How about a date this week, a movie in Houston?"

"Let's not go at this so fast. My father gave his approval for us to start dating again since the divorce is getting closer. My mother thinks I should wait awhile. She suggested sometime around February first closer to the actual date. I got a compromise out of them for about the first of the year." Eva replied.

"Ask them about one date this week and then I'll wait until the New Year."

"I'll do that and drop you a card."

"How about I save you that and stop by after school on Monday."

Eva nodded, "I hear you rented pasture again from Papa."

"I did as a matter of fact," Earl replied, "I just got back yesterday from the biggest cattle drive yet. I doubt if I have another this big, if ever. I don't see times getting any better. I did a good thing for a lot of farmers. I got nearly four dollars a head better than market. You may not have heard that the government is buying up herds and destroying them and burying the carcasses."

Eva looked across the street and saw her parents looking at them. She looked back at Earl, "I'll see you Monday. I'll have to explain that this was just a chance meeting."

Earl tipped his hat to her. He waved at Wayne and Rena. They did not return the gesture.

Chapter 20 -

Wherever You Go

Earl seized on hope for the future. He still relied on bootleg to beat down the other demons that haunted him. Despite his big success on the last cattle drive, he saw bad economic times in front of him in business. The state of the nation had fallen fast and far in two years. When would it get better? A severe drought was still gripping the West. Rain came only sporadically in Texas County. Enough rain had fallen in early November to restore the grass for the cattle. Another rain and snow in December was helpful and had delayed feeding hay earlier than necessary.

Earl went to Summersville on Monday after seeing Eva on Saturday. He sent Lonnie to the National Stock Yards with two loads of hogs from purchases he had made on Friday in West Plains and Willow on Saturday. The market had gone up a fraction on Friday morning. He hoped for a small profit.

He had continued taking some loads of cattle up on consignment percentage or on flat rate.

Earl had some inquiries about young Jersey or Guernsey cows bred or ready to breed. He though it might be somewhat lucrative. He knew he could deliver the animals for fifty cents or a dollar a head profit. He wanted only to buy as demand warranted it.

The price of cattle was so volatile and trending downward that Earl knew not to buy on speculation for a long time to come.

In Summersville Earl bought twenty dairy cows, all dry and bred. Most of his inquiries were for one to three cows. Earl even sold cows on payments to individuals he could trust to pay. He had select farmers, who had no ready cash, sign an IOU on the contract that Jim Holt had prepared for him. When Lonnie came back from East Saint Louis, Earl sent him home to sleep since he had been up all night. Earl asked Dillard to go and pick up the cows.

By late afternoon Earl was ready to head off for Stultz. When he got to the school and alit from the Plymouth, an angry, scowling sky was approaching from the Northwest. Earl went into the school and saw Eva with the pupil she was tutoring. Earl sat quietly in the back and listened. He was amazed at how bright and knowledgeable Eva was about the subject matter she was trying to instill into the student.

When the tutorial was finished Eva followed the young boy, who grinned knowingly at Earl. Eva stopped in front of Earl, who stood up quickly. The boy stopped at the door to watch the two of them.

"Shoo. Shoo," Eva said, "Go on home."

The boy smirked and turned to go.

Earl moved closer to Eva as the boy went out the door. He put his arms around her, she put her arms around him but not tightly. She evaded his kiss.

Eva broke away from the embrace, "Let's take this slow, Earl. I don't have complete agreement on how to go forward, if at all."

Earl's brow furrowed in thought, "Go forward. I don't understand."

"I don't have complete agreement or harmony on this between me, my father and my mother."

"How about the date we talked about?" Earl asked.

"You mean the date you talked about."

"Yes, that one," Earl said rather exasperated.

Eva smiled with an impish twinkle in her eye, "They said it would be okay for one time but to wait awhile for anything more."

"How about tomorrow? A movie in Houston?"

"No movie," Eva said, "My parents think they are the devil's workshop. Make it Thursday."

"An ice cream treat? Or you could come over to the house and we could pop some popcorn and listen to radio comedy shows," Earl said.

When they got outside, there was a biting, cold wind coming out of the Northwest. Earl said, "Get in and I'll drive you home so you won't freeze. I bet you didn't wear a coat with it so warm this morning."

Eva went to the passenger's side and got in. Earl drove Eva to the Morgan's. When Earl pulled up in front, he saw Belle looking out the window. "This will set tongues a wagging," Earl said.

Eva got out quickly. With the door open, she said, "What time?"

"About six-thirty, would that be okay?" Earl said.

Eva nodded and hurried inside.

When Earl got home he went to the barn to look at the cows. Dillard had fed them some grain but hadn't opened the gate. Earl opened the gate and let them out knowing they would find the spring down below the hill.

He went back to the house to look at his mail, more cards from farmers.

There was a disturbing letter from Judge D. L. Johnson. The essential item in the letter was a complaint by Jim Smith. He accused Earl of abandoning his grandchildren for days on end, that they were being raised by a woman who was not a relative.

Earl wrote a letter explaining his actions during the cattle drive. He admitted to being gone for fourteen to sixteen hours a day assembling the large herd. He emphasized that it was of major importance in providing financially for his family, his grandmother and to a lesser degree of his Aunt Pearl. He said that the profit from the cattle drive may have to provide for the family for several months because of the bad livestock market. He offered to come see the Judge in person if it would be helpful and signed the letter. He sealed it in an envelope. He would mail it first thing in the morning. It was an unsettling event.

Earl walked down to the mill building. It was getting really cold. He looked at the old thermometer on the wall of the building by the office door. It was already below freezing. He wished he had worn a coat. He went into the office, taking a bottle from his hidden cache. He opened a bottle and had a couple of long pulls. He walked over to the barn and saw the pigs had all entered the barn breezeway and were in a huddled mass of flesh. He went back to the mill office and drank some more bootleg. He knew that Glen and Lucille would probably be done with chores and supper would be on the table soon. He was reluctant to go back to the house after he had so much to drink. Remembering Fern's warning he walked down to his grandmother's house.

It was starting to snow, big fluffy flakes the size of a baseball. Earl entered the living room without knocking. Sarah had built a fire in the stove. It felt good. Earl was unsteady on his feet. He sat heavily in the overstuffed chair across the room from his grandmother who was seated in her usual rocker.

"Looks like you've been drinking again," Sarah said wrinkling her nose, "You smell like a saloon. Marcus would drink some and so did Elmer. I guess your dad got you started on the moonshine. Neither my husband or son drank like you have taken to."

Earl didn't answer immediately. Finally he said, "I got a letter from the Judge. Monkey Jim has been complaining that I went off and left the kids."

"Yes, Earl, he was over here nosing around and seein' the children after school. He was stayin' with Leroy Grogan. He's the one he wanted on as bondsmen and oversight of the estate, remember?" Sarah said, "I figured Grogan would be trouble when he was appointed, he and Jim Smith have been as thick as thieves for years."

"I wrote a letter to the judge about an hour ago. Lucille and Glen were still doing chores so I walked down to the mill and over by the barn to check on the hogs," Earl said, "I'm hungry and don't think I should go back up to the house yet." He took out his box of Sen-Sen and chewed on them.

Sarah frowned at Earl but said, "I can warm you up something'. There's fire in the kitchen stove yet, I recon." Sarah got up and went into the kitchen.

Earl followed her.

Sarah put some wood in the stove. Earl watched as she left the front of the little fire box open to produce more draft. He sat on one of the chairs by the kitchen table. The fire caught and Sarah closed the little door to the stove firebox.

Sarah went out on the porch and came back with some sliced baloney. She put a large skillet on the stove to heat. She took a covered pan out of the warmer oven. After a couple of minutes she put a little lard in the skillet and some baloney to fry. She cut two slices of homemade bread. The baloney browned. She put the three slices between the two slices of bread and put it on a small plate. She uncovered the small pot and ladled some soup into a bowl. She sat them in front of Earl and seated herself across from him.

Earl ate hungrily.

They were surprised to hear the front door open. Lucille entered the kitchen. She sat down in one of the chairs and said, "Earl, I'm so sorry. I happened to read the letter from the Judge. It's my fault."

Earl stopped eating, "I don't understand what you're talking about."

"When Pappy came over last Tuesday, he was waiting for us to get out of school and walked to the house with us. He 'was just over for a visit' he said. Then he was here again on Wednesday. He walked home with us again and we sat on the front porch and visited. I complained that you had been gone a lot, then he asked a lot of questions. He said he was going to go over to have a word with the Judge the next day. I'm so sorry," Lucille finished miserably.

"It's alright," Earl said reassuringly, "I wrote a letter to the Judge explaining that this was an opportunity that would probably not come up again and that it was for the long-term good of the family. It will be okay."

"Anyway, I'm sorry if I caused trouble." Lucille lamented.

"It will be okay," Earl repeated, "With the country going the way it is we're in for a long spell of really bad times. Hoover will be blamed for it even though it wasn't his fault. I pity the next President of the country. It looks like nothing will help. The government buying up cattle hasn't helped the price of beef. It has just continued to fall."

"Fern said you got up suddenly and left the house without a word," Lucille said, "I just knew something was wrong, then I saw the letter."

They sat in silence as Earl finished his sandwich and soup. He wiped his mouth on a cloth napkin. "It will be all right, Lucille. The letter I wrote will take care of it," Earl said, "Go back home and get ready for bed, I'll be along soon."

All three got up and walked to the front porch, the ground was covered with snow, at least an inch in a short time. Lucille's footprints in the snow led up past the harness shop on the corner. Earl went back inside with his grandmother. He was not so unsteady on his feet now.

Sarah sat in her rocking chair. "Earl, you have to get your drinkin' under control."

Earl glanced down at the toes of his boots and nodded his head. He got his hat off the arm of the chair where he had sat a few minutes before. He walked toward the door.

"Wait, let me get you one of Marcus' old coats," Sarah said. She rose and went into her bedroom and came back with an old mackinaw. Earl slipped it on and left with no reply.

He walked in the dark down toward the old Hotel where the Parmenter family now lived, around the old beer joint. The new house across the road was nearly complete, the roof on and the unusual stucco exterior was in place. They were still working on the inside. He walked back between the two silent, closed groceries. He glanced at the dark blacksmith shop and church on his left. The snow was falling so quickly that there was close to two inches. When he walked past the house where Ike Miller and his second wife lived, he saw the faint imprint of Lucille's shoes in the snow.

When he got back to the house, Lucille and Fern were awake, reading by lamplight. Earl stomped snow off his boots. He removed his coat and shook off the snow. He walked in and sank into his usual easy overstuffed chair.

Fern looked up and said, "Earl, Lucille told me about the letter. I'm so sorry."

"The letter I wrote and sealed before I left will take care of it. It'll be okay." Earl assured. "I think I'm going on up to bed. Tomorrow I think I'll go over to the sale in Mountain View."

"The radio forecast isn't good. They're talking about a foot of snow or more."

"I'll throw some chains in the truck in case I get stuck." Earl rose and went to the dining table and lit the small lamp he used to light his way up the stairs. When he got to the top of the stairs he looked in on Glen. He was sleeping with the lamp turned down low. He got a blanket out of the closet to put over Glen. Earl got a blanket for himself, undressed quickly, and was in bed before he could get chilled.

He woke while it was still dark. He fumbled around in the dark until he found a match to light the lamp. He looked at the clock on the chest of drawers. It was four thirty. He went downstairs. He started a fire in the heating stove in the living room. He found the two-day-old Sunday newspaper.

Earl read that the Cardinals were expected to have a good year in 1932 with their two new young pitchers, the Dean brothers. The news on the economic front was still grim. The government purchase of hundreds of thousands of cattle was deemed a failure. The price of cattle had continued to fall. Hog prices were up and down but was trending down. Earl knew he would have to take great care in his purchases of hogs. Corporations and banks were continuing to fail. The international news was grim. Japan was making noise of continuing colonizing in Asia. Italy had a new dictator and the news from Germany was troubling. Earl decided to turn to the funnies for a lightening of the mood.

Fern came in the room a little after five. Earl got up and went to the kitchen to start the five in the kitchen stove. He noticed that the wood for the stove in the wood box was getting low. He went out the back door to the wood pile and began to split wood. Earl noticed that the snow was pretty deep but no more was falling. Even though it was well over an hour before sunrise, the Eastern skies were already brightening and there was enough light from the snow reflection to work. When he had an arm load ready he carried it in the house. Earl left a small pile of split wood for later in the day.

Earl let the load of wood fall into the box in the kitchen.

Fern was at the stove, putting the coffee pot on to perk.

Earl returned to the living room. He knew the stock market report would be on at five thirty. He turned the radio on and tuned it in to KMOX. He caught the last few words of the news cast, "the economic news for the nation continues to be grave. Now a word from Standard Oil."

During the commercial, Earl picked up Capper's weekly, a farm magazine that Earl scanned occasionally. It had lots of advertising aimed at farm women in particular. After the oil commercial, the weather news came on. "There was snow last night, here in Saint Louis. We got about four to six inches but in the South part of the state they were hard hit. Springfield had ten inches but in Texas County we have reports of a foot or more. Houston and Raymondville sources said they had fourteen inches, Licking twelve, and Cabool says they have fifteen. This storm has moved off into the Ohio River Valley area bringing heavy snow but not as much as in southern Missouri. Here is the farm report:" Earl listened intently. The price of cattle had dropped closer to three cents a pound. When would it end, he thought, soon the farmers would have to give away their animals.

The clock struck five-thirty. Fern came in. "Earl, would you wake Lucille and Glen. It'll take longer to do chores with all this snow."

"It won't take as long because we won't have to carry water to cool the milk. I just hope Nick can get our milk with the snow. I hope he has chains for his truck."

Earl woke Lucille and Glen. He had a cup of coffee. He cooled it in the saucer, blowing on it and sipping from the saucer until he had finished it. He put on some rubber boots from the back porch. He trudged out to the haystack, in the Southwest corner of the field West of the house. He forked ten forks full over the fence into the larger field South of the milk parlor and hen house. After the milking was over he would let the milk cows have first chance at the hay and then he would bring up the other animals.

Earl walked on down into the fields above the spring. He knew he would find the cattle there. The cattle were standing around forlornly in the snow. He separated the four cows they were milking from the herd and started them up the field toward the milk parlor. The other cows he had bought the day before were following along behind. When he got near the parlor, he turned and herded the other cattle back toward the barn. He went to the barn and forked hay out into the barnyard. He carried the hay on his fork and tossed it into the field across the corral fence. The cattle and horses both noticed and came up to graze on the loose hay.

Dillard came trudging through the snow. "I couldn't get out of the driveway with the car."

"Go on back home, take care of things over there. I can feed the Hogs." Earl said.

"Since I'm here I might as well do it. Besides she sent me over with the key to the store to get some bacon for breakfast." Dillard knew he couldn't open the gate with all the snow so he just climbed over. He turned over the hog troughs to empty the snow out and got buckets of ground corn into the troughs. The hogs reluctantly left the shelter of the barn and began to eat.

Earl worked his way through the snow back to the house. Glen was particularly happy with the snow. He knew they could have a lot of fun sliding down the hill toward the boys' outhouse. Earl cautioned him to be careful. He had lost a tooth last year running into that little structure. The teacher had found it and jammed it back in place. It had rooted itself but was still discolored.

When the sun came out it was warm enough by noon that the snow began to melt. By Thursday the snow was nearly all gone except in deeply shaded places. Earl was happy about the snow because it would replenish the water table and help green up the grass again if it stayed warm.

* * * * * * * * * * * *

Eva, on Tuesday morning woke early to over a foot of snow. She knew that school would not be dismissed. The children all walked to school. They would just have to leave home sooner. Eva knew she only had eight days left. Eva would work hard to continue teaching her school children all she could. She would continue tutoring the eighth grade boy to help ready him for high school. Eva wondered, however, if the snow would have any adverse impact on her date with Earl on Thursday.

By Thursday the snow had mostly melted. Bell told Eva they had just a little more than twelve inches of snow.

It was getting close to five and a half months since she and Earl had gone anyplace together. She was in full anticipation. She dressed in one of her new purchases from the last weekend in Willow. It was still chilly so she wore a light jacket.

Earl was anxious. He was fifteen minutes early. He had to wait in the living room with Belle and George in attendance. They had a chance to have a nice talk. When Eva emerged, Earl was dazzled by her loveliness.

"Where you young people off to," George said.

"I think we'll go over to Cabool for a steak dinner and an ice cream treat afterward," Earl said.

They got in the Plymouth and Earl wound his was through to Elk Creek and over to the highway south to Cabool. The roads were gravel but well graded. The road between Stultz and Elk Creek had a lot of chuck holes from the snowstorm. Earl drove to a downtown café. Earl, good as his word, ordered steak but Eva chose fried chicken. Earl had coffee and Eva sipped a Pepsi Cola. They ate and chatted until the café was nearly ready to close. They hurried down the street to the Pharmacy before it could close. Both ordered malted milks, Earl vanilla and Eva chocolate. They sat and drank and talked until the owner said he usually closed fifteen past.

They drove home and were in front of the Morgan house by nine o'clock. Earl knew Eva got up early to help Belle. She went to the school early to get a good fire going before the children arrived.

Earl wanted to cuddle in the car a bit but Eva wasn't ready for that yet.

"Will I see you the weekend of Christmas, Eva."

"I don't think it's a good idea. Mama and Papa are still on outs over this. Why don't you stop by our house on the Saturday after Christmas. By that time we may have some resolution.

Eva got out of the car. Earl started to get out.

Eva said, "You don't need to walk me to the door."

"You didn't give me a chance to tell you," his frustration bled into his voice, "that I promised to take Lucille, Glen and Vivian somewhere between Christmas and New Year. I don't even know if I'll be back by that Saturday but I'll try."

"Do your best. I'll be at Clear Springs right down by your folks. I'll be staying at Ray and Mae McAllister's just a little over a mile from the school" Eva kissed her hand and blew it to Earl. Turning, she walked slowly to the door and inside.

* * * * * * * * * * *

Earl's brother and sisters decided they wanted to go to Bull Shoals Lake. Elmer and Sylva had taken them there in July a year ago. Lucille remembered they went to a new resort cabin near Pontiac right on the Arkansas line. Earl looked at a map and decided he probably could drive down in two hours on the Monday after Christmas.

After seeing Eva, the time dragged by until Christmas. Earl continued to work. He sent two truck loads of hogs the Monday before Christmas. He lost money on the trip. Hog prices took a sudden dive that Monday in the ring. Earl was thankful that he had the big payday on the cattle drive.

Little did Earl know how bad it would get before it got better.

During the week before Christmas a sudden interest in farmers wanting to upgrade their teams of horses came in by penny post card. Earl had heard the farmers who had lost crops in Kansas was selling off their work horses. He asked Lonnie to have George come by when he had a chance. On Wednesday morning George stopped in as Earl was eating breakfast. He explained his idea of going to Kansas to buy young working stock. Earl planned to send George by train to Garden City, Kansas, where they had a weekly auction barn where he could start.

George and Earl went to Raymondville and back to Cabool to catch a train for Garden City. He gave him seven hundred dollars to buy ten teams of horses and any other horses that George thought would be good to send to Peoria next spring. He instructed George to pay cash for bringing the horses back by rail if he could bring them back for a dollar a head. "Get receipts and stay in a good hotel but watch the money," Earl instructed.

When George had bought his ticket and was going into the waiting room. Earl gave him a bottle of his moonshine. "Buy yourself some more along as you need to. You don't need a receipt for that," Earl chuckled.

Earl saw a nice cedar that he thought would make a good Christmas tree. When he got back to the house he found a saw and took the truck back to get the tree. He got back home before school was out. He took some two by fours and made a stand and nailed the tree to the stand and supported it by four pieces of wire to the wood stand to keep it stable. He brought it into the living room.

Fern said, "That's a fine looking Christmas tree, Earl."

"We'll decorate it after chores and supper," Earl remarked, "I'll go upstairs and get the box of decorations. Tomorrow we'll go to Willow shopping for toys and other gifts for the kids."

"Since you'll be gone next week, I'd like to go home and spend some time with my family at Henry and Effie's. We're all getting together down at Mary and Charlie's on Christmas day."

Earl smiled, "In ways I wish I could be there with the family, too," A look of sadness crossed his face, "But that's not possible now."

"No, Earl, it's not. I'm so sad for you sometimes that life has taken such a vicious turn for you and your sisters and brother."

"I'll drop you off at Skaggs' on the way back from Willow. I just don't know how we could have gotten by without you the past few months," Earl said earnestly.

"Now don't you get me crying," Fern said pursing her lips as well as she could, "I have always loved you like a brother since we practically grew up together. I've grown to love your Lucille, Glen and Vivian. They are precious."

"They are at that, Fern."

"Earl, I want you to promise me something," Fern said, now very serious, "You must take them to church during Christmas and the New Year weekends.

"I'll take care of it." Earl turned and went upstairs to get the box of decorations.

* * * * * * * * * *

It turned out to be a good Christmas. Ira and Pearl came over Christmas Eve. Earl drove down and got his grandmother. They sat around the living room staying warm by the heat stove. They sang Christmas songs. Ira played his fiddle. Sarah slept on Lucille's bed, Lucille in Glen's bed and Glen slept with Earl. Ira and Pearl slept in Fern's bed. The children found the gifts Earl had bought in Willow the day before. They thought Santa had come.

The family went together to Big Creek to church that Sunday, Earl stayed at home to work.

On Monday morning they set out for Bull Shoals lake.

Earl rented a two bedroom cabin by the day on the lake. They rented a rowboat for fishing. The weather, when they arrived was warm. On Monday they caught enough fish for supper. The little cabin was furnished with a gas stove. Lucille had learned well from Fern. They had slaw and fried potatoes with the fish. They fished in the mornings on Tuesday and Wednesday. In the afternoons they played shuffleboard. They rotated teams. The most successful was Glen and Lucille together. On Thursday morning they awoke to sleet on the ground. The forecast was continued cold through the weekend. They decided together to check out and go back home.

When they got near Mountain Grove, it began to sleet again, by the time they were just north of Cabool freezing rain was coating the windshield. The rest of the way home was a slip-sliding adventure. The ford at Big Creek was treacherous. It was solid rock from shore to shore and the shores were solid ice. Earl kept the Plymouth moving and survived the crossing. He breathed a sigh of relief when they were back on the gravel covered road.

When Earl pulled up in front of his house, Glen, Lucille and Vivian headed immediately to get their sleds. A riding horse Earl recognized as one he had bought for Dillard was hitched to the front fence. Earl went inside and started a fire in the heat stove and went out back to find Dillard. He heard sounds of activity by the barn. He found Dillard feeding the hogs and forking hay out into the field for the horses and cattle.

Dillard was surprised to see Earl, "I didn't expect you back until Saturday or Sunday."

"Well, the weather didn't cooperate or we would have stayed," Earl said, "We couldn't catch many fish in this kind of weather. You can go on back home if you want."

"I'll take you up on that, Earl. I've been comin' over early in the mornin' to do your chores and before supper in the evenin'. You'll have to ease them back into a more regular schedule," Dillard handed Earl the pitchfork.

"Any problems?" Earl asked.

"Had a hog dead yesterday mornin'. I drug it down on the east end of the pasture and buried it by the tree line."

Earl knew that animals just up and died for no explainable reason. Another loss noted in his diary.

Earl finished up the chores by the barn. He saw Dillard reining his horse around to head west to where he was living now. He pulled out his pocket watch and made a mental note that he would have time to pick up his mail at the Kidd Store. He got his mail and the accumulation of three days of newspapers. Most of his post cards were ordinary requests. He settled in to read the newspapers and look at the livestock markets for Monday and Tuesday. Beef and pork prices were trending down sharply. Mutton and lamb were steady. Earl wished there were more sheep available.

There was a reply to Earl's letter from Judge Johnson, intimating that Johnson hadn't taken the complaints by Jim Smith too seriously. It reminded Earl that he probably should start compiling the last quarter report to the bondsmen and the court. I'll start that tonight, he thought.

His sisters and brother returned while he was doing chores with scrapes and bruises from sled wrecks. At least they hadn't run into the outhouse on the schoolhouse hill.

On Saturday morning he had a penny post card from Eva inviting him to the Weilers for Supper that evening. It was a pleasant surprise. He expected a hard grilling by Eva's parents. He and Lonnie went to the Willow sale barn and bought a truck load of pigs, boars and shoats, to begin feeding out.

* * * * * * * * * *

When Earl arrived at the Weiler's it was just past six o'clock in the evening he was dressed in a nice long-sleeved shirt, good khakis and his new flat heeled boots. Young Wayne B. opened the door for him and Ralph rushed over and grabbed Earl's forefinger and held on tightly.

Rena came from the kitchen and smiled grimly, "It's so nice you could come," She motioned toward an overstuffed chair, "Sit down, please. Eva is upstairs getting ready. Wayne, Clyde and Esther are up at the barn finishing chores."

Joyce sitting on the bed in the living room, smiled and looked at him in openmouthed wonder.

Earl settled into the chair and Ralph climbed up on his lap and leaned his head back on Earl's shoulder.

Wayne B. said, "He likes you"

Earl put his arm around Ralph and squeezed him lightly. If he had been a kitten he would have purred.

Earl heard steps on the stairs and his heart gave a lurch of anticipation.

When Eva entered the room she smiled beatifically and the whole room lit with her presence.

Earl wondered how anyone so lovely could be interested in him. He always thought his face and nose were too long, his chin too sharp.

"Ralph! Get down this instant," Eva scolded.

Ralph started to obey but Earl held him a little tighter, "It's okay," Earl said smiling, "We're friends. Empty laps are lonely."

Eva smiled, warming the room. She went on into the kitchen. Earl heard her asking if she could help. He heard the murmured reply by Rena and the sounds of silverware and china being placed on the table. A few minutes later Earl heard other voices. Clyde glided through with a knowing smirk of a smile. Esther passed through with a frown at Earl. Not a friend, Earl surmised. Wayne, on his way through to change from his work clothes, said, "Hello." Not unfriendly, Earl thought.

The meal was baked chicken with cornbread dressing, green beans and mashed potatoes with white gravy. It was served after Wayne had said a beautifully worded prayer. Everyone ate in a studied silence. After the meal was over, Wayne asked Clyde and Esther to take the younger children upstairs to play Chinese Checkers. "Clyde put a couple of sticks of wood in the heating stove," Wayne added.

"Ralph don't know how," Wayne B said.

Rena said, "Ralph doesn't know how, Wayne B."

"Yes that's right," Wayne B replied.

"Then you teach him how, help him to learn," Eva said.

Clyde said, "He and I will be partners. Right, Ralph."

Ralph nodded vigorously and they all got up and left the room. Earl heard their steps as they ascended to the upper floor.

Earl was armed and ready. He had taken his grandmother's Bible and read up on two of scriptures' greatest love stories.

The four sat at the kitchen table, sipping their coffee quietly. Finally Wayne cleared his throat and spoke, "Earl, we asked Eva to invite you over to appraise you of a decision that we made. In this case it was a rather reluctant decision." Wayne paused for a moment and continued, "My biggest concern is for the happiness and welfare of my daughter. Because of your past I was concerned that you would remain faithful to her if this relationship should lead to marriage. I have biblical reservations of my daughter continuing a relationship with a married man."

Rena took up a cudgel, "Earl it has been my conviction from the outset that you do not deserve to be seeing my daughter. Your past behavior, in my estimation disqualifies you. You are a married man and should not even be pursuing Eva."

Earl bowed his head in shame but when his eyes, piercing brown, met Rena's pretty blue eyes they were sincere, "You are right Missus Weiler. I don't deserve Eva. I led a selfish, wayward life in the past. I have given up that way of life because of Eva. I love her with a passion that burns in my heart like a fire. The last several months have been pure misery. If I could undo my past, I would but it will always be with me."

Rena said, "Earl, I believe you to be an honest man. Despite my reservations, Wayne and I have agreed that you can resume your relationship since you will be a free man in a few more weeks. Eva will be teaching at Clear Springs and you'll have a lot opportunity to see each other."

Eva said, "You and Papa have been so protective of my welfare and I appreciate that. I have been just as miserable as Earl with not being able to see him on a regular basis. I just couldn't go against your wishes. I love this man, Earl. You two know what true love is. I've seen that between you, Mama and Papa. Thank you. Thank you."

"I would caution you," Wayne said, "take it slowly and let your relationship be cool until Earl's divorce is final."

Earl said, "Your counsel is important to us. I came prepared with love stories I had heard of in Sunday School but now it won't be necessary to fortify my position."

Rena brightened considerably, "I would like to hear what you were going to offer, Earl."

Earl suddenly became shy about what he had been prepared to say but began anyway, "I was going to tell you about Ruth and Naomi and David and Bathsheba. Both love stories were born in the midst of death and intrigue. Ruth's husband had died and she became the Great-grandmother of David. David killed a man for the love of a woman who had become the mother of the next King of Israel."

Earl stopped speaking. Rena nodded and said, "Continue what you were going to say. I'm interested."

Earl gathered his thoughts and said, "I won't try to quote scripture but Ruth loved her mother-in-law so much that she wouldn't stay with her own family. She told Naomi 'wherever you go I'll go' and 'your people will be my people.' David, despite adultery and murder came to be 'a man after God's heart.' I've done some bad things. God may punish me for it but I'm hoping you won't keep me from the one I love because of it."

"Well said, Earl," Wayne said. "Thank you for your candor."

In an effort to let some levity into the situation, "Earl said I have a lot of things that require my attention beside chasing your daughter around." He chuckled and the others laughed nervously.

Eva spoke up quickly, "Earl has three families or fractions of family who look to him to keep the family business afloat after his sisters and brothers were so suddenly orphaned. His grandmother, his aunt and uncle and those little ones are all totally or partially dependent on his business knowledge. He has been appointed executor of a sizeable estate. It's not easy keeping it going. He gives a generous monthly stipend to his estranged wife."

"Yes," Rena said, "these are hard times and they won't get better anytime soon. That New York Governor, Roosevelt, is making noises like he wants to be President of the country. I'm not sure he's any better than what we have now. I'm just thankful that Wayne got that part-time job in Willow or I don't know how we would survive with all these young ones."

"Not to change the subject, Earl," Wayne said, "I need a new team of horses. My pair are getting up close to fifteen years old. You know where I can get replacements?"

"I just sent my 'horse man' George Bailey out to Kansas with instructions to buy ten teams of horses," Earl replied, "I've had enquiries from three other farmers beside yourself that are wanting new teams. I think I can come out on them if I take your team on in trade with five dollars a head to boot."

"That sounds really reasonable. I could have a new team for ten dollars. How can you do that?" Wayne asked.

"Would it surprise you if I told you that horsemeat is higher than beef? We would send your old horses off to Peoria, Illinois, for slaughter." Earl asked, "Would that bother you?"

Wayne shook his head.

Earl continued, "I'll probably hold on to them until it warms up in March and let George take them up. I pay him a dollar a horse and his expenses. He usually has some horses of his own he has traded for. He makes a little money on his horses and I make a little and everyone comes out."

"Would you mind if I have first pick?" Wayne asked.

"Not at all," Earl affirmed, "I expect to get a card any day when to meet him in Cabool. You can bring your team along and we'll make the trade right there at the train station where we'll be unloading them."

A few minutes later Earl left with Eva holding his hand. Before Earl got in the car Eva was in his arms, pressing against him, her arms about his neck kissing him with a passion he had not experienced from her before.

"I'll be seeing you in Clear Springs." Eva said her lips an inch or two away, "I've missed your family so much. It will be nice to see Mary and Charlie, Sarah, Lucille, Glen, Vivian, Aunt Pearl. Even that old lecher, Uncle Ira."

Earl kissed Eva much more lightly this time, "How do you know Ira is a lecher?"

"When you weren't looking one time he gave my rear end a caress with his hand."

"If he ever does it again," Earl said angrily, "slap his face really good. Tell him you'll set me onto him. If I catch him at it, pity him."

Earl said, "I'd better get going. I promised that I'd take the kids over to see Jim Smith tomorrow morning, They don't start school until Tuesday."

"How about me coming down Monday evening and going down to my mother's and Charlie's for supper?" Earl asked, "I can stop by on my way back from Arrol. If you can, I'll let them know we're coming."

"How about Tuesday evening," Eva answered, "Monday will be a get acquainted day and I'll be quizzing the students on what they learned the first half. After school I'll spend most of the evening looking at their books and getting prepared for their first day of actual school on Tuesday."

Earl left looking forward to the next phase of his relationship with Eva.

CHAPTER 21 -

If Wishes Were Horses

On Monday Earl drove by Big Creek on his way to Arrol to take the children to Monkey Jim Smith's. The children had a sudden urge to stop and see the new stone Earl had ordered back in August for their father and mother. It wasn't a pleasant experience, tears of sorrow had watered the clay soil of that City of the Dead. It had stamped its imprint on all their hearts. They didn't stay long.

When they crossed Big Creek for the second time, Earl told his sisters and brother that he was going to have Eva over to his mother's house for dinner. Lucille was particularly excited that their relationship had resumed.

It was close to eight o'clock in the morning when he dropped the kids at Monkey Jim Smith's. Smith was nowhere to be seen. Earl thought it was just as well he didn't have to deal with the man.

Earl went to Summersville to the sale but decided to make no bids. He sat and listened. He needed to go back to Tyrone and finish his report to the Judge and the bondsmen. Grogan would not have any room to complain for months to come.

Earl finished his quarterly rendition of his financial affairs dealing with the estate. He made an extra copy, hand written in ink. October and November didn't look too good but December was sensational. He sent one copy to Judge Johnson and the other to Bill Lawson. Bill's son Vess had been working out with the Clear Springs team late in the season. He would make a fine player sometime next year.

On his way back from the store to mail the report to the Judge, Earl went by his grandmothers's house. He told her he would be going down to his mother's and Charlie's for supper and that Eva would be there. A keen light lit Sarah's eyes and she said, "that's nice."

Fern was low key when Earl mentioned that Eva was going to have supper with him at his folks.

Earl enquired how her holiday week went. Fern said it was good to see her mother but the crowded little house made her glad to be back in the big roomy Sigler house.

Earl went to Ray and Mae's to pick Eva up at a little before five o'clock. Earl took his time driving to the turnoff to his folks' place to give Eva time to recount her last two days with her new students. She had met a young couple in their mid twenties with a child in the first grade. The Hansens had invited her over on Thursday to play cards and spend the night. They lived about the same distance from the school as McAllister's.

The road across the fields, to a ridge that led down to his mother's and Charlie's, was deeply rutted from the ice storm and snow in December. There was a gigantic mud puddle that Earl had gotten stuck in the winter before so he drove in the grass completely around it. There were only two people who lived on this township road and it was not a high priority for maintenance. Earl knew that Charlie had hauled a wagon load of rock and gravel and put in the puddle, but he wasn't going to take any chances.

With the days being so short, Charlie had finished his chores and was in the back room changing clothes after washing up a bit. Mary met them at the door and gave Eva a light little hug with little pats on the back. When Charlie came in he enveloped Eva with a grizzly bear hug.

"It's good to have you back again, Eva," Charlie said. "It's been too long."

Eva nodded, "It has."

"You're teaching the last half year in Clear Springs and staying at Ray and Mae's, I hear," Mary said. "I guess we'll see you at church on Sundays. Mae comes most Sundays with her boy and baby girl. They're Church of God people like the Beltzs' are but they don't want to drive all the way into Willow. Mama and Henry and Effie come here to church, too. They was raised in the Christian Church that was on the road over toward Grogan but it burned down a while back."

"Oh, Mary," Charlie said, "Eva don't want to hear all that stuff."

"I don't mind, Charlie." Eva said firmly, "My whole family, the Sweckers are all Church of God and Mae was a Swecker. Half the Willow church are Sweckers. My grandparents had a passel of children."

They had all seated themselves around the living/dining room. Charlie in his rocking chair, Mary by the stove and Eva and Earl on the Day Bed.

"'bout ten minutes the rolls will be done. I've got a pot roast and turnips simmering on the stove so we have time to sit a spell."

The next few minutes were filled with newsy information about families in the Clear Springs school. John, George and Raymond Bradford all had children enrolled. John had married the pretty Lola Patterson and they had a child almost every year since they were married nearly a dozen years ago. The boys, in particular, "were a handful," Eva said. "Dud and Bud."

"If it gets out of hand," Charlie said, "Let me know and it will be taken care of."

"I'm tougher than I look, Charlie," Eva replied, "I'll just told them I'll get permission to give them a whipping. You don't want your folks to hear I had to give you a whipping?" I asked them.

"I bet that settled them down," Charlie smiled.

Eva nodded, "That was on Monday and today they were just fine."

Earl, not wanting to be left out, said, "I bet it had a good effect on everyone in school."

"Children will get rambunctious once in a while, you just have to have reasonable control," Eva agreed.

Mary said, "The rolls are ready by now, find a seat."

Eva said, "I'll help you ….Mary." Eva almost said Mama inadvertently. She conjectured on how that might have been perceived.

Earl sat on the far side of the table across from Charlie and to the right of where Mary usually sat. Eva came back in carrying the pot of turnips in one hand and the rolls in her other. She set them on hot pads. Mary sat the pot roast surrounded by potatoes and carrots uncovered in the middle of the table on the largest hot pad.

Eva sat across from Mary and bowed her head and Mary bowed hers. Charlie looked straight ahead but Earl bowed his head without shutting his eyes. Mary prayed, thanking God for the meal and his everlasting goodness to his children.

They ate companionably with some small talk. Earl told everyone that he would be really busy the next couple of weeks. He mentioned the ten teams he had sent George Bailey off to Kansas to buy. He offered to bring his folks some mountain oysters he and Lonnie would be getting the next day.

"Bring 'em on down, Earl," Charlie smiled conspiratorially, "It'll give you an excuse to see this little girl," inclining his head toward Eva.

Eva chuckled and Mary smiled.

Mary said, "I might even enjoy seeing Earl, too."

Everyone laughed lightly.

Charlie swallowed a bite of food and said, "I don't need a pair I bought a young team a little over seven years ago. I'm hoping to get another half dozen more years out of them. They're almost like pets Now. I'll hate giving them up when the time comes. I'll pass the word around the community though."

"I have four teams spoken for," Earl said, "I recon they'll go pretty quick. You might want to spread the word around that I bought some young springer milk cows, heifers, bred to a Shorthorn bull. I got them very reasonable."

Charlie said quickly, "Now I'd talk about taking a couple of those heifers. You remember when I bought my cows right after we got back from Colorado. When you've milked a cow six to eight years, they just don't give as much milk as when they are younger."

"I'll tell you what Charlie, when I come down with the mountain oysters, I'll bring two of the best, both Guernsey. Dry your cows out after they drop their calves and have nursed a few months. Then I'll take them off to market. They're bringing about two and a half cents a pound. We'll sell the old cows and you give me the difference, if that's okay."

"Fair enough, Earl, but you've got time and gas in those heifers. How about I give you a half dollar each for delivery?"

Earl nodded his assent.

Eva and Mary went to the kitchen to do dishes. It was getting dark already as a heavy layer of clouds moved in. Charlie tuned in the radio to KMOX. The economic news was grim as the unemployment numbers were estimated nearing twenty percent. They listened to the farm report. Earl had gone to sit on the day bed that served like a sofa, leaning back against some very large pillows. The weather report came on and they reported snow falling west and north of Rolla.

Charlie turned down the radio and his voice rumbled to life, "Looks as if we'll be getting snow before daylight. Poor old Hoover is going to get blamed for all this mess. It was set to bring this on by the Wilson policies he started near twenty years ago. Jiminy Christmas, it ain't going to be pretty the next few years."

Earl nodded, "We're already in hard times and I don't see it getting better anytime soon."

Charlie turned the radio up a little and did a little more tuning as there was more static. As he worked the dial he got the station more clearly. The world news was about the same all over as the unemployment grew worse in Europe. There were reports of heavy fighting in China with the Japanese. A military warlord in China was having to fight the Japanese and Communists at the same time.

"Them dad gum communists are gonna take over the world, we don't watch out."

Eva had come back in while Charlie was talking. "We're a Godly country, Charlie," Eva said firmly, "they'll not make any headway here."

"Not unless we give it away. If Roosevelt gets in, he's just another Wilson."

Eva, showing great deference to Charlie's age, asserted, "You have a lot more experience in political matters. I won't vote for Roosevelt if he runs."

The comedy shows were starting so Charlie turned the radio up a little louder. Eva sat by Earl. Charlie put a couple of pieces of wood in the stove. Mary came and sat in her rocker on the far side of the stove, facing Eva and Earl. Fibber Magee and Molly were coming on, followed by Amos and Andy. The "canned" laughter induced a little laughter in the room. They made small talk during commercials. Ray and Lula Peabody's little boy, Calvin, had come down with a bad case of measles. Lula, the sister next to Mary in age, was a little older when she met Ray at Nagle school at a pie supper.

Church, pie suppers and chivarees were the big social events throughout the year. Hill people took their church seriously but it was a time to socialize, too. The pie suppers and raucous, noisy post marriage chivaree were just for fun. The pie suppers were to raise money and have fun. A crowd tried to disturb the bride and groom as they were getting ready for bed on the day of the wedding preferably. The groom usually had cigars to hand out to the men and the newly married couple sometimes served punch or some kind of drink to everyone. Eventually everyone left and the couple were left to their marital bliss.

After the third half hour of radio comedy, Eva rose, "I best get on back to McAllister's I don't want to keep them up too late."

When Earl pulled up in front of Ray and Mae's. Eva leaned over and kissed Earl lightly.

Earl said, "That's all."

"You heard Mama and Papa. They said take it slow," Eva opened the door and Earl walked up to the door with Eva. He could see the older couple sitting in the living room. Eva opened the door and went in. Earl walked slowly back the car, a note of dissatisfaction playing in his brain.

When Earl crossed the ford at North Jack's Fork, it was starting to spit snow. By the time he got to Tyrone and pulled up in front of the house there was over an inch of snow on the ground. He entered the front of the house through the west front door into the dining area. A lamp was burning on the dining table. Earl put two large pieces of wood in the stove and made up his mind to get up in the night to put more wood in to help keep the house warm. He lit the smaller lamp he usually took up to his bedroom and blew out the lamp on the table.

The dream he was having early in the night was pleasant as Eva inhabited this dream. He got up and went down to replenish the wood in the stove. Snow was still falling. The second half of his night wasn't so pleasant he awoke to his usual nightmare.

He fumbled his way through his pockets for a match to light the lamp.

When it was lit he looked at the clock on the chest of drawers, it was just after four. He knew he couldn't sleep anymore. He dressed and went downstairs, rekindling the fire from coals in the heating stove and went to the kitchen. He put some paper in the firebox with kindling on top and a few small sticks on top of that. All Fern would have to do would be strike a match. He sorted through the mail from the day before.

This last desultory task done, the tendrils of the dream like a toxic fog filtered through the cracks of his mind. He shrugged into a coat and donned a hat. He walked outside, considered going to the car to get a bottle behind the seat but he was cautious. He didn't want Fern seeing him. He trudged through over six inches of snow on down toward the mill building. He went in where he kept the box of bootleg. The reflection from the snow allowed Earl to find the lantern hanging from the ceiling. He lit it and a Lucky Strike. He smoked for a few minutes and the craving for liquor overcame him. He opened the box. There was one last quart, he made a mental note to pick up another box. He wrestled a full bag of ground corn up against the wall and sat on it with his back against the wall. He took several slugs, settling back against the wall comfortably. He alternated between the cigarette and the bottle until he had to put out the Lucky. He drank some more and became drowsy.

Full daylight coming through the door, opened by Dillard, awakened Earl. He looked up at Dillard blearily.

"Yer on the sauce already, Earl," Dillard said shortly, "That stuff will rot your guts and brain out."

"Dillard, if you only knew," Earl said quietly slurring his words, "how my night demons have got to me ever since the Fourth."

"I just know it ain't good for yeh. I cain't tell you how to solve it. Yer could do like Elmer done but that won't solve nothin'," Dillard said bitterly. "You been one of my best friends, goin' huntin' and fishin' together. I just don't want to see yer doin' yerself wrong."

"Thank you, Dillard, for your concern," Earl said wistfully, "I know I said we would mark those pigs this morning but as you can see I'm not up to it right now. I'm going down toward the school and walk this off. Would you stop by and tell Fern I went down to my grandmother's to have breakfast with her."

Dillard nodded.

"Thanks," Earl continued, "We'll mark the pigs," Earl pulled out his pocket watch and noticed it was already six o'clock, "at eight. Alright?"

"In this snow? I rode my horse over, didn't want to spin off in the ditch. I'll ride home for a little breakfast myself," Dillard replied, "I think I can make it back by eight."

"You're right," Earl said, "We can do it later in the week. You want to ride over to Licking and buy some more hogs with me. I'd like to have about another fifty to go to the Stock Yards. I'll send them up with those five we've got left in the corral."

"What time you want to go?"

"How about ten," Earl answered, "That'll give me time to stop by the bank on the way over."

Earl had made up his mind to make the next several trips up to East Saint Louis this winter. He didn't want his contacts up there to think he was out of the loop. He would drop in and thank Joe Sullivan for the nice heads up on the government buy of cattle. He hadn't been to the Stock Yards since early in October.

Sarah was surprised and glad to see him but she could tell he had been drinking again. It saddened her to see Earl get so dependent on alcohol. She knew he had the nightmares but now she wasn't so certain that he was up to the job he had been thrown into after all. But she knew Marcus had left home before he was even fourteen to make his own way in the world. He hadn't done to badly for himself. The best she could hope for was that it would just work itself out. She fed him a good breakfast and Earl trudged back up to his house in the snow.

The porch had been swept clear. Earl stomped off as much snow as he could and wiped his feet on the coarse mat by the door.

Fern was sure Earl had been drinking again but said nothing. He was used to him telling her where he was going for the day so she could pass it on to anyone who asked.

Dillard and Earl castrated the pigs on Friday. Dillard took home a bucket of mountain oysters and Earl took some up to the house. He told Fern he was taking some down home. Fern knew immediately what he meant, Charlie and Mary's.

At four thirty, before going to his mother's and Charlie's he went over to see Eva at McAllister's. Ray told him Mae and Eva had gone over to Houston shopping.

Earl left the mountain oysters with his mother and headed on back to Tyrone.

George Bailey sent a wire. It stated that he would be in Cabool at ten o'clock on Monday morning. Earl drove the truck to pick up Wayne Weiler at nine o'clock. They were at the Cabool station when the train arrived. George told Earl that the horses were on a siding about a half mile West of town. Earl loaded one pair on the truck and then Wayne's pick on behind the two in front. George took off the other eight teams. George rode one and led the others strung together. Earl dropped Wayne off at his house with his new team. Earl loaded Wayne's old team and delivered the other team near Pine Creek school.

Earl delivered horses to two other farmers who had asked for them. The horses had cost him more than he had anticipated. The farmers, other than Wayne, he asked six dollars difference. His enquiry by phone of price on horses was met with good news that the market was up almost a half cent.

Earl sold the other eight dairy cows that week. He made a dollar a head on them. He took a load of hogs up based on the price one day and the price had fallen when he got there. He lost nearly fifty dollars. The next week he sold two more teams of horses.

He stopped by Ray and Mae McAllister's and they said Eva was spending the night with some people by the name of Siegrist. He didn't know them and didn't want to just show up. On Friday afternoon he stopped by the school after delivering a team of horses over toward Mountain View. Eva was pleased to see him but they only had a couple of minutes together. Mae came to take her to Willow shopping. Eva invited him along but he didn't want to go shopping with two women. Was his love life fading away because of bad luck? What was all the shopping about?

Eva was convinced that Earl had been evading her since inviting her over to Mary and Charlie's or just not paying as much attention as he should. She couldn't fathom that he could be so busy he couldn't make more effort to see her.

Earl stopped, on his way to West Plains, before school on Friday to ask if she would like to ride over to Willow to the sale and do some shopping the next day.

"I won't go to Willow with you but you can take me by to see my folks Saturday. Papa can bring me back Sunday afternoon," Eva replied

"Okay, Eva. What time do you want me to stop by?"

"Is eight too early?" she said.

"Fine, see you then," Earl left with several children looking at him curiously.

Earl was there to meet Eva before eight o'clock Saturday morning. She bounced out of the house with a small satchel virtually trotting around the front of the truck and into the passenger side. She leaned across the seat and kissed him lightly on the lips. Earl sure would have liked a little more passion.

Eva thought she smelled something strange on Earl's breath. Earl had in fact had a couple of drinks of whiskey down at the mill where he had replenished his carton of bottles. He had chewed up several handfuls of Sen-Sen. Earl's craving for liquor wasn't always after his night demons, now.

Earl's attention was on his driving the first couple of miles before fording the South Jacks Fork. When he was back on the more level straight road before the Pine Creek Crossing, Earl said, "This week I'm going to be back and forth to Peoria every day. The market was up today on horseflesh. It is over ten hours driving and if I run into bad weather it could be twelve or more."

Eva scooted across the seat and cuddled up against him. Earl's heart raced.

"I better make up some time if I don't see you all week."

After they crossed Pine Creek it was only a short drive up the little valley to the Weiler house. When Earl stopped by the house, Eva asked, "Aren't you going to come in?" Smoke was coming from both chimneys.

"I saw your father just a few days ago and I'm not sure your mother likes me too much, yet."

"Okay, Earl. Have it your way. Can I at least say you said 'hi'?" Eva asked.

Earl nodded and Eva kissed him on the lips with a little more passion this time. Earl could see Eva's sisters and brothers looking wide eyed out the living room window.

* * * * * * * * * *

Monday through Friday passed like a rat through a maze. It was get up early, load up, drive to Peoria, eat greasy food on the road, get home go to bed, up early and do it all over again. Earl took George Bailey with him every day. George was the best man for handling horses Earl had ever encountered. Earl took two bottles of bootleg with him every day and they were finished off before they got home. On Friday George said he would like to stop in East Saint Louis and take Earl to a speakeasy he had been to. Earl had heard of them but they didn't have them in South Missouri.

It was on State Street nearly a mile away from the National Stock Yards. They drank whiskey. Earl particularly liked the Whiskey Sours. George preferred his neat.

Several hours passed by before Earl looked at his watch. It was past nine o'clock. He decided they should get back on the road. When they came back out, there were several inches of snow on the ground. Earl hadn't brought his chains to put over the truck tires.

"Let's go over to the National City Hotel and stay the night," Earl said, "I'd better not try and drive back with as much as I've had to drink and with this snow."

They took a room with two beds. George wanted to go back to the speakeasy. Earl wanted to eat supper in the hotel dining room. They had the best chicken fried steak with green beans, mashed potatoes and white gravy he ever had any place. They ate and went back to State Street.

By a little after ten they were back at a table. By eleven o'clock both had several drinks more. The later crowd had more women included. A small band played and there was dancing. A young woman in Earl's line of sight kept making eyes at him, even winking at him a couple of times. After the second wink, her companion looked back at Earl. He rose to his feet, a big hulking man of average height. He walked over to Earl and said, "You better stop it or I'll knock you head off." Earl started to get up but George grabbed his arm and held him down. The man returned to his table.

A few minutes passed and the woman was ogling him again. The husky man came toward Earl again. He didn't say anything, He grabbed Earl's shirt front and pulled him to his feet. It was a mistake. Earl's left hook would have made the Manassas Mauler proud. The man was on his knees. Earl backed away, waiting. The man shook his head, stood and moved toward Earl with his fists up.

Earl stepped in and hit him with a right cross that put the aggressor on his back. Two men at the man's table leapt to their feet. Suddenly three bouncers appeared, carrying leather encased saps, likely filled with double ought lead shot. The two men were felled with quick blows to the head. The other man was out cold from Earl's blow.

The bouncers started moving toward Earl. He held up his hands, "I'm leaving."

Earl started to turn away. One of the bouncers ran up behind him and hit him across his right shoulder. Pain shot through his arm, driving him nearly to his knees. He turned back to his attacker and the other two hit him in the face with their saps. George caught Earl before he could collapse to the floor. George was a smaller man but he was stronger than he looked. He walked with Earl hanging on to him. George turned at the door, "you three cowards should be ashamed of yourselves."

One of them spat out, "Get him out of here. We saw what he did to that big guy. We were just protecting ourselves."

George got Earl in the truck and he drove Earl to the Hotel. When they were up in their room, Earl examined himself in the mirror. He had an egg sized knot above his right ear, a dark bruise on his shoulder, a small cut over his left eye and a bruise on his right cheek bone.

Earl mumbled drunkenly, "I only remember being hit twice."

"The first one hit you again when you were about out cold." George said, "I caught you or you would have fell on yer face."

Earl washed the blood out of his eyebrow, undressed and went to sleep immediately. He awoke the next morning with a withering headache. He asked George if he could drive a while. They had breakfast in the Hotel café and started down the road before eight o'clock.

Earl stopped at the bank with checks for thirty horses totaling a thousand sixty five dollars. The horses had brought two and a half cents a pound. He gave George two hundred sixty four dollars for his eight horses. He figured he had cleared about a hundred and twenty dollars before his expenses. Not a lot for a whole week's work.

Earl had nearly four hundred dollars a month expenses: Dillard's pay, his grandmother, Fern, Ruth and Helen, part time help, food, clothing. He was barely meeting his financial responsibilities.

George and Earl had dinner at noon in Raymondville. Clouds were rolling in from the West-Southwest. When Earl took George to his house and returned freezing rain was glazing the windshield. Lucille, Glen and Vivian came out on the front porch to welcome him home.

They all hugged him with worried faces. Lucille said, "What happened to your face, Earl?"

Glen added, "We haven't seen you all week. Did you get in a fight?"

Vivian didn't ask any questions, "I'll kiss them well." and kissed him on both of his black eyes.

"Sometimes those horses can be pretty rough unloading and loading," Earl said without admitting anything but implying something he knew was false.

When they came in the house, Fern looked at him strangely but didn't have any more embarrassing questions. She wiped her hands on her apron. "I was just getting some ham and beans on for supper. I'll have cornbread, too."

"My favorite, Fern. Thanks." Earl said. "You kids will have some good sliding if it keeps on like it is now. I'm going up and change clothes so I don't smell like horse."

Earl walked up and changed into some work clothes. He looked at his face in the dresser mirror. He did look like he had been in a fight but no one had the courage to lay a fist to his face in anger. He really wanted to see Eva, to go to Ray and Mae's and find her. He couldn't truthfully face her questions. Maybe he would look better later in the week.

There was a card from Eva telling him of a singing at Clear Spring school on Tuesday, "hope to see you there." Eva knew he would be gone all last week. She was doing her part to see him. His mother and Charlie, the card said, had asked them to come on Thursday, implying she would see him there, too.

The card sent him into another spiral of self-pity. A desire for liquor was nearly overpowering. He fought in off and delved into his other mail. He had a letter from Jim Hart. The divorce date was set. Ruth had filed a counter suit. Hart said her attorney had told him she wanted to remarry.

There was a note from Bill Lawson, stating that the bondsmen were pleased with the income for the whole quarter.

Earl started feeling sorry for himself again. Here it was Saturday and he couldn't just up and go see Eva, not with the condition of his face. It was intolerable to even consider.

* * * * * * * * * *

Eva went to church Sunday morning at Clear Springs. She hoped Earl would be there. After church she saw the Skaggs and Mary and Charlie talking together animatedly. She walked up to listen in.

Henry was saying to Mary, "You should come with us to Nagle next Sunday. They've selected Floyd Baker as Elder and Ray Peabody and Arthur Shriver as deacons. They'll be having an ordination after church. The preacher from Willow will be there to officiate."

Mary said, "What they doing all that for?"

"They've totally reorganized the church. It will be called Nagle Christian Church, not just Nagle Church," Effie answered. "We grew up in the Christian Church and it will be good to have one close by."

Charlie said gruffly, "I don't get it. We're doing just fine here. Jiminy

Christmas, I don't get it." He reached into his pocket for a twist of tobacco and bit off a chew. He offered it to Henry and he shook his head.

"I'll have a smoke instead," Henry reached into his bib pocket and pulled out a pack of Camels and lit the cigarette.

"I thought Earl would show up today," Eva interjected.

"I hear he's been running back and forth to Peoria every day," Effie said. "Fern says he's been up at four o'clock every morning loading horses and getting back nine or ten o'clock at night sometimes. He's probably still resting up."

Eva said, "I wrote him a card about the singing on Tuesday night and that I was going down to Mary and Charlie's on Thursday. I bet he'll show up both times. I've sure been missing seeing him."

"Me, too," Mary said.

Eva went home with Mae and Ray. They played checkers and Chinese checkers most of the afternoon. Eva helped prepare the two meals at the McAllisters.

The evening of the singing came and Earl still wasn't there. Eva was puzzled. Surely he had gotten her card.

Eva went home with Siegrists and played cards until late. They taught her to play Pitch, a relatively simple card game but challenging.

The wiener roast on Thursday was a lot of fun. Eva thought it would have been more fun if Earl had come. The evening was chilly but not cold. It was nice to stand around the fire and cook wieners. What was happening? She asked herself. Had he found someone else?

Charlie and Mary came to bring Eva down to their house afterward. They fully expected Earl to be there waiting since he hadn't come to the wiener roast.

Mary said it first, "I don't understand why Earl didn't come. I sent him a post card on Monday."

"I sent a card last Thursday letting Earl know about the singing, the wiener roast and your inviting me down tonight," Eva lamented, "I'm puzzled, to say the least."

The evening was spent listening to the radio with a little uncomfortable conversation since they were avoiding questions about Earl's absence. Eva and Mary prepared the day bed for Eva to sleep on. Before Charlie and Mary went off to bed Eva asked for paper and an envelope to write a letter to Earl.

Clear Springs, MO
January 28, 1932   9:30
P.M.

Dearest Earl,

Gee, honey I was blue tonight. Came to the wiener roast and hoped you would be there but no Earl have I seen as yet. I'm down at your mother's now. You may not get this tho until after you see me.

I've done all kinds of things this week. Monday night I went over and stayed all night at Hansens. Tuesday I was playing ball and was catcher and I got an awful smack in the nose. It is still terribly sore. Tuesday nite I went to the schoolhouse to a singing when I went over it was pitch-dark had to almost feel my way. Went all by "my lonesome" too. The singing didn't amount to much and about 8:30 we went over to Siegrists and played pitch till 12:30. It was nice and moonlight going back. Then yesterday I hit my thumb and to-night the weiner roast.

Your mother said to tell you she missed you but she wasn't the only one who who missed you a whole lot.

Well, I'll quit as I don't have a good place to write and my thumb is all tied up too.

Lots and Lots of

(Its that big too)   LOVE,
                     Eva.

P.S.
Hope it don't rain before Saturday but
Charley says it will rain before morning.

Heres hoping not because Sweetheart, I
just must see you. good-night dearest.

Eva.

Friday, Eva taught almost like a robot. Her mind was too much on Earl. She had put her letter in Charlie's mailbox.

* * * * * * * * * *

Earl, on Saturday morning, told Fern he had to go to Kansas City. He just needed to get away from the prying eyes of the public and any questions about the condition of his face. He visited an old friend in the city and went to the stock yards to see what went on there. He went to a couple of movies. He told his friend that he had been bucked off a horse. He thought that would be a good excuse for anyone at home and went back to Tyrone on Tuesday.

Earl was lonesome to see Eva, too. By Wednesday the swelling was down and some of the really angry colors in his face was starting to fade but he still had two black eyes.

On Thursday Earl went over to see Jim Hart in response to a letter he had from the lawyer. When he got there he had to wait a while. When he got in the first thing Jim said was, "Whatever happened to your face?"

"A horse got the best of me, threw me off into a wood fence post," Earl answered.

It went so well with Jim that Earl decided that would be his excuse from now on.

"Your letter," Earl continued, "said that you have a court date set."

"Yes, the fifth of February. It's really just a formality now," Hart assured him, "Ruth's attorney has agreed to all our stipulations. We'll go in for the hearing and a couple of weeks we'll get the official decree that the marriage is dissolved. She has agreed to ten dollars for child support."

"It's my intention to continue the fifty dollars until she marries and then I will give more than the ten," Earl said.

On Friday Earl and Dillard went to West Plains. Earl drove the Plymouth and Dillard the truck. There were two lots of sheep there. Earl bought both since he thought he could come out on them. They double-decked them and Dillard drove them home to unload in the corral. Earl planned to feed them well and take them to the stockyards Monday morning.

Earl tried to time it to get there just before school was out. When the children hurried from the building and Eva appeared at the door, Earl's heart rate went up. Eva walked toward the car and Earl got out to go meet her. She was in his arms, quivering with emotion.

She kissed him and looked around. The children who remained were smiling broadly.

"Where have you been Earl?" Eva said a little angrily, "I thought I'd see you several days ago. And what happened to your face?"

Earl said, "Please don't ask me about it. It's embarrassing to talk about it."

Eva looked at him more carefully, "You got in a fight. I know how feisty you can get when somebody crosses you."

"It's not exactly like that. Enough said about it," Earl said firmly. He just couldn't lie to her.

"Okay."

"Would you like me to take you home?" Earl added, "Good news! I'll be a single man in about a week. It's all agreed to by Ruth. Hart told me she plans to remarry right after the divorce."

Eva put her arms around him and entertained the children some more.

"What about it, Eva?"

"Sure you can take me home to my Mama and Papa."

Earl looked a little aggrieved, "No about the news. Don't you think it's good news? I can get married, too."

"It's not bad news, that's for sure," a little understatement from Eva. "Did you have someone in mind to marry. I didn't know you had plans that way."

"Don't be difficult, please," Earl said tartly. "You know I'm crazy about you. I love you. I can't live without you."

"If that is a proposal, I might say yes after you and I have talked to my parents about it," Eva said softly. "Take me home. I'll have to go by Mae and Ray's to pick up a few things."

They drove to McAllister's. Earl smoked a Lucky while he waited and when he was done he chewed up some Sen-Sen.

When they got to the Weiler house, Wayne was out back splitting wood for the kitchen stove. Eva went straight to him. "Papa would you come in the house? Earl and I need to talk to you about something important."

"Sure, I'll come inside in a couple of minutes. I think Earl wants to talk to me first," Wayne said.

Earl nodded his head. As soon as Eva had gone inside, Earl said, "Yesterday I found out that my divorce is just a formality, now. Ruth, the woman I was married to, is wanting to marry as soon as the divorce is final. That should about a week from now. I would like to marry Eva, with your permission of course."

"Earl, my gut feeling is that I want to give you my blessing but Rena and I have to be in agreement on this," Wayne said, his one, good, left, blue eye glittering and friendly. Wayne had lost one eye a couple of years earlier in a hunting mishap when the twenty-two he was using to shoot a squirrel back fired. "Let's go inside and talk it over."

Earl helped Wayne carry in the split wood. When they got inside, the kitchen had been closed off with Eva's brothers and sisters in another room. The pots that were on the stove had been moved to the back. Earl and Wayne sat in two empty chairs. Earl deliberately sat so he could look at Rena face to face.

Wayne cleared his throat and began, "Earl has just asked if he could marry Eva. I told him that you and I must agree on this, Rena."

Rena turned to look at Earl. Earl met her look squarely. Rena's grey-blue eyes were hard with no malice in them, just determination. "I don't think you deserve my daughter's hand but if Eva and Wayne can convince me otherwise we'll invite you over in a few days. Eva comes home about every other weekend. Why don't you come for supper next Saturday."

"Thank you Missus Weiler. That's a very kind invitation," Earl said sincerely. "You must know this, I love Eva. I'll love her with the last breath I take on this earth whether I am allowed to marry her or not. It won't change anything."

Earl looked at Eva, tears were brimming in her eyes. She mouthed, "I love you."

Rena's look softened, "You're welcome to stay for supper today, too."

"Thank you so much for your invitation but I have to go home to tend to some sheep I bought today. Sheep are really kind of delicate creatures," Earl said regretfully. "I do wish things were different. I wish I hadn't done some things in my past."

Rena said, "There's that old saying. If wishes were horses, beggars would ride."

Earl rose with Eva close behind him. When he was ready to get in the car, Eva said, "I was so proud of you and so happy with what you said to Mama, it will carry a lot of weight in their minds."

"I'm not so sure after what your mother said," Earl said warily.

"You didn't notice that little smile after she said it. Mama has a quirky sense of humor."

Eva put her arms around Earl and gave him a good hard kiss. "Don't you worry, Honey." Eva said firmly, "I'm in charge now!"

"I hope to see you before next Saturday."

Eva smiled. "How about dropping by Mae's and Ray's on Tuesday and we go to the Pine Creek pie supper. You can buy whatever I bring. If you remember we met there about a year ago."

"I'll see you Tuesday, then." Earl got in the car and drove toward Tyrone.

CHAPTER 22 -

Weeds

The garden of life is cluttered with weeds like problems and crises. You can yank them out, only to find that they may proliferate once more.

The Book II title is a weed that has not been obliterated but it may be cast aside soon. The Sigler family saga will be cluttered with more weeds, too. The one big crisis Earl has encountered may be addressed if not eliminated.

God is in charge of all weeds. Will His best in life be allowed to flourish among the weeds if they cannot be pulled up by the roots and cast aide? Will Tyrone benefit from God, the Good Gardener?

The most insidious weed of all is pure evil the worst crisis of all. God knows about evil and the author of evil. Evil can destroy life as we have seen in this book. God with Jesus, his son (God in flesh), have the true answer to defeat evil and the evil one.

"Who is it that overcomes the world? Only the one who believes that Jesus is the Son of God."

I John 5:5 (TNIV)

CPSIA information can be obtained at www.ICGtesting.com
Printed in the USA
LVOW100356201211

260211LV00003B/1/P